D1042870

Critical acclaim for Madeline Baker's previous bestsellers:

CHEYENNE SURRENDER

"This is a funny, witty, poignant, and delightful love story! Ms. Baker's fans will be more than satisfied!"

—Romantic Times

THE SPIRIT PATH

"Poignant, sensual, and wonderful....Madeline Baker fans will be enchanted!"

—Romantic Times

MIDNIGHT FIRE

"Once again, Madeline Baker proves that she has the Midas touch....A definite treasure!"

—Romantic Times

COMANCHE FLAME

"Another Baker triumph! Powerful, passionate, and action packed, it will keep readers on the edge of their seats!"

—Romantic Times

PRAIRIE HEAT

"A smoldering tale of revenge and passion as only Madeline Baker can write....without a doubt one of her best!"

—Romantic Times

A WHISPER IN THE WIND

"Fresh, powerful, and exciting, a time-travel novel taut with raw primal tension and rich in Indian history and tradition!"

—Romantic Times

MADELINE BAKER

Winner of the *Romantic Times* Reviewers' Choice Award For Best Indian Series!

"Lovers of Indian Romance have a special place on their bookshelves for Madeline Baker!"
—Romantic Times

APACHE RUNAWAY

Jenny frowned as she peered intently at Fallon's wound. Even in the uncertain light cast by the moon, she could see the wound was swollen and angry looking. Tiny red streaks spread fanlike around the edges of the bullet hole.

"It's becoming infected," she whispered. "Are you in much pain?"

"No," Fallon rasped sarcastically, "I feel just fine."

"I have no medicine," Jenny told him regretfully. "Only this."

Reaching beneath the folds of the blanket, she withdrew a narrow-bladed Mexican dagger and a pint of cheap whiskey.

Fallon's eyes narrowed. "That's pretty primitive," he muttered dryly, "even for the Apache."

Jenny shrugged. "It's all I have."

Fallon shook his head. "Forget it and cut me loose."

Jenny threw him a look that said he was crazy. "You can't ride with that leg, and if the bullet doesn't come out soon, there'll be no point in removing it at all."

"I'll take my chances," Fallon hissed.

"If that bullet doesn't come out now," Jenny said flatly, "I think you'll be dead in a week."

Other *Leisure Books* by Madeline Baker:
BENEATH A MIDNIGHT MOON
CHEYENNE SURRENDER
WARRIOR'S LADY
THE SPIRIT PATH
MIDNIGHT FIRE
COMANCHE FLAME
PRAIRIE HEAT
A WHISPER IN THE WIND
FORBIDDEN FIRES
LACEY'S WAY
FIRST LOVE, WILD LOVE
RENEGADE HEART
RECKLESS DESIRE
LOVE FOREVERMORE
RECKLESS LOVE
LOVE IN THE WIND
RECKLESS HEART

MADELINE BAKER

LEISURE BOOKS NEW YORK CITY

A LEISURE BOOK®

March 1995

Published by

Dorchester Publishing Co., Inc.
276 Fifth Avenue
New York, NY 10001

Printed in the United States of America.

To
Budd "Rainbow Hands" Sherrick
and
Frank "Chief Grey Wolf" Salcedo—
two men who embody
the true Indian spirit

APACHE
RUNAWAY

Prologue

1868

It was spring and all the world was in bloom, but the woman standing at the water's edge was oblivious to the natural beauty surrounding her. Her thoughts were troubled, her eyes sad, and a long, shuddering sigh escaped her lips as she stared at the Indian lodges scattered across the valley floor.

Captured by Apaches! Once just the thought had made her blood run cold. But that had been two years ago; two long years since a dozen painted savages had attacked the stagecoach carrying her west to join Hank. The other passengers had been killed. At the time, she had considered herself lucky to be taken alive. But no more.

Her heart was heavy in her breast as she gazed at the high purple cliffs that enclosed the emerald valley like loving arms, their craggy peaks as impenetrable and confining as prison walls.

In despair, she raised her great green eyes toward heaven and whispered, "Oh, God, please send someone to rescue me from these savages . . ."

Chapter One

1870

Ryder Fallon reined his trail-weary gelding to a halt in front of the squat, unpainted building, shading his eyes with his hand to read the weather-beaten wooden sign that hung slightly askew over the sagging double doors.

ACE HIGH SALOON
LAST WATERING HOLE
THIS SIDE OF HELL

There was truth in that, Fallon allowed with a wry grin, seeing as how there was nothing but sand and cactus for over a hundred miles in any direction once you left the protection of the dilapidated Army post that crouched in the shadow of a tall yellow bluff less than a stone's throw away.

Dismounting, Fallon tossed the gray's reins over the hitch rack. Slapping the dust from his battered black Stetson, he entered the saloon, his mind set on a bottle of rye whiskey and maybe a friendly game of poker to while away the time until the sun went down and the desert was fit to travel.

The saloon was crowded with men, most of them clad in sweat-stained Army blue. At the bar, Fallon ordered a bottle of whiskey and after taking the edge off his thirst, he relaxed with his back against the bar. A wry grin played over his lips as he listened to a half dozen troopers at a nearby table complain long and loud about the new shavetail at the fort, then go on to gripe about the food, the weather, Indians, stubborn horses, rank mules, standing guard duty, and the idiocy of drilling in 115-degree heat.

A quarter of an hour later, Fallon bought his way into a card game. He nodded briefly as the players were introduced: Sergeant O'Hara, Corporal Donaldson, and Corporal Harris. O'Hara, Fallon noted, appeared to be the big winner at the table.

Sergeant Beauregard O'Hara grinned broadly as the stranger took a place at the table and produced a sizable bankroll. Old Beau was a big man, solid as a Kentucky oak. Clad in dusty boots and sweat-stained shirt, there was little to indicate he had once been a dandy. Or that he had once dealt for the house in the infamous Crystal

Palace in Dodge City. But that had been twelve years ago. Since joining up with the Army, old Beau played Sunday-school straight poker. Most of the time. But now and then he couldn't resist palming an ace, or sliding a few off the bottom, just to prove he could still do it.

And now was one of those times. China blue eyes twinkling like one of Santa's elves, his thick lips parted in a disarming smile, Beau adroitly manipulated the deck, assuring himself of a full house, aces over queens.

An hour later, Beau was still grinning, and still winning. Feeling generous, he called for a bottle, smiled graciously as he poured drinks all around.

"Southern Comfort," he purred, his soft drawl indicating roots in the Deep South. "You just can't beat it."

Hands moving swift and sure, O'Hara shuffled the deck and dealt a new hand: a pair of deuces to Harris, who would bet on anything; trash to Donaldson, a pair of sixes to the stranger, a straight for himself.

"Cards, gentlemen?" he drawled.

Corporal Harris asked for three, thinking he was a fool to stay in with nothing but a pair of deuces; thinking, too, that a good part of the money carelessly stacked in front of O'Hara had been his when the game started.

"I'm out," Donaldson growled, tossing his cards into the center of the table. "I haven't had a decent hand all night."

Muttering to himself, Donaldson pushed away from the table and elbowed his way to the bar.

O'Hara's placid gaze settled on Fallon. "How about you, stranger?"

"Two," Fallon requested mildly. "Off the top this time."

The smile on the face of Beauregard O'Hara froze and died there as the implication of Fallon's words struck home.

"Are you calling me a cheat?" the burly sergeant demanded in a voice aquiver with righteous indignation.

"I'm not calling you anything," Fallon countered evenly. "Just making a friendly suggestion. Deal the cards."

"Not until you apologize for your slander, sir!"

"No chance," Fallon replied in the same soft tone. "Deal the cards."

O'Hara rose stiffly to his feet, bristling like an enraged porcupine. "Why you dirty, half-breed sonofa—"

Ryder Fallon uncoiled from his chair with the easy grace of a sidewinder. "I don't care for the term half-breed," he interrupted, and now his voice was silky smooth, strangely at odds with the rising tide of anger visible in his midnight blue eyes.

O'Hara's face was livid. "I don't give a tinker's damn in hell what you like!" he roared furiously, and there was a sudden hush throughout the saloon as all eyes turned in his direction.

There followed a moment of taut silence as the red-faced sergeant and the cool-eyed half-breed glared at each other.

For all his outward bluster, O'Hara was as

cold as ice on the inside. During his years at the Palace, one of the first things he had learned was that a gambler who stayed calm gave himself an edge and usually lived longer than one who didn't. Some dealers liked to carry a sleeve gun, others preferred a knife, but old Beau put his faith in a .44 Remington and a fast draw. He was good, and he was fast, and he had no doubt he could outdraw the dusty half-breed saddle tramp facing him across the table. No doubt at all.

He was grinning confidently as his hand closed over the smooth, pearl-handled butt of the double-action revolver holstered at his side, and his last conscious thought was that he'd outgunned the arrogant redskin.

It was a thought shared by every other man in the room.

Until Ryder Fallon made his play. Later, no one remembered seeing him draw. One moment he was standing easy, his arms at his sides, and the next the Colt was in his hand dealing blood and death, as much a part of the man as his arms and legs. Or the color of his skin.

A startled look spread over O'Hara's face as the slug from Fallon's Colt slammed into his chest. Surprisingly, he stayed on his feet although his gun, suddenly too heavy to hold, slipped from his hand, unfired, and skittered across the rough plank floor.

"Well, I'll be damned," O'Hara drawled, and fell face down across the table. A bright red stain blossomed beneath him, soaking the faded green baize cloth, edging the cards and greenbacks with scarlet.

Ryder Fallon eyed the awe-struck crowd, but no one moved to take up old Beau's fight. Repelled by the bold challenge in the half-breed's eyes, they turned away, suddenly intent on their own business.

There was a quick resurgence of noise and conversation as the saloon's occupants gathered at the bar to rehash the shooting. Two troopers stepped forward and carried O'Hara's body out of the saloon.

Fallon was holstering his colt when the solid thrust of cold steel against his spine jerked him upright.

"Drop your piece, easy like," Major Darcy Miller ordered curtly. He jabbed the barrel of his service revolver a little deeper into the half-breed's back, adding emphasis to his words.

With an air of grim resignation, Fallon laid his .44 on the table and slowly raised his hands over his head.

The major relaxed visibly. "Corporal Harris, please bring Mr. Fallon's sidearm to my office immediately." Darcy Miller prodded Fallon in the back. "Move it," he commanded brusquely, and Fallon obligingly headed for the swinging doors.

The major's office was small and austere, consisting of little more than four whitewashed adobe walls, a badly scarred mahogany desk, a pair of straight-backed chairs, a filing cabinet, and a limp American flag.

Darcy Miller waved Fallon into one of the chairs before settling himself into the big black leather rocker that was the room's only concession to comfort. Wordlessly, he took a pipe from the rack on the desk top, silently chewed on the stem while he contemplated the man seated across from him.

Ryder Fallon was a big man, six feet two inches of bronze flesh stretched over a lean, hard-muscled frame. Broad-shouldered and narrow-hipped, with high cheekbones and a nose that proudly proclaimed it had been broken more than once, he was a man who looked as if he could hold his own in a fight. But it was his eyes that held Darcy Miller's attention. They were the coldest blue eyes the major had ever seen.

"Would you care for a drink, Mr. Fallon?" Miller inquired at length.

Fallon dragged the back of his hand across his bearded jaw. "Why not?" he said with a shrug. "It's your party."

Without taking his eyes from the half-breed, Miller pulled a bottle and a pair of shot glasses from the top drawer of his desk and poured two drinks.

"Water?" the major asked, nodding toward the carafe on the corner of the desk.

"Just like it comes from the bottle will be fine," Fallon allowed, reaching for the glass nearest him. It was good whiskey, better than what he'd been served at the saloon, and he sipped it appreciatively, wondering how Miller knew who he was.

"Do we know each other?" Fallon asked after draining his glass.

"We've never met," Miller replied curtly. "But I know all about you."

"That so?"

"Exactly so. Would you care for another drink? A cigar, perhaps?"

Fallon shook his head. "Just what is it you want from me, Major?"

Darcy Miller leaned forward. He was a tall, angular man with graying brown hair and wide-set brown eyes. A purple scar, souvenir of an Apache knife, puckered his left cheek, marring an otherwise handsome face. His service revolver, still clutched in his right hand, pointed at Fallon's chest like an accusing finger.

"I need a scout," Miller said, biting off each word. "A man who knows this country like the back of his hand. Perhaps you've heard that Kayitah and his cutthroats are on the warpath again? No? Well, they're raising hell from here to the Mexican border, burning homesteads, butchering innocent women and children, destroying everything in their path, including my last five scouts."

Miller's eyes glittered savagely, as if each incident of Apache treachery were a personal affront. "I want them stopped once and for all, if you know what I mean."

Fallon stood up, his head wagging slowly from side to side. "Get somebody else," he said flatly. "I won't scout against the Apache."

"You will," Miller countered firmly, "or I'll see

you hanged for the murder of Sergeant O'Hara."

Fallon snorted disdainfully. "There's no way on God's green earth you can make that charge stick and you know it. Hell, he drew first. There must have been twenty men, including yourself, who saw the whole thing."

"All true," Miller readily agreed. "But if I say it was murder, I think my men will back me up. I am, after all, in a position to make their lives, shall we say, uncomfortable, if they refuse to see things my way."

A thin, humorless smile curved the corners of Darcy Miller's mouth. "You will scout for me, Mr. Fallon, or you will be tried for murder tomorrow morning at seven by the clock, and hanged at precisely seven-fifteen!"

Fallon's eyes narrowed with impotent fury as he heard the major out. It was no idle threat. The man meant every word, there was no doubt of that. Darcy Miller was all the law there was in this part of the territory, and his authority was absolute.

Fallon muttered a vile oath, knowing the major had him right where he wanted him.

"I've been told your word is reliable," Miller remarked skeptically, "so I will accept your promise to lead my men to Kayitah's camp. Once they have sighted the hostiles, you're off the hook, so to speak. Do I have your word of honor?"

"You've got it," Fallon growled.

"Good. You will ride out at dawn with Lieutenant Terry. Your sidearm and your money will be returned to you at that time. Corporal Harris will look after your mount."

"Whatever you say, Major."

Miller nodded; then, knowing the half-breed would not like what he was about to do, Miller cocked his pistol and stood up. "Until that time," he said smoothly, "you will be a guest of the United States Army. Corporal of the guard!"

Ryder Fallon's face was a mask of bitter outrage as the corporal of the guard and two troopers entered the major's office, their rifles at the ready, their faces grim. Fallon had the distinct impression that the whole thing had been prearranged and that, one way or another, Darcy Miller would have maneuvered him into accepting his proposal whether he had killed O'Hara or not.

"Escort this man to the stockade and make him comfortable," Miller ordered tersely. His gaze lingered on the corporal of the guard. "If he escapes, I'll have your stripes."

Ryder Fallon fixed the major with a cold stare as the corporal of the guard cuffed his hands behind his back. "Dammit, Major, I gave you my word."

"I know," Miller said with a sigh. "But this way we'll both rest easier until morning."

"How the hell do you figure that?"

"It's quite simple," the major explained as he holstered his weapon. "I won't have to worry about where you are, and you won't have to spend the night resisting the temptation to hightail it out of the fort before dawn. Good night, Mr. Fallon."

Chapter Two

Ryder Fallon grimaced as he surveyed the countryside. Five days had passed since they'd ridden out of the fort, and now they were deep in the heart of the Apache homeland.

At first glance, the territory appeared to be a barren, inhospitable wasteland with no redeeming features. For countless miles, the desert stretched away in seemingly endless waves of shimmering sand, apparently populated by little more than snakes, Gila monsters, stunted cacti, and an occasional wild pig. A relentless sun commanded the vast blue sky, shining mercilessly over the desolate landscape, crushing man and beast alike beneath a heavy blanket of heat.

And yet, it wasn't all bad. There was water, if you knew where to look, and food, if you had a strong stomach and weren't too particular about what went into it. There were breathtaking sunsets and glorious dawns. And beyond the arid flatlands there was a hidden canyon sheltered between high purple cliffs, a secret place known only to Kayitah's renegade Apaches . . . and Ryder Fallon.

It was there, far from the grasping hand of the white-eyes, that the Indians holed up between raids. It was a much-needed haven of refuge where, if need be, a handful of well-armed warriors could stand off an invasion. Cool clear water and sweet grass were abundant, and game was plentiful. Deer, rabbits, bear, squirrels and wild turkeys could all be found within the high protective walls of Rainbow Canyon.

Fallon frowned as he glanced at the man riding beside him. Lt. John David Terry was a tall, good-looking kid with sandy brown hair and pale gray eyes. He was probably no more than 23 years old, Fallon guessed, though he carried himself with all the confidence of a seasoned veteran. Still, for all his West Point training and military bearing, he was as green as grass. This was his first Indian campaign, and he had nothing but disdain for the Apache—"uneducated, naked savages" he called them—and contempt for Fallon.

Stretched out behind Fallon and Terry, riding two by two, were 150 blue-clad troopers. The majority of the men rode slumped in the saddle, eyes half closed, wilted by the overpowering heat and the long hours in the saddle, more concerned with when they would find rest and water than with the whereabouts of an enemy they hadn't seen hide nor hair of in five days.

Only the veteran soldiers among them, and those were darn few, Fallon noted sourly, remained alert and on guard.

Fallon rose easily at the head of the column, his broad-brimmed black hat pulled low against the blinding sun. His narrowed eyes darted restlessly across the desert floor, undeceived by its apparent emptiness. The Apache were masters at the art of camouflage, able to disguise themselves with dirt and desert plants so effectively that they were virtually invisible. Until you were right on top of them.

The Apache was at home in the desert, able to carry what little food and water he needed. He could travel on foot over the roughest terrain, covering up to 70 miles a day. He was a power to be reckoned with when he had a bow in his hand, and could launch a fatal arrow up to 500 yards.

The Apache was an enemy to be treated with fear and respect, but Terry rode blithely forward, confident that his West Point education made him superior to a people who had been born and bred under the harsh desert sun.

Now and again, Fallon scanned the column's back trail, his keen eyes searching for any sign of dust or movement that would indicate they were being followed.

Nothing moved on the face of the land, and yet he knew they were out there, waiting. He could feel their eyes on his back, sense their hatred as they watched the bluecoats ride ever deeper into Apacheria.

Abruptly, Terry signaled for a halt. "How far to the nearest water, Mr. Fallon?" he asked curtly.

"Rock Springs is just beyond that shallow draw," Fallon replied, "but I think we'd best bypass the Springs and ride for Foxtail Creek."

Terry rubbed a thoughtful hand across his jaw. He was hot and tired, his throat was as dry as the dust at his feet. Only the thought of a promotion in the field made this campaign bearable.

"How far to the Springs, would you say?" he asked.

"Three, maybe four miles."

"And Foxtail Creek?"

Fallon sighed. "Closer to ten."

"Out of the question," Terry decided. "We could not possibly arrive at the Creek before dark. I do not wish to make camp after sunset. We shall ride for Rock Springs."

"You'll be riding into a trap," Fallon stated flatly.

"A trap?" Terry scoffed. "Set by whom? We've seen no sight of the hostiles in five days."

"And you won't see them!" Fallon snapped, irritated by the lieutenant's condescending tone. "Not until it's too late."

A pained expression flitted across Terry's face. "Please, spare me your tales of Apache cunning," he groaned. "And kindly remember that I am in command here. We will ride for

Rock Springs and make our camp there for the night."

Fallon felt his temper rise. "Don't be a damn fool," he said in a tight voice. "Kayitah knows we're here. By now he knows how many men you've got, and what you wear to bed. But, more important, he knows we're out of water. He'll be expecting us to ride for the nearest water and he'll be there, waiting."

Terry shot the half-breed a look of ill-disguised contempt. "You may be reluctant to meet these phantom savages, Mr. Fallon, but I am not. My men need rest and water, and I intend to see they have both before nightfall."

"They'll all be dead before nightfall!" Fallon growled.

"You need not be afraid to engage the hostiles," the lieutenant assured Fallon sarcastically. "I have a plan that will not fail. My men and I will execute it at the proper time. If that time ever comes."

Ryder Fallon muttered a vile oath as he urged his horse ahead, afraid if he stayed near Terry a minute longer, he would wring the man's insufferable neck. A plan! Hell, every man in the Army from the lowest recruit on up to General George Armstrong Custer had a plan, and they all boiled down to the same thing: exterminate the red man or pen him up on some worthless piece of ground no one else wanted.

General George Crook had once called the Apache the tigers of the human species, and Fallon could not argue with that description.

They were a fierce people, wild and brave. They rarely took male prisoners alive. Boys were adopted into the tribe, women and children were usually allowed to go free. But there were always exceptions. Sometimes, when their blood was up and the need for vengeance burned bright, all captives, male and female, were killed; sometimes a few prisoners were taken and tortured. But such occasions were rare.

There was a surprising change in the scenery as they neared Rock Springs, so named because of the massive boulders that surrounded the water hole on every side. A narrow passageway, wide enough for a single horse, was the only way in. And the only way out, at least on horseback.

It was a perfect place for an ambush, and Fallon felt a shiver of apprehension as he led the column toward the shimmering blue-green pool. Cottonwoods and lacy willows grew close together near the water's edge, providing welcome shade, and horses and soldiers alike perked up as they looked forward to rest and water at the end of a long day's travel.

Terry led his men boldly forward, blatantly ignoring Fallon's warning to advance with care. Once inside the high rock walls, the troopers threw caution to the wind. Like carefree children on holiday, they slid from their mounts and flung themselves down on their bellies around the water hole, splashing, shoving, cavorting like puppies as they greedily gulped great swallows of the cool clear water.

For many, it was their final act in life. As the last trooper vaulted from the saddle and hurried toward the water hole, a shrill war cry echoed off the high rock walls.

Before the first ululating cry had died away, it was answered by 50 voices, and then picked up by 50 more as a horde of paint-daubed Indians swarmed out of the rocky crevices and descended on the startled troopers. More Indians poured through the passageway, their voices raised in the same hideous wail as they rode toward the soldiers, until it seemed as though the whole world vibrated with the sound of their hatred.

Too late, the troopers began to move. They sprang to their feet, water still dripping from their mouths and chins, as they sprinted for their horses, grabbing with frantic hands for carbines foolishly left in saddle scabbards. But their horses reared and scattered, spooked by the inhuman shrieks of over 100 blood-hungry Apache warriors.

"Head for cover!" Fallon shouted. "Stay together!"

The troopers nearest the half-breed sprinted for the cover of the timber, firing blindly with their sidearms as they ran, wasting precious ammunition. There were Indians everywhere. Most of the warriors were on foot; others, still mounted, blocked the entrance, or rode down the milling troopers, counting coup. The sound within the rock walls was deafening as men and animals alike screamed with pain and fear. A heavy layer of gritty yellow dust and black powder smoke covered the water hole like a shroud.

Fallon was one of the few white men armed with a rifle, and he fired the Winchester as fast as humanly possible, providing covering fire for a handful of whey-faced soldiers as they made a frantic dash for a copse of timber.

Two-thirds of the column was wiped out in the first ten minutes.

Standing in his stirrups, Fallon searched for Lt. Terry, but it was impossible to locate one man in that churning mass of humanity.

And then Fallon forgot about Terry and everyone else as a bullet caught him high in the right thigh. With a grunt of pain, he wheeled his horse around and fired the Winchester point blank into the face of a screaming warrior.

The heavy .44/40 slug ripped through the Apache's skull. For an eerie moment, the dead Indian remained upright in the crude Apache saddle, his dark eyes blank and staring. Then his pony bolted and the corpse toppled to the ground.

Minutes later, Fallon's horse folded beneath him, its life's blood gushing from a gaping hole in its throat. Instinctively, Fallon jumped free of the saddle, but his wounded leg refused to support his weight and he fell heavily on his right side, striking the back of his head on a flat rock.

Lights exploded behind Fallon's eyes and the sounds of the battle receded into the distance as a hazy gray mist settled around him.

"I hope I come face to face with that jackass lieutenant in hell," he mumbled thickly, and then a deep black void opened beneath him, separating him from the rest of the world.

Chapter Three

"They come! They come!"

The village crier lifted his voice in a mighty shout as he walked through the village announcing the return of the war party.

Immediately, women and children and warriors who were too old for battle hurried out of their lodges, moving in a great wave toward the narrow mouth of Rainbow Canyon. Anxious eyes peered into the gathering dusk, striving to find a glimpse of that one particular face, to know for a surety that husbands, fathers, sons and brothers had come home safely.

Jenny Braedon put her sewing aside and went to join the others. Standing on tiptoe, she gazed into the growing darkness and breathed a sigh of relief. Kayitah, mighty war chief of the Mescalero Apache, rode tall and straight at the head of the returning warriors.

There were two women in the war party. Jenny watched as they dismounted and handed the reins of their war ponies to a couple of young boys. These women had no children at home and had gone with their husbands to prepare food, dress their wounds, and fight, if necessary.

Kayitah's women had elected to stay home. Alope had prayed for him every morning for the last four days; every time she pulled a pot of meat from the fire, she had prayed that Kayitah would get what he wanted: victory over the white-eyes.

Jenny had prayed, too, though her prayers were ambivalent. A part of her had hoped that Kayitah would not return, that she would at last be free of the warrior who owned her body and soul, even as she prayed for his safe return because she knew that, without his protection, she would be at the mercy of every man and woman in the rancheria.

Shouts of welcome rent the quiet of the evening as women, children and aged warriors gathered around the war party.

When the first jubilant shouts of greeting had passed and the cries of victory had subsided, Kayitah raised his hand. A hush fell over the crowd as he spoke the names of the warriors who had been killed in battle: Sanza, Codahooyah, Desalin . . .

Jenny shivered as the keening wail of bereaved women rose on the wings of the wind. From this night forward, the names of the dead would not be mentioned again lest their spirits be called back to earth.

Within minutes, the crowd dispersed. Jenny was turning to follow Kayitah to their lodge when she saw the prisoners. They were the first white men she had seen in two years, and she gazed at them intently, tears welling in her eyes. They were her people, her blood, and she knew they were all fated to die, and to die horribly.

With a shake of her head, she put such distressing thoughts from her mind. There was nothing she could do to help them, no way she could change their fate.

Trailing behind Kayitah, she watched as the warriors pulled the prisoners from the backs of their horses. One man, taller and broader than the others, caught her eye. There was no fear in this man's expression, only a kind of sadness as he glanced around the village. His right pant leg was stiff with dried blood, and she felt a swift surge of pity for him as he limped into the squat wickiup that served as a holding place whenever the men brought captives back to the village.

With a sigh, Jenny hurried to Kayitah's lodge. His first wife, Alope, was already inside, preparing her husband something to eat.

Jenny moved to the rear of the lodge. Alope was in her mid forties, as round and plump as a ripe tomato. Her long black braids were tinged with gray, her face wore a habitual frown. She was Kayitah's first wife and as such, ruled over the lodge. Her hatred for Jenny was as strong as the love she had for Kayitah, and as powerful as her jealousy.

Alope offered him a bowl of fragrant venison stew, brought him his favorite pipe, then sat at his feet, her black eyes openly adoring her husband.

But Kayitah had eyes only for his white captive, and Jenny felt herself grow suddenly apprehensive. He did not make love to her often, partly because he was well past the age when such things were of prime importance, and partly because of the trouble it caused with Alope, but Jenny feared he intended to share her bed on this, his first night home. The thought filled her with dread and revulsion.

Alope did not miss the look of tender affection that Kayitah bestowed upon the white woman, and she hated her all the more. Always, it was the white woman whose company he sought after a long absence. Always, she had the best robes, the first choice of hides, the place of honor at his right side.

Jenny cringed inwardly as the tension inside the lodge grew steadily worse. She had learned much about the Apache in the last two years, and she knew that Kayitah was a just and honorable man. She had learned that he had attacked the stagecoach in retaliation for a raid made upon a peaceful band of Apaches, and that the other woman in the coach had been killed because an Apache woman had been brutally raped and murdered. But that did not make her captivity any easier to bear.

Alope ordered her around as if Jenny were no more than a slave, never satisfied with anything she did, always criticizing, always complaining. More than once, Jenny had cowered beneath the Indian woman's sharp tongue; more than once, Alope had struck her. Jenny endured the older woman's abuse, afraid to complain for fear it would only make matters worse, afraid if she caused too much trouble in the lodge, Kayitah would cast her out.

"Golden Dove, come sit beside me."

Kayitah's voice, softly commanding, called to her, and she went to his side, obediently sitting beside him while he smoked the pipe Alope had brought him.

Jenny kept her expression impassive as he laid his hand on her thigh and gave it a gentle squeeze. "I will share your bed tonight, when the feasting is over."

Jenny nodded. She could feel the hatred radiating from Alope, could feel the older woman's eyes drilling into her back, as sharp as daggers, as deadly as the bite of a rattlesnake.

Head lowered, she picked at the fringe on her skirt. If only she could have persuaded Hank to stay back east where they belonged. If only she could escape. If, if, if . . .

Chapter Four

The prisoners exchanged apprehensive glances as they gazed around the lodge. The interior of the brush-covered wickiup was cold and dark, heavy with alien smells which somehow served to emphasize the seriousness of their predicament. Unconsciously, the eight soldiers moved closer together, leaving a clearly defined space between themselves and Fallon, who was, after all, a half-breed and an outsider.

"Hey, scout," Trooper Horn called. "Those are your brothers, aren't they? How 'bout palaverin' with them for our freedom?"

"Sure," Fallon replied sardonically. "Maybe I can get them to throw in a horse and a rifle, too."

Trooper Horn smiled ruefully. "Hell, I'd settle for a cigarette and a blindfold."

"Seriously, Fallon, what happens now?" The question came from a young trooper with a mild Texas accent.

As one, eight pairs of eyes swung in Ryder Fallon's direction.

"Well?" Trooper Horn asked impatiently, annoyed by the half-breed's seeming indifference. "Speak up, scout. You're the expert here."

"Reckon so," Fallon agreed. Leaning against the center lodge pole, he eased himself into a sitting position on the hard-packed dirt floor, swearing softly as his cool blue eyes flicked over the soldiers one by one.

Corporal Hunter stood nearest the doorway, his round face ashen, his pale green eyes void of expression. Dried blood from a nasty head wound made a dark splotch down his left cheek.

Sergeant Dryden met Fallon's gaze squarely. There was no mistaking the hostility or distrust in the sergeant's hard brown eyes, no doubt that he despised half-breeds as much as full-bloods.

Trooper Nephi Johnson was a grizzled veteran of indeterminate age somewhere between forty and sixty. He stood straight and tall, disdainful of the bullet wound in his left side. Like Fallon, he knew there were far worse things ahead than the minor discomfort of a .44 slug.

Trooper McNeil was staring blankly at the ground. His right arm had been broken in two places, and a piece of bone gleamed whitely in the lodge's dusky interior. He was humming a monotonous tune under his breath.

Trooper Horn was his usual cocky self, his head high, his mouth turned down in a sneer. He seemed to be unhurt except for a shallow cut over his left eye.

Fallon didn't know the other three troopers. But they were all young. So darn young. And scared.

"Well, scout?" Horn growled. "We asked you a question and we're all waiting for the answer. What are they gonna do to us?"

"Knowing what's coming won't make the waiting any easier," Fallon warned.

"Dammit, man, I asked you a question and I want an answer! We've got a right to know what to expect."

"Then chew on this awhile," Fallon snapped, angered by Horn's surly tone. "My guess is they'll cover a few of you with honey and toss you over an ant hill. And the rest of you will probably die pukin' your guts out over a slow fire. Now, does that answer your question, or do you want to hear more?"

"No! That's enough!" The strangled cry came from a freckle-faced youth with curly red hair and frightened brown eyes. Beside him, his equally young companion vomited quietly into the dirt. Even Horn looked a little green around the gills.

"Sorry, kid," Fallon said sympathetically. "But maybe Horn is right for once. Maybe you should know what's coming."

The wickiup grew uncomfortably quiet as each man digested Fallon's words and tried to accept the fact that he was going to die, that Death was waiting for them just outside the door.

One by one, the troopers sank to the ground, as if the weight of Fallon's words had drained the strength from their limbs.

Nephi Johnson sat cross-legged beside Dryden, his grizzled head bowed in an attitude of prayer, his voice soft and reverent as he began to pray.

"The Lord is my shepherd, I shall not want. He maketh me to lie down in green pastures, He leadeth me beside the still waters. Yea, though I walk through the valley of the shadow of death, I will fear no evil . . ."

The quiet power of the Twenty-third Psalm brought a measure of peace to the anxious troopers as they silently mouthed the rest of the words.

" . . . for Thou art with me; thy rod and thy staff they comfort me . . ."

Ryder Fallon listened impassively, hearing in his mind the lilting, musical voice of his mother as she tucked him into bed at night. Closing his eyes, he saw her kneeling beside his pallet in their lodge deep in the heart of the Cheyenne nation, smiling as he repeated the words to the Lord's Prayer.

As Nephi Johnson's softly spoken words of comfort and assurance whispered through the Apache lodge, Fallon's thoughts drifted back through the dim corridors of time, back to the golden years of his childhood. He heard his mother humming softly as she prepared their meals, saw her stand on tiptoe to kiss his father's copper-hued cheek. He saw his father, a mighty Cheyenne warrior, pause beside a meandering stream to pick a bouquet of wildflowers, saw the happy tears in his mother's eyes as she accepted the fragrant gift from her husband's hands. He smiled faintly as he recalled the feeling of love and security that had filled their lodge until the day a Pawnee arrow killed his father and broke his mother's heart.

Fallon's reverie was shattered by the frightened gasp of one of the troopers as two Apache warriors entered the wickiup. Wordlessly, they grabbed Corporal Hunter by the arms and dragged him outside.

Sergeant Dryden's hoarse cough echoed like thunder in the stillness that followed.

The seven remaining soldiers carefully avoided each other's eyes, ashamed of the swift surge of relief that flowed through them because they had been spared, if only for the moment.

Sweat tracked its way down grimy cheeks as each man strained his ears for some sound, some clue as to their companion's fate. Hearts pounded. Mouths went dry. Nervous fingers drummed on the hard earthen floor. Fear was a tangible presence in the lodge, as real as the harsh rasp of their breathing, as solid as the ground at their feet.

There was no sound from outside the wickiup.

Five minutes passed. Ten.

And still there was no sound.

Nerves already rubbed raw by the events of the day were frayed beyond endurance by the taut silence that hung over the Indian village. And then, when it seemed they would drift forever in a sea of silent uncertainty, a shrill scream shattered the quiet of the night, followed by a wail of such unspeakable agony that the camp dogs howled in sympathy.

"My God," breathed Trooper Horn, and quietly bowed his head, searching his soul for the courage to face whatever lay waiting for him.

The boy who had vomited toppled over in a dead faint. No one seemed to notice.

Fallon stretched out on his left side and gazed up at the tiny patch of sky visible through the blackened smoke hole of the wickiup. A solitary star winked back at him, shining clear and bright against the black velvet curtain of night.

With a sigh, Fallon closed his eyes and tried to clear his mind of the nightmare images that had been conjured up by Hunter's agonized scream. Of all the tribes in the Southwest, the Apache were the most skilled in the art of torture, often keeping their luckless victims alive for days at a time, long, pain-racked days and nights that undoubtedly seemed like endless years.

He swore softly. There was no possibility of escape, no hope of reprieve. He faced the fact squarely and accepted it. The best he could hope for was to face his tormentors defiantly, with his head high and his spirit unbowed. If he could endure their torture bravely, with dignity, as a warrior should, perhaps he could earn their respect again. Perhaps they might even grant him a quick death. Perhaps.

A wry smile touched Fallon's lips. It was doubtful that the People would go easy on him. Traitors died hard, and he was the worst kind of traitor. And with that thought in mind, he rested, knowing he would need every ounce of strength he possessed to meet the ordeal that lay ahead.

Surprisingly, he slept.

When he woke, it was morning and he was alone in the lodge with the freckle-faced boy.

"You look a little green, kid," Fallon observed dryly. "Just you and me left?"

The boy nodded weakly. "Y . . . yes."

"Saving the best for last, I guess," Fallon muttered, wincing as he struggled to sit up. For a moment the lodge spun out of focus, and he closed his eyes, waiting for the dizziness to pass.

When he opened his eyes again, he found the boy staring at him, a worried frown on his face.

"Are you all right, Mr. Fallon?"

Fallon snorted softly. "Yeah, I'm fine, kid. Just fine." *Except that my head feels like it was run over by a herd of buffalo and my leg feels like all the fires of Hades are kindled inside.*

"Just fine," he repeated dully, and wished he had a good stiff drink to ease the pain in his leg and wash the dryness from his throat.

A short time later an aged woman shuffled into the wickiup, a large bowl cradled in her gnarled hands. Murmuring to the boy in her own tongue, she offered him a spoonful of the bowl's contents, but the boy refused it with a violent shake of his head.

The old woman grunted her displeasure as she crossed the floor and knelt in front of Fallon.

A toothless grin lit her wrinkled features as he readily opened his mouth. The stew was hot, rich and thick, flavored with sage and wild onions and chunks of venison. He ate it all and wished for more.

"You should have eaten some, kid," Fallon remarked when they were alone again. "They aren't likely to offer you anything else."

"How can you think of food at a time like this?" the boy exclaimed angrily. "You know they're only trying to keep us strong so they can torture us later."

Fallon shrugged. "No sense dyin' hungry."

The boy groaned low in his throat. "Horn and the others are dead, butchered by those savages, and we're next!" He shuddered. "Horn lasted for hours. When I close my eyes, I can still hear him screaming. I don't know how you slept through it. I . . ."

"Get hold of yourself, trooper!" Fallon admonished sharply. "Horn and the others are dead meat, and none of your sniveling will bring them back!" He swore softly at the shocked expression on the boy's face. "I'm sorry, kid," he apologized gruffly. "Why don't you try and get some sleep? You look beat."

"Sleep!" the boy shouted. "Sleep!" His voice

rose hysterically. "After tonight, I'll be sleeping forever." Tears rolled down his cheeks.

"Take it easy, kid," Fallon said gently. "Everybody dies sooner or later."

"But not like this," the boy whimpered. "I'm scared."

"Yeah, I know the feeling."

"Are you scared?" the boy asked, genuinely surprised.

Fallon nodded slowly. He was scared, right down to the ground. More scared than he'd ever been, though it wasn't death he was afraid of; only that he might die badly.

Somehow, his confession seemed to make the boy feel better.

"What's your name, kid?"

"Cory, sir. Cory Mulhaney."

"How old are you, Cory?"

"Sixteen," the boy confessed. "I lied to get into the Army."

Fallon laughed ruefully. "I guess that proves honesty is the best policy, eh, Cory?"

"Yessir," the boy agreed, rewarding Fallon with a weak smile. "What did Sergeant Dryden mean when he said the Apache were your brothers?"

"Kayitah made me a blood brother to one of his warriors a long time ago. They adopted me into the tribe."

Cory looked confused. "Well, then, won't they let you go?"

Fallon shook his head. "I'm afraid not. I've been riding the white man's trail too long to have any friends left here now."

"I guess they won't like you scouting against them, either."

Fallon grinned. "Not much."

"Have you been scouting for the cavalry very long?"

Fallon's expression grew somber. "Less than a week."

"Why'd you sign on as a scout?"

"I guess you could say Major Darcy Miller 'persuaded' me."

Cory nodded, understanding the implication, and the two men exchanged glances of mutual dislike for Fort Bowie's commanding officer.

"You married, Mr. Fallon?"

There was a long pause before Ryder replied tonelessly, "No, kid, I'm not married."

"I got a girl in Tucson," Cory said wistfully. "We're gonna get married next year when I . . ." His voice trailed off as he remembered that, for him, there would be no next year.

Fallon looked away as the boy struggled to regain his composure. It wasn't easy to face the fact that your life was over before it had really begun. As for himself, Fallon shrugged fatalistically. He'd covered a lot of ground in his thirty-odd years, seen most of the country between the Atlantic and the Pacific, won and lost a dozen fortunes on the turn of a card, enjoyed the company of numerous beautiful women. He'd done most of the things he wanted to do, and there were few places he wanted to go back to. Still, while he wasn't afraid to die, he wasn't ready, either.

"What did you do before you were a scout?" Cory asked in a thin voice, disliking the silence that had settled over the wickiup.

Fallon smiled faintly, readily understanding the boy's need for conversation, his unwillingness to spend the long hours until nightfall sitting quietly, with nothing to do but think about what lay ahead.

"Just about everything, I guess," Fallon answered, shifting to a more comfortable position. "I busted broncs. Worked as a trailhand. Did some time in jail for robbing a bank over in El Paso. Tried my hand at gold mining in California. Did a stint as marshal in Kansas City. Tended bar in a fancy cathouse in Dodge. Even hired out my gun for a while, but I didn't cotton to that. Mostly, though, I just drift and hope the cards fall my way."

"Sounds exciting," Cory mused.

"It has been, from time to time."

"I wish I'd . . ."

"What?"

"Nothing," Cory said flatly. "What's the use of wishing for anything now?"

Outside, the shadows grew long, and as the setting sun turned the sky to flame, the low beat of the drum summoned the tribe to the center of the rancheria. Soon, the sounds of singing and dancing and merry laughter filtered into the darkening lodge. The smell of woodsmoke and roasting meat tickled Fallon's nostrils.

Cory had ceased his nervous chatter, and Fallon wondered if the kid had finally fallen asleep. Sitting there in the oppressive darkness, Ryder Fallon wished fervently for the strength and the courage to withstand whatever the fates held in store for him, and while he was wishing, he wished for a tall glass of Kentucky bourbon to ease the throbbing ache in his thigh, and for a cigarette to ease the tension that was tying his guts in a knot. But, like the kid had said, there was no use in wishing for anything now.

Outside, the village grew ominously still, as if a giant hand had suddenly choked off all sound, all movement. Even the dogs had ceased their endless snapping and snarling.

Cory began to sob quietly. "I don't want to die," he murmured piteously.

"Nobody does!" Fallon hissed. "Dammit, I wish they'd come and get it over with!"

The words had barely left his mouth when four warriors entered the lodge. Yanking both white men to their feet, the Indians shoved them outside.

A wordless murmur of anticipation rose from the waiting crowd.

For Jenny, the day had passed swiftly. Life with the Apache was hard and there was always plenty of work to keep her hands occupied. She had found several occasions to pass by the wickiup where the prisoners were being held, and her thoughts often strayed to the tall white man who had caught her eye the day before. She wondered who he was and if he had a wife to mourn for him, children who would cry for him.

With the coming of evening, she grew increasingly restless, and she finally went to the campfire, her steps reluctant. The Indians had tortured captives twice since she'd been a prisoner, but she had never watched. Now, a morbid sense of curiosity held her immobile as she waited in the shadows to see how the tall white man would react when the women began to torture him. Would he scream in terror? Would he weep? Would be beg for mercy when the pain grew unbearable? Intuition told her he would do none of those things, yet it was inconceivable that a man could withstand such agony without voicing the pain aloud.

She felt an ache in her heart as she watched the last two prisoners being dragged into the center of the village. The boy looked so young, so helpless and afraid, her heart went out to him. But it was the tall man who drew her gaze again and again. He did not look afraid. Indeed, he seemed to take a great interest in everything going on around him, as if he were merely a spectator to the event and not the main attraction.

In a matter of minutes, the two prisoners were spread-eagled on the ground on either side of the fire, their hands and feet securely lashed to stout wooden stakes driven deep into the earth. Two of the warriors drew their knives and began to cut away the tattered remains of the boy's Army uniform. The Indians laughed when they saw his long red underwear.

The two warriors were grinning and shaking

their heads with amusement at the strange clothing of the white man as they moved toward the half-breed. Dried blood from the bullet wound in his thigh had glued the prisoner's buckskin pants to his skin, and Jenny heard him curse softly as one of the warriors callously ripped the heavy material from the wound. A fresh trickle of blood oozed down his thigh.

Jenny swallowed hard. How could she stay and watch? The thought of what was to come made her stomach churn, yet she could not bring herself to leave. She felt strangely drawn to the tall man, though she could not say why. Just looking at him filled her with an odd fluttering in her stomach.

By mutual consent, the women chose Cory for their first victim. Jenny understood why the women behaved as they did. It was their way of exacting vengeance for the deaths of their husbands and sons, fathers and brothers, and yet it was cruel, so very cruel.

She felt a wave of revulsion sweep through her as the older girls and women swarmed around the boy like ants over a gumdrop, poking at him with knives and sharp sticks, hitting him with their hands and fists, digging their fingernails into his pale cheeks. They laughed derisively at his pale skin, and at the wispy, ginger-colored hair on his chest.

Jenny shook her head. She knew these women. They were loving wives and gentle mothers. They laughed when they were happy and cried when they were sad. But now, caught up in the light of the dancing flames, they looked like crones from hell.

The boy made a valiant attempt to be strong and silent in the face of their relentless attack, but as the sharp knives and sticks pierced his tender flesh again and again, his courage deserted him.

"Stop, please," he begged. "Somebody, help me." He tugged futilely on the ropes that held him down, struggling until he was breathless and covered with sweat. Tears welled in his eyes and coursed down his cheeks. "Oh, God," he sobbed brokenly, "this can't be happening."

His tearful cries filled the women with disdain. Eyes filled with contempt for his weakness, they lashed out at him.

Jenny longed to run to him, to take him in her arms and comfort him as a mother might comfort a frightened child, but she remained hidden in the shadows, knowing there was nothing she could do. To interfere would not save him.

And then, to Jenny's relief, one of the warrior women made her way through the crowd gathered around the boy.

"His cries make me weary," she said in a loud voice, and drove a feathered lance into the boy's heart, killing him instantly. There was a murmur of disapproval from the other women, but none dared challenge Ziyah's decision.

Fallon let out a long sigh. The kid had got off easy, he mused. And then he forgot about the boy as the women turned their eyes on him. More wood was tossed onto the fire, and as the flames blazed higher and higher, Ryder Fallon broke out in a cold sweat.

There was an atmosphere of tense anticipation as an incredibly ugly warrior swaggered into the center of the crowd and stood beside the prisoner. A streak of yellow lightning zigzagged across the warrior's chest. Similar symbols were painted across each cheek. His black eyes, narrowed and close set, flashed angrily as he strutted around the prisoner, recounting Fallon's treachery in guiding the soldier coats into the rancheria. His voice swelled with the force of his hatred as he described the battle at Rock Springs and declared that the prisoner had sent no less than six brave Apache warriors on the road to the World of Spirits.

The warrior's tirade increased the hostility radiating from the tribe, and Fallon felt their animosity rushing toward him, hotter than the flames that danced and crackled near his head.

In a swift, graceful movement, the warrior plucked a long burning brand from the heart of the fire. Swinging it in wide circles above his head, he walked around Fallon, chanting his war cry:

"Death to all white-eyes! Death to all white-eyes!"

And then, in a sudden move that caught Fallon completely off guard, the incensed warrior lunged forward and laid the smoldering stick across his naked belly.

Fallon gasped as the brand seared his flesh,

swore under his breath as the warrior withdrew the stick, taking a layer of skin with it.

Jenny covered her nose and mouth with her hand at the smell of singed flesh, but she never took her eyes from the prisoner. Sometimes, if a man was extraordinarily brave in the face of death, his life was spared, and Jenny found herself whispering, "Don't scream, don't scream," as his body went rigid with pain. But no sound escaped his lips, and the watching Indians shouted their approval. Traitor though he might be, the half-breed had courage.

The warrior heated the brand a second time, then advanced toward the prisoner again. Fallon watched him warily now, his muscles bunched in anticipation of the pain to come, his hands tightly clenched.

He swore softly as the Indian drew near.

"Niyokahe, wait!"

The warrior frowned as an aged squaw hobbled into view.

"Wait," the woman said again. She stopped in front of Niyokahe, her frail body placed between the warrior and the half-breed. "This one is of the blood. Do you not recognize Kladetahe, blood brother to Delshay?"

"Be silent, old woman," hissed a voice from the back of the crowd. "Do not speak my brother's name again lest his spirit become angry."

"Your brother would not see Kladetahe punished unjustly," the old squaw retorted.

"My brother's blood cries out for vengeance," the angry voice replied curtly.

"Kladetahe is no longer a brother to the Apache," Niyokahe proclaimed in a loud voice. "He has betrayed the People to the white-eyes, and the penalty is death!"

The warriors shouted their approval. There was no place in their ranks for a traitor, red or white.

The old woman held her ground, patiently waiting for the outcry of the warriors to die down before asking in a reasonable tone, "Would you kill a brother without hearing his side? That is not the Apache way. Every man is allowed to defend his honor."

"A traitor has no honor," Delshay's brother exclaimed vehemently. "I say kill him!"

Scattered shouts of approval and shouts of "Kill him, kill him, kill him!" rippled through the crowd.

The blood of the warriors, stirred by Fallon's betrayal, ran hot with hatred for all white-eyes, especially for the bluecoats, but also for the Mexicans, who offered a bounty on Apache scalps.

"Cat-ra-ra ata un' Innas 'u un' Nakai-ye!" Niyokahe cried passionately, and the cry was picked up and repeated by every warrior present until the shout echoed and re-echoed off the high canyon walls like thunder: "Curses and destruction on all white men and Mexicans!"

The old woman paid no heed to the heated words and threats rising all around her. Instead, she focused her rheumy old eyes on the face of the man who was striding briskly toward her.

Kayitah was tall for an Apache, standing almost six feet. He was naked save for breech-clout and moccasins. The firelight glistened on his broad, copper-hued chest. A necklace of bear claws circled his throat. His hair, showing more gray than black, was held away from his face by a wide strip of red cloth. His torso was rife with scars, mute evidence of innumerable battles fought and won.

"Ugashe!" he commanded the old woman. "Go!"

The old woman held her ground a moment more, then, her rheumy old eyes still defiant, she returned to the sidelines.

Fallon stared at the Apache chief. There was an aura of strength and power about Kayitah that demanded respect. It was apparent the moment he arrived on the scene, and Fallon felt it now as the Indian regarded him through hostile, deep-set black eyes.

"Kladetahe was once welcomed by our people as a friend and a brother," Kayitah remarked coldly. "He slept in our lodges and ate at our fires. He married one of our women. He fought our enemies. But that was long ago. Now his heart has turned against us. He no longer deserves to be considered as one of us. Let his fate be that of his companions."

Fallon had not realized he was holding his breath until Kayitah's words crushed the slender ray of hope spawned by the old woman's interference on his behalf.

Now, glancing at the implacable hatred reflected in the chief's ebony eyes, and facing the certainty of a long and horrible death, Fallon's pent-up breath escaped in a deep, shuddering sigh. Fear's icy hand clamped tightly around his insides, creating a cold lump in the pit of his belly, bringing a fresh sheen of sweat to his brow, a cold clamminess to his clenched fists.

"Wait!" A sturdy old man joined Kayitah, and a respectful hush fell over the Indians as they waited for the *diyi* to speak.

Jenny eyed the man intently. Perhaps there was still hope for the prisoner. Cochinay was the Apache medicine man. His was always the last word in any dispute, the deciding vote in any decision that affected the tribe. Villages were moved, hunts were started or postponed, all on the strength of the shaman's say-so.

"It is a bad thing for one Apache to kill another," Cochinay intoned sonorously. "It has been forbidden since the beginning of time. Therefore, we will let Usen decide Kladetahe's fate."

The medicine man paused dramatically, his bony arms raised skyward; then he pointed at an old deadfall on the outskirts of the camp near an abandoned sweat lodge.

"We will tie the prisoner there," he commanded. "Let no one go near him. If he is yet alive in five days, we will know it is Usen's will that Kladetahe become the slave of whoever cuts him free." Cochinay stared at Fallon. "If he dies, that, too, will be Usen's will."

Jenny stared at the prisoner. He had been badly wounded, but he looked strong and fit. Would he be able to survive for five days without food and water and medical attention?

Kayitah nodded in agreement, and then his gaze swept the crowd in a long warning glance. "Let no one aid him but Usen!"

Two warriors stepped forward and cut Fallon free. Pulling him roughly to his feet, they shoved him toward the fallen log. But Fallon's wounded leg refused to support his weight and he fell heavily.

"Fear has drained the strength from his limbs," Niyokahe sneered contemptuously.

"It ain't fear," Jenny heard the prisoner mutter as the two warriors dragged him toward the deadfall. "It's lead."

Within minutes, Fallon was trussed up like a Christmas turkey, his ankles bound tightly together, his arms drawn up behind his back and secured to the deadfall in such a way that he would be forced to remain sitting up when he wanted nothing so much as to lie down and sink into blessed oblivion.

Jenny walked slowly toward Kayitah's lodge, reluctant to leave the prisoner, though she could not say why.

Inside the wickiup, she slipped out of her dress, then drew on the loose-fitting garment she wore to sleep in. Sitting on the robes that made up her bed, she began to brush out her hair. For the first time since her capture by the Indians, she felt a glimmer of hope. If the white man survived, and if he would help her, she might yet win her way to freedom. She would promise him anything if he would only help her escape, anything at all.

With a sigh, Jenny slipped under the buffalo robes and closed her eyes. From outside came the sound of celebrating as whiskey bottles looted from wagon trains and cavalry patrols were opened and passed around. Long shadows danced on the sides of the wickiup as warriors strutted back and forth, bragging about their courage in battle, boasting of enemies slain and coup counted. Jenny felt her eyelids grow heavy as the laughter and the drumming slowly lulled her to sleep.

Ryder Fallon watched the dancing through heavy-lidded eyes, remembering warm summer nights when he had walked into the dusky shadows with a raven-haired maiden at his side.

He closed his eyes, seeking sleep, but he was not to be left alone. Kayitah and Cochinay had warned that the prisoner was not to be killed, but that did not mean the Indians couldn't torment the traitor as they saw fit. Robbed of his death, the people vented their anger by hurling insults at him, and when they derived no satisfaction in that, they jabbed him with sharp sticks and pelted him with rocks and dirt clods until the novelty wore off and they drifted back to the fire and the whiskey and the dancing.

Only then did Ryder Fallon give voice to his misery. Lifting his eyes toward heaven, he let out a long low moan filled with pain and despair. Five days, the *diyi* had said.

"Five days," Fallon muttered, and knew he'd

never make it, not in his present condition, not unless he got help, fast. He was weak from hunger and loss of blood. His thigh ached dully, monotonously, and there was a steady pounding in his head. The burn across his belly throbbed anew with each labored breath. But, more than anything, he yearned for a drink of water. Oh, Lord, for just one drink to ease the awful dryness in his throat.

A shadowy figure drew Fallon's eye and he found himself staring up into the swarthy face of Delshay's younger brother, Chandeisi. The warrior cradled Fallon's Winchester in the crook of his right arm. The desire to use the rifle burned bright in Chandeisi's glittering black eyes, and in the cruel twist of his mouth.

I should have let Miller hang me, Fallon thought bleakly. It would have been better than seeing the contempt on the face of this old friend.

Chandeisi stood there, not speaking, for several minutes. Then, slowly and deliberately, his dark eyes glinting with malicious intent, he jabbed the butt of the rifle into the half-breed's wounded thigh.

Pain skyrocketed the length and breadth of Fallon's right leg, but his pride, as deep and strong as his old friend's hatred, stilled the anguished cry that rose in his throat.

Teeth clenched against the pain, he choked back the vomit that burned in his throat. Waves of nausea assailed him as he stared at the bright red blood welling from his thigh, and suddenly the whole world dissolved in a crimson sea and he felt himself sinking, drowning in a scarlet tide of pain. . . .

The campfire was out, the celebration long over, when he regained consciousness. His arms and shoulders were numb from being forced into an unnatural position for so long. There was a searing ache in his thigh, and when the pain became more than he could bear, he retreated into the friendly darkness that hovered all around him.

There, in the last dreary hour before dawn, Death beckoned to Ryder Fallon. Her voice was soft as new grass, as entreating as the whisper of a young lover as she promised him peace and rest.

Come, Death whispered sweetly. *Why linger here in pain and misery when I can end your suffering?*

"Why, indeed?" Fallon thought ruefully, and leaned toward Death's outstretched arms.

Immediately, the pain in his body receded and he smiled. "No more pain," he mused, pleased. No more hunger. No more thirst.

He burrowed deeper into Death's comforting embrace. No more fights. No more killing. No more snide remarks about his mixed blood.

No more rides across the vast sunlit prairies. No more shady ladies or busthead booze . . .

He began to frown.

No more peaceful nights under a blanket of stars. No more laughter. No more buffalo hunts with the Cheyenne. No more rivers to cross . . .

"No!" The word was a groan on his lips as he twisted out of Death's dark snare.

Instantly, the pain returned, all the harder to bear for the brief respite.

"No," he whispered hoarsely. "No, no, no!"

Desperate now, he held fast to the pain, clinging to it as a frightened child clutches his mother's hand.

And now he relished every agonized moment, for pain meant life.

Chapter Five

Fallon woke, shivering, as the first faint rays of the sun streaked the eastern horizon. The air was bitterly cold, the ground beneath him harder than an old whore's heart.

The first day, he mused grimly. Looking down, he contemplated his injuries. The burn across his belly, though painful, didn't look particularly serious. The ache in his head was almost gone. But the wound in his thigh was red and swollen and sore as hell. At the moment, it didn't look infected; at least there were no ominous red streaks. Yet. If he could manage to survive the five days decreed by the old medicine man, and if he could figure out a way to get that chunk of lead out of his thigh before it festered, and if he didn't freeze to death lying naked in the cold, he might yet win his way to freedom.

They were mighty big ifs, he acknowledged bleakly, and yet men had lived through worse things. Dave Logan had been scalped alive by the Lakota and lived to tell the tale. Fred Winslow had been attacked by a grizzly, and though he had been badly mauled by the ferocious beast, he had managed to crawl away to safety. Later, he'd gone back and killed the bear. Big Jim Blake, blood brother to the Cheyenne, had been forced to run the gauntlet when he was caught in the buff with another man's wife. Banished from the tribe, naked and unarmed and bleeding from numerous cuts, he had managed to survive.

"Hell," Fallon muttered through clenched teeth, "if they could do it, so can I."

Slowly, the village came to life. Women poked the ashes of their cook fires, warriors emerged from their lodges and plunged into the icy river, seeking relief in the chill water from the after-effects of too much whiskey and too little sleep. Small children gawked at the naked white man, always careful to stay close to the ready protection of their mothers' skirts in case the white man grew another arm to grab them with and gobble them up like the Monster Elk who lived in the forest.

After breakfast, a group of young boys surrounded him, pointing at him, poking at him with sharp sticks as they counted coup on a living enemy, which was the greatest coup of all. One boy, older and braver than the others, drew blood with a sharp stone. His comrades crowed with delight.

Later, a handful of maidens walked by on their way to the river to draw water. One paused to stare openly at the half-breed's nakedness, brazenly admiring his broad chest and shoulders, the thick muscles in his arms and legs. After much whispering and giggling, they hurried away.

Women went out of their way to pass by him, raking their nails across his bare flesh, reviling him in their native tongue as they bloodied his face and chest.

Only the warriors ignored him, scorning his presence with their silent contempt.

As the sun climbed higher in the clear azure sky, a sultry stillness settled over the rancheria. Children sought relief from the heat in the gurgling coolness of the river. Babies napped in their *tsochs,* shaded by the spreading leaves of the trees that protected them like umbrellas. Ancient ones nodded outside their wickiups, enjoying the soothing warmth that chased the ache from old bones. The warriors lounged in the shade, half-heartedly repairing their weapons, or gambling.

Fallon closed his eyes against the sun's glaring brightness, quietly damning Major Darcy Miller and his blackmail tactics. Why hadn't he let that hard-nosed bluecoat hang him? At least that would have been relatively quick. Better than dying of thirst, or baking to death beneath a relentless summer sun. Better than waiting for the bullet lodged in his thigh to fester and send its slow poison winding through his veins to rob him of his strength, then his senses, and finally his life.

Discouragement spread her mantle over him, and he lacked the strength to cast it aside.

Jenny sighed as she walked down the valley looking for firewood. She hated living with the Indians. She hated their way of life, where every day was a struggle for survival. She missed her cozy home back in Philadelphia, missed the creature comforts she had once taken for granted, missed her friends and neighbors, like old Mrs. Craddock who had brought her fresh eggs every morning, and spry Mr. Johnson, who had given her flowers from his garden whenever she passed by. She missed the joy of Christmas, the bounty of Thanksgiving, the promise of new life on Easter Sunday. She missed birthday parties and dances on New Year's Eve, heart-shaped valentines, and pumpkins on Halloween.

Again and again she had begged Kayitah for her freedom, but he turned a deaf ear to her pleas. He would gladly give her anything she desired, anything but her freedom. He was happy with his white captive, fascinated by her long blond hair and green eyes.

Jenny sighed again as she sank down beneath a shady pine. She hated her life. She hated the hard work. She hated the food. She hated the clothing. Tanning hides was disgusting. Jerky and pemmican were less than appetizing, and yet, in the dead of winter when there was little else available, she ate it gladly. Venison wasn't too bad, but she often longed for a thick juicy steak that didn't taste wild or gamey. Some nights she dreamed of pork chops smothered in gravy and fluffy mashed potatoes, of cold milk and hot apple pie. She longed to bathe in a real tub and wash with fragrant soap instead of washing in the river. She yearned to sleep on a feather mattress between clean linen sheets that smelled of sunshine instead of sleeping on the ground beneath blankets made of hides. She longed to shop, to wander through Hadley's Dry Goods Store and Martha's Millinery Shoppe, to buy a pretty dress of sprigged muslin, to don a perky straw bonnet bedecked with ribbons and flowers.

But what she missed most of all was a home of her own. It was crowded in Kayitah's lodge, and living with Alope was a constant irritant. The woman was domineering and loud and as jealous as a shrew.

Kayitah had promised Jenny a wickiup of her own, but somehow it never materialized, and she knew he didn't trust her to live by herself, though how she would escape on her own remained a mystery.

Leaning back against the tree, Jenny closed her eyes and for perhaps the hundredth time that day found herself thinking of the prisoner. If only she could find a way to ease his pain, perhaps he would help her escape. But how to help him without jeopardizing her own safety? As much as Kayitah doted on her, she knew he would not be lenient if she were caught in a deliberate act of disobedience.

And yet, there had to be a way.

By day's end, Fallon was exhausted. Never in his life could he remember being so dirty, or so thirsty. Helpless anger raged through him as he bore the humiliation of the tribe's abuse in stoic silence, and yet he could not fault them for their hatred. He had betrayed them to save his own skin. Whatever they did to him was no more than he deserved, but it did not make the pain of his wounds, or the humiliation of captivity any easier to bear.

After a while, he slept.

Jenny sighed heavily as she saw the prisoner's head loll forward. He had drawn her gaze again and again during the course of the day. She had spent much of the afternoon watching him, always from a distance, of course, lest someone remark on her interest in the white man and mention it to Kayitah. It would not do to arouse the chief's suspicion or jealousy.

She knew the prisoner was in pain, yet he had made no outward sign of discomfort, either by word or expression. He bore the physical abuse of the women and children in tight-lipped silence, did not waste his breath begging for food or water. Or mercy.

Watching him, Jenny was convinced he was a brave man possessed of a strong stubborn streak coupled with a fierce desire to survive, and it occurred to her that, if he survived, he would not be content to remain a slave for very long.

If he survived. Jenny was not a doctor, but she knew he would die without help. And she did not intend for him to die. Not while there was a chance, however slight, that he might help her escape.

With a heavy heart, she knew she would have to defy Kayitah's edict. She would have to give the prisoner food and water and whatever medical attention she could manage, or he was going to die. And if he died, all her dreams of escape would die with him.

That night she lay awake long after Kayitah was asleep. If only she could somehow get away on her own. But no matter how many times she imagined such a thing, she knew it was impossible. Even if she managed to elude the sentries posted at the entrance to the canyon, there was no way she could hope to find her way through the crazy-quilt pattern of hills and canyons and desert that stretched for miles beyond the rancheria's high purple walls. No way she could hope to survive in the wilderness alone.

Two hours after midnight, Jenny summoned every ounce of courage she possessed and tiptoed out of Kayitah's lodge.

The village lay quiet under a cloak of darkness as she padded noiselessly toward where the prisoner was being held. Twice, dogs came toward her, stiff-legged with suspicion until they recognized her scent.

In moments, she was within sight of the half-breed. He was awake. He looked cold and tired and terribly uncomfortable, and she heard him swear softly as he shifted his weight on the damp ground.

Jenny smiled faintly. It was good to hear her own language again, even if the words were obscene.

Gliding soundlessly through the shadows, Jenny knelt beside the prisoner. "Shhh," she whispered at his startled look. "I've come to help you."

"Really? Why?" he asked suspiciously.

"Please, be still," Jenny begged. "I must not be caught here."

Fallon nodded, then winced as the woman ran her hand over his injured thigh.

Jenny frowned as she peered intently at the wound. Even in the uncertain light cast by the moon, she could see that the wound was swollen and angry-looking. Tiny red streaks spread fanlike around the edges of the bullet hole.

"It's becoming infected," she whispered. "Are you in much pain?"

"No," Fallon rasped sarcastically. "I feel just fine."

"I have no medicine," Jenny told him regretfully. "Only this."

Reaching beneath the folds of the blanket that covered her head and shoulders, she withdrew a narrow-bladed Mexican dagger and a pint of cheap trade whiskey.

Fallon's eyes narrowed. "That's pretty primitive," he muttered dryly, "even for the Apache."

Jenny shrugged. "It's all I have."

Fallon shook his head. "Forget it and cut me loose."

Jenny threw him a look that said he was crazy. "You can't ride with that leg, and if the bullet doesn't come out soon, there'll be no point in removing it at all."

"I'll take my chances," Fallon hissed.

"If that bullet doesn't come out now," Jenny said flatly, "I think you'll be dead in a week."

Fallon scowled as he heard his own thoughts put into words. "I think you're right," he agreed glumly. "Go ahead and cut it out."

Jenny held his gaze for a long moment. "If you cry out, we'll both be dead in a week," she muttered, and when Fallon made no reply, she began to brush the dirt from his thigh.

"I only hope you are as brave as you seem," she murmured under her breath, and uncorking the whiskey bottle, she dribbled a little of the amber liquid over the blade of the knife.

"Wait!" Fallon whispered. He nodded at the bottle in her hand. "Give me a swig of that."

The woman hesitated a moment, then held the bottle to his lips while he took a long swallow.

Ryder grimaced as the rotgut burned a path down his throat and pooled in his belly like liquid fire.

"Go on," he rasped, "cut the damn thing out."

With a supreme effort of will, Jenny put everything from her mind but the task at hand as she carefully guided the point of the slender blade into the malodorous hole. She swallowed hard as dark red blood and thick yellow pus oozed from the wound.

He's got to live. He's got to live. She repeated the words in her mind as she probed for the bullet, trying not to think of the pain her unskilled hands were causing him, trying not to let the knife cut into healthy tissue, trying to ignore the warm wet blood that stained her fingers.

Waves of nausea assailed Fallon as the woman probed blindly for the slug buried deep in the meaty part of his right thigh. Too weak to resist the rising tide of vomit that rose in his throat, he turned his head to the side and retched.

With a low groan, he felt himself slipping into blessed oblivion as the keen-edged blade bit deeper into his quivering flesh.

"I've got it!" Jenny whispered triumphantly.

The words pulled Fallon from the brink of unconsciousness and he let out a long breath, felt his taut muscles begin to relax as the tension slowly drained out of him.

Jenny wiped the perspiration from her brow, her eyes warm with compassion as she let the wound bleed for a moment, letting the bright red blood carry away the last of the pus.

Without warning, she emptied the contents of the whiskey bottle into the gaping hole in his thigh.

Fallon swore under his breath as the raw whiskey sizzled through him like liquid fire, sending long fingers of flame shooting up and down his right flank.

Quick as a cat, Jenny covered his mouth

with her hand. "Please be still," she implored as she cast an anxious glance at the sleeping village. Fear made her weak. Discovery would mean death at the worst, a severe beating and humiliation at the least.

Moving hurriedly now, she pressed a strip of clean cloth over the wound to stem the bleeding, then bent to examine the ugly blister on his flat belly.

"Forget that," Ryder rasped impatiently. "Get me some water."

Jenny nodded, a little irritated by his imperious tone. She was reaching for the waterskin at her side when a movement from a nearby wickiup caught her eye. With a wordless cry of distress, she snatched the cloth from the prisoner's thigh and disappeared into the shadows.

Fallon swore under his breath as a warrior emerged from a nearby lodge and relieved himself.

Scowling blackly, Fallon searched the shadows for some sign of the woman, but she had gone, taking the water with her.

Cursing the luck that had brought the warrior out of his lodge at such an inopportune time, he closed his eyes and was quickly asleep.

The second day.

Fallon woke with dawn's first light to see upwards of a hundred warriors assembled at the center of the village, all armed and painted for war. The *diyi* chanted a few brief words as he sprinkled a handful of *hoddentin* to the four corners of the earth, entreating the Apache gods to bless the *Dineh* with victory over the white-skinned invaders.

With a whoop, Niyokahe vaulted onto the back of his pony and raised his rifle high overhead. "Ho, brothers!" he cried in a loud voice. "It is a good day to die!"

Wheeling his prancing mount in a tight rearing turn, the warrior sank his moccasined heels into the animal's flanks and sent it galloping down the valley. The warriors raced after him, their war cries filling the air.

"Zas-tee! Zas-tee! Netdahe! Netdahe!"

The rousing cry trailed after the warriors like smoke in the wind as they rode out of the rancheria.

"Kill! Kill! Death to all intruders! Death to all intruders! Death to all intruders!"

Fallon wondered fleetingly where they were headed, and why Kayitah had chosen not to lead them. Then, remembering the night past, he glanced at his thigh. A fine layer of dust had been sprinkled around the wound lest someone notice that his right thigh was conspicuously cleaner than his left.

Fallon grinned. So, she had come back after he'd fallen asleep.

She hadn't been a dream, after all.

The morning dragged on with agonizing slowness. And still three more days to go. It seemed a lifetime. The smell of roasting rabbit and ash cakes set his empty stomach to rumbling, and his mouth watered as he stared at an ugly yellow hound gnawing on a bone heavy with raw meat. Damn! He was hungry enough to eat the bone, and the dog, too!

But worse than his hunger, worse than the growing numbness in his shoulders, worse than the nagging ache in his thigh, was the driving need for water, a desire that grew increasingly stronger as the hours went by.

The moon was waning when Jenny again made her way to the prisoner's side. Seeing that he was asleep, she touched his shoulder lightly.

Fallon came awake instantly, surprised by her unexpected presence. She was taking a big risk, coming to his aid. What could she possibly hope to gain by putting her own life in danger?

"I've brought water," Jenny whispered.

"Thank God."

"How badly do you want it?"

The gentle compassion of the night before was noticeably absent from her voice.

Fallon's eyes narrowed to mere slits, and he swore under his breath. What the hell was she up to, anyway?

"Dammit, lady," he growled angrily, "I'm in no mood to play games."

"Nor am I," Jenny retorted. "I need your help."

Fallon stared at her. "You need my help?" He snorted incredulously. "How in the hell can I help you when I can't even help myself?"

"I have been watching you these past two days," Jenny replied urgently. "I do not think you will die. And I do not think you will like being a slave, either. Sooner or later you will try to escape, and when you do, you will take me with you."

"Like hell!"

"You won't change your mind?"

"Damn right. A man would have to be crazy to agree to such a . . ."

But he was talking to the wind.

The third day was long and warm. Warmer still for the fever that burned through him. His throat was dryer than dust, his tongue heavy and swollen in his mouth. Silently, he cursed his quick words of the night before, cursed the mysterious woman who had offered him relief only to snatch it out of his grasp, cursed the sun that was slowly leeching the moisture from his body, increasing his thirst until he could think of nothing else.

The woman came to him again that night. Wordlessly, she examined his wound. Her hand was gentle, cool against his fevered flesh.

"I will not ask you again," Jenny warned softly. "Will you take me with you?"

"Who the hell are you, anyway?" Fallon asked irritably.

"There's no time for that now," Jenny admonished. "Will you take me with you?" She held up a waterskin, shook it to tempt him.

Fallon's pride urged him to tell her to go to hell, but he couldn't ignore the inviting sound of the water sloshing inside the waterskin, could not withstand his body's incessant demand for water. Water to ease the choking dryness in his throat, to replace the moisture drained away by the sun and his own sweat.

As if sensing his inner struggle, the woman shook the waterskin again.

"All right, dammit, I'll take you with me."

"I have your word? As a warrior?"

Fallon scowled. "Yes, but for God's sake, give me a drink before our friend with the weak bladder shows up again."

Suppressing a grin, Jenny held the waterskin to his lips, cautioning him to drink it slowly. The water was sweet and cold. He didn't know she had left the filled container submerged in the river all day to keep it cool; he knew only that it tasted better than anything else the world had to offer.

When he had taken the edge off his thirst, Jenny offered him a slice of succulent tenderloin, then another drink.

Fallon studied the woman closely while she fed him, but try as he might, he couldn't quite make out the features shadowed in the folds of the blanket that covered her head.

She offered him a second slice of meat, a third, gave him one last drink from the waterskin, and then she was gone.

Fallon let out a contented sigh. Whoever the hell the woman was, he was grateful for her help.

Feeling better than he had in days, he closed his eyes.

Two more days.

* * *

The fourth day of Fallon's captivity passed much the same as the others. Little girls pointed and giggled, little boys pelted him with rocks and dirt clods. The women taunted him, making jokes about his manhood, the rough beard that covered his jaw.

The warriors ignored him.

The sun burned down relentlessly.

The fifth day dawned cold and wet as a summer storm watered the canyon. Huge raindrops fell sporadically at first, and Fallon breathed a silent prayer of thanks as he threw back his head and let the life-giving water run into his mouth and over his face.

An hour later, the rain stopped and a pale sun broke through the clouds. Gradually, men and women began emerging from their lodges, all attention focused on the prisoner as the people waited to see if Winter Snow would claim the white man as her slave.

But it was Alope who crossed the muddy ground and cut Fallon free. "Come," she said curtly.

"Wait!" Kayitah strode toward his wife, his face dark with anger and astonishment. "What are you doing?"

"I wish to have this man as my slave."

"Why?"

Alope shrugged. "*You* have a slave," she remarked. "Now *I* have one."

"I forbid it."

"Then get rid of the white woman. Give her to Niyokahe, or trade her to the Comanche."

Kayitah glared at his wife, aware that they were being watched.

"Do as you wish with the white man," he replied coldly. "But know that you will regret it."

Turning on his heel, he returned to their lodge.

Alope watched her husband walk away, pleased by his anger. He was jealous. It was a good sign.

She nudged the white man with her foot. "Come," she said again.

Fallon rubbed his aching wrists as he slowly stood up. He felt as weak and helpless as a newborn pup. His legs were like rubber, his muscles stiff and sore. He stood for a moment, swaying slightly, aware of the eyes upon him.

Taking a deep breath, he drew himself up to his full height and then, with his head high, followed the Indian woman into her lodge.

Jenny glanced up, her eyes widening in surprise as Alope entered the wickiup, followed by the white man. She glanced at Kayitah, who was sitting beside the fire, his expression ominous. She had not questioned him when he returned to the lodge. If he was angry with her, she would find out soon enough.

Puzzled, she studied the smug expression on Alope's face and realized, abruptly, what had caused Kayitah's foul mood. Alope had claimed the prisoner.

Jenny's gaze flew to the white man's face. Did he recognize her? What if he said something? But when he looked at her, his expression was blank.

Alope tapped Fallon on the arm, then gestured toward a moth-eaten robe spread in the rear of the lodge.

"Rest," she said curtly. "You will need your strength to work. If you do not work, you will not eat."

Fallon nodded. Mindful of his wounded thigh, he eased himself down on the robe and closed his eyes, thinking that a fluffy cloud in heaven could not have pleased him more.

Chapter Six

Jenny stared thoughtfully at the white man while he slept. His face was drawn and haggard even in sleep, his breathing shallow and uneven. Sweat dotted his brow, and when she bent to touch his forehead, it was warm with fever.

With a sigh, she knelt beside him, glad for this time to be alone, with just the white man for company. Kayitah had gone hunting, Alope had gone with the other women to look for the narrow-leafed yucca plant which would be roasted on a bed of live coals. It was a staple of the Apache diet. Dried, it could be stored for up to a year, or pounded into a mixture with berries.

Alope had ordered Jenny to stay behind with the prisoner, obviously thinking Jenny would view such a task as a hardship when, in truth,

Jenny was glad to stay behind, glad to have some time to herself.

She remained at the prisoner's side all that day while the fever caused by exposure to the sun and loss of blood burned through him. With infinite patience, she mopped the sweat from his face and neck, replaced the blanket when he cast it aside, forced spoonfuls of thick, nourishing soup into his mouth.

He was a big man, with strong arms and broad shoulders and long, muscular legs. And as she cared for him, she knew he would live. He had to live. He was her only hope of escape.

Fallon stirred restlessly, hovering in a netherworld where memories of the past rose up to haunt him. Wandering through the mists of time, he saw his mother, forever beautiful, teaching him to read and write in the white man's way. He saw his father, strong and tall and proud, patiently teaching him to read the signs of the deer and the elk, of the wolf and the bear, the coyote and the rabbit, to interpret the signs of the sun and the moon and the stars.

Once again, he roamed the mountains and valleys with Delshay and Chandeisi, sharing their laughter as they raced their fleet ponies across the sun-bleached desert, or swam naked in a chill high-mountain stream.

And once again he saw Nahdaste, her belly swollen with his child, her ready smile brighter than the sun at noonday. Nahdaste, with hair like black silk and dark eyes warm with love and desire. Once again he held her close, begging her not to die. And once again, he lost her.

And then he was running, running through the mists of time, running from the wickiup where she had died in his arms. Running from the sympathetic faces of his friends. Running from her memory . . .

He woke with a start, her name a cry on his lips. A cool hand reached through the darkness to wipe his fevered face and offer him a cool drink of water. Soft words encouraged him to rest, to sleep, to forget . . .

Jenny sat back on her heels, wondering what demons haunted his dreams, what ghosts caused him to thrash about.

She glanced up as Kayitah entered the lodge. The Apache chief had been in a foul mood since Alope had brought the white man into their lodge. Now, as he locked a set of ancient shackles around the prisoner's ankles, he smiled for the first time in days.

"I have never seen a white man in chains," Kayitah remarked. "Only Indians." His grin widened. "This is better."

The lodge was cold and empty when Fallon woke the following morning. The village was quiet, and only the soft patter of the rain and the whisper of the wind broke the stillness.

He sighed, stretching, and there was an ominous rattle beneath the buffalo robes. He swore softly as he lifted the blanket, scowled at the rusty iron shackles fastened around his ankles.

Scowling blackly, he unleashed a string of obscenities. The heavy chains would not hinder him as he worked for the chief's wife, but they would sure as hell put a crimp in any attempt he made to escape, and Kayitah knew it. The chief knew he'd try to escape first chance he got, but he wouldn't get far dragging leg irons. Their infernal clanking would arouse every dog in the camp.

In a burst of anger, Fallon threw off the blanket, noting that someone had thoughtfully provided him with an elkskin clout to cover his nakedness. There was also a heavy buckskin shirt, and a pair of knee-high moccasins.

Rising, he pulled on the clout, and moccasins and left the lodge.

Jenny was returning from the river when she saw the white man step outside. Dressed in a clout and moccasins, he looked very much like an Indian himself except for his dark blue eyes and the heavy beard that covered his jaw.

Fallon's gaze met Jenny's as she drew near the lodge, and he knew somehow that she was the woman who had cut the bullet from his leg. It made sense now. She wanted to escape and she'd saved his life, then bribed him with the promise of water. She shook her head, silently begging him not to speak to her, not to mention that she had disobeyed Kayitah.

Fallon nodded imperceptibly as he read the fear in her eyes.

Jenny emptied the waterskin she had filled at the river into the kettle set on a tripod outside the wickiup, then added chunks of venison and wild vegetables, as well as a handful of herbs for seasoning.

Stirring the soup, she kept one eye on the white man, who was sitting in the sun, his long legs stretched out before him, his eyes closed.

Jenny smiled faintly. It was a beautiful day. The clouds had fled and the sky was wonderfully blue and clear. The whole valley sparkled, as bright and green as it must have been on the first day of creation, and Jenny felt her heart soar with hope. The white man was alive and well. Soon he would be strong again; soon he would try to escape, and she would go with him.

It was early afternoon when the war party returned to the village. It took but one look to know that the gods had blessed the Apache with victory. But it had not come cheap. Eleven Indian ponies carried lifeless burdens.

Jenny listened as Niyokahe intoned the names of the dead for the last time, shivering as the keening wail of bereaved wives and mothers floated down the valley.

Trying to block the sound of grief from her mind, Jenny let her gaze drift down the line of warriors. The Indians had attacked an Army supply train, looting it for blankets, rifles, ammunition, coffee, sugar and a keg of whiskey. They had stolen the Army mules, too. Jenny shook her head sadly when she saw the prisoner who stumbled in the wake of the mules. His head was bowed, his shoulders slumped in defeat. His uniform was in shreds.

When the war party reached the center of the village, two warriors took hold of the prisoner and tied him to the same deadfall where they had dragged Fallon. One of the warriors kicked the prisoner's legs out from under him while the other deftly secured his arms behind his back. With a final tug on the man's bonds, the two warriors hurried toward their lodges where their wives would be waiting with clean clothing and a hot meal.

Jenny stood beside Kayitah as he listened to Niyokahe's report, trying not to let her revulsion show as Niyokahe bragged of how the Apache had wiped out the Army supply train, and then ridden on to attack the fort.

"The whites are stupid," Niyokahe said contemptuously. "They sent too many soldiers to guard the supply train. Taking the fort was easy. We made the soldier chief watch while we killed his men. He cried like a weakling child."

Jenny turned away, feeling sick. How many men, red and white, would have to die before the red man and the white man learned to live together in peace and harmony? Would they ever learn? The soldiers did not think of the Indians as human and killed them without compunction, often slaughtering whole villages in their eagerness to exterminate the red menace. Of course, the Indians fought back, but more often than not they lost their battles, unable to match the Army's superior firepower or seemingly endless supply of fighting men.

Jenny sighed as she stirred the soup simmering in the big kettle. She thought of the miles and miles of empty land and wondered why there wasn't enough room for all men to live in peace. And once again she offered her silent prayer, asking God to help her escape from Kayitah and the Indians.

With the coming of night, the Indians began to gather in the center of the village. Jenny frowned irritably as she helped the other women serve the warriors. The Apache victory was being celebrated in the usual way, with drinking and feasting and dancing, and the air was heavy with the smell of woodsmoke and the tantalizing aroma of that most favored Apache delicacy, roast mule meat.

A blazing fire kept the dark at bay, and Jenny could see Niyokahe outlined against the flames, posturing wildly as he recounted the highlights of the attack on the white man's fort, boasting of coup counted and enemies slain in battle. He was a bully and a braggart, and Jenny heartily disliked him. More than once, she had thanked God that she had not been captured by Niyokahe. His naked torso glistened in the firelight and his face was distorted with hatred as he spoke of the whites, and of past treacheries the soldiers had committed against the People. The faces of the other warriors reflected the same intense hatred as Niyokahe's, and Jenny thought, regretfully, that there would never be peace as long as such hatred existed.

She was offering Kayitah a slice of mule meat when she happened to see the white man standing alone on the edge of the crowd, one arm draped over the makeshift crutch he had fashioned from a sturdy cottonwood branch. He looked up just then and their eyes met and held.

A curious warmth spread through Jenny as their gazes met, and she quickly glanced away lest he think she was flirting with him.

When she looked up again, he was gone.

Jenny left the celebration when they dragged the luckless prisoner into the camp circle. She did not want to see another man tortured and killed. She had seen enough death to last her a lifetime.

Leaving the village, she walked into the trees until the sounds of the celebration were far behind. She had been warned several times not to venture away from the village alone. There was danger in the dark for a woman on her own. Even the men rarely wandered far from the camp at night.

But she needed to be alone.

The woods were dark and quiet. The intertwining branches blocked the light of the moon, and she walked carefully, feeling her way through the darkness.

She knew suddenly that she was no longer alone. She froze in mid step, her eyes probing the night, her ears straining for some sound, her heart pounding wildly. She heard a rustle in the underbrush behind her and uttered a low exclamation of terror as a dark shape materialized out of the shadows.

Fallon chuckled softly. "Didn't anyone ever tell you it was dangerous to wander off alone at night?" he drawled.

Jenny felt her knees go weak with relief. It was the white man. "What are you doing out here?"

Fallon shrugged. "Probably the same thing you are."

"I wanted to be alone."

"Yeah. Me, too."

A faint cry, high and shrill and laced with pain, shattered the stillness of the night. Jenny shivered, her heart constricting in sympathy for the unfortunate soldier whose only escape from pain was a quick death.

"It'll be over soon," Fallon said quietly.

"That's the real reason I came out here," Jenny confessed. "To get away from that."

"I know."

She was glad suddenly that he was there beside her. His presence was comforting, and she wished she could spend some time with him, get to know him. It would be nice to speak her own language, learn what was going on in the world. But even now she was glancing into the shadows, fearful of being caught alone in the dark with a man. If Kayitah should find her . . . she shuddered, putting the thought from her mind.

"I've got to go," she said quickly.

"Wait." He laid a restraining hand on her arm. "I don't even know your name."

"It's Jenny. Jenny Braedon."

"Ryder Fallon. I never thanked you for saving my life."

"Just get me out of here," Jenny murmured. "That's all the thanks I need." And turning on her heel, she ran back toward the village.

As his strength returned, Fallon began strolling through the village, venturing a little farther each day, carefully noting the position of the sentries on the high canyon walls, their number, the hours when the guard was changed, all with one thing in mind: escape.

Fallon did not take kindly to being Alope's slave. She had a tongue sharper than a two-edged sword and a temper to match, and she took great delight in ordering him to do everything from finding her moccasins to brushing her hair. He was expected to draw water, gather wood, hunt for roots and berries, weed their garden.

The Apache children fell down laughing the first time they saw Fallon gathering wood. A warrior doing women's work? It was unthinkable! Unheard of!

"Stupid *pinda-lick-o-ye!*" they cried. "Stupid white-eyes."

The warriors turned away in disgust. Strangely, the maidens no longer mocked him. Some cast shy glances in his direction when they encountered him drawing water from the river or spading Alope's meager garden. Others admired him openly, staring unabashedly at his broad shoulders and long legs, for he was considerably taller and broader than most of the Apache men. A few of the young women flirted with him brazenly, not caring that he was a slave, seeing only that he was a man, and a handsome one, at that.

Fallon returned their smiles, but he made no attempt to encourage them. His longing for freedom far surpassed every other desire, even his need for a woman. Captivity was like a worm in his belly, gnawing at his pride, souring his disposition. He obeyed Alope without complaint, content to bide his time until he found a way to escape.

Still, slavery rankled deep in his soul, made worse by the shackles he was forced to wear. The only bright spot was Jenny Braedon. He'd had no chance to be alone with her since that night in the woods, but it was comforting, somehow, to have her there. She was a beautiful woman. Her eyes were the most incredible shade of emerald green, fringed by thick dark blond lashes. Her skin was smooth and unblemished, tanned to perfection. Her hair was long and thick and gold, a halo fit for an angel. Golden Dove, Kayitah called her, and the name suited her perfectly.

He was thinking of her a week later as he sat on the riverbank staring glumly at the swift-moving current. Freed of the restricting irons that hampered his every step, and with Jenny Braedon to share his lodge, life with the Apache would have been tolerable, even pleasant. He had lived with the Indians before, years ago . . .

He had been eighteen the day he had found Delshay lying half dead at the base of a tree. It was hard to believe that fifteen years had gone by since then, Fallon mused. It seemed like only yesterday. He had taken the wounded Apache back to his village, and when the boy recovered, the two had become blood brothers and Fallon had been adopted into the tribe and given a new name: Kladetahe. He had lingered at the Apache camp for several weeks, somehow reluctant to leave, and after a while it was assumed he would remain with the Apache indefinitely.

It was during that first cold winter that Fallon discovered Nahdaste. She was tall for an Apache, with straight black hair that reached to her waist and impish black eyes. Fallon had loved her from the moment they met, loved her with every fiber of his being.

There was a bittersweet pain in his heart as he thought of her now. But for the cruel hand of fate, he would have remained with the Apache for the rest of his life, content to spend all his days among Nahdaste's people.

But it was not to be. Less than a year after their marriage, Nahdaste had died in his arms. He had buried her high in the mountains beneath a sheltering pine, together with their tiny stillborn daughter, and then, overcome with grief, he had fled the rancheria in the dead of night. In retrospect, he supposed he had been running ever since. . . .

Fallon grinned ruefully as he ran a hand over his jaw. Even his beard was a form of running away, he mused, a way of hiding from himself.

"You'll never find a way to escape if you just sit there brooding like an old man," a familiar voice declared.

Fallon glanced over his shoulder, surprised she had sought him out. They had carefully avoided each other in the past week, both aware that Kayitah was very jealous of his blond wife.

"Do you think this is wise?" Fallon asked as Jenny sat down beside him. "People might think we're meeting on the sly."

"Don't be ridiculous!" Jenny retorted. But he was right. It was dangerous for them to be seen alone together, especially so far from the village. But she needed to get away, needed someone to talk to, if only for a minute.

She plucked a blade of grass and twirled it between her fingers, conscious of the man beside her. He was a handsome man, in a rugged sort of way, and she wondered what he would look like without the beard. He had a strong, arresting face, and a virile body corded with muscle . . . She felt her cheeks grow hot as she realized what she was thinking.

"So, tell me about yourself," Fallon said.

"There's nothing to tell. I just want to go home."

"Yeah," Fallon muttered and then, hoping to make her smile, he doffed an imaginary hat and held it over his heart. "Ryder Fallon at your service, ma'am," he drawled. "Gambler, drifter, ex-con . . ." His dark blue eyes raked her boldly from head to heel. "Rescuer of fair maidens in distress."

Jenny smiled in spite of herself. "Have you any idea how to get out of here?" she asked hopefully.

"There's only one way into this place," Fallon answered with a shrug. "And one way out, and that's through the passage at the mouth of the canyon. Unless you want to try scaling these cliffs."

Jenny looked up at the forbidding purple walls that hemmed them in and shuddered. "No."

"I didn't think so. The only other possible way out is through Diablo Canyon Pass, but I don't recommend that. Anyway, getting out is only part of the problem. First I've got to get shed of these irons so I can fork a horse. And then we'll need a couple of good mounts and supplies, not to mention a rifle." He shook his head ruefully. "Hell, maybe we'd better just forget it."

"No!" Jenny cried vehemently. "There has to be a way. I'll go mad if I don't get out of here soon." Her shoulders slumped as she thought of how miserable she'd been in the last two years, sharing Kayitah's lodge with a woman who despised and demeaned her, being forced to obey, to submit. She couldn't take it anymore. She just couldn't. There had to be a way out. She didn't care if she had to walk barefoot through Diablo

Canyon, just as long as she could go home.

She hadn't meant to cry, but once she started, she couldn't seem to stop.

"Hey," Fallon admonished gently. "Don't cry."

"Please get me out of here," Jenny sobbed. "I'd rather die in the desert than spend another night in this place. Please help me."

He could not ignore the despair he read in her eyes, the awful discouragement in her voice. Wanting to comfort her, he reached out to take her in his arms.

Jenny jerked away from him, her expression bordering on panic. Kayitah was the only man other than Hank who had ever touched her, and Kayitah had not always been gentle.

"I guess you've had a bad time," Fallon remarked quietly.

Jenny nodded warily.

"I won't hurt you," Fallon said, his voice softly reassuring. "I just thought it might help if you had a shoulder to cry on."

His voice was deep and low, strangely soothing. It was silly to be afraid of him, she thought. She would have to trust him if he was to help her escape.

Without quite knowing how it happened, she found herself in his arms, her face buried in the hollow of his shoulder. His touch did not repulse her as Kayitah's did, or leave her feeling empty, as Hank's did. Instead, she was filled with a sense of well-being, a sense of belonging. It was so unexpected, so disconcerting, she began to weep again, unleashing all the tears and frustration she had been holding back for so long.

Ryder Fallon frowned unhappily. He'd always been a sucker for a woman's tears.

"Don't cry," he murmured, stroking the golden head pillowed on his shoulder. "I'll think of something."

Chapter Seven

In the days that followed, the tension in Kayitah's lodge grew stronger and more palpable. Alope had hoped that the white man's presence would make her husband jealous enough so that she could win him back to her bed, but it hadn't happened. Kayitah's gaze continued to alight with favor on the white woman, and Alope's anger grew deeper and more bitter. She couldn't strike her husband. She didn't dare harm the white woman. But the white man was hers to do with as she pleased. She could beat him, she could kill him, and no one would care.

Now that his strength was fully returned, Alope had no qualms about venting her growing frustration on the white man. When he failed to obey one of her orders fast enough to suit her, she ordered him outside and whipped him unmercifully.

Fallon grimaced as a handful of children gathered around, their black eyes wide as they watched Alope whip her slave. Such punishment was unheard of for an Apache child. Children were prized by the People, raised with love and affection and a lack of control that white parents would have found appalling.

He flinched as the whip bit into his bare back. He was visibly trembling now, his legs weak and shaking, and still he refused to cower before her.

Alope's rage increased because he refused to cry out, because his pride was stronger than her arm, and she was forced to quit before she brought him to his knees. Frustrated beyond words, she brought the whip down across his shoulders one last time, then returned to the lodge.

As soon as she was out of sight, Fallon dropped to his knees, then stretched out on his belly in the dirt and closed his eyes.

It was Jenny who found him there, Jenny who carefully washed the blood from his mutilated flesh, then spread a thin coat of bear grease over his lacerated back.

He endured her help with quiet fury, not knowing which was worse, the pain of the whipping, the necessity of letting Jenny treat his wounds, or the humiliation of being whipped by a woman while a handful of children gathered around to watch.

"Why are you so stubborn?" she whispered.

"She would have quit if you weren't so bull-headed."

"And give her the satisfaction of knowing she was hurting me?"

"A slave can't afford the luxury of pride."

"I'm not a slave, dammit!" Fallon rasped.

He started to rise, but Jenny laid a restraining hand on his shoulder.

"You would be wise not to antagonize her," Jenny admonished softly.

"It's not me she's mad at," Fallon said wearily. "It's you. She's just taking it out on me."

Jenny stared at him in alarm. "What do you mean?"

"Are you blind? The woman's jealous of you; you must know that."

"She has no reason to be jealous of me," Jenny exclaimed vehemently. "I don't want her husband."

"But he wants you."

Jenny nodded, guilt rising up within her as she stared at Fallon's mutilated back. Everything he said was true.

As the days went on, things went from bad to worse. When Fallon broke one of Alope's favorite clay pots, she screamed that he was worse than a clumsy dog. That night, she dumped his dinner on the dirt outside the lodge, saying that if he was going to act like a dog, he could eat like one. He had gone to bed hungry that night, and the following day, as well.

Jenny had come to his aid in the early hours of the morning, sneaking him several strips of venison, but he had refused her offering, his pride rebelling at accepting her help yet again.

There were days when Alope pretended she had no work for him. On those days, she left him tethered to a tree from dawn till dusk, leaving him at the mercy of the sun and the flies. On those days, she refused him nourishment, saying that food and water must be earned.

The rope around his neck was worse than a noose, he thought bitterly. A hanging, at least, would have been quick. But this degradation was something no man should have to bear. It was not the scorn of the warriors, or the laughter of the women and children that rankled, but the sidelong looks of pity that Jenny spared him each time she passed by.

There were times when he knew she would have paused to speak to him, when she would have offered him something to eat or drink, but he warned her away with a harsh look. He could endure anger, scorn, ridicule, pain, hunger, the sting of the lash, the burning rays of the sun, but he could not endure the pity and compassion he saw in Jenny's deep green eyes.

He had been Alope's slave about a month the day she dropped a rope around his neck and made him spend the day on his hands and knees pretending to be a horse. To the delight of some of the older women, she led him into the woods where she placed a bundle of wood on his back, tied it in place with a length of rawhide, and then walked behind him as he made his way back to the village, poking him in the ribs and buttocks with a stick every step of the way.

Fallon was seething with anger and humiliation when they reached the wickiup. By damn, the woman's arrogance was not to be borne! But the consequences of disobedience forced him to hold his tongue. He wasn't sure why Alope had claimed him, though he suspected it had something to do with making Kayitah jealous.

Now, since her ruse had failed, he had a hunch she was looking for a way to get rid of him permanently, so he choked back the bitter words of rage that threatened to suffocate him and waited meekly outside the lodge while she called for Jenny to come and unload her "new horse."

Fallon kept his head down, the hot blood of humiliation heating the back of his neck as Jenny stepped out of the wickiup. He refused to meet her gaze, refused to face the sympathy he knew would be shining in her luminous green eyes.

Crouched on his hands and knees, his head hanging, he felt Jenny's fingers skim across his bare back as she untied the bundle of wood and began stacking it outside the lodge. Once, he felt her hand brush the back of his neck, her touch soothing, compassionate.

But still he refused to meet her gaze.

When the wood was unloaded, Alope sent him out to look for a large flat stone, to what purpose he didn't know, but he walked away from the wickiup without a backward glance, more angry and frustrated than he'd ever been in his life.

He kept remembering the sympathy in Jenny's beautiful green eyes, the touch of her hand on his neck, infinitely soothing, filled with compassion.

It wasn't pity he wanted from Jenny Braedon, he admitted bleakly. No, he wanted much more than that. He wanted the right to touch her the way Kayitah touched her. He wanted her at his side, wanted to see her smile at him, her eyes bright and clear, not shadowed with fear or sadness as they so often were. He wanted to hear the sound of his name on her lips . . .

He wanted her. The thought ripped through him like an Apache skinning knife. He wanted her as he had not wanted a woman in years, wanted to touch her, to taste her, to see those fathomless green eyes grow cloudy with passion and desire.

He wanted her, and that wanting made him hurt deep inside, made him ache with a soul-deep hunger that left him feeling empty and alone.

Fallon swore under his breath, and then he laughed, softly, bitterly. As well to desire the moon as the wife of the Apache chief, he mused. He had as much chance of obtaining the one as the other.

It was after dusk when Fallon returned to Kayitah's wickiup. He caught Jenny's worried gaze, endured the rough side of Alope's tongue as she cursed him for his lengthy absence, accusing him of shirking his duties, reminding him that his life depended on his strong back and her good will.

When Alope's tirade ended, Jenny unobtrusively handed Fallon a bowl of venison stew and a cup of black tea.

Kayitah did not miss the look of compassion and understanding that flickered in the white woman's eyes. For the rest of the evening he watched Jenny closely, surreptitiously, as she sat beside the fire sewing tiny silver bells to the sleeves of a new dress. He saw the way she looked up from time to time, her gaze constantly seeking the white man, her expression one of sympathy and concern.

Kayitah turned his attention to Kladetahe, who was sitting in the back of the lodge clumsily mending a tear in his shirt, apparently oblivious to everything, and everyone, else.

The chief frowned as he studied the white man. The half-breed was a man in his prime, a man handsome enough to draw any woman's eye. Kayitah knew that many of the maidens looked on the half-breed with favor. A few hoped that, in time, Kladetahe would be permitted to marry.

Kayitah spent the rest of the evening covertly watching the half-breed and his own young wife, but nothing unseemly passed between them, not looks, not words, and he breathed a sigh of relief. Perhaps he had been imagining things, after all. Perhaps it was only compassion his soft-hearted golden dove felt for the white man. And perhaps not.

The following morning, Alope sent Fallon to the far end of the canyon to search for pine nuts, warning him not to come back empty-handed.

Fallon left the lodge after the morning meal, eager to be away from Alope's nagging, away from the growing suspicion in Kayitah's eyes, away from everybody. Period.

Lost in thought, he wasn't sure when he realized he was being followed.

Glancing over his shoulder, he saw Jenny making her way toward him and he came to a stop, waiting for her to catch up.

"This probably isn't a good idea," Fallon remarked.

"Alope sent me to help you. I think she wanted some time alone with her husband."

Fallon grunted softly. He couldn't blame Alope for being jealous of the chief's second wife. Jenny was as pretty as a spring morning in the high country, as easy on the eyes as a clear summer sky.

"You wouldn't look at me yesterday," Jenny said reproachfully, "or talk to me last night. Why?"

Fallon let out a long breath. "Can you blame me? Dammit, I don't think I can stand much more of Alope's little games."

But that was only half the truth. It was Jenny's sympathy he couldn't tolerate much longer.

He looked down at his hands, his fingers curling into tight fists. He had strong hands, capable hands. He smiled faintly as he imagined those hands wrapping around Alope's throat, squeezing tighter, tighter.

"A horse, indeed!" he muttered bitterly.

"It was a cruel thing to do."

"Yeah, well, I've got a feeling things will get a lot worse before they get better."

If they ever get better, he mused ruefully.

He started walking again, the shackles on his ankles clanking noisily, shortening his naturally long stride so that Jenny had no trouble keeping up with him.

They were well away from the village now, and there were few people about. An eagle soared effortlessly overhead, making lazy circles in the sky as it searched the ground for prey. The horse herd grazed in the distance, covering the canyon floor like a multicolored blanket.

Jenny walked beside Fallon, quietly content just to be near him. There was an aura of strength about him that made her feel safe, protected. She didn't stop to wonder how odd that seemed. He was a prisoner, just as she was, yet she sensed the tightly leashed power that emanated from him, and knew that he could be a valuable friend, or a formidable foe. She knew he was also a man of his word.

"Have you given any more thought to getting out of here?" she asked.

"I might be able to disguise myself as a horse," Fallon muttered under his breath.

"I'm serious," Jenny said impatiently.

"I know."

Fallon gazed up at Jenny. The sun highlighted the gold in her hair and washed over her skin like a caress. Her brows were delicate and finely shaped; her eyes were deep and dark and green, like winter leaves. His gaze lingered on her mouth. It was full and red and he dragged his gaze away, resisting the temptation to draw her into her arms and see if she tasted as sweet as she looked.

Damn, but she was a beautiful woman, and his body reacted instinctively to her nearness.

To hide the evidence of his rising desire, he dropped down on his haunches, his back against a gnarled pine, his arms resting on his bent knees.

"You been here long?" he asked, hoping to turn his thoughts in another direction.

"Two years," Jenny answered, wondering at the husky quality of his voice.

Fallon grunted softly. It wasn't a terribly long time and yet he knew that, to her, it probably seemed like forever.

"You married, or anything?" he asked casually.

Jenny nodded, her expression suddenly wistful. "I guess Hank thinks I'm dead by now."

"Maybe not," Fallon remarked.

So, she was married. He shook his head ruefully, surprised to find he was more than a little jealous of Jenny's husband, whoever he was. But then, he was jealous of Kayitah, too, and he knew with bitter regret that he'd be jealous of any man lucky enough to call Jenny his own.

Jenny sat down beside him. "Are you married?" she asked.

A muscle worked in Fallon's jaw, and something that might have been pain flickered in the depths of his eyes and then was gone.

"No, I'm not married," he said tersely.

Jenny gazed at him, her curiosity piqued by his curt reply, and by the odd expression she'd seen in his dark eyes, but before she could ask any more questions, he stood up and reached for her hand.

"Come on, I've got work to do."

Jenny smiled at him, hoping to banish his bad mood. "You're not afraid of Alope, are you?" she teased.

"No," Fallon replied with a wry grin, "but I am afraid of her husband."

He gazed down at Jenny, conscious of her hand, so small and fragile, in his, of the sudden change in her breathing as he drew her close, his arms slipping around her waist.

"Fallon . . ." She looked up at him, her eyes wide with confusion.

"Shhh." He covered her mouth with his fingertips. "I just want to hold you for a minute, Jenny. Just one minute."

Slowly, she relaxed in his arms. He was her friend and he needed her. With that thought in mind, she rested her cheek against his chest and closed her eyes, the beat of his heart strong and comforting beneath her ear. She felt the warm sweep of his breath against the side of her face.

Fallon released a deep sigh, his craving for a woman, for this particular woman, burning bright and hot within him. But stronger than desire was the simple need to hold Jenny close, to breathe in the scent of her, to feel her warmth, to know she cared, that he wasn't alone.

Standing there, with his arms around her, Fallon knew that, right or wrong, his life had become irrevocably entangled with hers.

Chapter Eight

The next morning after breakfast, Fallon followed Jenny out of the lodge and down to the river for water. Other women were already there, laughing and talking as they filled their waterskins. The married women looked at Fallon with disdain. He was a traitor to the People and beneath their contempt. But the maidens . . .

Jenny frowned as she saw the way the younger women stared at Fallon, their slow smiles filled with invitation, their dark eyes alight with appreciation as they openly admired the spread of his shoulders, the broad expanse of bronzed bare skin above the brief elkskin clout he wore, his long, muscular legs.

Jenny's mouth thinned. He should be ashamed, running around without a shirt and leggings, she thought, and then felt her cheeks flame with self-disgust as she realized she was staring at him just as intently as the Indian girls were.

She glared at him when he smiled in her direction.

"I'm going for wood as long as I'm down here," he said. "Wanna come along?"

Jenny nodded, acutely aware of the envious glances of the other women as she followed him downriver. They passed several women bathing their children before they turned inland, toward the forest.

Jenny was about to tell Fallon he should be more discreet in his attire in the presence of young women when a shrill scream pierced the air.

The sound had come from the river, and when she whirled around, she saw Fallon hurrying in that direction, his steps hampered by the chains on his feet.

Dropping the waterskins she'd been carrying, Jenny ran after him.

She came to an abrupt halt at the river's edge. Several women were gathered together, and as she drew near, she could see a small child lying on the ground. His mother sat beside him, wailing softly.

"What happened?" Fallon asked one of the women.

"The son of Ziyah fell in the river. He is not breathing."

Without another word, Fallon put his mouth over the child's and began to blow into its lungs. Several moments passed, and nothing happened.

In desperation, Fallon picked the boy up by the heels and gave him a sharp whack across the back. A small chunk of mud flew out of the boy's mouth, he coughed once, and began to cry.

The women all began to talk at once as they touched the boy, assuring themselves he was all right, thanking Fallon over and over again before they carried the child back to the village.

"You'll be a hero now," Jenny remarked.

"I doubt that."

"Ziyah's husband will probably give you a horse for saving his son's life."

Fallon shrugged.

"Maybe Kayitah will remove your chains," Jenny said, her voice becoming excited at the prospect. "Maybe he'll even give you your freedom!"

"I doubt it," Fallon replied dryly. "Don't get your hopes up."

But it was too late. It was all she could think of.

Kayitah stared at Kladetahe thoughtfully that night. Ziyah's husband, Katuhala, had offered the half-breed a fine black stallion in appreciation for saving his son's life, and the Apache chief had allowed Kladetahe to accept it, knowing Katuhala would be offended if his gift were refused. But now the white man had a horse. And the admiration of the People. And Kayitah did not like it. Nor did he like the way the white man stared at Jenny when he thought no one was looking.

That night, Kayitah took Jenny to his bed, reminding the woman, and the white man, that she belonged to him.

Fallon stared into the darkness long after everyone else was asleep as he calculated the odds of getting away unscathed with the chief's favorite wife in tow.

"Slim and none," he murmured wryly, but even so, he knew he would not leave her behind, knew that if he left the canyon without Jenny Braedon, he would be forever haunted by the quiet desperation he had seen in her deep green eyes.

Such beautiful eyes, he mused. She had been in his thoughts continually since the night they met, he admitted, and even now he felt the desire rise quick and hot within him as he glanced over his shoulder and saw her blond head pillowed on a square of stuffed rawhide.

He remembered how neatly she had fit into his embrace that day by the river, how perfectly her body had molded itself to his.

With complete clarity, he recalled the silk of her hair beneath his hand, the feel of her breasts against his chest, the rich velvet of her voice.

And he remembered, with growing anger, the smug look in Kayitah's eyes when the chief had taken Jenny to bed that night. He'd never been a jealous man, but it had taken every ounce of self-control Fallon possessed to keep his hands from wrapping around the chief's throat.

He tossed restlessly on the buffalo robes, and the muffled clatter of chains reminded him of the biggest obstacle in his path to freedom. Until he found a way to rid himself of his leg irons, he wasn't going anywhere, with or without Jenny.

Once he managed to rid himself of his shackles, there would be other problems to contend with, like a horse for Jenny, food, water. And he would need a weapon of some kind.

Pondering each item separately, it all seemed easy enough. Stealing a horse was no problem, food could be hunted along the way, water could be found without much difficulty if you knew where to look, unless they decided to go south through Diablo Canyon Pass. But that way was suicide. No white man and few Indians had ever ventured into that barren wasteland and lived to tell the tale.

He could steal a weapon. Kayitah's bow, perhaps, or better yet, his rifle.

With the coming of dawn, Fallon slipped out of his blankets, shrugged into his shirt, and left the wickiup. Outside, the air was crisp and chill, reminding him that *chawn-chissy,* winter, was not far off.

The eastern sky gradually mushroomed with color as the rising sun climbed over the canyon walls, streaking the craggy peaks with fiery shades of orange and vermillion, edging the wispy clouds with pink and silver lace.

Fallon watched the spectacular display appreciatively, frowning as it occurred to him that, should his plan fail, he would probably not live to see the dawn of another day.

It was a sobering thought.

Pensive now, he reconsidered the plan he had formulated in the black hours just before dawn. Last night, his plan to rid himself of his shackles had seemed like a pretty good idea, but now, in the cold light of day, he was not so sure.

The success of his plan hinged on three things: his ability to correctly predict how Alope would react to a given situation, his own ability to withstand whatever punishment Kayitah decreed, and the Apache's almost fanatical admiration for courage.

Perhaps more than any other tribe in the Southwest, the *Dineh* respected a brave man. More often than not, a warrior's courage was measured by his ability to withstand pain, to laugh in the face of certain death, or meet it in stoic silence. The West was replete with tales of men, both red and white, who, on the verge of certain destruction, had cheated death at the hands of the Apache by a last desperate show of bravado.

The smell of ash cakes and looted Army coffee intruded on Fallon's thoughts. The rising sun caressed him with a delicious warmth. A child's carefree laughter bubbled from a nearby lodge, while a multitude of birds sang hymns to welcome the birth of a new day. A doe-eyed maiden smiled at Fallon as she made her way to the river for water.

Fallon sighed heavily as he drank in the beauty of the morning. Pondering the wisdom of setting his plan in motion, he decided to forget the whole thing. Life was too good to throw away, he mused, especially when he was risking it for a woman who would never be his.

But then Kayitah stepped out of the lodge, his arm around Jenny's shoulders, and Fallon knew he couldn't take it much longer. He couldn't go on living in the same lodge with Jenny. Couldn't go on watching her share her bed with Kayitah. Just seeing the warrior touch Jenny was enough to tie his guts in a knot. Sooner or later, he'd do something stupid, say something stupid, and Kayitah would kill him for it, and maybe Jenny, too.

Alope stepped out of the lodge a few minutes later. "We need wood," she said curtly. "Get it."

Ryder Fallon took a deep breath. "No."

Alope stared at Kladetahe, her mouth dropping open in astonishment. He had never refused to obey her before. Why did he have to do it now, when Kayitah and the white woman were watching?

Aquiver with indignation, she jabbed her finger in Kladetahe's direction. "You will find wood, now," she snapped. "And then you will go to the river for water."

Fallon shook his head. "Not today. Not tomorrow. Not ever again."

Anger suffused Alope's cheeks. "If you do not work, you will die," she reminded him, and felt a twinge of regret. Now that her anger at him had passed, she knew she would miss his strong back. But she had her pride, and she would not back down, not with Kayitah watching her.

"Death to dishonor," Fallon muttered under his breath, in English.

Alope frowned at him. "What?"

"I said no." Fallon glanced at Jenny, thinking again how beautiful she was. She wore a tunic of bleached elkskin. The skirt was ankle-length, the bodice and sleeves decorated with rows of blue and yellow porcupine quills. Her hair fell to her waist in soft golden waves.

Alope turned to her husband. "He will not work."

Kayitah nodded, mildly surprised by the defiant expression on the face of the half-breed.

"Work or die, Kladetahe," Kayitah said succinctly. "The choice is up to you."

"A Cheyenne is as much a warrior as an Apache," Fallon replied flatly. "No longer will I do the work of women." He drew a deep breath and expelled it slowly, hoping he wasn't making the worst mistake of his life. "If I cannot live as a warrior, then I will die like one."

Jenny listened in stunned silence as the man she had pinned all her hopes of escape on calmly talked about dying. Had he gone mad?

"Brave words," Kayitah remarked at last. "We shall see if there is substance in your words, or if they are empty, like the words of the white man. Gopi! Sanza!"

The two warriors summoned by the chief came forward, nodding their understanding as Kayitah issued his orders.

Jenny felt her insides turn to ice as Sanza produced a length of rope and quickly tied Fallon's hands together. That done, he tossed the loose end of the rope over a tree branch, then both warriors took hold of the rope and pulled, lifting Fallon off his feet. A few quick turns of the rope secured it to the trunk, leaving the half-breed dangling in midair.

"An Apache warrior endures pain in silence," Kayitah remarked as he drew his knife from his belt. "We will see if a half-breed Cheyenne can do as well."

Jenny held her breath as Kayitah cut away Fallon's shirt and stripped off his leggings. With deliberate slowness, the chief dragged the point of the blade across Fallon's shoulders and chest, opening several long, shallow cuts. When there was no reaction from the prisoner other than a sharp intake of breath, Kayitah raked the edge of the blade down the length of Fallon's thighs, slicing just deep enough to draw blood.

Looking satisfied, Kayitah stepped back a few paces and hunkered down on his heels. Gopi and Sanza sank down beside him.

Kayitah smiled faintly as he stared up at Kladetahe. Once, they had been friends, but no more. Once, Kladetahe had been one of them, a warrior as fierce and loyal as any of the men in the village, but no more. He had betrayed that trust. Better he should die now than betray that trust again, as surely he would, sooner or later.

News of Kladetahe's defiance spread quickly through the village, causing a great deal of excitement among the warriors. So, the half-breed had finally found the courage to act like a man! Well, that was something to see, and one by one, the men left their lodges and gathered around the half-breed, laughing and making jokes as they speculated on how long the prisoner's newfound courage would last.

Jenny ducked into her lodge and emerged a few minutes later carrying a pair of unadorned moccasins. Taking a place in front of the wickiup, she began to decorate the moccasins with dyed porcupine quills, but it was Fallon who held her attention. Whatever had possessed him to defy Alope? What did he hope to gain by making her angry? Surely he had known he would be punished. It was only the fact that he had been willing to be her slave that had kept him alive this long.

Ten minutes passed. Fifteen. Twenty.

Fallon's gaze swept over the sea of dark brown faces until he saw Jenny sitting near the door of Kayitah's wickiup, her head bowed as she worked on a pair of winter moccasins. Her long golden hair gleamed like the sun itself, and when she raised her head, he saw that her eyes were dark with worry. He wished fleetingly that he had stolen a kiss when he had the chance. Even now, hanging from a tree like a side of beef, he could feel himself wanting her.

He glanced at Kayitah's impassive countenance. What if he had misjudged the Apache chief? What if Kayitah decided to kill him outright? What if he had misjudged his own ability to withstand the chief's punishment?

He shook his doubts aside and focused on Jenny, and what he hoped to gain.

Thirty minutes slipped by. Thirty-five.

The muscles in his arms and shoulders began to protest at the strain of bearing his weight. Despite the cool breeze that whispered through the camp, sweat poured from his body, the salty moisture stinging the cuts Kayitah had inflicted.

Sixty minutes, and it seemed like sixty years. The rough hemp sliced into his wrists, and the flies deserted the blood drying on his shoulders and thighs to feast on the warm red rivers trickling down his forearms.

Jenny blinked back tears of sympathy as the minutes ticked by. Ninety minutes had passed now, and she knew that each second must seem like a lifetime to Fallon. Again, she wondered why he had defied Alope. Did he find slavery so unbearable that even death seemed better?

The watching warriors had lapsed into silence, their thoughts unfathomable as they stared at the half-breed.

Two hours passed, and Fallon's suffering was clearly reflected in Jenny's eyes. Sweat sheened his entire body now, trickling down his chest and belly to gather in shallow puddles on the ground at his feet. It was an effort for him to breathe, and his breath came in hard, short gasps.

Three hours, and Fallon marveled at the Apaches' ability to sit motionless for so long; at the patience that held them immobile as they waited for him to break, to scream, to plead for mercy.

He remembered lying on top of a rise with a number of warriors years ago, waiting to ambush a Comanche camp. They had remained motionless for hours, but that had been a matter of life and death. What held the Apache now?

Jenny stared at Fallon, the moccasins in her lap forgotten long ago. He was truly a brave man, she mused, to endure such pain without a murmur. Indeed, he might have been dead save for the labored rasp of his breathing. Her heart went out to him, and she yearned to go to him, to offer him a drink of cool water, to wipe the blood and sweat from his punished flesh. She hardly knew him, yet she ached for his pain, yearned for his touch.

Four hours passed, and now knifelike pains darted down Fallon's back and sides. His wrists were raw, his shoulders throbbed with aching monotony. He closed his eyes and clenched his teeth, and only his stubborn pride and the faint remembrance of what he hoped to gain stilled the animal-like cry of anguish that rose in his throat.

Jenny held her breath as Kayitah rose to his feet.

"You have only to ask for mercy," the chief advised the half-breed as he unsheathed his knife, "and I will send you swiftly to the land of your ancestors."

Jenny's hand went to her heart as she waited for Fallon's reply. Would he surrender his pain for a quick, merciful death? How much longer could he hang there before he gave voice to his agony, before he begged for relief?

"No," Fallon rasped, and Jenny felt herself go weak with relief. As long as he lived, so long as he could endure, her hope of escape lived also.

A strange half smile flitted across the chief's swarthy face as he laid the knife's keen-edged blade against Fallon's throat.

Fallon sent one quick glance in Jenny's direction, wanting to imprint her image on his mind so that he might carry it with him into the afterlife, and then he stared impassively into Kayitah's eyes, felt the muscles in the back of his neck grow taut as he waited for the chief to slit his throat.

Instead, Kayitah raised the knife and severed the rope binding Fallon's wrists.

He hit the ground hard, stumbled, but did not fall. There was a new pain in his arms and legs as the creeping numbness that had set in began to recede, but he kept his face blank, betraying none of what he was feeling, or thinking.

"Follow me," Kayitah ordered curtly, and walked briskly toward his lodge, his admiration for the half-breed stronger now than his hatred.

It was Jenny who followed them into the lodge, Jenny who, with gentle hands, wiped the blood from Fallon's legs and chest, bound the cuts with strips of cloth that had been soaked in warm water and aloe. Not once did she speak or meet Fallon's eyes, but he was keenly aware of her presence. The touch of her hands on his flesh made Fallon wonder anew what it would be like to hold her close, to feel the warmth of her body against his own, to run his hands through the golden silk of her hair, to caress the womanly sweetness hidden beneath the shapeless doeskin tunic.

Once, looking up, he saw Kayitah watching them, his dark eyes thoughtful.

Jenny was acutely conscious of Fallon's eyes watching her. His skin was warm beneath her fingertips; his nearness made her insides quiver strangely even as a flood of heat suffused her. He was so very handsome, so very male. She was sorely tempted to let her fingers explore his hard-muscled arms, to feel them close around her. The very thought sent a thrill down her spine. It was disturbing, the effect he had on her, and she was suddenly grateful that Kayitah was there to protect her from her own foolishness.

When she finished treating Fallon's wounds, she left the wickiup, relieved to be away from the man who stirred her emotions in ways she did not care to examine too closely.

Fallon watched Jenny leave the lodge, all else forgotten until Kayitah spoke.

"You have proved you still have the heart of a warrior," the chief acknowledged grudgingly. "No longer will you work with the women."

The words "thank you" were seldom spoken by the Apache people, and Fallon did not voice them now. Instead, he lifted his gaze toward heaven in the traditional sign of thanksgiving, thereby acknowledging Usen's hand in all things.

For a time, the two men studied each other; then Kayitah bent down and unlocked the shackles on Fallon's feet and tossed them aside.

"Though you are no longer a slave, you are still a prisoner," the chief said tersely. "Apache ears are sharp. Our eyes are keen. Our memories are long. We do not forget those who have wronged us. If you betray us a second time, you will wish for death a thousand times before it comes for you."

Fallon nodded, his dark eyes expressionless. Running away with the war chief's favorite wife would, he supposed, be considered the worst type of betrayal.

Kayitah rose smoothly to his feet. "Come, let us refresh ourselves in the sweat lodge," he suggested.

It was the first indication of Fallon's new status with the tribe.

Chapter Nine

"How could you take such a terrible chance?" Jenny demanded furiously. "Kayitah might have killed you!"

"Well, he didn't!" Fallon snapped, annoyed by her outburst. "Anyway, it was my neck on the line, not yours."

Jenny choked back the hot words that sprang to her lips, but her thoughts were easily read in her bright green eyes, and in the sudden flush that stained her cheeks. If Fallon died, all her dreams of escape would die with him.

Ryder Fallon scowled into the distance, bemused by his anger. And he was angry, not because she had been giving him the rough side of her tongue for the last ten minutes, but because he knew that, once he got her away from Kayitah, she would no longer give a damn whether he lived or died. And he wanted her to care.

"Don't worry, sweetheart, I won't cash in until I get you out of here," he muttered irritably, and a hostile silence fell between them.

Jenny glanced warily over her shoulder, making sure they were still alone on the riverbank. She did not like to think what would happen if Kayitah found her alone with Fallon. The Apache chief had been very possessive lately, even more so than usual, watching her, sometimes coming to look for her if he thought she was gone too long.

"I'm sorry," she murmured after a while. "It's just that . . ."

"I know. Forget it," Fallon growled. "Damn, I wish I had a cigarette."

"I wish I was home."

Fallon skimmed a small flat stone across the placid water, his anger forgotten. She sounded so forlorn, so heartbreakingly sad, he longed to take her in his arms and kiss away the tears that glistened in the corners of her eyes. Instead, he asked, "Where's home?"

"Widow Ridge. Hank went ahead to find us a place to live. I was on my way to meet him there when the Apaches attacked the stage." Jenny shuddered with the recollection. "I was taken prisoner. Everyone else was killed."

Fallon nodded sympathetically. He could only imagine how scared she must have been, even as he felt a quick surge of gratitude that Kayitah had spared her life.

"Oh, Ryder, will I ever get away from here?"

"Sure, honey," he drawled softly, thinking that her eyes, no longer flashing fire, were as green as emeralds, as deep as a high mountain lake.

Jenny sighed. "I'd love to go home, but that's silly, isn't it? I've never even been there. But, oh, how I'd love to sleep in a real bed again, and take a hot bath in a real tub with real soap. I want to wear dresses again, and petticoats, and real shoes. And I'm dying for a glass of cold milk, and a slice of hot apple pie."

Her voice dropped to a whisper. "And I want to see Hank again." Tears stung her eyes, and she covered her face with her hands. It would be so good to see her husband again, to live with a man who desired nothing more of her than companionship and affection.

"Oh, Hank," she sobbed, "I miss you so!"

Ryder Fallon looked away, moved by her tears, touched by the aching loneliness in her voice. It had been a long time since a woman loved him the way Jenny Braedon appeared to love her husband.

"Ryder?" She didn't look up, and her voice was muffled by her hands.

"I'm listening," he answered quietly.

"I've been Kayitah's prisoner for over two years. If you were Hank, would you . . . would it make any difference?" Jenny held her breath as she waited for Fallon's answer. Did he think she was ruined because she had lived with an Indian? Would the fact that she'd been Kayitah's wife change her relationship with Hank?

"It won't matter, Jenny," Fallon assured her. "Not if he loves you."

"I've been telling myself that every day for the last two years," Jenny confessed, "but somehow it sounds more convincing coming from someone else." She made a vague gesture with her hand. "I don't know why I'm so worried. Hank's probably forgotten me by now."

Fallon shook his head. "He'll still be waiting."

"How can you be so sure?"

"Because you're worth waiting for," Fallon replied, certain that no man who had once known Jenny Braedon would ever forget her.

With a last sniffle, Jenny wiped the tears from her eyes, then gazed at Fallon, a mysterious smile playing over her lips.

"You gonna let me in on the joke?" Fallon asked, and Jenny burst into giggles.

"I was just thinking that when I was first captured, I prayed and prayed for someone to come and rescue me, and when no one came right away, I guess I gave up hope. But now you're here." Jenny smiled and gave a little shrug. "I guess it just takes longer for some prayers to be answered."

"I doubt I'd be considered the answer to anyone's prayers," Fallon retorted with a wry grin.

For a moment, they smiled at each other and then, gradually, their smiles faded.

He had wanted her for so long. All he had to do was take a step forward and fold her in his arms.

Jenny gazed into the depths of his eyes, her

heart reaching out for this man who had become her friend. She felt the need to lay her head on his chest, to be held in the arms of someone she cared for. Someone who cared for her in return.

"Ryder . . ."

Ignoring the inner voice that warned him he was on dangerous ground, Fallon opened his arms.

She felt a wondrous sense of well-being as his arms closed around her. Funny, she thought, she knew nothing about him except that he was a half-breed drifter, yet she felt utterly safe in his embrace. There was a solid dependability about Ryder Fallon, a deep well of inner strength and confidence that she found reassuring. He never seemed ill at ease or unsure of himself. Even when the Indians were torturing him, he had been in control of his emotions. She had never known a man who possessed such self-assurance. Or one who was so outrageously handsome. His hair was long and black. His eyes were a dark, dark blue. Sometimes they were as expressive as print on a page, and at other times completely unfathomable. Often, she found herself wondering what he would look like clean-shaven. In truth, she spent far too much time thinking about him, period.

Fallon frowned as Jenny snuggled trustingly into his arms. Did she have any idea of the powerful longing her nearness aroused in him? His nostrils filled with the scent of her, and a quick heat flared in his belly and spread downward with astonishing speed. He had not had a woman in a long time; her nearness was the sweetest kind of torment.

He swore under his breath, chiding himself for being all kinds of a fool. No matter how their intended escape turned out, Jenny would never be his. If they failed to make it safely out of Rainbow Canyon, he would be killed by inches and she would be forced to return to Kayitah's lodge. If, by some miracle, they managed to reach civilization, she would hasten to her husband's arms.

Jenny stirred in his embrace. "I'd better get back before Kayitah comes looking for me," she murmured.

"Yeah." His voice was husky as he released her.

Jenny looked up at him for a long moment, all her senses urging her to stay. Instead, she gave him a quick smile of farewell and hurried back to the village.

Fallon watched her out of sight, admiring the gentle sway of her hips, the way the sun danced in her bright golden hair. No wonder she was the chief's favorite wife, he mused. Just looking at her made a man feel good.

Chapter Ten

Silent tears tracked Jenny's cheeks as she stared into the lodge's murky darkness, but she made no effort to wipe them away for fear of waking the man at her side. The Apache chief lay close beside her, snoring softly, his arm heavy across her breast.

Despair brought fresh tears to Jenny's eyes. Even when Kayitah was not in the mood for lovemaking, he shared her bed most often. Little wonder Alope hated her. She was obviously the chief's favorite, and Jenny wondered, as she had so many times, how he could find pleasure in a woman who made no effort to disguise the fact that his very touch repulsed her.

She cringed as Kayitah moved against her, his touch somehow possessive even in sleep. How she hated him! If only she had the courage to kill him while he slept, but the consequences of such an act filled her with terror. Unpleasant as her life was, she had no wish to end it.

Discouragement perched on Jenny's shoulder like a carrion crow, and she turned her thoughts toward home, wishing she could see Philadelphia again. She had been so happy there, living in her little white house, surrounded by friends and neighbors, working in the hospital. It was there she had first met Hank. He'd been wounded in the war and had been sent home to recover. Only he hadn't wanted to recover. He'd wanted to die.

One of the doctors had asked her to spend time with him, to try to convince him that life was still worthwhile, in spite of everything. She hadn't understood at first and then, when the doctor had explained that Hank could no longer function as a man, she had been overcome with embarrassment.

But once that had passed, she had been filled with sympathy for the handsome young man. She had spent hours at his bedside, talking to him, reading to him, or simply sitting there to keep him company. It had taken weeks, but eventually she'd managed to break through the icy wall that Hank had erected around himself and they'd become friends.

When Hank was well enough to leave the hospital, he began to call on her, assuring her that he wanted only to continue their friendship. He had no one left in Philadelphia now that his brother had gone West, and he was lonely. As she was. Her parents had been killed in a carriage accident only a few months earlier and she was still mourning their loss.

She'd been lonely, and he'd been lonely, and when, only three months later, he had asked her to marry him, she had accepted, even though they had known each other a scandalously short time. She had not minded that there could be no intimacy between them. She was a stranger to passion, to love. She had wanted only his companionship, someone to laugh with, to cry with.

At night, in Hank's arms, she had been content to be held. Gently reared all her life, she had never been alone with a man, never felt the faintest stirring of desire. Hank's chaste kisses had not aroused her, his touch had never left her yearning for more, and so they had lived together amicably, sharing everything but passion.

They might have lived happily ever after if Hank hadn't decided to go West to be with his brother, Charlie. A new life, he'd said, and nothing she could say could change his mind. A week later he'd quit his job at the bank and headed for Arizona Territory to go into business with Charlie. Three months later, she had boarded a stage, headed for a town she'd never seen, never even heard of. Widow Ridge. The very name had sent a shiver down her spine.

Fresh tears welled in Jenny's eyes and she blinked them back. Crying was useless, as useless as blaming Hank for her predicament. It wasn't Hank's fault the Apaches had attacked her stagecoach any more than it was her fault she had been forced to become Kayitah's woman. She supposed she should be grateful the Apache chief had taken her for his wife. At least she had been spared the cruel fate that had befallen the other woman on the coach. Even at this late date, she could hear the cries of that poor woman.

Jenny thrust the memory aside and tried to visualize Hank's face in her mind's eye, but she hadn't seen him in over two years and her mental image of her husband had grown fainter with each passing day, like a photograph left too long in the sun.

She had no trouble conjuring up a picture of Ryder Fallon, though. His bearded face danced before her in the dark lodge, his midnight blue eyes warm as he assured her that everything would be all right. She remembered the strength of his arms when he had held her close, how nicely she had fit in his embrace. He was every inch a man, from his broad chest and wide shoulders to his long lean flanks. She remembered how his muscles had bunched when Kayitah was tormenting him. So many muscles, she mused, so much lean bronze flesh.

She turned her head and glanced to where Fallon lay sleeping, only a few feet away. She wished suddenly that it was Fallon lying beside her, his arm across her breast.

Her cheeks grew hot and she put such thoughts from her mind, wondering instead how old he was. The beard and mustache made it difficult to judge his age, but she guessed him to be in his early thirties. Most men were married by then, and she wondered why he was still single, and then wondered what difference it made. He was nothing to her, only the means to an end. And that end was escape.

She breathed the word aloud, and the sound of it rose like a prayer.

"Escape." She murmured the word again as she closed her eyes, focusing on how wonderful it would be to get away from the Apache, to see Hank again.

But it was Ryder Fallon's image that followed her to sleep.

Chapter Eleven

Jenny watched with narrow-eyed envy as Fallon left the lodge the following morning. She was supposed to be Kayitah's wife, and Fallon, though no longer a slave, was still supposed to be a prisoner, but he had more freedom than she did!

He left the lodge early every morning, joining the other men at the river to bathe, then going off to train the big black stallion that Ziyah's husband had given him.

Jenny had, on occasion, sneaked over to watch Fallon exercise the horse. They were two of a kind, the ebony-colored horse and the dark-haired man. Both big and strong. Both still more than a little wild in spite of the reins of civilization. She had seen Fallon riding bareback across the valley, using only the sound of his voice and the pressure of his legs to guide the big black stallion. They were beautiful to watch. He was beautiful to watch . . .

She drew her thoughts from Ryder Fallon, wishing she had an excuse to leave the wicki-up, especially now when Alope was nagging her again, complaining that the tea was too strong and the berries not ripe.

She waited until Alope went out, and then, with a sniff of defiance, Jenny walked out of the lodge. If Alope and Ryder could come and go as they pleased, then so could she!

Fighting back tears of anger and frustration, she made her way to her favorite place along the river. How she hated Alope! The Indian woman's temper had not improved since Kayitah had declared that Fallon would no longer be considered a slave. Now that Alope could no longer vent her anger on the white man, she had taken to taunting Jenny again, her voice harsh and critical. More and more, Alope tormented Jenny, seeming to take great pleasure in making her angry.

Nothing Jenny ever did was right as far as Alope was concerned. There had been a time when Kayitah had interceded in Jenny's behalf, but no more. With typical male cowardice, he fled the lodge at the first sign of trouble, leaving the two women to settle their disputes without benefit of his counsel.

With a wordless cry of despair, Jenny flounced down on the grassy riverbank. Cradling her head in her hands, she began to weep. It wasn't fair, she thought petulantly, wishing she had the nerve to fight back, to call Alope all the unkind names that stuck in her throat, but she had never been given to violence, either physical or verbal. A proper lady did not resort to such things. But, oh, she was so tired of feeling worthless and unwanted.

Sunk in the depths of her despair, she didn't hear Fallon's footsteps coming up behind her.

"Anything I can do to help?" he asked.

Startled, she glanced over her shoulder, then relaxed. "No." Raising her head, Jenny wiped the tears from her eyes with the hem of her skirt. "Darn that old witch. She makes me so mad!"

"Which old witch is that?" Fallon queried, dropping down on the grass beside her.

"Alope!" Jenny answered vehemently. "She criticizes everything I do."

Fallon chuckled softly. "Why don't you learn to do things right?"

"I do them right!" Jenny snapped. "I can cook and sew and tan hides just as good as she does, but she's always finding fault with me, even if she has to make things up."

"Jenny, take it easy," Fallon said soothingly. "I was only kidding."

"I know," she said contritely. "I'm sorry."

"Don't let her walk all over you. She'll never respect you if you don't fight back. Next time Alope starts to give you the rough side of her tongue, tell her to shut up. Or slap her face."

"Slap her!" Jenny gasped, horrified by the thought of striking the other woman.

"Hell, yes. Slap her silly. Once she knows she can't bully you, she'll stop."

Jenny glared at him, appalled, and then angry. "You mean stand up to her the way you did when she was treating you like a horse?"

Fallon mumbled an oath under his breath. "That's not fair, and you know it."

"I know," Jenny admitted, instantly penitent. "I'm sorry."

She had no right to insinuate that Fallon had been afraid to stand up to Alope. If Fallon had openly defied the Indain woman, she probably would have killed him, and taken great pleasure in the deed.

Jenny sighed. No matter how bad things got, she knew she didn't have to fear for her life, because Alope would never dare lay a hand on her, not so long as Kayitah was there.

"Forget it. Listen, Jenny, you've got to trust me on this. I know what I'm talking about. If you stand up to her, she'll back off."

"I'll try," Jenny said resolutely. "Thanks for the advice."

"Any time."

Toying with the folds of her skirt, Jenny covertly studied Ryder Fallon. What was there about him that made her blood sing whenever he was near? It was more than just his rugged good looks. No man had ever made her feel so feminine, or so vulnerable. She knew she had no business thinking about him in any way that was remotely personal, and yet he filled her thoughts by day and crept into her dreams at night.

She couldn't help wondering what it would be like to feel his mouth on hers. He was tall and strong and handsome, and though she knew it was dreadfully wicked, she could not help wondering what it would be like to feel his hard muscular body next to her own, to feel his hands in her hair, the touch of his lips brushing her skin . . .

She felt a sudden wave of heat wash into her cheeks as all the thoughts that had kept her awake the previous night came back to haunt her. She was a married woman, morally and legally bound to her husband, yet she was forever daydreaming about another man, a man she hardly knew. It was shameful, disgusting.

With a sigh, she fell back on the grass and gazed up at the clear blue sky, forcing her thoughts away from Ryder Fallon. It was beautiful here by the river, peaceful and secluded. If only she could stay here forever, away from Kayitah, away from his sharp-tongued wife.

If only she were free . . .

Frowning, she closed her eyes. She would catch the devil from Alope for staying away from the lodge for so long when there was so much work to do, but sometimes she just had to get away, to be alone with her thoughts.

But she wasn't alone.

A dark shadow blotted out the sunlight. Opening her eyes, Jenny saw Fallon leaning over her, his midnight blue eyes smoky with desire, his mouth descending on her own.

She whispered, "No, don't," but she made no move to resist as his mouth covered hers. His lips were warm and firm, undeniably hungry as he kissed her with a passion she had never known. His mustache tickled her upper lip as his tongue probed the warm secrets of her mouth. Such unexpected intimacy should have made her cringe; instead, she shuddered with pleasure as a quick heat shot clear through her, then settled in the center of her being, filling her with a delicious glow. His beard was soft and strangely sensual as it brushed against her cheek.

Caught up in the wonder of his touch, Jenny did not stop to think about what she was doing. She knew only that she had never experienced such a surge of emotion or known such delight, had never yearned so deeply to be held, or to feel a man's hands caressing her.

Moaning softly, she slid her arms around Fallon's neck and drew him closer, wantonly pressing her body against his, reveling in the sheer masculinity of his chest and thighs. The passion that had lain untouched within her sprang quickly to life in response to the touch of Ryder Fallon's hands and lips. Hank's chaste kisses had never aroused her to such fever pitch. Kayitah's occasional caresses had filled her with revulsion, but Fallon's touch was exquisite and she gloried in the tutelage of his hands as he lightly stroked her breasts and gently massaged her belly, igniting little fires of pleasure wherever he touched.

She closed her eyes, shivering with wonder as wave after wave of sensation washed over her, arousing her, engulfing her.

She was drowning in a sea of honey. His mouth was warm against the side of her neck, his tongue like a silken finger of flame as he teased her lips, then dipped into her mouth to sample the nectar within.

A soft moan rose in her throat, a sob of mingled pleasure and exquisite pain. She was going to die, she thought. Any moment now, she was going to burn up and die from the sweet fire of his touch. Already, her blood had turned to flame and her limbs had gone weak. Like butter left too long in the sun, she was sizzling, melting.

Fallon held Jenny tight, amazed at her response. He had not expected her to return his kisses, had, in fact, expected a slap in the face.

Her quick surrender fired his blood and urged him to taste and touch and explore every inch of the delectable body which had been tormenting him for weeks. He knew he should stop, knew he should release her and run like hell before it was too late, but he could not bring himself to let her go. Her kisses were as intoxicating as brandy, her skin was like soft satin beneath his hands.

Heat engulfed him, arousing him to such a

state there could be no doubt of what he was feeling, what he was thinking, wanting . . .

The sudden pressure of his manhood against her thigh brought Jenny suddenly back to her senses. With a little cry of despair, she pushed him away.

She was both disappointed and relieved when he let her go without a struggle.

"I'm sorry, Jenny," Fallon said thickly. "You looked so pretty lying there, and I . . . oh, hell," he said gruffly. "I'm sorry."

Jenny refused to meet his gaze. How would she ever be able to face him again? He must think she was no better than a harlot!

"Jenny."

"What?"

"Look at me."

"I can't."

"Look at me."

She faced him sullenly, her cheeks hot with shame. Why didn't he just go away and leave her alone? He had stirred feelings she had never experienced before, feelings that made her feel vulnerable and confused.

Feelings she had never had for her own husband, or any other man. Guilt washed over her, hot and bright. She had betrayed Hank, betrayed her marriage vows.

"It's all right, Jenny," Ryder said with an understanding smile. "You're lonely and unhappy, and I'm . . . hell, I'm lonely, too."

"I'm so ashamed."

"Don't be. You haven't done anything wrong."

"No, but . . ."

"But?" Fallon's dark eyes watched her carefully, almost as if he knew what she was thinking.

But I wanted to. The words thundered in her mind, and she blushed furiously. For the first time in her life, she had wanted a man to hold her, caress her. She had wanted to feel Fallon's hands on her flesh, taste him and touch him in return. And he knew. That was the worst of it. He knew it.

Ryder placed his fingertip under her chin and forced her to look at him. "But?"

She stared up at him, wondering at the curious expression that lurked in the depths of his midnight blue eyes.

"Never mind," she said irritably. "I've got to get back."

Ryder let out a deep breath, refusing to acknowledge that he wanted anything more than her companionship.

"Still friends?" he asked, grinning at her.

Jenny's heart skipped a beat. Did he know how remarkably handsome he was when he smiled like that? It made her heart pound and her blood race. She clenched her fists to keep from reaching out to touch him one last time, to confirm that his chest was rock hard, to measure the width of his shoulders, the length of his thigh, to run her fingers through his hair.

"Still friends," she agreed.

His grin was infectious and she smiled back at him. How could you stay mad at such a man?

"Good." He rose easily to his feet. For a moment, he stood there gazing down at her. "Give 'em hell, honey," he drawled, and with a wave of his hand, he walked away.

Jenny watched him go, feeling strangely bereft. He was a handsome man, tall and lean and virile, with a smile to break a woman's heart. How many women had he loved? How many women had loved him?

Rising, she smoothed her skirt over her hips, patted her hair into place. Kneeling at the river's edge, she splashed cold water over her face and neck, wishing she could douse the fire Ryder Fallon had ignited deep within her.

Alope looked at Jenny sharply when she returned to the wickiup, but instead of shying away from the other woman's gaze or making excuses for her prolonged absence, Jenny glared back at her, her expression openly defiant, almost as if she were daring Alope to start something.

"We need wood," Alope said. "Get it."

Only yesterday, Jenny would have backed down. But that was yesterday. *She'll never respect you if you don't fight back.* Fallon's words echoed in her mind. *Once she knows she can't bully you, she'll stop.*

Jenny squared her shoulders and took a deep breath. "Get it yourself."

Disbelief flickered in the Indian woman's eyes as she took a threatening step forward.

"You dare to defy me?" Alope exclaimed.

"I'm not defying you," Jenny replied calmly, though her insides were shaking like a leaf in the wind. "I got the wood this morning. I've gotten the wood every morning, and every night, for the last two years." She sent Alope a sugary smile. "Now it's your turn."

A gleam of something that might have been respect flickered briefly in Alope's black eyes and then was gone.

"Very well," Alope said, conceding defeat. "I will gather the wood in the evening."

Jenny nodded, her expression impassive, but inwardly she was turning somersaults. Fallon, bless him, had been right!

That night, for the first time since Jenny had been taken prisoner, there was peace in Kayitah's lodge.

Later, in bed, Jenny surprised herself and Kayitah when she pushed him away.

"I don't want to," she said firmly, then held her breath, waiting to see what his reaction would be.

Kayitah sighed heavily as he rolled onto his side and closed his eyes. It had taken a long time, but his little white captive had become a wife.

The last days of summer gave way to fall. The nights grew longer, the sun lost its warmth. The trees put away their emerald garb and flaunted vivid gowns of gold and red and orange, but the beauty of the changing seasons was lost on Jenny as what had started as a niggling suspicion grew into certainty. She longed to confide in Ryder, who had become her closest friend and confidant, but she was afraid of what his reaction might be, afraid he'd change his mind about helping her escape if he knew.

They met in secret whenever they could both get away without being missed.

At first, Jenny had been reluctant to be alone with Ryder. The recollection of his kisses, of her reaction to them, still burned bright in her memory. But Ryder never mentioned what had happened between them, and she began to think maybe she had read more into his kisses than he'd intended.

Still, it was hard to be near him and not touch him. The feelings he had aroused in her were so new, so wonderful, it was hard to ignore them, to pretend she didn't remember how her whole body had come alive at his touch. She loved looking at him, being with him, hearing his voice. She tried to tell herself it didn't mean a thing, that she was just hungry for companionship, for the sound of her own language, for someone to share secrets and memories with.

She tried to convince herself that she would have felt the same if Ryder were old and ugly, instead of breathtakingly handsome. But it was a lie, and she knew it.

Ryder had praised her for standing up to Alope, and Jenny had basked in his approbation. It had been so long since anyone had complimented her, so long since she'd heard kind words, that she'd almost wept with pleasure. And while standing up to Alope had been one of the hardest things Jenny had ever done, she had to admit it was also the best thing she could have done. The other woman no longer nagged her unceasingly, and while they hadn't become friends exactly, they had decided to share the work between them.

Alope did the cooking because she enjoyed it, and Jenny fetched wood and water. They shared the task of sewing for Kayitah, and took turns tanning the hides he brought them.

Fallon's status with the tribe was also changing. He was no longer viewed as an outcast. Daily he became more popular with the warriors and he was often included in their games. He gambled with them in the evening, danced at celebrations, and rode with them when they went hunting. He often gave his share of the hunt to the old woman who had stepped forward and intervened in his behalf. Her husband was old and unable to hunt, so she was dependent on others to provide her lodge with meat.

At first, Jenny had viewed Fallon's increased status with the tribe with hearty approval. After all, if he were free to come and go as he pleased, it would make their escape that much easier when the time came. And she had to get away, soon, before it was too late.

But then Fallon began to court one of the Apache maidens, and a new fear crept into Jenny's heart. She knew that Ryder had lived with the Indians once before and had liked it. What would happen to her dreams of escape if he suddenly decided to marry Codahooyah's daughter and settle down? He wouldn't be able to spirit her away and then return as if nothing had happened.

The thought of living with the Indians for the rest of her life tormented Jenny. She saw herself growing old, older, having Indian children, and eventually becoming an Indian herself.

It was a thought that filled her with dread. If she didn't find a way to escape, she would never live with her own people again, never go to a concert or the theater. She'd never be able to attend church and partake of the word of the Lord. Never know what was going on in the rest of the world. Never enjoy a fine meal served on linen and crystal. Never wear anything but animal skins and moccasins. She'd never see Hank again. . . .

When her doubts and fears grew too heavy to bear, she sought out Fallon, hoping he would alleviate her growing concerns, but he managed to avoid being alone with her until the day she trailed him to the river.

"You've been avoiding me," Jenny accused without preamble. "Why? I thought we were friends!"

Fallon flinched at the hurt in her eyes. It was true. He had been avoiding her, which was no easy task when they shared the same lodge. During the day, he spent as much time as possible away from the lodge, hunting with the warriors or working the big black stallion. He had taken to sleeping outside at night, making his bed beneath the stars because it was getting harder and harder to watch Kayitah share her bed. She was forever in his thoughts, in his dreams, and it was driving him crazy. He yearned to hold her close again, to inhale the sweet womanly fragrance that was hers alone, to touch her hair, caress her cheek. Make her his woman. But he could not tell her that. She thought of him as a friend, nothing more. And he wanted to be so much more than her friend.

"I'm sorry, Jenny," he said at last, "but it's dangerous for us to be seen together. You know that."

"Is that the only reason?" she asked suspiciously.

Fallon frowned. "What's that supposed to mean?"

"It looks to me like you're enjoying it here," Jenny answered sourly. "Enjoying it and thinking of staying."

Fallon snorted. "Don't be ridiculous."

"I'm not!" she fired back, arms akimbo. "You're thick as thieves with the warriors, especially since you went on that raid last week. And now you're courting Cadahooyah's daughter like she's Juliet and you're Romeo! And last night, I heard Kayitah talking to Marteen about taking you back into the tribe . . ."

Jenny's voice trailed off as she realized what she'd let slip out.

Fallon lifted one black brow as he read between the lines and quickly understood what was really bothering Jenny. She was afraid he might decide to stay with the Apache instead of taking her home, as he'd promised.

Fallon's mouth twitched at the corners. "If I didn't know better," he teased, "I'd think you were making noises like a jealous woman."

"Jealous!" Jenny sputtered. "Why you . . . I never . . ."

"Calm down, honey," Fallon said, laughing. "I was only kidding. But listen, Jenny," he said, serious once more, "we really can't take a chance on getting caught down here alone. Not now. And for your information, I have no intention of settling down here or anywhere else, not now, not ever. But you're right about one thing," he allowed, grinning broadly. "I have been enjoying myself. I'll try to watch it in the future."

"You're incorrigible," Jenny said, pouting. But she was secretly relieved that he was not serious about the Apache maiden. She could not bear to think of him being married, holding someone else . . . She shook the thought from her mind. "Can we leave soon?"

"Soon," he promised, noting the anxiety in her eyes. "You look a little pale, honey," he remarked. "Are you feeling all right?"

"Yes, I'm fine," Jenny said quickly. She took a step back and folded her arms over her stomach. "Just anxious to get away."

Fallon studied her briefly, wondering what was really bothering her. She had been awfully quiet in the last few weeks, eating little, keeping to herself. She'd even managed to put Alope in her place and now there was peace in the lodge, something both men appreciated.

"We'll leave as soon as we can," Fallon said at last. "When the time is right, we'll meet in the old sweat lodge an hour after midnight."

Jenny nodded. For the first time, it all seemed real.

"You'd better go now," Fallon said. "We shouldn't meet again unless there's a change in plans."

Jenny nodded, one hand worrying a lock of her hair.

"What is it?" Fallon asked, concerned by the troubled look that flitted across her face.

"Nothing," Jenny lied.

"Are you sure?"

"Yes. I guess I just can't believe it's true, that we're really going to go."

"We'll do it all right," Fallon promised. Or darn well die trying.

Chapter Twelve

The fall hunt was over and the Apache had meat to see them through the coming winter. A raid into Mexico supplied them with horses, blankets and warm clothing, as well as flour and other foodstuffs, including a large supply of coffee and several boxes of thin black cigars.

Jenny didn't care for coffee, preferring tea, but Fallon drank several cups the first night it was available, and then sat back and lit a cigar, more content than he'd been in months.

Days passed and the trees lost their autumn leaves and the grass withered and died. The horses' coats grew long and shaggy.

It was a busy time of year, with the men hunting and raiding and the women drying great quantities of meat. Fallon continued to spend as much time as possible away from the lodge, his hunger for Jenny growing with the passage of each day. Often, he stayed outside until everyone else had gone to bed, preferring the cold weather to the sight of Kayitah sitting beside Jenny, touching her hair, sleeping in her bed.

The few times he spent any time around her, he noticed she looked a trifle pale, was considerably more irritable than he'd ever seen her, and often seemed to be lost in thought, but he supposed that was only natural, what with the time of their proposed escape drawing nearer with each passing day.

Secretly, he prepared two makeshift saddlebags and filled them with jerky and pemmican for their journey. He ran a knowing eye over the horse herd and selected a rangy chestnut gelding for Jenny, wondering if she could ride astride with only a blanket. There weren't any sidesaddles in the rancheria; in fact, there were few regulation saddles of any kind.

Roping the chestnut, he ran expert hands over its legs, paying special attention to its feet, making sure the walls of each hoof were firm, the frog clean and sound. It was not an idle saying that as the foot went, so went the horse.

He worked the black stallion each day, more pleased than he could say with Katuhala's gift. The black was a remarkable animal, swift, intelligent, easy to train.

Satisfied that both horses were sound, he turned them out in the corral with a casual remark to the herd boy that he would be using both the black and the chestnut in the future.

* * *

He learned the cause of Jenny's disquiet on a day in late November. He'd gone hunting, intending to be gone most of the day, but his bow had cracked and he'd returned to the lodge early. Stepping inside, he caught Jenny changing clothes. In profile, the reason for her increased irritability was obvious.

She was pregnant.

It hit him like a blow to the groin.

"How far along are you?" he asked flatly.

Jenny grabbed her dress and held it in front of her as she whirled around to face him. "I don't know what you mean."

"You're pregnant. How far along are you?"

"I'm not sure." Jenny placed a hand over her abdomen. Due to worry and a lack of appetite, she had gained very little weight. "About six months, I think."

He let out a long sigh. "Well, that tears it," he muttered.

"We're still going, aren't we?" Jenny asked, her eyes filled with alarm.

Fallon shook his head ruefully. "No."

"You promised."

"I didn't promise to take a pregnant woman."

"Please, Ryder, I've got to get away before the baby's born. Please. I don't want my child born here. I don't want him raised to be an Apache." She gazed up at him intently, willing him to understand. "This baby will be Kayitah's first child. He'll never let me go if the child lives. Never!"

Fallon shook his head again. "I'm sorry, Jenny, but the answer's still no."

She lifted her chin stubbornly. "I risked my life to save yours," she reminded him. "And you gave me your word, as a warrior, to get me out of here."

Ryder Fallon swore softly. "Dammit, woman, are you out of your mind? Do you think escaping from here is going to be a picnic? We'll be traveling hard and fast. We won't have much time to stop and rest. Kayitah will be after us the minute he finds out you're gone." He glanced pointedly at her swollen belly. "Especially now."

"I never said I thought it would be easy," Jenny argued. "But think about this. The trip will be easier if there's just the two of us. If we wait until the baby's born, it's liable to cry while we're sneaking out of the village, and we'd have to stop to feed it along the way."

He took a deep breath, his anger rising as he realized he was neatly caught in a trap of his own making. He had promised to take her, and while he'd done a lot of despicable things in his life, he'd never broken his word. But he was sorely tempted to start now.

Jenny reached out and laid her hand on his arm. "Please, Ryder." He heard the soft note of pleading in her voice, but it was the quiet desperation he read in the depths of her green eyes that changed his mind.

"All right, Jenny, if you're sure this is what you want to do."

"I'm sure."

"We'll leave right away. I'll get everything ready and then we'll go."

He ducked out of the lodge before she could thank him for what he knew was a big mistake.

It was in his mind to leave the following night, but Kayitah decided to go on a quick raid across the border and insisted that Fallon accompany him.

They were gone for three weeks, and when they returned, there was a feast and dancing. The following day, Kayitah decided to take Jenny and go away for a few days.

Fallon spent the days with Nahthletla, reminiscing with her about the old days when he had lived with the People. They talked of Chandeisi and his brother. It had been in a skirmish against the soldiers that Delshay had been killed. Chandeisi had blamed Fallon for his brother's death. He had accused Fallon of being a coward, claiming that Fallon had turned and run when he could have stayed on the field of battle and saved Delshay's life, but Delshay had already been dead when Fallon reached him. Chandeisi was right about one thing, though. There had been no time to take the body and get away alive. Right or wrong, Fallon had left Delshay's body and run for cover.

Nahthletla spoke of her children, of her daughter who had died of the coughing sickness, of her son who had died in the same battle that had taken Delshay's life. They spoke of the days before the white man came, of the uncertainty of the future now that the white man was here to stay.

The only thing Fallon refused to speak of was Nahdaste. Even now, the memory of her death filled him with bitter despair.

But it wasn't the memory of Nahdaste that tormented him at night. It was the thought of Jenny lying in Kayitah's arms, being held against her will, being kissed by another man, being touched by the Apache chief when he, Fallon, longed to touch her. He told himself he had no rights where Jenny was concerned, none at all. She was married to another man, a man she loved, a man she desperately yearned to see, but he couldn't ignore the jealousy that burned through him like a hot branding iron, couldn't deny the fact that he wanted her as he had never wanted another woman. It was ironic, he thought, that after all these years he'd finally found a woman he desired, and she belonged to someone else.

Each morning and evening he expected to see Jenny and Kayitah return to the rancheria, but each dawn brought only sunrise, and each night brought only darkness. Alope's expression grew more and more sullen as the days slipped by. Fallon stayed out of her way as much as possible, for her temper was short and her tongue sharp.

It was two weeks later when Jenny and Kayitah returned. The Apache chief looked rested and happy; Jenny looked anxious and afraid.

She sought Ryder out at the first opportunity. "We've got to go. Now. Tonight."

"What's wrong? Did he hurt you?"

"Of course not. He never touched me."

Fallon nodded curtly. He'd been torn by jealousy during Jenny's absence, imagining Kayitah holding her, kissing her, caressing her, even though most Indian men didn't have intercourse with their women once it was known they were pregnant.

"So," he asked, "what's your hurry?"

"He's getting too possessive. He hardly lets me out of his sight, and I'm afraid it will only get worse."

"Yeah." Fallon's gaze skimmed over Jenny's belly. She'd gained only a little weight, so little he found it hard to believe she was almost eight months along. Pregnancy agreed with her, he thought ruefully. Her color was good, her eyes were bright and clear. But it seemed like sheer folly to undertake such a venture, and he said as much.

"I want to go," she replied firmly. "As soon as possible."

"All right, Jenny," he promised, frightened by the determination he saw in her eyes and afraid she might try to run away on her own. "It'll be coming on winter in another two weeks. We'll leave the night of the first good storm and hope the rain will cover our tracks."

"You promise?"

"I promise," he said heavily, and felt as though he'd just signed his own death warrant, and hers, as well.

Chapter Thirteen

The sound of rain pelting the sides of the wicki-up roused Fallon from a deep sleep. The first storm of the year had come.

Cautiously, he sat up and looked around the lodge. The fire had gone out, but he could see Kayitah curled up beside Alope and he breathed a sigh of relief. Maybe Usen would smile on this venture, after all. Glancing to the left, he saw that Jenny was awake and watching him.

He nodded, then slid out of his blankets and after pulling on his moccasins, he shrugged into a heavy buffalo robe coat and slipped outside. Padding noiselessly toward the corral, he stopped to retrieve his saddlebags from their hiding place.

A fledgling warrior stood guard at the corral. The boy made a dark forlorn silhouette as he huddled beneath a sodden blanket.

Not liking what he was about to do, Fallon lowered his gear to the ground, then crept through the shadows until he was behind the boy. Wrapping one arm around the boy's neck, he choked the young warrior into unconsciousness, then tied the boy's hands behind his back and lashed his feet together.

Moving quickly now, Fallon took the boy's bow and quiver of arrows, picked up his saddlebags, and entered the corral. The horses eyed him balefully but made little fuss as he spoke to them in the Apache tongue. In minutes, his black and the chestnut were bridled, a blanket was in place on the gelding's back, and the saddlebags were draped across the stallion's withers.

So far, so good, Fallon thought as he made his way toward the sweat lodge. After a hasty look around, he ducked into the wickiup.

Jenny was a dark shadow against the far side of the wickiup, her golden hair hidden beneath the folds of a black Spanish shawl that had been a gift from Kayitah, her figure lost in the voluminous folds of a blanket.

"Ready?" Fallon whispered.

"Yes."

"Then let's go. The sooner we get out of here, the better."

"Wait, I have something for you."

Jenny fumbled beneath the folds of the blanket and withdrew Kayitah's favorite rifle and a bag of ammunition. Smiling, she handed them to Fallon.

"Good girl," he said approvingly, and his hands caressed the smooth rosewood stock of the Winchester as lovingly and tenderly as a man might stroke a woman's flesh. "Can you handle a rifle?" he asked, checking to make sure the Winchester was loaded.

"Yes."

Fallon grunted as he handed her the rifle. "If anything happens to me, you ride like hell. There's a town about forty miles north of here. Don't stop until you get there, savvy? Then let's make tracks."

Outside, he lifted Jenny onto the chestnut's back, then paused, one hand on her knee. "Are you sure, Jenny?"

"I'm sure."

"All right, let's go."

Single file, they rode down the valley. Dark clouds shrouded the moon, the hiss of the rain smothered the sound of their passing.

Jenny rode behind Fallon, her heart pounding in her breast. "Please, God," she prayed urgently. Just those two words, over and over again, as she followed Ryder toward the narrow passage at the head of Rainbow Canyon. She knew as well as he did the risk they were taking, the consequences if they were caught.

Two dark shapes loomed at the mouth of the canyon. As they drew closer, one of the warriors left the shelter of a rocky overhang to meet them.

It was Niyokahe.

Fallon smiled wolfishly as he recognized the ugly warrior who had wielded the burning brand with such enthusiasm. He was still smiling as he nocked an arrow to his bowstring.

"Perico, you are early," Niyokahe said. "Is anything wrong?" He peered into the darkness. "You are not Perico," he exclaimed in surprise, and then frowned as he recognized Kladetahe. "What are you doing here . . ."

The words died in the warrior's throat as Fallon's arrow pierced his heart. A second arrow followed the first, quickly disabling the second sentry.

"Let's get out of here!" Fallon shouted above the roar of the storm, and slammed his heels into the stallion's flanks.

The two horses galloped headlong through the narrow passageway and out into the open desert. A wild elation filled Ryder Fallon as they thundered through the night, ignoring the taunting voice of his conscience that told him he was a fool—a fool to bring Jenny, a fool to risk his life for a woman who would never be his, a fool for not killing the herd boy, who was probably hollering his head off by now, rousing every able-bodied man in the rancheria. But there was no help for it. Killing Niyokahe was one thing; killing a kid was something else.

As the moon broke through the clouds, Fallon urged the black on, and the stallion bellied out in a ground-eating run. Glancing over his shoulder, Fallon saw Jenny riding close behind him. She was clinging to the reins with one hand and to the gelding's mane with the other. The rifle was snugged under her left arm. Her face was a pale oval in the dim light of the moon. The shawl had slipped from her head and her long golden hair streamed behind her like a battle flag.

Jenny smiled as the wind stung her eyes and cheeks. At last, she was free! She kept her eyes focused on Ryder's broad back, silently thanking God for sending her a man like Ryder Fallon. He was strong and smart and resourceful. He knew the country. If anyone could get her home, he could.

As they veered northward, the landscape underwent a gradual change. Tall trees and scattered clumps of brush reared out of the darkness, their hulking shapes looming menacingly on all sides. Jenny shivered as her imagination began to play tricks on her, turning every swaying tree and dancing shadow into some frightful creature ready to devour her without mercy. Hard sand gave way to thick black mud that sucked hungrily at the horses' hooves, forcing them to slow their pace.

And then, just when Jenny was certain they would escape without a hitch, her horse went down.

Fallon heard her frightened cry above the wail of the wind, and a quick chill skittered down his spine as he reined the stallion in a tight rearing turn.

He swore softly as he saw Jenny sprawled in the mud. A short distance beyond, the chestnut was struggling to its feet. He knew, deep in his vitals, that the horse had a broken leg.

Suppressing an oath, Fallon rode back to Jenny. Sliding from the stallion's bare back, he knelt at her side.

"Are you all right?" he asked. "Is anything broken?"

"I don't think so," Jenny replied, touched by the concern in his voice.

"Good. We'll have to ride double. Your horse has gone lame. Come on, I'll help you up."

Jenny nodded, offering Fallon her hand as he stood up. She had almost gained her feet when the pain sliced through her. In the dim moonlight, Fallon saw her face go pale, saw the fear rise in her eyes. Gently, he lowered her to the ground.

"What is it?" he asked, knowing, and dreading, the answer.

"The baby," Jenny gasped. "It's coming."

A great weight, heavy as the hand of doom, settled over Fallon. For a fleeting instant, he thought of swinging aboard the black and riding like hell, away from Jenny, away from the slow, agonizing death Kayitah had promised him.

But he could not leave her. Jenny had saved his life. She had brought him water when he would have sold his soul for one precious drop. No matter what her motives had been, she had disobeyed Kayitah, and put her own life in jeopardy, to help him. He could not abandon her now.

Jenny smiled faintly as Ryder laid a comforting hand on her shoulder.

"Take it easy, honey," he said reassuringly. "Everything's gonna be all right."

Jenny watched Fallon through pain-glazed eyes as he stripped the blanket from the back of the chestnut gelding and spread it beneath a stand of timber that offered some degree of shelter from the rain. She moaned softly as he carried her to the blanket, gasped as a sudden gush of warm liquid soaked her skirt.

She stared up at Fallon, embarrassed to be sharing such an intimate moment with a man who was not her husband.

"I'm sorry," she murmured helplessly.

"Forget it." He eased her down on the blanket and covered her with his heavy buffalo robe coat.

He tethered the stallion to a sapling, then put the chestnut out of its misery with a single well placed shot.

"Ryder!" Jenny called his name as a sharp pain threatened to tear her apart.

Fallon hurried to her side, his brow furrowed with concern.

"You've got to go," Jenny gasped. "Now, while there's still time."

"Don't try to talk now," Fallon admonished softly. "Just take it easy. Try to rest between the contractions."

"No, please, you've got to go before it's too late. Kayitah will kill you."

"Save your breath, Jenny. I'm not going anywhere."

Jenny smiled weakly as she reached for his hand.

"I knew you wouldn't leave me," she whispered tremulously, then squeezed his hand as another contraction caught her unaware.

"It hurts," she murmured. "I didn't know it would hurt so much."

Fallon nodded, wondering what he could say to comfort her. Childbirth could take hours, perhaps days. And there was a good chance she'd been injured inside by the fall. How would she survive if there were complications? And what about the child?

He looked at Jenny and for a moment he saw Nahdaste lying there, her eyes dark with pain as she struggled to bring their daughter into the world. The keening of the wind reminded him of the sound of her cries when, after hours of labor, their daughter had been born dead. A short time later, Nahdaste had died in his arms.

Jenny squeezed his hand again and Fallon swallowed the fear rising within him. He'd always been a man in charge of his own life, able to deal with whatever life dumped in his path, but now he felt totally helpless and inadequate. Jenny needed a woman to care for her, perhaps a doctor, not a half-breed drifter.

Jenny gasped as another pain knifed through her. "Talk to me," she implored. "I'm so afraid." So afraid, she thought bleakly. Afraid of the pain, afraid of death, of the night that seemed to be closing in around her. "Talk to me, please."

"What about, honey?"

"Anything. Tell me about you."

And so, to please her, Ryder Fallon reached back into his past and told Jenny about his childhood with the Cheyenne, of his first battle against the Pawnee when he was fifteen. How, less than a year later, his father had been killed in a raid by the Crow; how his mother had died six months later.

Pausing, Fallon glanced down at Jenny. Her eyes were closed, her mouth a thin white line of pain.

The rain stopped and the only sound was the rasp of Jenny's labored breathing and the steady splash of a million raindrops as they slid down the leaves and branches of the surrounding shrubbery to collect in tiny pools on the rain-soaked earth.

Jenny groaned and clutched his hand tighter. "Please go on," she begged, desperate for the sound of his voice, for anything that would take her mind from the awful pains that tormented her.

"Sure, honey," Ryder said, and he told her how, after his mother's death, he had decided to leave the Cheyenne and visit the land of the white man. He told her of his first impression of civilization, how he had found rough towns overflowing with tough men. Mule skinners, buffalo hunters, miners, trappers, bounty hunters, gamblers, con men and lawmen. He met them all and found that, regardless of race or occupation, they were all hard men, and most of them smelled incredibly bad.

He told her of cheap saloons brimming with rotgut whiskey and games of chance; some honest, some crooked as a dog's hind leg. He told her how he had discovered poker and found that he had a natural feel for the game.

He didn't tell her of the brothels that filled those towns, or of the scantily clad, heavily painted women that plied their trade in the tiny cribs.

He told her instead of how he found an old Colt's Dragoon and practiced with it for hours on end until he could draw and fire a six-gun as quickly and accurately as he had once used a bow.

He discovered he was a man with an itchy foot, never happy to remain too long in one town, one place.

He lapsed into silence as Jenny's contractions came harder and faster, and he thought he would rather suffer torture at Kayitah's capable hands than have to endure the pains of childbirth.

Jenny clasped Ryder's hands tighter, tighter, her nails diggings into his palms, as the pains grew stronger and came closer together. She rolled her head from side to side, moaning softly. She was going to die. The thought filled her with sorrow. She would never see her child, never know if it was a boy or a girl.

She kept her gaze focused on Ryder's face, telling herself that everything would be all right so long as he was there beside her. He was so strong, so brave; surely he would not let her die.

"Scream if it will help, honey," Fallon urged. "There's no one to hear you but me."

"You never screamed," Jenny murmured, her body rigid with pain. "Not once. He cut you, but you never screamed."

"I wanted to."

She did scream, moments later, as the baby's head emerged.

Quickly, Fallon threw back the buffalo robe coat and caught the tiny head in his callused hands. "Push, honey," he coaxed gently. "Push."

Gathering the last of her strength, Jenny managed one last thrust, and the baby slid into Fallon's waiting arms.

It was a boy, with tawny skin and a thatch of thick black hair. A thin wail floated across the stillness of a new day as the infant drew its first breath.

"Thank God," Fallon murmured. Cutting the cord, he tied off both ends, wiped the baby dry with a length of cloth Jenny had packed for just that purpose. Then, wrapping the infant in a blanket, he laid the child in its mother's arms.

"It's a boy," Ryder said, answering the unspoken question in Jenny's eyes. "A beautiful boy."

"Ryder?"

"What is it, honey?"

"Is it . . . is it hard, being a half-breed?"

Half-breed. How he had come to hate the word, the sarcastic remarks and taunts, the snide looks that invariably accompanied it.

It was only hard in the white world, Fallon thought bitterly. The Indians didn't place much emphasis on a man's skin color, but most of the white people he'd met couldn't see past the color of a man's skin, and the only color they accepted was lily white. But he couldn't tell Jenny that, not now, when she was cradling a new life in her arms. She would find out for herself soon enough, because people would scorn her, too, for being the mother of a half-breed. Decent women would shun her, and the men would call her dirty names.

"Go to sleep, honey," he said at last. "We'll talk about it in the morning."

"It's bad, isn't it?"

"Jenny . . ."

"I want to know."

"It's bad." He thought of the half-breeds he'd known over the years. Most of them, himself included, were caught between two worlds, and never quite at home in either one. Many of them, unable to accept their lot in life, turned outlaw, or daily drank their way into oblivion, unable to cope with the constant abuse meted out by an intolerant society.

Jenny gazed down at her son, so beautiful, so perfect, and wondered if perhaps she should have stayed with the Apache. Her son would have been loved there. No one would have belittled him because his mother was a white woman.

She let out a long sigh, too weary to worry about it any longer. With her son lovingly enfolded in her arms, she closed her eyes.

Ryder couldn't stop looking at Jenny. Sitting there, with the rifle close at hand, he felt a vague sense of loss, a longing for something that had once been his, long ago. With some surprise, he realized that Jenny reminded him of Nahdaste. She had the same ready smile, the same innocent air of sensuality that made a man aware of, and immensely pleased with, the difference between male and female.

Seeing her lying there, sleeping peacefully beside her son, he was suddenly conscious of just how empty and meaningless his life had been since Nahdaste's death. A wave of loneliness swept over him as he sat there, listening to the gentle patter of the raindrops and the quiet swish of the wind through the trees.

Overhead, the clouds moved east, revealing a golden sun and an azure sky. Raindrops sparkled in the treetops like diamonds tossed aloft by a careless hand. Birds lifted their voices to greet the new day; in the distance, a lone hawk circled high in the sky.

The shrill whinny of the stallion brought Fallon to his feet, the rifle cocked and ready in his hands. He glanced at the black, saw that it was staring into the trees, its nostrils flared as it sniffed the wind, its ears pricked forward.

"I hear them," Ryder muttered, and laying the Winchester aside, he carefully eased the baby from Jenny's arms. Then, muttering an oath, he drew his knife and laid the edge of the blade against the infant's throat.

And that was how Kayitah found them when he rode up a few minutes later, flanked by twenty heavily armed warriors.

The Apache chief took in the scene at a glance: the dead gelding, Jenny sleeping soundly, the blanket-wrapped infant cradled in the crook of the half-breed's arm, the long blade of a skinning knife at its throat.

"You have a son," Fallon said tersely. "Tell your warriors to drop their weapons, or the child goes to its ancestors."

Kayitah glowered at Fallon. "If you spill a drop of my son's blood, I will take your life an inch at a time."

"Your son will still be dead. My hand grows weary. Take your warriors and go home."

"I will not leave without my son."

Fallon shook his head. "No. The child will assure us a safe journey from the land of the Apache."

"No." Kayitah nocked an arrow to his bow and sighted down the shaft. Jenny was his target. "Give me my son," he demanded softly, "or the woman dies now, and then you will die, slowly, cursing the mother who gave you life."

"And if I give you the child?"

"You and the woman are free to go. But I will peel the skin from your body an inch at a time if you ever return to the rancheria."

Fallon nodded. Then, with a heavy sigh, he sheathed his knife and handed the infant to Kayitah.

"Ryder, no!"

He glanced over his shoulder to see Jenny sitting up, her arms outstretched.

"Jenny . . ."

"No!"

"Jenny, there's nothing I can do."

She turned her desperate gaze on Kayitah, her arms still outstretched. "Please."

"He is my son," Kayitah said.

"I'm his mother."

"No."

"Then take me with you."

Kayitah nodded in Fallon's direction. "You have chosen the path you will travel," the chief said, his voice harsh and cold. "I give you the freedom you have begged for so often. The white man will guide you back to your people."

"Let me hold him just once more," she said, sobbing.

"No."

"At least let me feed him before you go."

Kayitah paused for a moment, then nodded curtly. He could not deny his son nourishment.

Tears streamed from Jenny's eyes as she put her son to her breast. She blocked everyone else from her mind, her gaze focused on her child's face as she stroked his downy cheek with her fingertip. His eyes were dark, his nose tiny and perfect, his hair like ebony-colored silk. He gazed up at her through dark eyes fringed by fine black lashes.

"I love you," she murmured brokenly. "You'll never know how much."

Too soon, Kayitah took the child from her arms.

Fallon stood beside Jenny, watching the silent tears course down her cheeks as the Apache chief rode away, surrounded by his warriors.

When Kayitah was out of sight, Jenny curled into a ball and began to sob, her cries tearing at Fallon's heart.

For a moment, he stood there, filled with a sense of helplessness and impotent rage. Maybe he should have refused to give Kayitah the child. Maybe he should have called the chief's bluff, but he'd lacked the nerve to gamble with Jenny's life. And in his heart, he knew the child would be better off with the Apache. In the rancheria, the boy would grow up surrounded by people who would love him in spite of the white blood in his veins. He would not be so readily accepted in the white man's world. But what could he say to Jenny?

"It's all my fault," Jenny sobbed. "All my fault. I was afraid to have my baby in the village. I wanted a nice clean bed and a doctor to help me, and now I've lost him."

"Jenny, don't . . ."

"I've lost him. I'll never see him take his first steps, never hear his voice . . ."

"Jenny, don't blame yourself. If you need to blame someone, blame me. I was a fool to bring you with me."

"Who'll take care of him?" she wailed softly. "Who'll feed him and tell him stories and kiss his hurts? Oh, Ryder, what have I done?"

He had no answers to her questions, no words that would comfort her. Instead, he took her in his arms and held her close. And suddenly it was Nahdaste in his arms, bleeding to death from a child that had been born too soon.

Fallon glanced apprehensively at the blood-soaked cloths bunched between Jenny's thighs and felt his heart go cold.

Twenty minutes later he was riding north with Jenny cradled in his arms. With luck, they'd reach the nearest town before dark tomorrow.

Chapter Fourteen

The town of Broken Fork lay nestled in a narrow valley surrounded by rolling hills. A cutting wind whipped between the whitewashed buildings that lined the main street, stirring whirling dust devils around the stallion's hooves. There were few people in evidence, and those that Ryder saw stared openly at the two mud-spattered figures riding double on the big black stud.

Fallon ignored their curious glances as he reined the black to a halt at the hitch rack fronting the Hendrix Hotel.

Dismounting, he lifted Jenny from the stallion's back, dismayed by the dark smudges under her eyes and by the total lack of color in her face.

"You okay?" he asked doubtfully, but she turned her head aside, refusing to meet his worried gaze.

Frowning, he scooped Jenny into his arms and carried her into the hotel lobby.

Jason Orley peered over his newspaper as the hotel door swung open, admitting a long blast of cold air and two disreputable-looking patrons clad in travel-stained buckskins.

An angry scowl darkened Jason's pinched features when he got a good look at the man's face. *Half-breed,* he thought derisively.

Fallon crossed the room in three long strides. "I need a room, quick," he said, ignoring the clerk's unspoken animosity.

"The management don't . . ." Orley began, then swallowed hard as the half-breed's narrowed eyes took on an ominous glint. "I mean . . . that is . . . I, uh, we're full up."

"I need a room," Fallon repeated. "A room for the lady, and if I don't get one, now, the management will be in need of a new clerk. You savvy my meaning, fella?"

"Yessir," Jason answered meekly. "Take room fourteen, at the top of the stairs. First door on your right."

Fallon grunted as he took the key from the clerk's trembling hand. "You got a doctor in this town?"

"Yessir, and a good one, too," Orley babbled nervously. "Doc Findley. Elias Findley. Lives in a two-story green house down at the east end of Main Street."

"Obliged," Fallon rasped, and moved toward the carpeted stairway, his arms tightening around Jenny as he took the stairs two at a time.

Room fourteen was clean and neat. Somber-hued wallpaper covered the walls. A double bed, a commode, a four-drawer chest and a straight-backed chair crowded the floor. Frilly white lace curtains seemed strangely out of place amid the austere mahogany furniture and brown rag rug.

Fallon lowered Jenny onto the bed, carefully removed her blood-stained tunic and mud-caked moccasins, then covered her with the patchwork quilt folded across the foot of the bed.

For a moment he stood beside the bed gazing down at her, his dark eyes clouded with worry. She looked so pale and worn out, so fragile. So sad. Had be been wise to move her so soon? She had endured the grueling ride without complaint, her great green eyes closed, her mouth compressed in a tight line of sorrow and pain.

Releasing a heavy sigh, he took up the Winchester and left the room.

Dr. Elias Findley was frowning over his account book when his housekeeper, Emma Flaherty, bustled into the room.

"You've not even touched your supper," she scolded, arms akimbo. "I don't know why I bother to cook for you at all!"

"Now, Emma . . ."

"Don't be wasting your sweet talk on me, Elias Findley. Save it for your patients. And why you waste your time with that book is beyond me. Half the people in it can't afford to pay you, and the other half don't seem to be in any hurry."

"Now, Emma, would you have me refuse to help some poor soul just because he can't afford to pay me?"

"It's not my place to tell you how to run your practice, but if it's charity cases you're looking for, you'll be delighted to see the gent waiting in the parlor. I'll wager my back pay that he hasn't got a penny to his name."

"Well," Findley said with a grin, "send him in and let's find out."

Elias Findley listened without interruption as the bearded man in travel-stained buckskins related the details of the difficult delivery. After asking a few pertinent questions, the doctor grabbed his hat and medical bag and accompanied Fallon to the hotel, politely but firmly requesting that Fallon wait in the hallway while he examined the patient.

Fallon paced restlessly outside Jenny's room, hoping Findley knew what he was doing. He'd told the sawbones that the child had died, because it seemed easier and less complicated than telling the truth.

He paused to stare at the door. What was taking so long? He had little faith in doctors, white ones anyway, and would have preferred some of Cochinay's Apache magic. He had seen Indian medicine men perform more than one miracle. And that was what he needed now, he mused ruefully, a first-class miracle that would ease the hurt in Jenny's heart and erase the soul-shattering pain from her eyes.

After what seemed like hours, Findley stepped out into the hallway.

"How is she, Doc?" Ryder inquired anxiously.

"She's going to be fine, just fine," Findley murmured absently as, head cocked to one side, he studied the half-breed with a practiced eye, noting the deep lines of worry and fatigue etched in the man's lean face. "I'm not so sure about you, though," the doctor added with a smile. "When's the last time you had a decent meal and a good night's sleep?"

"I'm fine."

"Maybe, but in my opinion, you look like a man who could use a good stiff drink."

"Thanks, Doc, but I—"

Findley brushed Fallon's protests aside with a wave of his hand. "Strictly medicinal," he said sternly. "And I'm buying."

"Okay, Doc," Fallon agreed with a wry grin, and followed the doctor out of the hotel and across the street to the saloon.

At the bar, the doctor ordered a beer for himself and a shot of whiskey for Fallon. "Are you planning to stay in town long?" Findley asked affably.

"Just passing through."

"I'm aware of the fact that personal questions are taboo in these parts," Findley said with a shrug. "But are you in trouble with the law?" There was no condemnation in his tone, only concern.

"No, Doc. Just dead broke. And you sure Jenny's gonna be all right?"

"Certain sure. She's young and strong. A few weeks in bed will put her right as rain. I give you my word on it." Findley placed a kindly hand on Fallon's shoulder. "Trust me, son. Time's the best healer of all."

"Yeah. Listen, Doc, about the bill—"

"Plenty of time to worry about that after your missus is on her feet again."

Your missus . . . Ryder let the doctor's assumption go uncorrected. He was in no mood to explain what he and Jenny were doing together, or how they had gotten together in the first place.

Findley drained his glass, then wiped the suds from his mouth with the back of his hand. "I'll be by to look in on Mrs. Fallon first thing in the morning. Don't fret if she sleeps all night and a good part of tomorrow. I gave her a pretty potent sedative."

"Thanks for everything, Doc."

Findley nodded, then summoned the bartender with a wave of his hand. "Give my friend here another drink and put it on my tab."

Alone, Fallon stared pensively into the mirror that spanned the wall behind the gleaming mahogany bar. With Jenny taken care of, his next problem was money—money to pay the doctor, to pay for Jenny's room at the hotel, for food, for new clothes for the two of them, for hay and lodging for his horse.

Frowning at his reflection, he drained his glass in a single swallow, then dragged the back of his hand over the coarse black beard that covered the lower half of his face. He was in dire need of a bath, he mused. And a shave.

With a sigh, he stared thoughtfully at Kayitah's Winchester. It was a good rifle, nearly new. He'd likely be able to get a fair price for it.

Chapter Fifteen

The brilliant yellow sunlight streaming through the window coaxed Jenny awake. For a moment, she stared up at the whitewashed ceiling, unable to remember where she was, and then, in a rush, it all came back to her: the midnight escape from the rancheria, their headlong flight through the rain-swept night, the gelding's fall, the concern in Ryder Fallon's eyes as he knelt beside her in the mud, the knifelike pains that had threatened to split her in two, the unbelievable miracle of birth.

Hot tears sprang to her eyes as she recalled the tiny infant Fallon had placed in her arms. Her heart had swelled with love as she gazed into her son's dark eyes. What peace, what contentment, she had known as she cuddled that tiny bit of humanity to her breast. Almost, she could have loved the father, so thrilled was she with the child.

A sob tore at her throat as she relived the horror of watching Fallon hand her son to its father. Willingly would she have gone back to the rancheria to be with her baby, but Kayitah had refused to take her.

She pressed her hand to her mouth to stifle the urge to scream. She'd lost her son as surely as if he had died, and it was all her fault. She should have known Kayitah would come after her, that he would never let her go while she was carrying his child. But she'd wanted so badly to go back to her own people, she'd had to take the chance when it came. And she'd been so afraid of having her baby in the wilderness . . . Oh, if only she'd known how things would have turned out, she would have stayed with Kayitah. Even now, she'd go back to him for the sake of her child, only she knew Kayitah would never take her back. She had spurned him in front of his warriors, and he would never forgive her for that.

Burdened by a horrible sense of loss, Jenny gave in to the rising tide of grief that welled deep within her breast. Sobbing uncontrollably, she poured out her sorrow and anguish in a torrent of bitter tears. Her child had been taken from her and she'd never see him again. Her arms were empty, so empty; her breasts were heavy with milk.

Overcome with grief, she closed her eyes and sought relief in the sweet oblivion of sleep.

* * *

When she woke again, it was late afternoon. Feeling listless, she sat up, then stared at the man standing at the foot of the bed, her sorrow momentarily forgotten. Gone was the bearded drifter in travel-stained buckskins, and in his place stood a clean-shaven, ruggedly handsome man. He was dressed in black whipcord britches and a gray wool shirt. A black kerchief was loosely knotted at his throat, a black Stetson was pushed back on his head. The moccasins on his feet had been brushed free of dirt. A .44 Colt with plain walnut grips nestled in a holster low on his right thigh.

"How are you feeling?" Ryder asked.

Jenny shrugged and looked away. Fallon had been her best friend, her only friend. She'd trusted him, depended on him, and he'd given her son away. She would never forgive him for that. Never.

Fallon took a deep breath, dismayed by the silent accusation in her eyes. "Are you hungry?"

"No."

"You should eat."

Jenny shook her head, wishing he'd just go away and leave her alone.

With a sigh, he gathered the packages he'd dropped on the floor and tossed them on the bed. "I thought you might like to get dressed," he remarked flatly. "Go ahead, open them. They're all for you."

Jenny gazed at the paper-wrapped parcels. It was in her mind to refuse them, to tell him the only thing she wanted, the only thing she needed, was her son.

"Jenny, there was nothing else I could do."

"Wasn't there?"

"He threatened to kill you if I didn't give him the baby. I couldn't take that chance."

"Why not?" Tears washed down her cheeks. "Oh, why didn't I stay with him?" She buried her face in her hands as the tears came faster.

"Jenny." Her cries tore at Fallon's heart. Sitting on the edge of the bed, he drew her into his arms.

She stiffened at his touch, hating him for what he'd done, hating herself.

"Jenny . . ."

His voice was filled with tenderness and concern, his touch so gentle she felt herself relaxing in his arms. She needed to be held, needed it now more than ever in her life. She was lost and alone.

"Jenny, maybe it's for the best."

"No."

"He'll be well taken care of, Jenny. Kayitah will see to that. You know how the Apache are. They love children, and they don't care if they're Indian or Mexican or even white. Try to put your own feelings aside and think about what's best for your son. He'd never be accepted by your people."

"I'd have made it up to him. No one will ever love him as much as I do." She took a deep breath and let it out in a long sigh. "Oh, Ryder, it hurts so much."

"I know," he said quietly, and for a moment he was back in the rancheria again, saying a last goodbye to Nahdaste and his stillborn daughter, certain that his life was over. "Time will dull the pain, Jenny. And you'll have other children."

"No."

"Sure you will, honey. You're young, and—"

"No," she said again, more vehemently.

"Jenny—"

"No!"

She screamed the word and rose to her feet, railing at the cruel hand of fate that had taken her child from her, the only child she would ever have.

Hank couldn't father a child. When she had married him, it hadn't seemed important. She had never been one to fall to pieces at the sight of a baby. But now . . . now she knew what it was like to carry a new life beneath her heart, to hold that child in her arms. Certainly no other love was as strong, as enduring or as satisfying as that of a mother for her child.

Her first child. Her only child . . .

"Jenny . . ." Ryder reached for her, aching to hold her, wishing he could draw the pain from her heart, erase the sorrow from her eyes.

"Leave me alone!" Overwhelmed by grief, she pushed him away, pummeling his chest with her fists, wanting to hurt him, needing to hurt him.

He didn't try to avoid her fists, only stood there until the strength went out of her arms and she collapsed on the bed, weeping softly.

"All right, Jenny," he said heavily, "have it your own way. But you can't stay in this room forever. And you've got to eat. I'm going over to the restaurant to get you some dinner."

Wiping the tears from her eyes, she watched Ryder leave the room, then gazed at the packages piled at the foot of the bed. Listlessly, she reached for the nearest one and opened it to find a blue cotton nightgown trimmed in fine white lace. A second package held a green dress that exactly matched the color of her eyes. There was a white shirtwaist, a tan riding skirt, a pair of shoes and two pairs of stockings, a bar of lavender-scented soap, a pair of handsome black boots, a hairbrush, and a heart-shaped box of chocolates.

They were all there, all the things she had mentioned that day by the river, all the things she had said she missed the most. All that was missing was the milk and apple pie.

She glanced up as the door swung open and Ryder entered the room carrying a covered tray.

Wordlessly, he placed the tray on her lap and lifted the cover, revealing a plate piled high with roast beef and mashed potatoes smothered in gravy. There was half a deep-dish apple pie, and a tall glass of cold milk.

Jenny stared up at Fallon, the wall of ice around her heart melting a little in light of his thoughtfulness even as she told herself again that she could never, never forgive him for what he'd done.

Her son was gone and she had nothing else to live for.

Chapter Sixteen

A week slipped by, and then two. Fallon spent his days with Jenny, talking to her, reading to her from the pages of the Broken Fork *Gazette,* trying to get her to take an interest in life again, but she responded to him in monosyllables or ignored him completely. It pained him to see the haunted look in her eyes and know he had put it there, but he'd had no other choice.

Rest and lots of good food quickly restored her health, though she remained pale and listless.

Nights, after she fell asleep, he could be found sitting on the hotel veranda, staring into the darkness, or sitting at one of the gaming tables at the Silver Saddle Saloon.

But now it was afternoon and he was sitting in Jenny's room, wishing he could think of a way to put the light back in her eyes.

"Did I ever tell you about my mother?" he asked, hoping to turn her thoughts away from her son.

Jenny shook her head, her attitude one of complete disinterest.

"Her name was Dorinda Lee Fallon and she was a hell of a woman. She came from a wealthy Boston family. You know the type, very proper, very high-class. Her mother was a prominent socialite, her father was a pillar of the community. Dorinda was sixteen when her mother died. After a short period of mourning, her father, Douglas Fallon, closed down a thriving medical practice, sold everything he owned, and headed west, dragging his daughter by the hand. Seemed he'd always had a secret longing to see what lay across the Mississippi.

"Somehow he managed to get himself appointed the post surgeon at one of the forts near the Cheyenne hunting grounds. I've forgotten which one.

"Anyway, Dorinda took to the West like a duck takes to water. Much to her father's horror, she discarded all her Boston training. She burned her corset and gave all her fancy silk dresses away and refused to wear anything but pants and a shirt. Caused quite a scandal, I guess."

Ryder slid a glance at Jenny, pleased to see that she was hanging on every word.

"My father was scouting for the Army back in those days. I remember my mother saying she was completely captivated by him the first time he rode into the fort. She said she tried every way she could think of to get his attention, but he didn't seem to have any interest in a white woman."

Fallon grinned. "Of course, my mother didn't take kindly to being ignored. She was a bit of a spoiled brat, I'm afraid, and the next time my father rode into the fort, she accidentally tripped and fell in front of his horse."

"Accidentally?" Jenny asked, curious in spite of herself.

"That's what she always claimed. Anyway, my father jumped down to see if she was hurt. After that, it was just a matter of time. I remember my father telling me he'd fought the Utes and the Pawnee, but there was no way to fight the look in my mother's eyes."

"Didn't she ever miss her own people?"

"I don't know. She never mentioned them much. Her father disowned her for running off with a savage. Years later, he sent her a message by way of another Indian scout, begging for her forgiveness and asking her to come and see him at the fort, but she refused to go. He died soon after that. I never heard her mention his name again."

"Was your mother happy, living with the Indians?"

Fallon nodded. "I think my folks were two of the happiest people I ever saw."

Jenny found it hard to believe that anyone could be happy living with Indians. The women did all the work except the hunting. They raised the children until the girls married and the boys were old enough to go with the men. The women did all the packing when the village moved. They set up the lodge in the new location, cooked the meals, carried the water and the wood. It was a life she hoped never to live again.

"The doc says you can get up today," Fallon remarked. "I thought maybe you'd like to go out to dinner."

It was in her mind to refuse, but when she saw the hopeful look in Fallon's eyes, she nodded. He'd been so patient with her, so kind, surely it wouldn't hurt to have dinner with him.

"I'll pick you up about six. You get some rest now, hear?"

At loose ends, Fallon wandered aimlessly through the town, thinking about his mother, remembering how happy she'd always been. Summer or winter, in good times or bad, she had never been without a smile, a word of hope, the sure conviction that things would get better. She had embraced the Cheyenne way of life with all her heart, learning the language, accepting the Cheyenne beliefs as her own. He had been six years old before he discovered she was a white woman. Even now, he could remember how surprised he had been to learn she was not one of the People by blood. But it didn't matter. In her heart and soul, she had been Cheyenne.

Fallon grinned. Dorinda Fallon hadn't been more than five feet two inches tall, but she had been a formidable woman just the same. Fallon had adored her, but then, they all had.

His father, Nahkohe, had treated her with unfailing respect, seeking her advice, listening to her counsel. The love that Nahkohe and Dorinda had shared had lasted a lifetime, growing ever stronger. Nahkohe had nursed Dorinda through snakebite and fever, comforted her when she lost a child; Dorinda had spent three days at Nahkohe's side when he was wounded in battle, feeding him, loving him, forbidding him to die.

And they had loved their son, totally and completely. Fallon had found that kind of unswerving devotion with Nahdaste, too. He'd never thought to find love again after Nahdaste died. Indeed, he had never looked for it, certain he would never find it again.

And then he'd met Jenny Braedon and discovered that it was possible to love again. . . .

Fallon swore softly, cursing the fact that Jenny was married to another man. He remembered the sweet fire of her kisses that day by the river. He hadn't meant to kiss her, hadn't meant to hold her so close, but she had melted like butter in his arms, her warmth too seductive to resist. He had caressed her in ways he had no right to do, but, like a drowning man clinging to a tiny piece of life, he had kissed her, and kissed her, unable to let her go. Not wanting to let her go.

And now he was going to have to let her go again. He wondered briefly what she would say if he told her he had decided not to take her back to her precious husband, that he was going to find a place where they could settle down, just the two of them. But he couldn't, wouldn't, do such a thing. He'd promised to take her home, and he would.

He swore softly as a sharp stab of jealousy knifed through him. Hank Braedon must be a hell of a man, Ryder thought, for Jenny to be so in love with him, so eager to see him again. She'd spent two years with Kayitah, holding onto her husband's memory, letting it see her through the bad times, the lonely times. She deserved some happiness, and if taking her back to her husband would make her happy, then he'd do it, and gladly. But damn, he was going to miss her.

He was heading back toward the hotel when he heard a small whimper of pain.

Turning down the alley that ran behind Brewster's Saloon, he saw two figures struggling in the dirt.

The man was big, broad through the shoulders, with arms the size of young trees.

The woman was a half-breed. Fallon's gaze swept over her, noting that the beadwork on her moccasins and the star pattern on the collar of her gingham dress were Cheyenne.

"Let her go."

The man grunted and looked up. "Who the hell are you?"

Ryder shook his head. "Nobody."

"Then get the hell out of here."

"Not until you let her go."

"Listen, 'breed, mind your own business."

Fallon glanced down at the girl. She was young, fifteen or so, and badly frightened. He thought of Nahdaste, of the child that had died with her, and a knot of cold rage wrapped around his heart. Had Nahdaste's daughter lived, would she have been subjected to this same kind of abuse? Would this man, with his greasy hair and his filthy hands, have thought he could paw her so disrespectfully just because she was a half-breed?

It sickened him to think of what might have happened to this girl if he hadn't come along when he did.

"I'm making this my business," Ryder said, his voice harsh with barely suppressed anger. "Let her go."

The man stood up, dragging the girl with him. "She's just a whore," he said. "I bought her fair and square, and what I do with her is none of your concern."

"That's a lie!" the girl cried.

"Shut up!" the man roared. He wrenched her arm behind her back, giving a cruel twist that made her cry out in pain.

Fallon spoke to the girl in Cheyenne, his eyes never leaving the man's face. "Do you belong to this man?"

She shook her head, obviously afraid to speak again.

"Do you want to stay with him?"

She shook her head again, more vigorously this time.

Fallon rested one hand on his gun butt, outwardly calm. Inwardly, he was spoiling for a fight.

"I'm gonna ask you nice, just one more time. Let her go."

The man stared at Fallon through narrowed eyes, taking in his easy stance, the way his hand seemed to caress the butt of the Colt holstered low on his thigh.

"Now listen, mister," he said in a conciliatory tone, "she ain't nothing but a little Injun whore. If you want a piece of her when I'm done . . ." He shrugged. "Hell, I'll let you spend an hour with her for a couple of dollars."

"You've got ten seconds to turn her loose," Fallon warned. "One . . ."

"Go to hell," the man exclaimed.

Shoving the girl forward, he dropped to one knee, drew a derringer from inside his shirt, and fired.

The girl screamed. Dropping to her knees, she folded her arms over her head and screamed again.

Ryder swore as he felt the heat of the bullet whiz past his cheek. With the speed of long practice, he drew his Colt and fired, the echo of the gunshot reverberating off the walls.

The slug caught the man in the chest and slammed him backward, and the girl screamed again.

Ryder pulled the girl to her feet. "Are you all right?"

She nodded, tears streaming down her face.

Removing his kerchief, Fallon thrust it into her hands.

The man was dead. Fallon didn't have to look at him twice to see that.

By now, a crowd had gathered at the end of the alley. Fallon paid them no mind as he led the girl toward the street. "Where do you live?"

"With my folks. Above the newspaper office. My father is the editor."

"What's your name?"

"Cynthia McDonald."

"Come on, Cynthia, I'll take you home."

Slipping his arm around her shoulder, Ryder led her through the crowd, ignoring the excited questions that rose all around him.

"Thank you for what you did," Cynthia said softly. "My father warned me not to cut through the alley behind the saloon, but I didn't listen."

"You won't do it again," Ryder remarked.

"No," she said, smiling shyly. "I won't."

He left her outside the newspaper office, declining her offer to come in and meet her parents.

A red-faced deputy flagged him down as he was making his way back to the hotel. "You're under arrest," the lawman said.

"Arrest? For what?"

The deputy, a young man with brown hair and a smattering of freckles, tried to look tough, and failed miserably.

"You killed a man. That's a crime in this town."

"It was self-defense."

The deputy swallowed hard. "I still have to take you in."

"I don't think so."

A red flush crept up the lawman's neck. "But—"

"Is the sheriff in his office?" Fallon asked.

"No, he's out of town. Won't be back until later tonight."

"Listen, kid, I'm staying at the hotel. If the sheriff wants to see me when he gets back, that's where I'll be."

The deputy didn't like it, not one bit, but he'd only been a lawman for a couple of months and he was too young and insecure to try to take on a man who wore a gun like it was part of him.

"Well, I . . . ah, don't leave town."

"I'll be here," Ryder said.

The hotel clerk, Jason Orley, had his nose buried in a newspaper when Fallon entered the lobby. Orley sent a furtive glance at the half-breed, tugged nervously at his cravat as the tall man passed the desk on his way to the stairway.

News of what had happened in the alley was spreading through the town like wildfire. Some folks thought he ought to be strung up for what he'd done; others, who knew the dead man's unsavory reputation, thought the gunman deserved a medal.

Jenny was sitting on the edge of the bed when Fallon entered the room.

"You're late," she remarked.

Fallon nodded curtly. "Are you ready?"

She stared at him a moment, wondering what was wrong. His voice was hard and flat, and there was an odd expression in his eyes, but she was too wrapped up in her own misery to wonder about it for long.

"Jenny?"

"I'm ready."

She stood up, and Fallon felt his heart slam against his ribs as he got a good look at her. The green gown he had bought her outlined every delicious curve. The bodice emphasized the fullness of her breasts, the sash circled a waist he could have spanned with his two hands. Her golden hair, freshly washed and brushed to a high sheen, gleamed like spun gold in the lamplight.

She was so beautiful it made him ache inside. "Jenny . . ."

She turned toward him, her green eyes devoid of expression, of feeling. "What?"

"Never mind. Shall we go?"

She nodded, letting him take her arm as they walked down the hallway toward the stairs. She didn't want to go out, she didn't want to see people, but it was too much of an effort to protest.

Jason Orley stared at the couple in open-mouthed astonishment as Jenny and Fallon walked past the desk. Was that the same woman who had arrived in a filthy buckskin dress, her skin as pale as death, just two weeks ago?

His mouth hung open as his gaze moved over her from head to heel. He glanced at Ryder Fallon, thinking what a lucky devil the half-breed was, and the expression in Fallon's eyes chased every other thought from his mind. There was a thinly veiled warning in the half-breed's cold blue gaze. Orley tugged at his shirt collar, grown suddenly tight, as he turned his back to the couple and busied himself with sorting the mail.

Fallon took Jenny to the town's best restaurant, ordered her the finest meal it had to offer, and bullied her into eating every bite. He kept her wineglass filled, hoping it would relax her, hoping it would put some color in her cheeks.

After dinner, he insisted on a walk around town.

Jenny walked beside him, her thoughts turned inward. Her son was gone, lost to her as surely as if he had died. But she still had Hank. He was the one constant in her life, and she was suddenly anxious to see him again.

Hank was safe. He wouldn't make demands on her. He wouldn't expect anything of her that she couldn't give. She would never have to feel anything again.

"I want to go home," she said abruptly. "How soon can we leave?"

Fallon felt a twinge of regret. He was going to miss looking after Jenny once she was safely back in her husband's arms.

"Whenever you feel up to it."

"Tomorrow, then."

Fallon nodded. "Tomorrow," he agreed.

Chapter Seventeen

By noon the following day, the town of Broken Fork lay far behind them. For Ryder, the two weeks they'd spent in the town had been profitable, to say the least. Using the money he'd won at the poker table, he'd purchased a good used saddle for the black, a pair of saddlebags, a new Winchester repeating rifle, plenty of .44/40 ammunition, and the Colt riding easily on his hip. In addition, he'd bought ponchos and bedrolls for himself and Jenny. Even after all the necessary purchases, he was almost a thousand dollars ahead.

The sheriff had been waiting at the hotel when they returned from dinner the night before. The lawman had listened intently to Ryder's side of the story, agreed that it sounded like self-defense, and left without saying much, though he was careful to add that he was glad to hear Fallon was leaving town.

Fallon took a deep breath, savoring the fresh sweet scent of the outdoors. It was good to be on the move again, good to be riding across unfenced country, surrounded by prairie and gently rolling hills instead of whitewashed buildings and four-rail corrals.

It was even good to be back in his worn buckskins, brushed clean now of mud and trail dust.

He glanced at the woman riding beside him. Mounted on a sleek piebald mare, Jenny seemed to be lost in thought as she gazed into the distance. She hadn't said a dozen words since they left town. Thinking of her son, he supposed, or maybe about her husband. He wondered, not for the first time, what kind of man Jenny had married.

"Is it far?" she asked after a long while. "Widow Ridge, I mean?"

Fallon shrugged. "We should be there late tomorrow if the weather holds." He grinned inwardly, wondering if Red Carlisle was still tending bar at the Double Eagle. "Think you can put up with me for another day?"

Jenny nodded, her stomach churning with apprehension. One more day before she had to face Hank. Would he still look at her with love, or would she see revulsion in his eyes, or worse, pity?

Suddenly, she wished the trip would take longer. She hadn't seen Hank in two years. Two years! What if he no longer wanted her for his wife? They had only been married a few months when Hank had decided to go west. Two years had passed since she last kissed him goodbye. She was no longer the shy innocent girl he had married. She was a woman now. She had been another man's wife in every sense of the word, borne his child . . .

She choked back the tears that were never far from the surface. Would Hank be able to accept her as she was now? And what about the townspeople? Would they accept her, or view her as an object of curiosity?

There were no answers to her questions, only a constant stream of doubts and fears that continued to plague Jenny as they rode westward. What if Hank rejected her? What if he laughed at her for thinking she could just waltz back into his life after two long years? What if he had left Widow Ridge? How would she ever find him?

Plagued by these and a hundred other worrisome thoughts, she didn't notice the troubled expression on Fallon's face as he scanned the darkening land for a place to bed down for the night.

Scattered Indian sign made him cautious, and he chose a secluded campsite well away from the shallow waterhole located within a circle of cottonwoods. He insisted on a cold camp, and Jenny, caught in the web of her own thoughts, didn't think to question his decision.

Dinner was a silent meal save for the lonely lament of a coyote as it serenaded the moon, and the throaty croak of a bull-frog.

There was a quiet rustle of wings as a questing owl flew by in search of prey. Jenny shivered apprehensively, suddenly overcome by the haunting darkness. The Apache believed that good people went to the underworld when they died, but the souls of bad people went into owls. The hoot of an owl often signaled that someone was about to die.

"Cold?" Fallon asked.

"No." She glanced at the darkness that flanked them on all sides. "I wish we could have a fire, though."

"Too risky." He didn't mention the Indian sign he'd seen earlier in the day.

"Do you ever think about death?"

"No. I reckon it will find me soon enough. Why do you ask?"

"I don't know." She wrapped her arms around her body, chilled by her fears, by the loneliness that wouldn't let her go. "Kayitah saw a vision of the hereafter once. It was . . . strange. He said he passed a mulberry tree that was growing out of a cave in the ground. He said there was a guard at the entrance to the cave, but when he showed no fear, the guard let him pass. He said he went deep into the earth until he came to a narrow passage that gradually grew light even though there was no sun.

"After a while he came to a passageway guarded by two huge serpents. They hissed at him, but let him pass when they saw he wasn't afraid. As the passage grew wider, he saw two mountain lions, and later on he saw two grizzly bears, but he spoke to them and they let him pass.

"And then he reached a valley where there were a lot of Indians and lots of game. He said he saw his parents there, and a brother who had died. He said he was sorry when he woke up."

"Are you afraid of dying, Jenny?"

"I'm afraid of being alone."

"You're not alone. I'll have you home soon."

Jenny nodded, missing the easy camaraderie they had once shared. He'd been her best friend, her only friend. How could he have let Kayitah take her son?

She gazed at his profile, silhouetted in the bright light of the full moon, and felt a peculiar catch in her stomach as she remembered the day by the river when he had held her in his arms. She wished she could curl up in those arms now, wished she could put her head in his lap and go to sleep. Why had be betrayed her? Why had he been so quick to let Kayitah take her son? She hadn't even had a chance to give her child a name, and now she'd never see him again.

"Jenny."

As if reading her thoughts, Fallon held out his arms, inviting her inside.

Jenny shook her head, though she wanted, needed, to be held.

"I didn't have any other choice, Jenny," he said, his anger under tight control. "Would you rather be dead now? Kayitah wouldn't have hesitated to kill you, and your death wouldn't have accomplished anything."

"You saved your life, too, Mr. Fallon," she reminded him, her voice thick with contempt.

"Damn right."

"How could you?" she sobbed. "How could you?"

Fallon swore under his breath as he pulled Jenny into his arms, holding her tight as she flailed against him, covering her mouth with his hand when she began to scream that she hated him, that she would never forgive him.

He rocked her back and forth as a father might rock a distraught child, whispering to her that he was sorry for what had happened, telling her, truthfully, that he would do the same thing again to spare her life.

Gradually, Jenny's sobs ceased and she relaxed in his arms. For all that she hated him, he was as solid as the distant mountains, as dependable as the sunrise.

As she grew quiet in his arms, Fallon became aware of the softness of her skin, the silklike texture of her hair, the warmth of her breasts against his chest. He felt his blood heat at her nearness, felt the sharp talons of desire uncurl within him as she slowly drew back and met his gaze.

Jenny's breath caught in her throat as she looked up and saw the hunger in Fallon's eyes. Once, she would have welcomed that look. Once, she had dreamed of having him make love to her. But no more.

She seemed incapable of movement as he slowly leaned toward her, unable to think of anything but the growing desire in his midnight blue eyes, of the taut muscles in the arms that imprisoned her. She took a deep, frightened breath and her nostrils filled with the scent of leather and sweat and tobacco.

She was alone with him, completely at his mercy, but the thought didn't frighten her nearly as much as it should have.

"Jenny . . ."

Her heart was beating wildly, like that of a rabbit caught in the jaws of a wolf, as his head lowered toward hers. Her eyes remained open as his mouth covered hers. The warmth of his kiss spread through her like liquid fire, igniting a sudden desperate need deep within her.

For one brief, gloriously breathtaking moment, she surrendered to the pleasure of his touch, returning his kiss with all the ardor she had denied Kayitah, with the passion that Hank would never claim. Fallon's flesh was warm and firm beneath her fingertips, and she marveled at the sleek muscles that bunched beneath her hand.

And then, with a muffled cry, she twisted out of his embrace, her dark green eyes ablaze with hatred. "Don't ever touch me again!"

A muscle twitched in Fallon's jaw as he drew back. "You wanted it as much as I did," he said, his voice cruel.

She felt her cheeks flame at his accusation, hating herself because it was true, hating him for knowing it.

"I despise you," she said, her voice hissing like water thrown over hot coals.

"I know."

Rising to his feet, he grabbed his hat and rifle and walked into the darkness, leaving her alone with her anger and her tears.

Chapter Eighteen

Jenny's gaze darted from side to side as she rode down the main street of the town that was to be her home.

Widow Ridge appeared to be a thriving Western community, inhabited by saint and sinner alike as evidenced by the two whitewashed churches at either end of town and the five saloons sandwiched between.

Riding down the dusty road, Jenny noted a smithy, a livery barn, several restaurants. She saw a Chinese laundry, a newspaper office, a barber shop, two banks, a large false-fronted hotel, and a dozen other small shops.

A large sign midway down the street on the left-hand side proclaimed in bold black letters:

BRAEDON'S GENERAL STORE & SALOON

Jenny gazed at the store in awe as she reined her horse to a halt at the hitch rack. It was an impressive building, two stories high, with a lot of fancy lattice work and bright green shutters at the windows. A narrow veranda, painted the same shade of bright green, skirted the second floor.

Dismounting, Fallon tossed the black's reins over the hitching post, then turned to help Jenny from her horse.

"Smile, honey," he admonished with a lop-sided grin. "I'm sure the Christians weren't half so pale when they went out to meet the lions."

"I'll bet they weren't as scared, either," Jenny retorted.

Squaring her shoulders, she took a deep breath and walked up the steps to the board-walk. At last, after two long years, she was going to see Hank.

She heard the soft fall of Fallon's footsteps behind her as she approached the door. Inex-plicably, knowing he was there made her feel better.

When she was just inside the entrance, Jenny's courage deserted her and she ducked out of sight behind a rack of ladies' ready-to-wear dresses. There was nothing to be afraid of, she reminded herself. This was Hank's store, and she was his wife, and . . .

Her hand went to her throat as the man standing behind the counter turned around. It was Hank, looking just as tall and handsome and blond as the day they'd married.

She was here, she thought, really here, in Widow Ridge. It wasn't a dream. Never again would she wake up in an Apache lodge. Never again would she have to listen to Alope's endless complaints, or surrender to Kayitah's touch.

Fallon stood behind Jenny, studying the layout of the store. Shelves and counters lined the walls and crowded the floor, stocked to overflowing with bolts of cotton, gingham, chambray and muslin, harnesses, canteens, saddlebags, horse blankets, guns and ammunition, candy, soap, sacks of sugar and flour, salt and seed. A row of red flannel underwear added a splash of color along the back wall.

A shelf behind the counter held a variety of patent medicines: Dr. John Bull's Worm Destroyer, Ayer's Cathartic Pills, Dr. Kilmer's Female Remedy and Blood Purifier, Dr. Rose's Obesity Powders.

Fallon whistled under his breath, impressed by the abundance and variety of goods on display. Several customers, mostly well-dressed women, moved through the store browsing, while others thumbed through mail order catalogs from back East. A couple of men were hunkered over a barrel, discussing the merits of Hostetter's Stomach Bitters.

Hank Braedon was sitting on a gold mine, Fallon mused. He was pleased by the thought that Jenny's husband would be able to take good care of her, and irritated by the twinge of jealousy that stabbed at his heart as he imagined Jenny spending her husband's money, living in his house, lying in his arms . . .

He closed the door to that line of thinking as he gazed down at Jenny. She was staring at the man behind the counter, and from the rapt look in her eyes, he knew they'd found Hank Braedon.

Jenny's husband was the kind of man every mother hoped her daughter would marry. He was lean and fit, outrageously handsome, ambitious, young, with a kind of boyish charm most women found irresistible. He had thick blond hair that curled down over his collar, a wide forehead, a nose that had never been broken. When he smiled, he displayed teeth that were white and even and perfect. But it was his eyes that first drew attention. They were a clear bright blue, forthright and honest.

Fallon took an immediate dislike to the man.

One by one, the customers made their purchases and bade Hank Braedon a pleasant good night, until only Jenny and Fallon remained in the store, still out of sight behind the rack of ladies' ready-to-wear dresses.

Hank Braedon sighed as the last patron left the building. Discarding his white work apron and protective black sleeves, he plucked his coat from the rack behind the counter and stepped into the main aisle.

He was reaching for his hat when Jenny stepped out of her hiding place.

"May I help you, miss?" Hank asked politely.

"I hope so," Jenny replied tremulously. "How are you, Hank?"

Braedon's face was a study in disbelief as he murmured, "Jenny? Jenny, is it really you?"

"Yes."

"I don't believe it." He took a step toward her, then stopped, his brow furrowed in confusion. "The stage . . . the Army said you'd been killed by Apaches. I . . . oh, Jenny!" he breathed, and swept her into his arms.

From his place behind the dress rack, Fallon watched Braedon's face, saw the love and happiness in the man's expression, the hint of tears in his eyes.

"We've got a lot to talk about, Jen," Hank murmured, releasing her. "Let's go home."

"Home." Jenny sighed. "Oh, Hank, you have no idea how good that sounds." She smiled up at him as he took her arm and they started toward the door.

Jenny came to an abrupt halt when she saw Fallon standing beside the dress rack.

Hank frowned at the tall, dark stranger, his gaze lingering for a moment on the gun at the man's hip.

"May I help you?"

"Hank, this is Ryder Fallon," Jenny said. "He's the one responsible for getting me away from the Indians. Ryder, this is my husband, Henry Braedon."

The two men shook hands briefly.

"I'm deeply indebted to you, Mr. Fallon," Hank said sincerely. "I don't know how I can ever repay you for what you've done."

"It isn't necessary," Ryder replied curtly.

"If there's ever anything I can do for you," Hank went on, "please let me know."

Fallon nodded, his gaze intent on Jenny's face. He hated to leave her like this, but perhaps it was for the best. She had made it perfectly clear that she would never forgive him for what he'd done.

"Perhaps we'll see you around town," Hank remarked.

"Perhaps," Ryder mused. He nodded at Jenny, then turned on his heel and left the store.

Jenny stared after Ryder, her thoughts turbulent. He had been her friend, a shoulder to cry on, a bulwark against the loneliness she'd known in the Apache camp. And then he had given her son to Kayitah, and though she knew she would never, ever, forgive him for that, she knew that she would miss him, that he would forever hold a place in the deep recesses of her heart.

Feeling confused, she turned toward her husband. He was smiling at her, his deep blue eyes filled with happiness, and Jenny smiled back at him. For two years, her goal, her dream, had been to escape from the Indians and return to her husband. And now she was here, with Hank, where she belonged. They had been happy before; they would be happy again.

"Come on, Jen," Hank said eagerly. "I want to show you our house."

A home of her own. The idea excited Jenny and she put her hand on Hank's arm as he led her out of the store and helped her into a rather elegant black carriage with a fringed top and bright red wheels. Her heart was pounding with excitement as she settled back against the soft leather seat. At last, she was going home.

Jenny gasped when Hank pulled up before a large, two-story house. It was like a palace, she thought. Bigger than any of the other houses on the shady street, it boasted a wide veranda, a large flower garden, a neatly manicured lawn, and a fresh coat of sparkling white paint.

"This is home, Mrs. Braedon," Hank said as he lifted Jenny from the buggy.

Taking her hand, he led her up the stairs.

"Oh, Hank," Jenny murmured as he opened the front door and escorted her inside. "It's lovely. Just lovely."

The rooms that Hank showed her were spacious and sunlit, decorated in gleaming mahogany and lustrous oak. The settee in the parlor was of dark blue damask, the chairs a rich blue print. Expensive paintings hung on the walls, costly rugs muted her footsteps, crystal chandeliers and Tiffany lamps provided light.

Her head spinning, Jenny followed Hank from room to room, unable to grasp it all. The house seemed overwhelming, almost garish, after the years she'd spent in Kayitah's rude wickiup.

"The store must be doing very well," she mused aloud as she followed Hank up the carpeted stairway.

"Yes," Hank replied after a slight pause. "Very well."

He cleared his throat as he opened a large oak-paneled door. "This is my . . . our room."

The bedroom was as large as the parlor downstairs. An oversized bed dominated the room. The dark mahogany furniture was massive, the carpet fully two inches thick, the drapes were of deep green velvet. Green and white striped paper covered the walls.

Jenny sighed as she let her hand drift over the plush bedspread, wondering if she would ever get used to such luxury.

"I'm glad you're here, Jen," Hank said. He put his arms around her waist and gave her a squeeze. "I've been lonely without you."

"I missed you, too."

"Was it awful, living with those savages?"

"Yes."

"Did they . . . did anyone . . . ?"

She knew immediately what he was thinking. "I'd rather not talk about it."

A muscle worked in Hank's jaw as he realized what Jenny wouldn't say. She'd been with a man. Jealousy raged through him. But she was his wife. He'd be the envy of every man in town when they saw Jenny on his arm.

* * *

Ryder Fallon was scowling when he left Braedon's General Store. Meeting Jenny's husband had left a bad taste in his mouth, and he angled down the street toward the Double Eagle Saloon, hoping a good stiff drink would make him feel better.

He paused briefly at the saloon entrance, surveying the crowd inside before making his way to the bar. The Double Eagle wasn't fancy. There were no lavish trimmings here, no plush chairs or gilt-edged mirrors, but Fallon knew the whiskey was uncut and the cards came off the top of the deck.

As was his wont, he took a place at the end of the bar where he could keep an eye on the door, and where no one could creep up behind him unawares.

"Ryder? Tarnation, it is you!" The bartender's face lit up as he pumped Fallon's hand. "I hardly recognized you without your chin hair."

"Hi, Red. Still selling firewater to Indians?"

"To a select few now and then," the bartender replied, chuckling. He pulled a bottle and a glass out from under the counter. "What brings you to town after such a long absence?"

"Just passing through," Fallon answered. "What do you know about Hank Braedon?"

"Hank?" Red rubbed a thoughtful hand across his jaw. "He came to town a little over two years ago and went into business with his brother, Charlie. There was some talk that Charlie made a killing running guns to the Indians and that he was using the store as a front." Red shrugged. "No one could ever prove anything, and then Charlie up and left town and no one's seen him since."

"Charlie Braedon." Fallon's eyes narrowed. "I've heard that name."

"Yeah, he earned himself quite a rep as a fast gun while he was here. Hank's good, too."

"Hank? He wasn't packing any iron when I saw him at the store."

"Never does, not when he's working." Red poured Fallon another drink. "Bad for business. Makes the ladies nervous, you know. But he keeps a loaded shotgun under the counter. He's good, Ryder. Damn good."

"Think I should go into hiding?" Fallon asked dryly.

Red chuckled. "Oh, I reckon you can still handle yourself okay. I manage to keep up with your exploits. Hell, I heard Ben Ladera hired you to clean up Parksville, and now the place is quiet as a church."

"Yeah," Ryder admitted, grinning. "That's why I left."

Jenny sat across the table from her husband, listening as he told her about the store and the people in town. He'd made a place for himself in the community, she thought with pride, but she couldn't help worrying about what people would think once they learned she'd spent the last two years living with Indians. Would they accept her? Or shun her?

And how would she adjust to living in a house again, to having people wait on her? Hank had a housekeeper and a cook, both of whom Jenny had met earlier that day.

"Where's Charlie?" Jenny asked during a lull in the conversation.

"He, uh, left town almost a year ago."

"Really? Why?"

Hank shrugged. "Wanted to move on, I guess."

"But the reason you wanted to come west was to go into business with him."

"We are in business."

Hank stared into his coffee cup, wondering how much to tell Jenny, wondering how she'd feel if she knew that her brother-in-law had been selling guns to the Apache. It had been profitable, there was no doubt about that. It had provided Charlie with the means to buy the store and the house, but after a while there had been rumors and a lot of ugly talk about traitors and a hanging. In the end, Hank had convinced Charlie to leave town before it was too late. And for once, Charlie had shown some good sense and skedaddled, leaving Hank in charge of the store. Every couple of months, Hank went over the books, divided the profits, and sent Charlie's half to a bank in West Texas.

Hank sipped his coffee. He had made a good life for himself in Widow Ridge. Everyone in town knew that his wife had been killed by Indians. The women had done their best to comfort him. As time went on, a few of the unmarried ones had flirted with him openly, but he'd never paid them any mind. They still fussed over him, inviting him to dinner, to socials, nodding with supposed understanding when he refused their invitations. They thought he was still in mourning, and everyone said how devoted he was to stay faithful to his wife's memory after all this time. If they only knew, he thought bitterly. If they only knew.

And now Jenny was back, but she had changed, somehow. She was still beautiful, even more beautiful than he remembered, but she had changed. He supposed that was only natural after all she'd been through, but there was something about her, something that went deeper than pain.

She'd been with a man. He knew it, and the knowledge was almost unbearable. She had been with a man, a whole man. He would lose her now, he thought bleakly. Now that she knew what a farce their marriage had been, she would leave him for a man who could be a husband in the true sense of the word, a man who could give her children.

She'd been with a man, and nothing would ever be the same again.

Jenny was exhausted when she retired to bed later that night. The pillowcase was cool against her cheek as she closed her eyes and waited for Hank to come to bed, praying that they could resume their former closeness, that they could recapture the warmth and friendship they had once shared.

She felt herself tense as he slid into bed beside her, and then she reminded herself that this was Hank, and she had nothing to fear. He wouldn't force himself on her. Once, this had been her favorite time of day, a time when they had talked about the day's events and made plans for the future.

"Jenny, I know you don't want to talk about what happened, but I need to know."

"Please, Hank . . ."

He slipped his arm around her in an unconscious gesture of possession. "Was there another man?"

"Not in the way you mean."

She felt his arm tighten around her shoulder. "Who was it?"

"His name was Kayitah. He was the chief of the tribe, and he made me his second wife. I hated it, Hank, and I hated him, and I don't want to talk about it."

"All right, Jen. I'm sorry."

He felt a surge of relief so sweet it was almost painful. Perhaps he wouldn't lose her after all. And then he recalled the way Jenny had looked at Ryder Fallon, and the way Fallon had looked at Jenny. He had to know. No matter how much it hurt, he had to know.

"What about Fallon?"

"What about him?"

"Did he . . . was he . . . ?"

"He was a prisoner, just like me, that's all. Please, Hank, I just want to forget about it."

"I won't mention it again, Jen, I promise. Good night."

Jenny remained awake, staring into the darkness, long after Hank had fallen asleep. She was home, where she'd dreamed of being for so long, but nothing was the same. She'd been a girl when she left Philadelphia, innocent in the ways of men, untouched by life, by desire.

But she wasn't a naive young girl any more. She was a woman now. She'd known pain and grief. She'd seen death and vengeance firsthand. She'd lived with hunger and fear. She'd been a wife, she'd borne a child and felt it suckle at her breast. She had felt the first stirrings of desire in Ryder Fallon's arms . . .

Fallon. Where was he now? She tried to push his memory from her thoughts, but his swarthy image remained, his midnight blue eyes haunting her. Damn him! Why had be come into her life? He had shown her what passion was, had given her a hint of what love could be like between a man and a woman. She had never craved a man's touch until he had kissed her, had never known what passion was, or realized what she had been missing with Hank.

I hate him. I hate him. She repeated the words in her mind, wishing she had never met him.

But for Ryder Fallon, she would have remained untouched by passion, by desire.

But for Ryder Fallon, she never would have left Kayitah. She would never have lost her son.

Suddenly, her arms ached to hold her child. Tears welled in her eyes as she looked into the future and saw nothing there but loneliness.

She would never see her child again, and she would never have another.

There would be no desire to warm her nights, no afterglow of passion to carry through the coming days, only Hank's chaste affection.

There would be no children to fill her house with laughter, no grandchildren to bring her joy and comfort in her old age.

Choking back a sob, she stared out the window into the darkness of the night, into blackness as deep as the pain in her heart, as empty as her arms. And wished that she had let Ryder Fallon make love to her just once.

Chapter Nineteen

Fallon spent a restless night. Every time he closed his eyes, he imagined Jenny in her husband's arms, kissing him, loving him, pleasuring him as only she would know how.

The thought drove him crazy, and he finally gave up all hope of sleep and left the hotel. He paced the dark street for twenty minutes before he turned down the road that led to the house that Red had described as belonging to Hank Braedon.

He whistled under his breath when he saw the big white house. The place was as big as some of the mansions he'd seen back East, well cared for, expensive.

With a rueful shake of his head, he turned away and headed back to Main Street. Even if he'd been able to persuade Jenny to leave her husband, he'd never be able to give her a place like that. Hell, he couldn't afford to buy one room of a place like that, let alone the whole shebang. It was a moot point anyway, he mused as he stepped into Red's saloon. Jenny was in love with her husband, and she was never going to forgive him for what he'd done.

Sunday morning found Ryder Fallon lounging idly on the steps of the Double Eagle Saloon, bleary eyed after another sleepless night.

As the courthouse clock chimed ten, the townspeople began to wend their way toward the tidy white church that dominated the south end of town.

One family in particular caught Fallon's eye. The father and mother walked ahead of their brood, looking somber and straightlaced. Behind them, slim and lovely in blue dresses with crisp white sashes, came their twin daughters. Trailing the girls were three boys, their well-scrubbed faces marred by frowns of displeasure that grew steadily deeper as they neared the church.

Fallon grinned, knowing the boys would rather be out hunting or fishing than suited up for Sunday school. Well, he could sympathize with them. He had never been able to find Usen inside the four square walls of a white man's church, either.

His thoughts came to an abrupt halt as Hank and Jenny Braedon rounded the corner of Main Street. Hank looked prosperous in a dark gray suit and neatly tied cravat. Expensive black boots, polished to a high shine, reflected the early morning sun. He smiled expansively at several elderly ladies rocking sedately on the porch of the Regency Hotel.

But it was Jenny who held Ryder's gaze. She looked stunning in a pale pink dress of watered silk. Her long golden hair was partially hidden beneath a perky straw bonnet bedecked with pink satin roses and gaily colored streamers.

A sudden warmth pulsed through Fallon at the mere sight of her, and he cursed his weakness for her even as he returned her smile.

Hank Braedon scowled as his wife's steps slowed and then stopped, her gaze focused on the half-breed. Hank didn't miss the flush that rose in her cheeks, or the sudden sparkle in her eyes. It was a look he coveted for himself.

Fallon felt the force of Jenny's gaze, and it drew him like a magnet.

Rising, he walked down the steps and crossed the street to Jenny's side. "'Morning."

Jenny nodded, the sound of Ryder's voice flooding her with an emotion she dared not name. "Good morning." Now that he was there, so close she could almost touch him, she didn't know what to say. She was supposed to hate him, yet just seeing him made her feel alive for the first time in days.

"Good morning," Hank said politely. "It's nice to see you again."

"Thanks."

"We're on our way to church," Braedon said. He took Jenny's arm possessively. "Let's go, Jen. We'll be late."

Jenny nodded. "Good day, Mr. Fallon."

"Ma'am."

He stood there, his fists clenched at his sides, as he watched Hank and Jenny walk away.

She's his wife, he reminded himself. *You've got no claim on her. None at all.*

Turning on his heel, Fallon headed for the saloon. He needed a drink. Maybe two. And then he'd leave town before he made a complete fool of himself over another man's wife.

Desert gave way to gently rolling hills as Ryder Fallon left the town of Widow Ridge far behind. A chill wind flattened the yellow prairie grass and caused the slender willows to bend in supplication to its power.

Hunched in his buffalo robe coat, Fallon rode warily, ever on the alert for Apaches, though it was doubtful they'd be raiding this far north.

The stallion snorted and shook its head against the wind's wintry breath, and Fallon grinned, taking pleasure in the coiled power of the big black stud. The black was prancing now, its long neck arched, its muscles quivering with the urgent need to run after spending the last few days in a box stall.

Fallon gave the black its head, leaning low over its neck as the stallion lined out in a dead run.

Reveling in the surging power of the horse and in the invigorating sting of the wind in his face, Fallon threw back his head and let loose with the Cheyenne war cry. The shrill, ululating cry spooked a jackrabbit from cover, and the frightened animal fled in panic before the stallion's thundering hooves.

Guiding the horse with the pressure of his knees, Fallon pulled the Winchester from the saddle boot, sighted down the long barrel and squeezed the trigger.

It was a lucky shot, nothing more. The heavy slug caught the buck at the base of the skull, nearly severing its head from its body.

Grinning, Fallon brought the black to a halt, slid from the saddle to retrieve his kill.

"Well, that takes care of dinner," he muttered. "All we need now is a place to bed down."

Swinging into the saddle, he urged the black into a lope, scouting the terrain until he found a place that offered protection from the wind. There was good graze for the stallion and ample shelter for himself. After a dinner of roast rabbit and hardtack, Fallon squatted beside a thrifty fire and rolled a cigarette.

Watching the cigarette smoke spiral skyward, he kept a tight rein on his thoughts, refusing to let himself think of Jenny, of what might have been if he'd met her sooner, under other circumstances.

Grinding out the cigarette, he rolled into his blankets, one hand resting on the butt of the Winchester.

Picketed nearby, the stallion stood silhouetted against the gray sky, a dark outline that gradually merged with the gathering darkness as night spread her cloak across the empty land.

The next day dawned cold and wet. Fallon sought shelter in a cutbank arroyo and spent the day staring moodily at the cloud-darkened sky. Thunder rolled across the heavens, causing the earth to tremble. Great slashes of lightning lanced the clouds.

Lost in thoughts he could no longer hold at bay, Fallon was oblivious to the fury of the raging storm as Jenny's image danced in his mind, her great green eyes now dark with concern as he endured Kayitah's punishment, now glinting with anger when he threatened to leave her behind, now dark with loathing as he surrended her son to Kayitah.

"I had to do it, Jenny," he muttered. "I didn't have any choice."

He dreamed of her that night, and in his dreams she was smiling at him again, her beautiful green eyes warm with desire, her arms outstretched. In his sleep, he reached for her, hungry for her touch, her forgiveness, but she only laughed and slipped from his grasp.

He woke muttering an oath as her image faded from his mind, only to lie awake the rest of the night, smoking one cigarette after another.

Dawn found him riding further north.

Jenny stared at her husband. "Left town?" she repeated. "Are you sure?"

Hank nodded. "Couple people I know saw him ride out late yesterday afternoon. Does it matter?"

"No, of course not," Jenny said. She forced herself to smile as if it didn't matter, wondering why it did. She never wanted to see Ryder Fallon again. He was a constant memory of a day she longed to forget.

In the days that followed, Jenny made an effort to pretend that nothing had changed. She rose early in the morning to prepare breakfast for Hank before he went to the store. She kept the house spotlessly clean. She took great pains with her appearance. She often met him in town for lunch, met him at the front door each evening.

And the friendship they had once shared bloomed again. They spent their evenings at home because Jenny was shy about meeting people. They took turns reading the paper to each other. Hank told her about his day at the store; she complained that she couldn't make a decent pie crust.

She'd been home about three weeks when Hank asked her to go to a church social. She agreed reluctantly.

Jenny dressed with special care that night, choosing a modest gown of dark blue velvet. She was as nervous as a new bride when they walked into the hall.

Everyone in town knew she had spent the last two years as a prisoner of the Apache, and even though Jenny knew the townspeople were too polite to ask her what awful trials she had endured, she knew they were wondering.

She could feel the men eyeing her speculatively, wondering if she had been forced to pleasure the Apache bucks. She could see the women wondering, too. Outwardly, they were sympathetic, but Jenny feared that, inwardly, they were condemning her. Any decent woman would have killed herself rather than allow a savage to defile her.

Hank slid his arm around her shoulder. "Relax, Jen," he whispered. "Give them a chance. They're nice people. You'll like them. And they'll like you."

Jenny nodded doubtfully.

Over the next two hours, she met most of the people in town. And just as Hank had said, she liked them, and they liked her. A few of the men leered at her, a few of the women looked down their noses at her, but for the most part the townspeople accepted her with smiles of welcome. She was Hank's wife, and everyone liked Hank.

Later, lying in bed beside her husband, Jenny wished that she had a real marriage, that Hank could take her in his arms and make love to her.

She bit down on her lower lip, cursing Ryder Fallon for coming into her life. If she'd never met him, she'd be perfectly happy to be Mrs. Hank Braedon, perfectly happy with things the way they were, the way they'd always been. After enduring Kayitah's touch, she would have been content to live a chaste life. But Ryder had awakened her desire, stirred the sleeping embers of passion that had lain dormant within her.

She looked at her sleeping husband. She loved him deeply, loved him as a sister loved a brother, as a woman loved a good friend. But it wasn't enough.

It would never be enough.

She was suddenly thankful that Ryder Fallon had left town. He was far too appealing, too handsome, too virile. He had never made any secret of the fact that he found her desirable. In spite of the fact that she hated him for what he'd done, she was suddenly afraid she might have been sorely tempted to betray her husband and her marriage vows for one night in Fallon's arms.

Chapter Twenty

Clearwell was a remote island of civilization set amid a vast sea of grass. Once a flourishing boom town, it was now reduced to poverty, its only redeeming feature and reason for existence the well from which it derived its name. Many a weary traveler, saddle sore and lost in a seemingly endless world of sun and thirst, had found new life in the depths of the clear spring that gurgled in the center of the ruined town.

Only two buildings remained standing: a rundown saloon that served beer when it was available, and a fire-ravaged hotel that had three rooms still intact, including, miraculously, the glass in the windows.

The town's only permanent resident was Vic Linderman, who owned the saloon.

Linderman was a short, stocky man with

sparse gray hair, sunken cheeks, a long crooked nose. He stood behind the bar, idly polishing a shot glass with a towel that had once been white, his gaze fixed on his only customer. The man was playing solitaire. Between moves, the tall half-breed took long pulls from a bottle of cheap whiskey, a bottle that had been full when he arrived and was now nearly dry.

Linderman had wanted to object when the man sat down and started working his way into a bottle that had been purchased elsewhere, but one look into the breed's cold blue eyes had stilled Linderman's objections.

Ryder Fallon ignored the barkeep's mute disapproval as he slapped a black jack on a red queen, a red ten on the jack. But his mind was not on the cards, or the old man. He was far away, 200 miles to the southwest, in Widow Ridge.

For months he had drifted aimlessly from one cow town to another, losing too much at cards because he was drinking too much, spending too much time with too many women in a futile attempt to forget one woman. But, try as he might, he couldn't outride the memory of her smile, couldn't drown the sound of her voice in the endless bottles of busthead booze he swallowed without tasting.

"Damn you, Jenny," he murmured thickly. "Damn you, damn you, damn you!"

Hoofbeats drew Linderman's attention from the taciturn cardplayer, and he glanced over the top of the swinging doors to see two men riding in from the east. Minutes later, they entered the saloon, slapping the trail dust from their clothes with their hats.

Vic Linderman eyed the pair warily. The man on the left was tall and lanky, with slicked down black hair and a pencil-thin mustache. A deep scar puckered his right cheek. His eyes were hard and cold, like the matched six-guns strapped to his thighs, butts forward for a cross draw.

The second man was no more than twenty. He had a thatch of unruly brown hair and long sideburns. His fair skin was soft and unblemished, like a newborn babe's, but there was nothing soft in his cold yellow eyes, or in the heavy Walker Colt shoved into the waistband of his trousers.

Troublemakers on the prod, Linderman thought uneasily. No doubt about it. Fumbling beneath the bar, he set two glasses before the sour-faced pair, shrugged his regret that he had nothing stronger than lukewarm beer.

"Not much of a town, eh, Roy?" drawled the scar-faced man disdainfully.

Roy shook his head in disgust. "For sure, Jake. I seen outhouses in Texas bigger than this dump. And they were sweeter smellin'!"

Jake's laugh was as brassy as the bray of a mule as his gaze wandered over the run-down saloon, coming to rest on the saloon's only other occupant. The man seemed totally ignorant of their arrival, his attention apparently focused on the cards spread on the table.

Noisily, Jake gulped down the last of his drink, wiped the foam from his mouth with the back of his hand as he swaggered toward the half-breed.

"Mind if I sit down?" Jake asked, and when there was no response, he tossed his hat into the middle of the table, scattering the cards.

"Yeah, I mind a lot," Fallon retorted. He didn't look up as he picked up the man's hat and sent it sailing across the room with a flick of his wrist.

Jake's eyes glowed with anticipation. "Hey, Roy, we got us a uppity half-breed over here. Think we should light a spell and teach him some respect for white folks?"

"It's our duty," Roy sang out. "Our Christian duty!"

At that, Fallon looked up, his eyes boring into those of the younger man. "You know what happened to the Christians, don't you?" he asked pleasantly.

Roy's brow furrowed as he tried to make sense of the half-breed's remark.

Jake was better versed in Bible history. "An uppity Injun with a smart mouth," he sneered.

"What'll we do with him?" Roy asked, enjoying the game.

"We could make him a good Injun," Jake suggested with a sly grin.

A good Indian, as any five-year-old paleface child knew, was a dead Indian.

Fallon's only visible reaction to Jake's implied threat was a faint tightening of his facial muscles as he eased the chair away from the table and stood up.

"Where do you think you're going?" Jake demanded arrogantly.

"Anywhere I damn well please," Fallon snarled,

shoving the man aside. "Get outta my way!"

Behind him, Fallon heard Roy yell, "Let's take him, Jake!"

Jake looked startled, but Roy was already reaching for his gun. Excitement and overconfidence spoiled his aim.

Fallon heard the bullet whine past his left ear as he clawed the .44 from his holster, turned and fired, all in the same smooth, practiced movement. The slug drilled Roy neatly between the eyes. Blood spurted from the wound, staining the lower half of Roy's face with crimson as he dropped dead in his tracks.

Fallon whirled around, his gun seeking another target, but Jake stood with his hands well away from his guns.

"Well?" Fallon asked.

Jake shook his head, his courage as dead as his partner.

"Go on, get out of here."

"Sure, sure," Jake said. Keeping his hands up, he backed out of the saloon.

Vic Linderman swallowed hard as he stared at the gun clutched in the half-breed's hand. Smoke curled from the end of the barrel, spiraling upward. The ominous black muzzle yawned before him, as big as a cave, smoke still curling from the barrel. All at once the bartender's muscles seemed to melt and the glass he'd been furiously polishing for the last ten minutes crashed to the floor.

The sound of breaking glass was thunderous in the deathly stillness of the saloon.

Fallon grimaced as the barkeep jumped a foot.

"Relax, old man," he muttered dryly. "I rarely kill more than one a day."

Chapter Twenty-One

The sun was low in the sky when Fallon rode down the main street of Widow Ridge. The town appeared to be pretty much as it had been when he'd left four months earlier, he mused.

Dismounting, he hitched the black at the rail in front of the Double Eagle Saloon, paused at the swinging door. There were only a few customers inside at this time of day.

Pushing through the doors, he took a place at the end of the bar.

Red grabbed a bottle and two glasses and ambled toward the half-breed, grinning affably.

"Tarnation," the bartender boomed. "Unusual for you to make an appearance twice in the same year. Kinda like seeing old Saint Nick drop down your chimney two nights in a row."

"You gonna talk my ear off or pour me a drink?" Fallon asked.

Red chuckled again as he filled Fallon's glass, and then his own.

"You forget something when you were here last?"

Fallon scowled, then shook his head. That was the trouble, he thought ruefully. He hadn't forgotten.

Red eyed the tall man thoughtfully for a moment, and then sighed. "You want to be alone?"

Fallon nodded. "Yeah. Leave the bottle, will you?"

"Sure."

"Thanks, Red."

Ryder sipped his drink in brooding silence. He had not intended to return to Widow Ridge, not for a long time, if ever. There was no point in it. Jenny was married, happy to be back with her husband. But he couldn't get her out of his mind.

He let out a long sigh. After the shootout at Clearwell, he'd intended to ride to Dakota Territory and spend the summer with the Cheyenne, see if he couldn't find his center again. But the need to see Jenny one more time had drawn him like a magnet, so here he was, feeling as foolish as a boy with his first crush.

"Hi, honey," purred a soft voice at his shoulder. "All alone?"

He didn't look up. "That's right."

"Wouldn't you like some company?"

"Not really."

"Buy me a drink?" she coaxed, her voice low and sultry.

Fallon turned to face her, surprised to find she was almost pretty. Her hair was long and red, her eyes blue and heavily outlined with kohl. For a moment he thought of grabbing her arm and hauling her upstairs, but he knew it wouldn't do any good. He didn't want just any woman. He wanted Jenny.

"Just one drink?" she said, smiling.

"Sure." He slid his glass toward her, filled it, then lifted the bottle in a silent toast.

"My name's Lilah," she said, batting her eyes at him. "Wanna go upstairs for a while?"

Fallon shook his head.

"Maybe it's me," Lilah said with a sigh. "Maybe I'm losing my touch."

"It's nothing personal," Fallon said. "I'm just not in the mood."

"Yeah. Well, I sure can pick 'em. If I had to depend on you and that store owner, I wouldn't get any action at all."

She shrugged, then drained the glass. "At least he paid me, even though he couldn't do nothing."

"Maybe he had too much to drink," Fallon suggested.

"Hank? Why, he hardly drinks at all."

"Hank?" Fallon's eyes narrowed. "Hank Braedon?"

"Yeah. Do you know him? Poor thing."

Fallon filled her glass again, watched as she tossed it down in a single gulp. "What's the matter with him?"

The girl shook her head. "I'm not supposed to say."

Fallon filled her glass again. "Is he sick?"

"No." Her voice was slurred now. "He was hurt. In the war. He can't . . . you know? He used to come see me every Friday night so's people would think he had the same urges as other men, but we never did it, 'cause he can't."

She held out her glass and Fallon filled it again. "He don't visit me no more since his wife came back." She smiled sympathetically. "I feel sorry for her. All that money and a handsome husband . . . too bad."

Fallon stared at the girl, his mind whirling. Why hadn't Jenny told him? Muttering an oath, he thrust the half-empty bottle into the girl's hand and left the saloon.

Outside, he drew a deep breath, remembering Jenny's near hysteria when he'd tried to comfort her by telling her she'd have other children. She must have loved Hank Braedon an awful lot to marry him, he thought jealously, to be willing to spend her life with a man who couldn't give her children, who couldn't . . .

Ryder shook his head. It was none of his business. If she hadn't been happy with her husband, she wouldn't have been so anxious to return to him. It was none of his business.

He walked down the street, his hands shoved in his pockets, hardly knowing where he was going until he saw the sign that hung over the boardwalk: Braedon's General Store.

And there, standing under the sign, was Jenny. She was wearing a dress of jade green, a white straw hat, white gloves. Her face, in profile, was more beautiful than he remembered. The shock of seeing her was like a blow to his gut.

He stared at her, remembering that she'd saved his life at the risk of her own, remembering the day by the river when he'd held her in his arms, the worry in her eyes when Kayitah had tried to break his spirit, the loathing in her expression when he gave her son to its father.

Jenny. He'd tried to forget her for the last four months, but nothing had worked, not drinking, not other women. Nothing. He loved her. He admitted it for the first time.

Jenny turned, took a step, then came to an abrupt halt when she saw him standing there. For a moment they stared at each other, the memories flowing between them.

"Ryder . . ."

"Jenny."

He looked older, she thought, thinner, more haggard. She wondered where he'd been for the last four months and three days, who he'd been with, why he'd left, and why he'd come back. She thought of all they had shared in the Apache camp, how he'd risked his life to help her get away, how he'd cared for her even when she screamed that she hated him for giving her child to Kayitah. She would never forgive him for that. Never. Every day she thought of her son. And every day her hatred for Ryder Fallon grew deeper, stronger.

And yet, looking at him now, she felt a peculiar

catch in her heart, a suspicious burning behind her eyes.

"Excuse me," she said brusquely. "I have to go home."

"Jenny, wait."

"We have nothing to say to each other."

He was as tall and handsome as she remembered. And his voice, that deep husky voice, caressed her like rumpled velvet, making her shiver with longing.

He fell into step beside her. "Let me walk you home."

"No."

"Please, Jenny."

He held his breath as he waited for her answer, knowing he'd follow her home on his hands and knees if she asked him to.

Jenny glanced over her shoulder, then shrugged. "All right."

"How've you been, Jenny girl?" he asked. It grieved him to see the hatred in her eyes when she looked at him.

"Fine, thank you."

She walked briskly, as if she couldn't wait to be home, to be rid of him.

"And Hank?"

"He's fine. The store is prospering."

"Are you happy?"

She started to say yes, of course she was happy, but the words wouldn't come.

"Jenny?"

"How are you, Ryder?" she asked, hoping to change the subject.

"Just getting by."

"Why did you come back here?"

"To see you."

The longing in his voice threatened to weaken her resolve. Looking straight ahead, she continued walking.

"Oh? Why would you want to see me?"

He grabbed her arm and whirled her around so that they were standing face to face. She felt his fingers dig into her arms, felt the heat of his touch spread through her, warmer than the rays of the sun.

"Why do you think?" He growled the words.

"I'm sure I haven't the faintest idea."

"Jenny, I . . . Dammit, Jenny, I've spent the last four months trying to forget you, but it didn't work. I kept thinking, hoping . . ."

He shook his head, wishing he was as handy with words as he was with a .44 Colt.

"I had to see you, to know you were happy. Are you, Jenny? Just tell me yes, and you'll never see me again."

"I'm happy," she said, not meeting his eyes. "I have everything I've ever wanted. Except my son."

"You'll have other children," he remarked, his gaze intent upon her face.

"Yes, of course," she said hoarsely. "Goodbye, Ryder."

"Jenny, wait. I know about Hank."

She stared up at him, her face suddenly pale. "You . . . how could you?"

"I just do. Are you really happy with him, Jenny? Do you want to spend the rest of your life living like a nun?"

"Yes . . . no . . . I don't know. Please, I've got to go."

"I'll be in town awhile if you change your mind."

She nodded, unable to speak past the lump in her throat. Turning on her heel, she hurried down the street toward home.

He had come back. Why did seeing him again make her feel suddenly alive? She hated him.

At home, she removed her hat and gloves, then stood in the middle of the parlor, her mind reeling. He was back.

Slowly, she began to pace the floor. He had come back because he couldn't stop thinking of her, because he wanted her. But she didn't want him.

Liar.

Sinking down on the sofa, Jenny closed her eyes and pressed her hands to her temples, trying to shut out the memories, the sound of his voice, the look in his midnight blue eyes. But all too vividly she recalled those times when he had held her in his arms—the day by the river when he had held her because she was missing Hank, the day he had kissed her and she had kissed him back, her whole being vibrating with desire. She recalled how he had held her hand while she struggled to bring her son into the world, the way he had held her while she cried.

He was the only man who had ever made her feel like a woman, the only man she'd ever yearned for, dreamed of. If only he hadn't betrayed her trust, she could have loved him with her whole heart. But she couldn't forget her son, couldn't forget the anguish of watching Ryder give her only child over into Kayitah's keeping.

Her son. He would be four months old now. Growing every day. Smiling. Learning to love someone else.

The tears she'd been holding back began to fall and she was powerless to stop them.

"Jenny? Jenny, what is it?"

The sound of Hank's voice infiltrated her despair. She tried to wipe the tears from her eyes, but she couldn't seem to stop crying. She heard his footsteps in the hall, and then he was there, in the room.

"Jenny, what's wrong?"

She looked at him helplessly, knowing at that moment that it was Ryder she loved, Ryder she wanted, in spite of everything.

Hank knelt before Jenny and drew her hands into his. "Jen, won't you tell me what's wrong?"

And she did. The words poured out of her. It felt so good to tell him everything, the whole truth, about Kayitah, about her son. The only thing she held back were her feelings for Ryder Fallon.

Hank stared at Jenny, not wanting to hear, not wanting to believe. He'd known she'd been some redskin's squaw, and he'd been able to live with that. But a child . . . the thought knifed through him. Jenny had borne a son to a heathen savage, a son that should have been his. A son he'd never have.

He stood up, quietly cursing the war, cursing the doctors who had saved his life, cursing Jenny for making him believe his impairment didn't matter, that they could have a life together.

His gaze moved around the room. Things. He could give her things. Expensive paintings, elaborate furnishings, costly gowns, but he could never make love to her, could never give her a child to replace the one she'd left behind.

The knowledge cut deep into his soul. And with the pain came an unreasoning jealousy, a need to hurt as he was hurting.

"It's him, isn't it?" Hank said flatly. "Mrs. Johnson told me she saw you walking with Fallon."

"It has nothing to do with Ryder," Jenny replied quickly.

"You're lying." All the doubts, all the fears, exploded to the surface. He'd seen the way women looked at Fallon. Despite the man's reputation, women were taken with him, drawn to his dark good looks, to the mystery that surrounded him. "Tell me the truth, Jen. You owe me that."

"Hank, please . . ."

He crossed the floor in two angry strides. "Tell me the truth!" he demanded.

He stared down at her, all the old hurt, the old anger, flaring to life once again. He remembered how she'd come to see him every day in the hospital, always smiling, always assuring him that it didn't matter. She'd told him she loved him, that his disability didn't matter. They could always adopt a child. She'd made him hope, made him believe. . . .

Before he realized what he was doing, he slapped her, and then slapped her again and again, sickened because he wanted to hurt her, because he needed to hurt her.

"Slut!" he roared, his anger feeding on itself. "You slept with him, didn't you?" He slapped her again, harder this time. "Didn't you?"

Jenny shrank back against the sofa, the ache in her heart far worse than Hank's blows. Slowly, she shook her head.

"Hank, please, don't do this."

He drew a deep shuddering sigh. Horrified, he stared at Jenny, at the vibrant red marks his hands had left on her cheeks.

"I'm sorry, Jenny," he said hoarsely. "So sorry."

And turning on his heel, he left the room, unable to endure the pity and remorse in her eyes a moment longer.

The tension between them grew worse in the next few days. Once Jenny admitted to herself that she loved Ryder, it seemed as if her whole world began to fall apart. Her marriage, which had been amiable if not passionate, seemed stifling, a mockery. She thought of Ryder constantly during the day, dreamed of him at night. She avoided going to town for fear of running into Fallon, for fear that Hank would accuse her of being unfaithful. And though she never mentioned Ryder's name, Hank seemed to know what she was thinking. She saw the knowledge in his eyes, in the dispirited slump of his shoulders.

He began coming home late, drinking after dinner. Often, she found him sitting in the library, a bottle in his hand, his eyes red-rimmed and dull. He accused her of sneaking off to meet Fallon, accused her of betraying their marriage vows.

His drinking led to violence. Sometimes he smashed the furniture. Sometimes he slapped her. He was always sorry, always ashamed.

Now, lying in bed, alone, she knew she had to do something. Perhaps divorce was the answer. Certainly they couldn't go on as they were. Their marriage was a failure. It was time to end it now, before they started hating each other.

She would tell him in the morning.

Her decision made, she closed her eyes, feeling at peace for the first time in weeks.

She woke with Hank's voice shrieking in her ear, calling her vile names, accusing her of unspeakable things.

She blinked up at him, confused. "What is it?" she asked. "What's wrong?"

She stared around the room.

"You've been seeing him on the sly, haven't you?"

Jenny sat up, drawing the covers to her chin.

Hank stood beside the bed, his face haggard in the early morning light filtering through the windows.

"Have you been drinking all night?" she asked.

"Don't try to change the subject, you tramp. You've been seeing him, haven't you?"

"No."

"Liar!" He choked back a sob. "You were calling his name. You reached for me, but you were calling his name. Dammit, Jen, how could you?"

"I didn't."

"Liar!" He grabbed her by her hair and dragged her across the bed. "You're no better than a whore!"

"Hank . . ." She cringed as he hovered over her, his eyes dark with jealous fury, cried out as he slapped her. "Hank, no . . ."

But it was too late. Drunk with whiskey and rage, he hit her again, and again until, abruptly, he let her go.

"Jenny . . . Jenny, oh God," he sobbed, and ran out of the room.

Chapter Twenty-Two

The sound of the door closing behind her husband sounded like a death knell in Jenny's ears, the death of her hopes and dreams, the death of her marriage. She had tried, she thought bleakly, but maybe such a marriage had been doomed to fail from the start.

She dried her tears on the hem of her nightgown and then, groaning softly, slipped out of bed.

Downstairs, she heated water on the stove, then filled the tub. She scrubbed herself thoroughly, as though she could wash away the hurt, the ugliness, the awful sense of failure that engulfed her.

Returning to her bedroom, she stared at herself in the mirror. A stranger stared back at her, a stranger with lifeless green eyes. There were livid bruises on her arms. Her face throbbed from where Hank had slapped her; her left eye was red and swollen.

Poor Hank. It would have been better for him if she'd never come back here.

She sat on the edge of the bed, too numb to think. She had to get away, she had to leave before Hank came back. She couldn't face him, not now.

She dressed quickly, then left the house. She had no clear idea of where she was going; she knew only that she had to get away.

Head lowered, she began walking, away from the neat rows of houses that lined the road, away from the town.

She walked all day, not caring which way she went, oblivious to the setting of the sun, to the sudden chill in the air.

"Jenny? Jenny!"

She looked up at him, her expression blank, her eyes red with tears that seemed to have no end.

"Jenny."

Ryder slid from the back of his horse, his eyes narrowing as he stared at the dull red imprint on her cheek. Her left eye was red and swollen.

"What the hell happened?" he demanded, his anger making his voice gruff.

"Nothing."

"Nothing? Dammit, what happened?"

She shook her head, two fat tears sliding down her cheeks.

"Jenny." He drew her close, felt her flinch as

he touched her arm. "Jenny, what happened?" he asked again.

"Hank. He . . ."

Fallon swore. "He hit you, didn't he? The bastard. I'll kill him for this."

"No. Please, Ryder."

"You're cold," he muttered. "Here," he said, removing his jacket, "put this on."

His coat was warm, fragrant with the scent of tobacco and man.

"Jenny, you shouldn't be wandering around out here alone."

She shrugged, past caring what happened to her. She didn't think to question his sudden appearance. From the moment she had met him, Ryder had always been there when she needed him.

Fallon muttered an oath as he stripped the saddle from his horse and spread the saddle blanket on the ground.

Jenny didn't resist as he sat down and drew her into his lap. With a sigh, she rested her head on his shoulder. It felt so right to be in his arms; how could it be so wrong?

The night was quiet, the sky alight with a million dancing stars and a pale yellow moon. A faint breeze stirred the tall grass, whispering good night to the trees.

"Do you want to talk about it, Jenny?"

She closed her eyes, wondering where to start. His hands, so big and brown and strong, were infinitely gentle as they stroked her hair. What a comfort he was! So understanding and sympathetic. She was tired of trying to hate him, of trying to fight her feelings for him.

"Jenny?"

She looked up at him, knowing that her sadness, her hunger, were mirrored in her eyes. Her hand reached up to caress the dark bronze of his cheek.

Just looking at him stirred something deep within her soul. His hair was long and thick, as black as the night, his shoulders were solid and wide, wide enough to carry the weight of the world. His arms were corded with muscle, strong enough to hold her, to protect her. And he had been kind to her, so kind.

"I wish . . ." She turned away so he couldn't see her face.

"What do you wish?"

"I wish I'd met you first, before Hank, before Kayitah."

She took a deep breath and let it out in a long sigh. "I wish you hadn't given my son to his father."

"I'm sorry, Jenny girl. I wish to hell things hadn't turned out the way they did, but there was nothing else I could do."

She nodded, too weary to argue. She was married to a man she didn't love, and she loved a man she'd sworn to hate. It just wasn't fair. She wished suddenly that she could forget it all, that she could run away and start all over again, free of old hurts, old memories.

Ryder smiled at her, his dark eyes filled with yearning.

"If you were a Cheyenne woman, I'd ask you to run away with me. And if you said yes, it would end your marriage to Hank."

"Just like that?"

"Just like that. Life among the Indians is a lot less complicated than life among the whites. Sometimes the new husband sends one of the old men to the first husband. The old man offers the injured party a pipe and asks him if he wishes something in exchange for his wife. A horse, perhaps, or a buffalo robe."

"Is a marriage undertaken with as little ceremony as divorce?"

"No. A couple usually court for a long time. Then the man sends horses to the girl's father. If she accepts them, they set a date for the wedding. On her wedding day, the girl rides her best horse to the lodge of the young man's mother. Some of his relatives spread a blanket on the ground. They place her on it and carry her into the lodge. In her mother-in-law's lodge, the girl removes her old clothing and puts on a new dress and moccasins. Her mother-in-law prepares a meal for the bride and groom, and then the young couple go to their own lodge. Sometimes a couple decides to run off together, especially if her parents don't approve her choice of a husband."

Jenny stared up at Fallon, her eyes suddenly bright. "Let's pretend," she whispered. "Let's pretend I've run away from Hank and we're eloping."

"Jenny . . ."

"Please, Ryder, be my husband for this night."

"For this night and every night," he replied fervently, and lowering his head, he kissed her.

She moaned softly as his tongue slid over her lips, shivered with delight as his hands moved over her back and shoulders, drifted lightly over her breasts, his touch trailing fire.

This was what it meant to be a woman, she thought, to be loved by a man. She'd been married to Kayitah, had borne his child, but she had never felt like this, as if her whole being was alive, glowing, ready to burst into flame.

She returned Ryder's kisses with a fervor never before known, whimpering for him to hurry as he undressed her, and then shed his own clothing.

This was what she had wanted, had needed since the first time she saw him in the Apache camp, a prisoner, badly wounded. He had stirred something deep within her, something that had lain dormant until he looked at her for the first time. Perhaps she had loved him even then. He was kindness and caring, love and security, and more, so much more. For this one night, she would be his, and he would be hers.

Fallon held Jenny close, unable to believe she was a reality in his arms and not just another dream. He had been on fire for her since he first laid eyes on her in Kayitah's camp, had wanted her desperately even though she had been forbidden to him. Sometimes he had thought of dragging her into the bushes and making love to her regardless of the consequences. She had haunted his dreams at night, filling him with a restless yearning, a hunger that nothing else could feed.

But now she was in his arms, warm and willing and eager. Her nails raked his back as he moved slowly within her, and it was like coming home. She was his now, his woman, the wife of his heart, as surely as if they had been joined together by a minister.

He needed no written words, no signature on a piece of paper. He knew how meaningless words and papers really were. His people had been cheated out of their lands by the worthless words and treaties of the whites. The Indian way was better, more honest. Jenny was his now and he would care for her, provide for her, protect her with his dying breath.

He whispered her name as he buried his face in the soft cloud of her hair. Her scent, the silk of her flesh against his own, the taste of her sweetness, all fired his blood, and he drove into her, possessing her, branding her as his woman for all time.

Jenny breathed his name as his hands and lips aroused her, filling her with a wild desire such as she had never imagined, wrapping her in layers of ecstacy until she was certain she would melt from the heat of it, the intensity of it, the sheer joy of his touch.

Higher, higher, they climbed, leaving the earth and its cares behind.

For Fallon, there was nothing but Jenny, nothing but the sweetness of her love and the soft sound of her voice in his ear as she whispered his name over and over again.

And for Jenny there was only Ryder. Ryder, whose very touch had the power to make her forget old hurts, old memories, old pains. Ryder, who had caused her such anguish, and brought her such joy.

She sobbed his name as her desire crested and broke, leaving her adrift in a sea of wondrous warmth and peace. She clung to Ryder as he arched over her, his whole body shuddering as his life spilled into her, binding them together in a way nothing else ever could.

And then, all too soon, reality returned. She stared up at him, wondering how many other women he had loved, wondering how she could ever look at herself in the mirror again. She had betrayed her husband, betrayed her marriage vows, all for one night of passion.

Ryder sensed the change in her immediately. "What is it, Jenny?" he asked, his voice guarded.

"I was just wondering how many other women you've made love to. Have there been very many?"

"A few," he admitted cautiously. "I made love to them, Jenny girl, but I was never in love with any of them."

"Oh."

She'd known he wasn't a monk, but she wished she could have been the first woman in his life, that he had been the first man in hers.

"It doesn't matter, Jenny," he said quietly.

"Nothing that happened before tonight matters now. You're my first woman, my first love. And my last."

She felt her heart swell until she thought it would burst. Taking his hand in hers, she pressed it to her lips.

"And you're my first love, my only love," she whispered, and wished it hadn't come too late.

She shook the thought aside and then, taking a deep breath, she asked the question that had plagued her for so long. "Why haven't you ever married?"

He didn't answer right away, and Jenny felt the subtle change in him, felt his body tense, then relax.

"I'm sorry," she said quickly. "It's none of my business."

"It's all right, Jenny girl, it was a long time ago."

She was suddenly sorry she had brought it up, and she held her breath, knowing she would be hurt by his answer, whatever it might be.

"I was married once, to an Apache girl. She died in childbirth, and my daughter with her."

"But you loved her? She was your first love, wasn't she?"

"Jenny . . ."

"Wasn't she?"

"It was a long time ago. I was just a kid."

A muscle worked in his jaw when he saw the tears in Jenny's eyes, but he couldn't lie to her.

"I loved her, Jenny, it's true, but it was so long ago. Don't let it spoil what we have."

He drew her close, his midnight blue eyes seeking her understanding, and suddenly it didn't matter that he had known love before. She was his, for this one night, and he was hers. She would take his love and hold it close, cherish it as one might cherish a rare flower that bloomed for one night only, knowing that in the morning it would be gone, that it would never bloom again.

Chapter Twenty-Three

Bleary-eyed, Jenny reined the black stallion to a halt, wondering if she was still headed in the right direction.

Ryder had made love to her into the wee small hours of the morning and she had reveled in it, shutting out the voice of her conscience, knowing that what they had shared was a precious gift she would never find again.

If only she could stay with him, love him, grow old at his side. But that was impossible. She was married to Hank. *In sickness and in health . . . for better or for worse . . . until death do us part . . .*

Her marriage vows, the very vows she had desecrated, rang in her mind. She had committed adultery with Fallon. It sounded ugly when she said it like that. No matter how wonderful it had been, how desperately she had craved his touch, she had committed a terrible sin.

She couldn't have Ryder, and she wouldn't go back to Hank. She'd never be able to face Hank again after last night, knowing she had committed the very sin he had accused her of.

She lifted a hand to her cheek, the memory of the anger and rage in Hank's eyes more painful than the faint bruise.

She shuddered as she remembered the ugliness of it all, the sound of Hank's bitter accusations ringing in her ears, the dull thud of his fists striking her as he screamed at her, calling her a whore. And now she had proved him right.

In the dark hours of the night, lying in Fallon's arms, she had reached a decision. A cowardly one, perhaps, but a decision nevertheless. She couldn't stay with Hank, not after what had happened. She couldn't count on being able to obtain a divorce. She couldn't live in sin with Ryder, or trust herself to stay away from him now that she knew what it was like to held in his arms, to be loved . . .

Resolutely, she pushed the thought from her mind. She was going back where she belonged, back to her son. The thought of seeing her baby again, of holding him, made the loss of Ryder's love easier to bear.

The decision had not been easily made. But it was the only one she could live with. She had been unfaithful to her husband, betraying her wedding vows for one night of passion, and she'd never be able to go home again, couldn't abide the thought of seeing the hurt and the accusation in Hank's eyes.

She wondered what Ryder had thought when he awoke to find her gone, and his horse and his clothing with her. It had been a cruel thing to do to the man who had given her a night of unbridled ecstasy, but she couldn't have him following her too soon.

It would take him at least two hours to walk back to town, and then he'd have to find a way to sneak into his hotel room unseen, dress, and find another horse. By then, she hoped to have a good enough head start that he wouldn't be able to catch her.

Of course, after what she'd done, he might never want to see her again. A wry grin tugged at her lips. He might not want to see her, but there was always a chance he'd come after his horse.

She urged the stallion into a trot, her stomach growling loudly. She would have to find something to eat soon, and water for herself and the horse. Living with the Apache had taught her how to live off the land. She thought she was heading in the right direction. If she was lucky, one of Kayitah's raiding parties would find her and take her to the rancheria. If necessary, she would beg for Kayitah's forgiveness, promise him anything, if he would only let her be with her son.

Fallon swore softly as he realized that Jenny was gone, and with her his horse and clothing.

Naked as the day he'd been born, he grabbed his gun and pulled on his moccasins, the only things she'd left behind, and began scouting the ground for sign.

It wasn't hard to find. She was riding south, and he knew deep in his soul that she was going back to the Apache, back to her son.

And it was all his fault. He'd driven her to it because he couldn't control his lust, because he'd had to make love to her, at least once, before she went out of his life forever. And now she was gone, driven away by her guilt at what they'd done. She was a decent, God-fearing woman and she'd broken her marriage vows, thanks to him. He knew her well enough to know she couldn't face Hank, and that she couldn't face him, either, so she'd run away, back to a life she hated, to be with her son.

He swore softly. She didn't have to stay married to Hank. The marriage had never been consummated. She could have the marriage annulled . . . Damn! Why hadn't he thought of it before?

Cursing softly, he headed for town, keeping well away from the road. Fortunately, it was too early for most people to be about, and he made it to his hotel unseen by anyone except the rheumy old man who cleaned the saloon next to the hotel.

The man stared at him, his jaws agape, but Fallon just shrugged and smiled and ran up the back stairs.

In his room, he washed and dressed in record time. Strapping on his gunbelt, he left the hotel and went to the livery, rousting the owner out of bed.

He was leading a big buckskin gelding out of the barn when Hank Braedon called his name.

"Fallon! Jenny's gone. I've looked everywhere. Have you seen her?"

"I've seen her," Fallon said. His hands held tight to the reins. It was all he could do to keep from smashing his fists into Braedon's face. "I've seen her," he said again. "And I saw what you did to her. I ought to kill you for that."

A deep red flush crept up Braedon's neck. "I . . . she told me she'd had a baby by that savage who kidnapped her. I . . . I'm afraid I haven't handled it very well."

Hank ran a hand through his hair and over his stubbled jaw. "I didn't mean to hit her. Afterwards, I went out and got drunk. She was gone when I came home."

Hank took a deep breath as he worked up his courage. "I saw how you looked at her that day at the store, the way she looked at you, and I thought maybe . . . I don't know what I thought."

"She left town," Fallon said. "Headed south."

"South?"

"She's going back to Kayitah, back to her son."

"No!"

"I'm afraid so."

"It's all my fault. I never should have married her. I never should have insisted we come out here. She didn't want to come, but I loved her. I thought . . . I should have known it would never work."

"We're wasting time," Ryder said curtly. "I'm going after her."

"I'll go with you."

"No."

"You can't stop me. She's my wife."

"I can make better time alone. Besides, you'll only get yourself killed."

"It doesn't matter," Hank said bitterly. "I'm not good for a damn thing anyway."

"Do what you want," Fallon muttered, swinging into the saddle. "I'm not waiting for you. I've wasted too much time already."

Hank cried, "Fallon, hold on!" but it was too late.

Ryder was headed out of town at a gallop, headed due south.

He rode hard, his heart pounding in unison with the buckskin's hooves. He couldn't let Jenny go back to Kayitah, not now, not after what they had shared. She loved him, he was sure of it even though she hadn't said the words. But he knew Jenny Braedon, knew she wasn't the kind of woman to give her body and not her heart.

As the miles went by, he wondered what Kayitah would do if Jenny managed to find the village. Would the Apache chief take her back, or kill her on sight for the sake of his pride?

Fallon knew what his own fate would be. It had already been decreed. *I will peel the skin from your body an inch at a time if you ever return to the rancheria.*

Fallon swallowed hard as he recalled Kayitah's words, but there was no going back. He had to find Jenny no matter what the cost, and with that in mind, he urged the gelding onward, praying that he'd find Jenny before the Apaches did.

Jenny drew the stallion to a halt and slid wearily to the ground. She had ridden hard all that day and now she wanted only to sleep. Too weary to be afraid, she unsaddled the black, tethered it to a tree, curled up on the horse blanket, and went to sleep, unbothered by the shifting shadows or the sounds of the night.

She woke at dawn, shivering and hungry. For a moment, she thought of turning around and heading home, and then, slowly, she shook her head. She'd missed too much of her son's life already.

She rode all that day, stopping at a stream to water the stallion and ease her own thirst. When that was done, she scooped some water into her hands and laved it over her face. Her left cheek was still tender from where Hank had hit her.

Poor Hank. She still couldn't believe he'd actually struck her. He'd always seemed so accepting of his condition. She'd never realized the depths of his pain, never truly understood what the war had deprived him of, until she'd made love to Ryder. Now, knowing how wonderful love could be between a man and a woman, she felt a deep hurt for Hank's anguish. She knew now how awful it must have been for him all these years because she knew how awful it was going to be for her, never to be able to be with Ryder again.

Knowing she needed to eat to keep up her strength, she dug some roots near the water. She'd never been particularly fond of them when she lived with the Apache, didn't even know what they were called. Now, biting into one, she hardly tasted it.

Riding southward, she wondered how Ryder had reacted when he woke to find his horse and his clothing gone. She smiled as she pictured him sneaking into town wearing nothing but his gunbelt and moccasins. It occurred to her again that he might come after her, if only to get his horse back.

Jenny stroked the black's neck. The stallion was a dream of a horse, easy to ride, and with the endurance to go all day and all night without tiring.

She slept under the stars again that night, her pity for Hank and her grief at leaving Fallon fading in the realization that she would soon see her son again.

She woke to the smell of roasting meat and the sound of masculine laughter. One voice cut across the others. A voice she recognized all too well.

Slowly, she sat up. "Hello, Kayitah."

He nodded briefly in her direction, his dark eyes giving nothing away. "Why have you come back here?"

"To see my son."

"You have no son."

"Kayitah, please. I was wrong to run away. Punish me if you must, but please let me see him."

"Eat." He shoved a chunk of meat into her hand.

Jenny did as she was told, her gaze never leaving that of the man who had been her husband. She could hear the other warriors moving about the camp, smothering the fire, burying the rabbit's entrails, readying their horses for travel.

Kayitah offered her a drink of water from a waterskin, then swung aboard his horse. Holding her head high, Jenny saddled the black and climbed into the saddle.

Kayitah took the lead and Jenny fell in behind him. They rode all that day, single file to make it difficult for anyone who came across their tracks to count their number.

At dusk, they rode through the narrow defile that led to the valley. For a moment, Jenny was filled with dread, and then she took a deep breath and squared her shoulders. She wasn't a frightened little girl, she was a grown woman. She knew the Apache way, the language, the customs. This would never be home, but it was her son's home, and she intended to be a part of it.

The warriors dispersed to their own lodges when they reached the village. Jenny followed

Kayitah to his tipi, her heart beating double time as Alope stepped outside to greet her husband.

The smile of welcome died on the Indian woman's face when she saw Jenny.

"Why have you brought her here?" Alope demanded angrily.

"I did not bring her. She has come back on her own."

Alope's dark eyes burned into Jenny. "Why?"

"She wishes to see the child."

"He is my son now. Send her away."

"He is my son," Jenny asserted with a calmness she didn't feel.

"No! He belongs to Kayitah, and to me. He will never be yours."

Jenny felt her anger rise. She was tired and uncertain. And she was afraid, though she refused to admit it. "I want to see my son."

Alope shook her head, and something inside Jenny snapped.

With a cry, she jumped off the black and hurled herself at Alope. The Indian woman stumbled backward and the two women fell to the ground in a tangle of arms and legs. Alope was older, heavier, but Jenny was filled with anger and fear and she fought as though she were possessed by a demon, until Alope screamed for help.

Only then did Kayitah interfere. Smothering a grin, he grabbed Jenny by the arm and pulled her away from Alope.

Alope scrambled to her feet, her eyes blazing with hatred. "I will kill her! I will carve the skin from her bones an inch at a time!"

"You will not lay a hand on her," Kayitah warned. "She had the courage to come here alone. She has bested you in a fight. I say she has earned the right to see her son."

Kayitah looked at Jenny for a long moment, and then nodded toward his lodge. "Go."

Heart pounding, Jenny entered the lodge. She could hear Alope arguing with Kayitah, heard Kayitah tell Alope that Jenny deserved some time alone with her son.

Her son. He was lying on a pile of soft robes, cooing softly as he watched a narrow shaft of sunlight dance over the lodge skins. For a moment, she could only stare at him, marveling at how big he'd grown. He was naked save for a clout, his skin a deep golden brown. His hair was black and wavy, his eyes were dark.

"Hello, darling," Jenny murmured.

Gently, she scooped him up in her arms and held him close, breathing in the scent of him. Tears filled her eyes as arms that had been empty for so long held her son close to her heart.

Later, she examined him carefully, touching each tiny finger and toe, marveling at the smoothness of his skin. He smiled up at her, and she imagined that she saw forgiveness in the depths of his eyes.

"I've missed you," Jenny murmured, stroking one downy cheek. "You'll never know how much

I missed you, but I'm here now, and I'll never leave you again."

She laughed softly as the baby reached for her finger.

"His name is Cosito."

Jenny glanced up to see Kayitah staring down at her, his expression guarded.

"Cosito," Jenny repeated. "He looks well, Kayitah. Thank you."

"You did not think I would harm my son?"

"No, of course not."

"You will have to share him with Alope. She has grown to love him as her own."

"I understand."

"I have missed you, Golden Dove."

Jenny gazed up at Kayitah. For the first time, she saw affection in his expression.

"I would not have come back if it weren't for my son."

"I know. I have always had feelings for you, Golden Dove. That is why you are still alive. I will let you return to my lodge, but only as my wife."

He stood there, his arms folded across his chest, waiting, watching as the full implication of his words sank in.

Jenny nodded once, curtly. "I understand."

"I have many hides. You may erect a lodge of your own if you wish. Perhaps it will make your life here more pleasant."

"Thank you, Kayitah."

"Alope will help you."

Jenny nodded.

Kayitah's dark-eyed gaze trapped her own. "Know this, Golden Dove, I will not let you go again. You are here to stay."

The following day, Alope enlisted the aid of a dozen women, and by late afternoon, Jenny's lodge was completed.

Kayitah gave her robes and blankets for a bed; Alope gave her several cooking utensils and pots, and Jenny set up housekeeping.

By the time she went to bed that night, it was as if she'd never been away. She was a prisoner again, albeit a willing one this time, and as she cradled her son in her arms, she was content for the first time in months.

The next couple of days passed quickly, peacefully. To her surprise, Jenny found herself slipping easily into the Apache life that she had once hated. She found a kind of peace in searching for wood, in drawing water from the river, in cooking over an open fire. Even the jagged cliffs that she had once thought as impenetrable as prison bars no longer distressed her. She no longer viewed them as walls keeping her in, but as a bulwark to keep the rest of the world out.

Resigned to spending the rest of her life with the Indians, she made an honest effort to be friendly with the other women, only now realizing that it had been her own aloofness, and not their dislike, that had kept them from being congenial before.

But it was Cosito who warmed her heart and made each day worthwhile. She could hold him, feed him, play with him to her heart's content, even though Kayitah had refused to allow her to keep the child in her lodge overnight after the first night, no doubt fearing she might try to run away again.

Jenny didn't even mind sharing her son with Alope, and that was most surprising of all, but Jenny had no doubt that the Indian woman loved the child as deeply as she did.

To his credit and Jenny's relief, Kayitah left her alone, though his gaze always sought hers when they were together. Had he always looked at her like that, his dark eyes filled with affection? In two years, she had never noticed the yearning in his eyes when he looked at her, and it occurred to Jenny that much of the unhappiness she had endured in Kayitah's lodge had been of her own making.

When he asked her to walk with him, she agreed without hesitation. He spoke to her of Cosito, of how proud he was of the child.

"I had never thought to have a son," Kayitah said, taking her hand in his. "Each day, I thank Usen for my son, and for the woman who gave him life."

Jenny gazed into the Apache's eyes, not knowing what to say.

"I know you were unhappy here before," Kayitah said. "I will try to make it more pleasant for you now." He paused, gazing down at their joined hands. "I will not force you to my bed," he promised, his voice low, "but I hope, in time, you will come to me of your own accord."

Jenny looked at his bowed head, unable to believe this was the same arrogant man who had forced himself upon her.

He raised his gaze to hers, his expression pensive, hopeful.

"Perhaps, in time," Jenny replied, and knew that the day would come when she would go willingly into this man's arms. Ryder had awakened her to passion, and though she knew she would never love Kayitah or any other man as she had loved Fallon, she realized that, given time, she might learn to care for the man who had fathered her child, to tolerate his touch, not because she loved him, but because she so wanted to be loved.

Kayitah smiled then, and she realized for the first time that he was quite a handsome man.

"Come," he said, his hand squeezing hers, "let us go and see if our son is awake."

Hand in hand, they walked back to the village. And for the first time in months, Jenny felt she might have a chance for happiness after all.

Chapter Twenty-Four

Fallon sat atop a craggy bluff, his gaze scanning the valley. He had no trouble finding Jenny. Her hair stood out like sunshine on a cloudy day, making it easy to follow her as she moved through the village.

He'd been watching her for four days now, and his nerves were strung out from tension and lack of sleep. He rested only moments at a time, afraid to relax completely for fear of being taken unawares by one of the scouts that patrolled the area. He'd been lucky so far, but he knew it couldn't last.

Sitting there, he'd tried to think of some way to enter the village unseen, grab Jenny and the kid, and get away without anyone being the wiser.

So far, he hadn't been able to think of a thing.

It was near dark when two white men rode into the village. The man on the right led a pack horse laden with boxes that Fallon guessed contained rifles and trade goods.

Ryder cursed under his breath as he leaned forward, wondering if his eyes were playing tricks on him in the fading light, because the man on the left looked remarkably like Hank Braedon.

Fallon frowned, remembering something Red had said about Charlie Braedon, something about a rumor that he'd gotten his start selling guns to the Apache.

Fallon watched as Kayitah came forward to greet the two white men, clasping the hand of the man Fallon believed to be Charlie Braedon. It was obvious, from the smiles on the faces of the two men, that they'd known each other a long time.

Fallon shook his head, remembering how well armed the Indians that had attacked Terry's column had been. No doubt Charlie Braedon had sold the Apaches the rifles they had used that day. And probably the rifles they'd used to attack Jenny's stage, as well.

Jenny stared past Kayitah to the two men who had followed him into her lodge, wondering how Hank had found her. She glanced briefly at the second man and knew immediately that it had to be Hank's brother, Charlie. They looked enough alike to be twins even though they'd been born several years apart.

"Prepare food," Kayitah said. He gestured for his visitors to sit down, then offered them his pipe.

Charlie Braedon took the pipe and smoked it, then passed it to Hank, who stared at it, a blank look on his face.

"Smoke it," Charlie urged in English. "Old Kayitah here will be offended if you refuse."

Hank nodded, took a short puff, coughed once, and passed the pipe back to Kayitah. He watched Jenny move around the lodge while Charlie and the Indian talked. This was the man who had defiled Jenny, who had planted his seed in her belly. His hand fairly itched to grab his gun and blast the heathen redskin between the eyes. Instead, he sat quietly, hoping that Charlie knew what the hell he was doing and didn't get them both killed.

Jenny served Kayitah first, then offered food to Hank and Charlie before resuming her seat in the back of the lodge, her mind whirling.

Hank ate without tasting a thing, his gaze riveted on Jenny and the dark-haired baby nestled in her arms. She'd told him about the kid. It hadn't seemed real then, but it was real enough now.

He'd wired Charlie soon after Fallon left town, telling him that Jenny had run off and that he thought she'd gone back to the Apaches. Charlie had arrived on the next stage.

Hank had never really believed they had a chance to find Jenny, but when he'd mentioned

Kayitah's name to Charlie, Charlie had laughed and said not to worry. He knew where Kayitah was holed up. And now they were here, in the midst of an Apache camp, and Charlie was talking Apache gibberish and smiling at the chief as if they were the best of friends.

After dinner, Kayitah showed Hank and Charlie to another lodge where they would spend the night.

"It's no good," Charlie said when they were alone. "I offered him money. I offered him guns and ammunition, but it's no go. He won't trade for Jenny."

"Damn. What are we gonna do now?"

"How bad do you want her, little brother?"

"I want her."

"Why? She's no good to you in bed. Hell, she ran away from you to come back here."

"I want her, Charlie. She's my wife, and . . . and I love her."

Charlie nodded. "Then we'll just have to take her."

"Take her? How?"

"Tonight, when everyone's asleep, we'll grab her and make a run for it. It'll be risky as hell, but with a little luck, we'll make it." Charlie grinned. "I've got some new repeating rifles that'll give us plenty of firepower."

Hank stared down at his hands, wondering why he wasn't afraid. From the time they were kids, it had always been Charlie who was ready to try something new while Hank had hung back. But he wasn't afraid now.

Surprisingly, he was looking forward to a fight. He might not be able to make love to his wife, he thought bitterly, but he could fight for her.

"Well?" Charlie said.

"Let's do it!"

"All right!" Charlie slapped Hank on the shoulder in a gesture of brotherly affection. "Let's get some rest."

But they were too keyed up to sleep and they spent the next couple of hours talking about the past and then the present, with Charlie bringing Hank up to date on his business dealings in Texas, and Hank telling Charlie about the store.

For a time, they were silent, and then Charlie cleared his throat.

"Did you ever find a doctor who could help you with your problem?"

"No."

"And your wife never complained that you couldn't . . . that you couldn't?"

"No."

"So that's not the reason she left you?"

"She came after the baby."

Charlie grunted. "Are you planning to take the kid with us?"

Hank nodded. "I don't think she'll go without him."

"It's gonna make things more difficult."

"I know, but I can't leave her here. She said she hated it here, hated him."

"Kayitah?"

"Yeah."

"He's not a bad sort as long as you don't cross him."

Hank stared at his brother in amazement. "Not a bad sort! He kidnapped my wife, Charlie. Kidnapped her and raped her and gave her a bastard child."

It was three hours after midnight when Hank and Charlie slipped out of the lodge and saddled their horses, which were tethered near the doorway. Armed with new Winchester repeating rifles, they glided silently through the night until they reached Jenny's lodge.

"Hurry," Charlie whispered, and followed Hank into the tipi.

Kneeling beside Jenny, Hank placed one hand over her mouth, then softly called her name.

She woke with a start to find Hank bending over her. "Hurry. We're getting out of here."

"No!"

"Dammit, Jenny, I don't have time to argue. We're leaving."

"I can't! Alope has Cosito in her lodge."

"What?"

"Kayitah won't let me keep him here. He's afraid I'll try to run away."

"We don't have time to argue about this," Charlie hissed. He dropped his hand over Jenny's mouth. "If you cry out, Kayitah will string us up by the short hairs, if you get my drift. But you'll die before we do, because sure as I'm gonna burn in hell, I'll slit your throat if you so much as make a whimper. You understand me?"

Jenny nodded. Throwing back the blanket, she pulled on her moccasins and followed Hank outside. He lifted her onto the back of his horse, took the reins, and began walking toward the head of the valley. Charlie followed behind.

Jenny's heart was beating a wild tattoo. Of all nights for Kayitah to stay in Alope's lodge, why did it have to be this one? She didn't want to leave her son, didn't want to go back to Widow Ridge with Hank. Most of all, she never wanted to see Charlie Braedon again.

As they made their way through the village, she kept waiting for one of the sentries to shout a warning, but nothing happened. The night was dark, the moon shrouded in drifting layers of clouds. A faint wind rustled the leaves of the trees, muffling the sound of hoofbeats.

And then all hell broke loose.

She heard the sentry at the mouth of the canyon demand their identity. There was a gunshot as the sentry materialized out of the darkness, and hard on the heels of the gunshot she heard a shout, and then another gunshot as Charlie fired at the second sentry and missed.

Charlie yelled, "Get the hell out of here," as he swung onto the back of his horse.

Before the words were out of his mouth, Hank had vaulted up behind Jenny and was kicking the horse into a run.

It was like a bad dream from which she couldn't awake. There were more gunshots. She heard the hiss of an arrow, heard Charlie curse as he was knocked off his horse.

Hank hesitated when he saw his brother fall, and Jenny screamed at him, fear rising up to choke her as she glanced over her shoulder and saw a half dozen mounted warriors racing toward them.

The moon broke through the clouds and she recognized Kayitah riding at the head of the warriors. He was naked save for his clout, and his eyes seemed to pierce the darkness like twin flames. She could feel the heat of his gaze and she drummed her heels into the horse's flanks, breathed a sigh of relief as the animal surged forward.

Moments later, she heard Hank cry out in pain, felt him slump in the saddle behind her.

"Hank, hold on!" she cried, but it was too late.

She felt his grip on her waist grow slack, and then he tumbled over the horse's rump.

She tried to haul back on the reins, but the horse took the bit in its teeth and bolted, frightened by the sporadic gunfire and the scent of blood.

Jenny sawed on the reins, trying in vain to turn the horse's head, to go back to her son. She screamed as a man mounted on a big buckskin materialized before her, emerging out of the shadows of the night like a ghostly centaur.

Leaning toward her, he grabbed her horse's reins and then they were racing down the narrow passageway and into the desert.

It was a nightmare, a hideous ordeal over which she had no control, a familiar scene that had been played once before.

"Hang on, Jenny girl."

His voice reached out to her through the darkness, dissolving her fears, making her heart pound, not with terror but relief. He was not a specter of death, but an angel come to deliver her.

Legs clamped around the horse's sides, she held on to the horse's mane and prayed that the animal wouldn't step in a hole, that they wouldn't be followed, that Hank was all right.

On and on they went, riding as if all the hounds of hell were at their heels. She could feel her horse's labored breaths, feel the heat of its body.

Finally, when she thought they would go on forever, Ryder found a place to spend what was left of the night.

She was too weary to ask questions. Wordlessly, she sank down on the blanket Ryder spread for her and closed her eyes. She tried to fight the tears that burned in her eyes, but she didn't have the strength. Hank had come to save her and in so doing, he had only made things worse. He was probably dead, and his brother with him, and she knew she'd never find the courage to go back to Kayitah, not after tonight. He would never trust her again.

"Jenny . . ."

"What are you doing here? How did you find me?"

Fallon shrugged. "It didn't take much of a genius to figure this was where you'd gone when you left Widow Ridge."

"Oh, Ryder, Hank's ruined everything."

"He just wanted you back, Jenny girl. I can't blame him for that."

"He just made everything worse, and now he's probably dead, and I'll never see my son again."

Fallon drew Jenny into his arms as great sobs racked her body. He didn't care if Charlie Braedon was dead, didn't care if Hank suffered hours of pain and torment at the hands of Kayitah's warriors. All he cared about was Jenny. She was safe in his arms and he didn't intend to ever let her go.

"It'll be all right, Jenny girl." He stroked her hair, his hands gentle and caring. "Kayitah will take good care of your son, and Alope will love him as her own. As for Charlie Braedon, he's been selling guns to the Apache for years. As far as I'm concerned, he got what he deserved."

Removing the kerchief from his neck, Ryder wiped the tears from Jenny's face.

"I'm sorry about your husband," he said quietly. "It sounds like life dealt him a bad hand."

"He was a good man, Ryder. Kind and gentle. Not like Charlie."

She shuddered as she recalled the look in Charlie's eye when he warned her to keep silent. "I never met Charlie before, but I could tell that he was mean clear through."

Ryder nodded. "I knew him by reputation, and it was a bad one."

Jenny sniffed, suddenly conscious of Ryder's hand moving in her hair, of the fact that she was sitting in his lap. His breath was warm against her cheek, and she thought how good it was to be held in his arms. She felt safe there, comforted somehow.

Her eyelids were heavy, so heavy. She closed them for a moment and rested her head against Fallon's shoulder. She was tired. It hurt to think that Hank might be dead, to know that she would never see her son again . . .

Fallon's hand stilled in Jenny's hair as he felt her relax against him. Soon, the even rise and fall of her chest told him she was asleep.

He held her for a long time, breathing in her scent, reluctant to let her go.

Jenny woke with the dawn to find Ryder sitting beside her, a rifle resting on his bent knees.

"You're here," she murmured. "I thought it was a dream." She sat up, pressing a hand to her back. "Hank was shot. Charlie, too. Do you think they're dead?"

"I hope so."

Jenny stared at Fallon, shocked by his response, and then she realized what he was saying. If Hank and Charlie survived their wounds, the Apaches would surely torture them to death, especially if Kayitah suspected their only reason for being in camp was to kidnap his wife and child.

"We should be going," Fallon said.

Rising, he helped Jenny to her feet. For a moment, he held her close, and then he went to saddle the horses. He didn't think Kayitah would come after them. After all, the man had his pride, but it wasn't a chance Fallon was willing to take.

Jenny stood behind him, watching as he smoothed a blanket over the back of his big buckskin, swung the saddle in place, and tightened the cinch. "Where are we going?"

"Does it matter?" he asked as be began saddling her mount.

"No."

He glanced over his shoulder to find Jenny staring at him. "What?"

"Why did you come after me?"

His dark blue eyes gazed deep into her own. "Don't you know?"

Jenny nodded, the sadness in her heart lifting a little as she remembered the words he had spoken to her after they had made love.

Nothing that happened before tonight matters now, he had said with quiet sincerity. *You're my first woman, my first love. And my last.*

She took a deep breath. "I just wondered . . . if you still felt the same?"

A faint smile played around the corners of his mouth. "That was a dirty trick, you know, running out on me like that."

"I know," Jenny said contritely. "And I'm sorry."

"Yeah, well it gave the old man who cleans the saloon quite a start, seeing me come strolling into town wearing nothing but my moccasins, I can tell you that."

"I'll bet," Jenny said, grinning as she imagined Ryder trying to sneak into town buck naked.

"I'm sorry about your horse. I know how much you liked him."

"I got another horse, Jenny."

"You could get another woman, too."

He went suddenly still. "Is that what you want me to do, find another woman?"

"No."

He didn't realize he'd been holding his breath until it whispered past his lips in a sigh of relief. He wanted to take her in his arms, to brand her with his love, but he sensed she needed time; time to grieve for Hank, for the child she had been forced to leave behind, again.

"We'd best be making tracks. Here." He handed Jenny his canteen and a strip of beef jerky. "This will have to do for breakfast."

Jenny nodded. It was time to move on, and this time there would be no going back.

Chapter Twenty-Five

Twin Rivers was a small but thriving community that owed its existence to Fred and William Howard, two brothers who had married Comanche women. The Howards had not intended to establish any kind of town when they stumbled into the valley fifteen years earlier. They had merely been searching for a place to live in peace, a quiet place to raise their children. Shunned by whites because they had married Indian women, dissatisfied with the Comanche's nomadic way of life, the brothers had set out to find a piece of ground where they could live and farm without interference from their neighbors.

Twin Rivers was located in a verdant valley cradled between gently sloping hills. The streams for which the town had been named were crowded with fish, the soil was rich and brown, timber was abundant, the winters were mild.

Working side by side, the brothers had quickly built two small cabins, planted their crops, and dreamed of peace.

By and by, other wanderers had found their way into the valley: an outlaw looking for sanctuary; a woman running away from an unhappy love affair; a drifter who happened by and fell in love with the woman; a retired sheriff and his wife; a priest who had tired of preaching to people who didn't listen and set out to find a flock that needed him; a Negro and his wife looking for greener pastures. The brothers welcomed them all with no questions asked.

In the early years, paint-streaked Apaches had scouted the settlement, troubled by the arrival of the whites, bewildered at the sight of white men, Indian women, and black people living and working together. Henry Johnson, the retired sheriff, rode out one fine spring day under a white flag to parley with the Indians. Speaking in their native tongue, Johnson had welcomed the warriors and offered them tobacco and corn as a sign of friendship, assuring them that the people of the valley wanted only to live in peace with their red brothers.

Thereafter, the Apaches came often, sometimes bringing their women and children, eager to trade furs and hides for guns and ammunition, for cloth and candy.

Mace Carson, the outlaw-turned-trader, gave the Indians a square deal on their pelts, let them wander through the store at their leisure. After a while, Mace took himself an Apache wife and fathered a brood of raven-haired daughters.

The inhabitants of the town tended to be friendly without being nosy. Since most of the people who settled in Twin Rivers were on the dodge or hiding something unpleasant, they were careful not to pry too deeply into each other's pasts.

It was to this quiet valley that Fallon brought Jenny. The little town had grown considerably since Fallon's last visit almost five years ago. In addition to the combination trading post and saloon, there was a pint-sized church and a bright red schoolhouse. Thirteen cabins lined the valley where there had once been only two. Children, red and white and in between, laughed and played together in the warm afternoon sun. White-faced cattle grazed on the lush hillsides. Horses stood head-to-tail, lazily swishing flies as they cropped the fragrant clover at their feet. Dogs sprawled in the shade. A speckled hen paraded down the dusty road, clucking anxiously to a brood of yellow chicks.

As he drew rein at the trading post, Fallon guessed the town now housed about fifty people.

Mace Carson confirmed his estimate. "Fifteen adults and more than twice that many young'uns," the reformed outlaw said proudly. "You plannin' to settle here?"

"If nobody minds," Fallon replied. "Does it matter where we build?"

"Shucks, no. Jest pick an empty spot." Carson scratched his head and grinned. "Say, now, the cabin at the far end of the valley is vacant. I reckon you could just move on in. It's been empty for nigh onto six months, so I don't reckon anybody else wants it."

Fallon expressed his thanks and the two men shook hands.

"Could we look at it now?" Jenny asked.

Mace Carson grinned amicably as he nodded in Jenny's direction. "Now, ain't that jest like a woman. Can't wait to get moved in and start tidying up."

Ryder threw Jenny a quizzical glance. "Is that right?"

Jenny shrugged, and then smiled, not at all certain of what she wanted.

"Women are all alike in some respects," Mace remarked, chuckling. "If she works you too hard, you jest come on back here and I'll draw you a cold one."

"Thanks, I'll remember that," Fallon promised as he opened the door for Jenny. "Say, who do I pay for the cabin?"

Carson shrugged. "Beats me. The previous owner jest packed up and lit out, so I reckon it's yours till somebody says otherwise."

The cabin sat alone at the end of the valley, a squat wooden square against the flowering hills. A split rail fence, badly in need of repair, separated the cabin from the broken-down corral in back and the road in front. Tall brown weeds rustled as Fallon and Jenny walked up the path to the front door. A rabbit scurried for cover as they neared the cabin.

The shanty had two rooms. The main room served as both parlor and kitchen, the smaller room was a bedroom. There was no furniture in the house save for a square oak table and three rickety chairs in a corner of the main room. A fireplace with a raised hearth took up most of the east wall. A narrow window looked out on the dusty path that led off into the trees at the north end of the valley.

Fallon frowned as he surveyed the cabin's dismal interior. It was a far cry from the rich surroundings and fancy furnishings Jenny had known in Widow Ridge. A thick layer of dust covered the table and raw plank floor. Lacy cobwebs hung from the beamed ceiling. Scattered piles of leaves and dead grass bore mute evidence that more than one rodent had nested inside the fireplace at one time or another.

Slowly, Ryder shook his head. "I don't know, Jenny. What do you think?"

"It'll be fine as soon as we clean it up a bit."

"Are you sure?" Ryder asked dubiously. It was more than he was used to, but Jenny was a city girl at heart, and in spite of the two years she'd spent with the Apache, he couldn't help but feel that she expected more, deserved more. "Maybe you'd rather go back to Widow Ridge. With Hank and Charlie dead, the store and the house belong to you now."

"No, I don't want to go back there."

Ryder crossed the floor and took Jenny's hands

in his. They hadn't really talked about the future; he wasn't even sure that Jenny wanted a future with him.

"Jenny, we don't have to stay here."

"I don't mind," she said, and then looked away as color suffused her cheeks. Didn't he know she'd rather be here, with him, than live in the finest mansion with anyone else? Even though she knew it was wrong to live with him without benefit of marriage, she would do it, because she loved him, because she never wanted to be away from him again.

"What is it, Jenny girl?"

"Nothing."

"Jenny, I don't want there to be any lies between us. Tell me what's wrong, and I'll fix it if I can."

"I . . . we're not . . ." She bit down on her lower lip, then took a deep breath. "What will people think, about us living together?"

"I don't much care what anybody thinks," Ryder said. "Only what you think."

"I want things to be right between us," Jenny said, not meeting his eyes. "I married Hank, and it was a mistake. I lived with Kayitah because I didn't have any choice, and it was awful. This time I'd like a real marriage with the man I love."

"Jenny!" He swept her into his arms and crushed her close. "Will you marry me?"

"Yes, today, if you like, unless you think we should wait."

"Wait? For what?"

"People usually wait a year after the death of a loved one before they remarry."

"Your marriage has been dead for over a year," Ryder remarked. "But if you want to wait, I'll wait."

"I can't wait," Jenny admitted shyly. "I don't care what people think."

"Good. I'll go talk to George and see if he'll marry us today."

Jenny looked down at her buckskin dress and moccasins. "But I don't have anything to wear!"

"You look fine to me."

"All right, then," she agreed, her whole being thrumming with exitement. She was going to be married, married to a whole man, a man who loved her.

She walked through the cabin after Fallon left to find the preacher, seeing the dreary little shack with new eyes. Some curtains, a rug here and there, a lamp or two, and the abandoned cabin would become a haven of refuge where she could live with the man she loved.

The man she loved. It felt good to admit how she really felt at last. For so long, she'd tried to pretend she hated him. Perhaps it had even been true, for a short time. But now she felt her affection for him bubble up within her, a wellspring of love with no beginning and no end. He had been her friend, her confidant, her ally. Her lover.

Warmth spread through her as she recalled the night they had made love outside of Widow Ridge. He had been tender, caring, gentle, and she had gloried in his touch. And tonight, tonight he would take her in his arms again and their joining would be better than ever, because he would be her husband, and she would be his wife.

She whirled around, a smile of anticipation on her lips, as the door opened and Ryder stepped inside, followed by a tall man with a mane of white hair and a beard that reached his chest.

"Jenny, this is Father Link. Father, this is Jenny Braedon."

"It's a pleasure to meet you, Father," Jenny said.

Father Link nodded as he took both of Jenny's hands in his. "The pleasure is all mine, my child. This rascal tells me you've agreed to marry him. Is that true?"

"Yes, Father."

"Well, I'm glad that someone who could tame him finally came along. What's your full name, child?"

"Jennifer Marie Braedon."

Father Link nodded as he placed Jenny's hand in Fallon's. "And your full name, my son?"

"Ryder Fallon."

"Do you have a ring?"

Ryder shook his head. "I'm sorry, Jenny."

"It doesn't matter." He might have doubted her words if it hadn't been for her smile, and the love he saw shining in the depths of her eyes.

The priest cleared his throat. "Do you want the long ceremony or the short one?"

"The short one's fine," Ryder said.

"Very well. Ryder Fallon, do you take this woman to be your lawfully wedded wife?"

"I do."

"And do you, Jennifer Marie Braedon, take this man to be your lawfully wedded husband?"

"I do."

"Then by the power and authority vested in me by Holy Mother Church, I hereby pronounce you, Ryder Fallon and Jennifer Marie Braedon, husband and wife so long as you both shall live. I would admonish you to be fruitful and multiply and to cherish one another. May God bless your union, in the name of the Father, and the Son, and the Holy Ghost. Amen."

"Is that it?" Jenny asked.

"That's it, my child. Just as binding as if your vows had been spoken in a grand cathedral in front of the Holy Father himself." He smiled at Jenny. "Take good care of your husband, my child. Remember to put him first in your life. And you, Ryder Fallon, you be good to this beautiful young woman. Put her wants and needs before your own, and your marriage will endure."

"Thanks, Father."

"Yes, thank you, Father," Jenny repeated.

"Good day to you, then. And I'll expect to see you both at Mass on Sunday."

Jenny nodded, her heart brimming with joy as she waved goodbye to the priest. A new marriage. A new start. She felt suddenly as if she'd been given a second chance at life, at love.

Fallon shut the door, then turned to face Jenny. His wife. "I'm sorry about the ring."

"It doesn't matter, honestly." Jenny gazed up at him, a shy smile playing over her lips. "Aren't you going to kiss me?"

"Jenny!" He swept her into his arms, then swore softly as he remembered there was no bed in the place.

Putting Jenny on her feet, he went out and unsaddled the horses. Carrying their saddles inside, he spread one of the bedrolls on the floor, locked the door, then took Jenny in his arms once again.

"Welcome home, Mrs. Fallon," he whispered as he carried her down to the blankets.

"Welcome home, Mr. Fallon," Jenny replied, her pulse racing as Ryder rained kisses on her face and neck, his breath warm against her skin. She gasped as his mouth traveled to her breasts, the heat of his lips penetrating her buckskin dress.

"Jenny." His voice was ragged as he breathed her name. He made love to her as he had always dreamed of doing, letting her know with each kiss and caress that she was his, that she would always be his. Only his from this day forward. He marveled at her beauty as he removed her dress and moccasins, exploring the delicate texture of her skin, pausing now and then to claim her lips in a gentle kiss of promise, still finding it hard to believe that she was here, that she was his.

Jenny eagerly returned each kiss and caress, reveling in the arms that held her, the hands that turned her flesh to flame. She felt small and vulnerable in Ryder's embrace, yet strangely powerful at the same time. It was exhilarating to know she pleased him, that he desired her, that she had the power to arouse him, to make him tremble with longing.

Her hands wandered lovingly over his hard-muscled flesh. His chest was as solid as a rock wall, his arms and legs were long, corded with muscle, and she delighted in the strength sleeping beneath her fingertips. She would never be afraid again. He was her strength, her courage, and she gave herself to him completely, eagerly, basking in his touch, in the sound of his voice as he whispered her name.

Her blood ran sweet and hot as their bodies came together. He was hers, for now and for always. She would fall asleep in his arms each night for the rest of her life, kiss him each morning.

She cried his name, her nails raking the length of his back, her teeth nipping at his neck, as his life poured into her, filling her, hearts joined life to life, and soul to soul.

Chapter Twenty-Six

The little town of Twin Rivers welcomed Jenny and Ryder with open arms. Mace Carson was an old friend and he gave them a slightly worn settee and an overstuffed chair that he assured them was just gathering dust in the back room of the trading post.

Linda Johnson, wife of Sheriff Henry Johnson, dropped by with a dozen jars of strawberry preserves, two loaves of fresh-baked bread, and a smile of welcome.

The drifter and his wife, Abel and Laura Patterson, gave them a set of dishes. True, the plates and cups didn't match, but they were pretty and unchipped.

Father Link stopped by and left them a sack of seed corn, a Bible, and his blessing on their new home.

Fred Howard, a widower now, stopped by one evening and handed Jenny a box filled with his wife's pots and pans, insisting gruffly that he didn't need them any more.

The Negro, Elijah Brown, offered them a spotted heifer and a gallon of fresh milk.

Jenny was deeply touched by the generosity of her new neighbors. She'd had friends back East, she'd made a few friends in Widow Ridge, but none of them had been as generous as the people in Twin Rivers, welcoming her simply because she was there, not because her husband was a rich man.

Under Jenny's loving hands, the little cabin at the end of the valley underwent a remarkable transformation. Red gingham curtains appeared at the kitchen window, a matching cloth covered the scarred oak table. A rag rug brightened the floor in front of the hearth. Lace doilies camouflaged the worn arms of the settee.

Changes were taking place outside, too. With the help of some of the men, Fallon tore down the old corral and built a new one to house their stock. Fred Howard helped lay in a supply of firewood, and his brother lent Fallon the tools he needed to patch a hole in the cabin's roof.

The days raced by, each one better than the last. Never had Jenny been as happy as she was living in the little cabin with Ryder. She woke early in the morning, eagerly looking forward to another day. She sang cheerfully as she did her chores, never complaining about their poor furniture, the hard work, or their lack of creature comforts. She cooked and cleaned and sewed as though such tasks were fun instead of hard work.

It was such a joy, to be able to look out the window and see Ryder working in the distance. Watching him, watching the effortless way he moved, and the way his muscles rippled in the sunlight, did funny things in the pit of her stomach. He was a wonderful man, solid, dependable as the sunrise. He never got angry with her, never uttered a cross word, never raised his voice. In fact, nothing ever seemed to rile him or ruffle his composure.

Jenny had never known such happiness existed, had never dreamed it was possible to live in such harmony with another person. There was no tension between them, as there had been between herself and Hank, no distrust, as there had been between herself and Kayitah, only love.

Just looking at Ryder filled her with such an overwhelming sense of well-being and love that she sometimes thought she would burst with the sheer joy of it. Often she found herself laughing for no apparent reason except that she was blissfully happy with her husband.

It was only sometimes, at night, when she was too tired to sleep, that her joy dimmed and her arms ached for the son she had left behind. She tried often to tell herself that he was better off with his father, that he'd never known her and wouldn't miss her, but it didn't help. She missed her son terribly. He would be sitting up soon, walking, talking, and she wouldn't be there to see it. She'd never hear the sound of his laughter, never dry his tears. He would grow up to be a warrior, never knowing who his real mother was, or that she had loved him deeply. He would never know how often she thought of him, or how many nights she wept in the darkness, aching to hold him just once more.

She managed to keep her sadness at bay during the day. Now, as she prepared Ryder's midday meal, she thought only of her husband. She wondered how long the excitement would last, how long they would live together before the magic was gone and they started to take each other for granted, the way other married couples did. But she wouldn't mind even that, she mused, so long as it was Fallon taking her for granted.

Ryder smiled at her as she brought him his lunch, and Jenny felt her heart skip a beat. He was so handsome, and she loved him so much.

They ate together, sitting side by side in the shade of an ancient oak. Jenny had a hard time concentrating on her food. Fallon was naked from the waist up, and the sight of his broad chest, sheened with perspiration, excited her in a very unladylike way. She had a wild impulse to run her tongue over his sweaty flesh. The thought brought a quick flush to her cheeks.

Ryder raised an eyebrow at her. "Are you plotting mischief of some sort?" he queried lightly. "You look guilty as hell. You haven't poisoned my noonday meal, have you?"

"Of course not," Jenny murmured. "I was just thinking that . . . oh, never mind."

"Thinking what, Jenny girl?"

"Thinking how nice it would be to . . . you know."

Whispering her name, Fallon swept Jenny into his arms and carried her swiftly into the cabin. Inside, he placed her on the robes that served as their bed, then began to undress her slowly, deliberately, his mouth moving hotly over each new area of bared flesh.

Jenny sighed with contentment as he shrugged out of his pants and moccasins and lowered his long body over hers. He smelled of earth and sweat and she breathed in the scent of him, savoring the musky male smell as if it were the finest wine. Her fingertips moved tantalizingly over his shoulders and arms, then slid down, down . . .

Fallon sucked in a ragged breath as Jenny's hands moved over him, teasing, caressing, giving promise of the pleasure to come.

He felt a sudden wave of pity for Hank Braedon, who'd never been able to take advantage of Jenny's passionate nature, and for Kayitah, who'd taken her body but had never touched her soul. She was his, wholly his, and the thought pleased him beyond words.

When he was on fire for her, he became the aggressor, fondling all the soft secret places that only he knew, arousing her to fever pitch, her passion igniting his own.

They came together with a knowledge all their

own, each pleasuring the other, straining together until there was nothing in all the world but their need and the wondrous ecstasy that blended a man and a woman into one flesh.

For a time, they didn't move, content to lie in each other's arms. Ryder stroked Jenny's hair, loving the feel of it, the way it curled around his hand, as if her hair had a life of its own.

Jenny sighed deeply as she kissed Ryder's cheek. How marvelous, to feel so loved, so cherished. Her fingertips traced the curves and planes of his face, lingering on his lips. She gave a little cry of pretended pain when he bit her finger.

Pouting playfully, she jerked her hand away and made a face at him.

Fallon laughed, a deep rich sound filled with happiness. Then, yawning hugely, he put her away from him and bounded to his feet.

"Come on," he said, reaching for her hand. "Let's go for a swim."

It was a day to remember forever. They swam and splashed and swam again, then stretched out on the cool grass to dry. Lying on his side, Ryder toyed with a lock of Jenny's hair. She looked like Eve, he thought, pink and perfect in the Garden of Eden.

They played by the river the rest of the afternoon, swimming, wrestling, then walked along the shore. Jenny laughed as Ryder waded into the water and caught a fat trout with his bare hands.

"Laugh at me, will you?" he growled, and soon had her shrieking in protest as he threatened to drop the wriggling fish down the front of her dress.

"Uncle, uncle!"

"Do you admit that I am a mighty fisherman?" Fallon demanded, straddling her thighs, the fish held a few scant inches from her nose.

"The best in the world!"

"Do you admit that I am also a mighty hunter?"

"The mightiest," Jenny gasped breathlessly. "And also the heaviest. Ryder, do get up. You're squishing me."

"You didn't complain about my weight in bed," he purred wickedly.

"That's because you're also a mighty lover," Jenny declared with a grin.

"That's true," Ryder agreed with a salacious grin. Tossing the fish back into the stream, he helped Jenny to her feet.

Happily weary, they walked hand in hand toward the cabin as the shadows grew long. Jenny sighed as they reached the house. The setting sun bathed the ugly little shack in a warm golden glow, magically transforming the crude structure into a thing of beauty. But Jenny hardly noticed the change in the cabin's appearance. To her, it was home, and it was always beautiful.

For Fallon, the days were achingly sweet. Not only did he have Jenny for his own, but for the first time in his life, he found himself accepted for what he was: a man trying to make a life for himself with the woman he loved. There were no derogatory remarks about his Indian blood, no insulting comments, no looks of contempt. If the townspeople knew he had once been a roving gambler, or that he had killed more than his share of men, they didn't seem to care. He wasn't a gambler or a gunman now, just a farmer.

He worked hard during the day, clearing the land, chopping wood, pulling weeds, feeding the stock, and went to bed feeling tired but content.

Like now. He held Jenny close, thinking that it was time to try to build a bed. The robes were cozy, but the floor was hard, and would seem harder and colder come winter.

Jenny sighed and nestled closer to Ryder, her fingers toying with the thick pelt of black hair that curled on his chest. What had she ever done to deserve such a man, such happiness? Was he as blissfully content as she?

"Happy, Jenny girl?" Ryder asked, for his thoughts had been following a similar path.

"Happier than I've ever been," Jenny answered softly. "So happy it frightens me. I'm afraid I'll wake up one day and it will all be gone, like a dream." Lifting herself on one elbow, Jenny gazed down at Ryder. "Are you happy here? Do you miss the freedom of your old life?"

Fallon's gaze moved toward the window. Outside, the night was dark and quiet save for the distant yap of a coyote.

"Sometimes," he admitted honestly. "There's

a lot of pretty country out there, Jenny girl. Hidden canyons rich with grass and game. Sparkling rivers. Mountains so high it takes your breath away just to look at them. Wild places where a good horse and a good rifle are worth their weight in gold."

He lifted a lock of her hair and pressed it to his cheek, a faraway look in his eyes. "You know, this is the first real home I've had in fifteen years. It takes a little getting used to."

Jenny buried her face in his shoulder, troubled by his words, afraid he would see her tears. Had she detected a note of longing in his voice when he talked of distant places? Was he regretting his decision to stay here, with her? Unhappily, she remembered his words at the Apache camp: *Don't worry, Jenny,* he had said, *I've no intention of settling down here or anywhere else.*

In her mind's eye, she saw him riding across the vast untamed wilderness that he loved, a tall man clad in fringed buckskins and knee-high moccasins, as free as the wind and the red-tailed hawk. Was he sorry, deep down, that he had traded the endless prairie for a few acres of ground in this valley? Would he find their little cabin too small, too confining, after the wandering life he'd led? Would he grow to hate it, and her, too? Was he already longing for the wild places, wishing he was stretched out beside some lonely moonlit trail, as carefree as the moon and the stars?

Her thoughts made her heart heavy, and her throat ached with unshed tears. And yet, even if her worst fears came true and he tired of her and rode out of her life forever, she would always treasure the memory of these warm summer days of laughter, and the intimate nights they shared beneath the furry robes.

"I'll never tie you down, Ryder," she promised solemnly. "I'll understand, if you have to leave here one day."

"Leave? Jenny, what in the great green hell are you talking about?" Fallon demanded, and when she refused to answer, he cupped her face in his hands and forced her to look at him.

Her eyes reflected her thoughts as clearly as print upon a page. There, behind the tears she tried to blink away, he saw her love for him, and the unspoken fear that he would tire of life in the valley and ride away, alone. His heart swelled with love for the golden girl lying at his side. How well she knew him! But there was one thing she apparently didn't understand, and that was how much he loved her.

"I'll not leave you, Jenny girl," he vowed fervently. "Don't you know that by now?" He wiped the tears from her cheeks with his fingertips, kissing each damp spot, and then a slow grin spread across his face and a spark of deviltry danced in his eyes. "I'm afraid you're stuck with me," he murmured as his hand slid down her thigh. "You've got hills and valleys that put the *Paha Sapa* to shame."

It was as though he'd pulled a thorn from her heart. "Be serious," Jenny scolded with mock severity.

"I've never been more serious in my life," Ryder drawled, rising over her. "Never more serious in my life . . ."

The warm summer days paraded by, filled with love and laughter. Like two children on holiday, Ryder and Jenny spent the balmy summer days swimming in the stream, or riding in the woods. Sometimes Jenny packed a picnic lunch and they hiked into the foothills, or backtracked the southern stream to the waterfall that spawned it.

There were dances at the schoolhouse, family picnics on the meadow near the pond. There were pot luck dinners and social gatherings, a barn raising for a new couple in the valley, a rousing Fourth of July celebration that lasted until dawn.

In August, Laura and Abel Patterson, who had five daughters, became the proud parents of twin boys, and Abel threw the biggest party the valley had ever seen. There were a lot of men with hangovers the next day, and a lot of women who sadly shook their heads at their foolish husbands, who thought they could drink all night and not pay the price.

But it was not all play. There was a cow to milk, eggs to gather, weeds to pull. There were clothes to be washed and ironed and put away; they were crops to tend, animals to feed and water, wood to cut, fences that seemed to need constant repair, land to be cultivated for the next crop.

Sometimes Jenny saw Ryder staring, bemused,

at the fertile fields that lay behind the cabin. It was not hard for her to divine his thoughts. Who would have thought that Ryder Fallon, that no-account half-breed drifter, would ever settle down in one place long enough to plant a crop, let alone harvest it? Or that he would hang up his gun. Or find contentment in the arms of just one woman.

Or that he would engage in anything as frivolous as dancing. Jenny had been appalled when she discovered her husband couldn't waltz or polka.

"Anyone can learn to dance," she had assured him when he seemed less than enthusiastic to learn. "Even you."

Fallon didn't care much for dancing, but he was in favor of any activity that put Jenny in his arms. Bless the girl, he mused as they whirled around the cabin, what a delightful change she had wrought in his life.

Summer slipped into fall. The days grew shorter, the nights longer and colder.

With the changing seasons, a restlessness took hold of Jenny. She couldn't seem to stop thinking about her son. He'd soon be a year old, and she didn't even know what he looked like. Was he happy? Was he walking? He'd call Alope mother and Kayitah father, he'd run around naked in the heat of summer, splashing in the river, eating wild plums and berries.

In the winter, he'd slide down the snow-covered hills on a sled made of buffalo bones and sit around the campfire while the old men told thrilling tales of battles won and lost.

He'd worship heathen gods, and never know about Easter, or Thanksgiving, or Christmas. He'd never hear the wonderful stories of Jesus, the miracle of His birth, His life, His death and resurrection. He'd fall asleep listening to the exploits of Coyote the Trickster, instead of the fairy tales she'd heard growing up.

She threaded a needle and began to sew a rip in one of Ryder's work shirts. It was funny, she mused. Not long ago she had been afraid that he would leave her and now she was thinking of leaving him, of going back to Kayitah in hopes of seeing her son. It would be foolish, dangerous, and yet she couldn't put the thought out of her mind.

She caught Ryder watching her at odd times during the next few days, his midnight blue eyes thoughtful.

It was on a cool night a week later while they were walking in the moonlight that he took her in his arms and kissed her, a soft gentle kiss.

"What is it, Jenny?" he asked, gazing down into her eyes. "What's wrong?"

"Nothing."

"Don't lie to me, Jenny girl. You're no good at it. If you're not happy here, tell me."

"I am happy," she said quickly. "Honest, I've never been happier in my life. But, oh, Ryder, I miss him so!"

He let out a long breath as he drew her into his arms and held her tight. He'd seen the look of yearning in her eyes when she held one of Laura

Patterson's baby boys. He'd heard her whisper to the child, soft, meaningless words that were as universal as motherhood. The Patterson house drew Jenny like a magnet, and she often offered to sit with the twins to give Laura a rest.

"What do you want to do, Jenny? What do you want me to do?"

"I don't know."

"You can't go back to the rancheria, you know that."

"Why?" She looked up at him, her great green eyes filled with pain. "I didn't do anything."

"I know, but Kayitah might not give you a chance to explain about Hank and Charlie."

Two tears welled in her eyes, hovered there for a moment, then slid down her cheeks.

"You don't understand," Jenny murmured, then bit back her words because he did understand. He'd lost a wife and a child. At least her son was still alive. She could be grateful for that.

"Let's go inside," Ryder said. "I'll fix you a cup of coffee."

She sat in the kitchen, watching him, knowing that she couldn't leave him. He'd risked his life to get her away from the Apache, had sat beside her through the long hours of labor, endured her anger and her hatred, all because he loved her. And she loved him, loved him too much to hurt him.

She took the cup he offered her and set it aside; then, taking him by the hand, she led him into the bedroom and drew him down on the bed he'd made for them.

"Love me, Ryder," she whispered. "Make me forget everything else."

"Jenny." He murmured her name and she melted into his arms.

He rained kisses on her face and neck, his eyes moving over her in silent adoration as he undressed her and then removed his own clothing.

He made love to her with exquisite tenderness, hoping she'd know, with every caress, how much he loved her. He tasted the salt of her tears as he kissed her cheeks, her eyelids, and knew the ache in her heart would never truly heal, and he vowed to make her happy in every way he could. He only hoped that his love would be enough; that, in time, she would learn to accept her loss, as he had accepted his.

Jenny drew Ryder close, her body molding itself to his, as she merged her life with his, giving all she had to give.

Later, wrapped in the security of her husband's arms, she bid a silent farewell to the son she knew she would never see again.

Chapter Twenty-Seven

Fallon rose early that sun-swept morning and padded out to the corral. The gelding stamped and snorted as Ryder slipped a horsehair bridle in place, swung effortlessly onto the horse's bare back.

Armed with a bow and a quiver of arrows, and the knife sheathed on his belt, Fallon reined the buckskin down the dusty trail that led to the forest that reared up at the northern end of the valley, off to spend a day hunting, Cheyenne style.

Deep in the heart of the sun-dappled woods, he dismounted and left the stallion tethered to a tree. On foot, he glided soundlessly over the moss-strewn ground, his eyes and ears alert to every sound, every movement.

Alone in the deep green cocoon of the forest, surrounded by a silence broken only by the hum of winged insects, the shrill cry of a jay, and the gentle whisper of a sun-kissed breeze, he felt at home and at peace.

As he rounded a deadfall, he spotted a fine three-point buck grazing on a patch of thick grass. Deftly, Ryder pulled an arrow from the hide quiver slung over his left shoulder, nocked it as the buck raised its head.

For a moment, the deer looked directly toward Fallon's hiding place, its liquid brown eyes probing the shadows, its flared nostrils testing the breeze.

For a stretched second of eternity, Fallon and the deer stood frozen in time. Then, with a sigh, Ryder lowered the bow and sheathed the arrow. They didn't really need the meat, and it was too lovely a day to kill just for the sake of killing.

"Perhaps another time," he muttered aloud, and the sound of his voice sent the buck leaping gracefully out of sight.

Ryder spent the rest of the day in a shady thicket, stretched out beside a shallow pool, content to be a part of the tranquil atmosphere of the forest.

It was early evening when he returned home.

Hanging his bow in the shed beside the corral, he slipped the bridle from the buckskin and forked it some hay.

A lamp burned cheerfully in the front window of the cabin and he experienced an overwhelming sense of peace as he pictured Jenny inside, humming to herself as she stirred up something good for supper.

He was whistling softly when he opened the door and stepped inside.

Jenny was standing near the hearth, her face pale. She shook her head, her eyes wide with alarm.

His hand moved instinctively toward his right hip, only to close on empty air, and he mouthed a silent oath as he visualized his Colt hanging useless and out of reach on the back of the bedroom door.

"What is it?" he asked. Too late, he sensed someone behind him.

Jenny took a step forward, then froze as a deep voice spoke out of the shadows between the hearth and the bedroom door.

"Stay where you are, ma'am," the voice warned. "Fallon, you make one wrong move and she's liable to get hurt in the crossfire."

Ryder stayed where he was, his hands balled into tight fists, his gaze on Jenny's face.

"I see we understand each other," the voice remarked. "Put your hands up, nice and slow."

Without hesitation, Fallon did as he was told.

Immediately, someone stepped up behind him and lashed his hands together.

"Search him, Vince."

"What's this all about?" Ryder spoke through clenched teeth as the man called Vince relieved him of the knife sheathed on his belt.

"It's okay, Jed. He's clean," Vince announced confidently.

Only then did the other man step out of the shadows.

"Ryder . . ."

"It's all right, Jenny."

Fallon studied the face of the man who had stepped out of the shadows. Jed was a big man, his skin weathered from years in the sun, his eyes deep set in a tanned face. He wore a pair of canvas pants, a buckskin shirt, and boots that had seen better days.

"I asked you a question, mister," Ryder said curtly. "I'd like an answer."

"It's about this," the man called Jed replied. He pulled a crumpled sheet of paper from his pants pocket and tossed it at Fallon.

The handbill was creased and torn, but the message was still clear:

WANTED
RYDER FALLON
FOR THE MURDER OF ROY TRAHERNE
$200 REWARD
DEAD OR ALIVE

There was also a physical description and a fair pen and ink sketch of his face.

"What's going on?" Jenny asked. "I don't understand."

"I killed a man a while back," Ryder said, his gaze still on the bounty hunter.

"Ain't much of a reward," Jed remarked with a shake of his head.

"He wasn't much of a man," Fallon retorted.

Jed shrugged. "Times being what they are, we can't afford to pass it up."

"Ryder, what's this all about? What man?" Jenny frowned. "You're not talking about the man you shot in Broken Fork, are you? They said that was self-defense."

Ryder shook his head. The shooting in Clearwell had been self-defense, too, he mused.

"Ryder?"

"It's a long story, Jenny."

"Well, we ain't got no time for any long stories now," Vince said, dragging a tobacco-stained hand through his hair.

"That's right, lady," Jed agreed. "So how about fixin' us some grub so we can be on our way?"

"Fix it yourself," Ryder said curtly.

"We can do this easy, or we can make it hard," Jed remarked affably. "I don't cotton to hittin' women as a rule, but I can make an exception. It's up to you."

Fallon's gaze locked with the bounty hunter's cold gray eyes. The man wasn't bluffing. Fallon knew it without a doubt.

"Do what he says, Jenny."

"Vince, you go along and keep the little lady company. Make sure she doesn't get a sudden yearning to hightail it into town." Jed jerked his head toward the sofa. "Fallon, why don't you sit down? We'll all have something to eat, and then we'll be on our way."

Ryder sat down on the edge of the sofa, his hands testing the rope that bound his wrists. There was no slack, no way he was going to slip free.

"Where are you taking me?" he asked.

Jed lifted one big shoulder and let it drop. "El Paso, I reckon."

"And my wife?"

"She stays here." Jed grinned, exposing a mouthful of crooked teeth. "Don't worry, we ain't gonna hurt her none. I don't hold with abusin' them that's weak or helpless."

Ryder glanced toward the kitchen. "And your partner?"

"Don't worry none about Vince. He won't touch her."

Only partly mollified, Ryder stared at the floor, wondering if the bounty hunter was as easy-going as he appeared, or if he could expect a bullet in the back once they were out of the valley. The wanted poster said dead or alive, and he had a feeling Jed and his partner would rather take him in tied face down across the back of his horse than have to worry about his trying to escape along the way. He wasn't afraid of death. It was an unknown shadow that awaited every man, but prison . . .

The very word left a bad taste in his mouth, calling to mind memories of long ago, of the six months he'd spent in a Mexican jail.

He shuddered with the memory. All his life, he had been free, like the buffalo and the hawk, free to cross the endless prairie, or ride alone in the high country. Free to come and go like the wind, tied to nothing, neither land nor home nor clocks. Free as only an Indian is free—until the Federales caught up with him.

Six months. He no longer remembered why

they had arrested him, but he vividly recalled the horrors of life behind bars: the constant stink of sweat and excrement, the vile odor of stale air and unwashed bodies, of vomit, and death.

The unending clink of chains. The dismal, never-ending groans of the sick and the dying; the nightmare cries of men locked in solitary confinement, the tortured screams of men writhing under the lash.

Six months of seeing little more than dull gray walls and thick iron bars, emaciated bodies, and gaunt faces wiped clean of hope.

Six months of cold worm-ridden food, slimy green water, and lice-infested blankets.

Six months of being hungry, not just for a decent meal, but for a hot bath, clean clothes, the feel of a gun in his hand, the sight of buffalo stampeding across the plains, for the sight and scent of trees and grass and dirt. For the touch of a woman.

Jenny . . . but it wasn't Jenny he was worried about. He knew that the people in the valley would look after her in his absence, knew that she would wait for him, no matter how long he was gone. No, he didn't have to worry about how Jenny would get along without him. But what would he do without her?

He swallowed hard, remembering the long days behind bars. It had been sheer hell. The men were chained together in groups of four during the day. Nights, they were confined to individual cells so small that he could sit in the middle of the floor and touch all four walls.

When he couldn't take any more, when even the prospect of death under the lash became preferable to another day behind bars, he had plotted an escape with the three men who shared his chain. It had been ridiculously easy, so easy he wondered why they hadn't thought of it sooner.

They had been working on the side of a hill outside the prison walls, clearing it of boulders and weeds so the warden's *puta* could plant flowers. At a prearranged signal, the man nearest the edge of the rocky slope keeled over in a mock faint. When he fell, he rolled down the incline, dragging Fallon and the other two prisoners with him.

When the guard came down the hill to check on the "unconscious" man, one of the other prisoners strangled him with his bare hands. Fallon dug the key out of the dead man's pocket, removed his irons, and ran like hell. He never knew, or cared, what happened to the other three men.

And now it looked like he'd be going back . . .

He glanced up as Jenny entered the room. "Dinner's ready," she announced.

"Vince, you go ahead and eat while I keep an eye on Fallon and the woman."

"Right, Jed."

Jenny stared at the bounty hunter for a moment, then crossed the room and sat down on the sofa beside Ryder. "Aren't you hungry?"

"No." Right now, food was the last thing on his mind.

"What are we going to do?"

Fallon shook his head. "Looks like I'm going to jail." Damn!

He felt his heart turn over as Jenny placed her hand on his thigh. "I'm going to El Paso with you."

"No, Jenny."

"I want to."

He shook his head. "Somebody's got to stay here and take care of the place."

"The Howards will keep an eye on things while we're gone."

"Jenny, if they don't hang me, I could be facing a long prison sentence. What are you going to do in El Paso while I'm locked up? Take in laundry?"

"I'll do whatever I have to."

"No, Jenny."

She didn't say anything, but he saw the stubborn look in her eye and feared he was wasting his breath.

Ten minutes later, Jed went into the kitchen to eat. Vince stood near the door, a shotgun cradled in the crook of his arm.

"You might want to pack your husband a change of clothes," Vince suggested. "And maybe some grub for the trail."

Jenny looked at Fallon, and he nodded. In spite of himself, Ryder felt a slim ray of hope. Maybe he would make it to El Paso alive.

Vince stood at the bedroom door where he could keep an eye on the two of them.

Ryder studied the other man. Vince was maybe five years younger than his partner, but his face wore the same hard, lean expression. They were men down on hard times, Ryder thought, and that made them dangerous.

Jenny returned to the parlor a few minutes later, one of Ryder's saddlebags draped over her arm.

A few minutes later, Jed sauntered into the parlor. "Good cook, your wife," he remarked.

"Yeah. How'd you find me?"

Jed chuckled. "Just luck. Saw you in Carson's store yesterday." He shrugged. "I got a good memory for faces, and I recollected I'd seen yours. Me and Vince took a look through the wanteds, and sure enough, yours was there."

Ryder swore softly. Luck, he thought bitterly. That's not what he called it.

Jed scratched his armpit. "You about ready to go?"

"Do I have a choice?"

"'Fraid not."

Ryder stood up. "Mind if I say goodbye to my wife?"

Jed shook his head. "Make it quick."

Jenny thrust Fallon's saddlebags into Jed's hand, then hurried across the room to throw her arms around Ryder. She pressed her face against his chest, breathing in his scent as she fought back her tears. She couldn't imagine Ryder locked behind bars. He'd hate being locked up, hate the loss of his freedom.

"I love you," she murmured.

"I know." He kissed the top of her head. "I

love you, too, Jenny girl. Stay well. I'll write as soon as I can."

It hit her then, really hit her for the first time. He was leaving. She might not see him again for years. "Please let me come with you."

"No."

"Please, Ryder."

"No. Dammit, Jenny, I want to know you're here, safe. Please."

She heard the concern beneath the rough tone of his voice and knew he didn't want her to be at the mercy of Jed and Vince. They didn't seem like the types to abuse a woman, but if she was wrong, Ryder wouldn't be able to do anything to protect her.

"Please, Jenny?"

How could she refuse him? "All right."

She rose on her tiptoes, pressing her lips to his, her hands moving restlessly over his back and shoulders. "You'll write as soon as you get there, promise me?"

"I promise."

"Is there anything I can do?"

"I don't think so."

"I'll write every day."

"Jenny, I . . . damn!" He blinked hard against the tears that burned his eyes.

"I know," she murmured, her hand stroking his cheek with infinite tenderness and understanding. "I know."

Jenny turned to face the bounty hunter, her hand going out in a gesture of pleading. "Please don't do this."

Jed cleared his throat. "I'm sorry, ma'am, but times is hard. I got a family of my own to feed." He looked at Fallon and jerked his head toward the door. "Let's go."

One last kiss, and he was gone. Jenny stood in the doorway, her throat aching with unshed tears as she watched Jed and Vince boost Ryder into the saddle, and then he was riding away, flanked by the two bounty hunters.

He turned back for one last look and Jenny forced a smile, knowing he wouldn't want to see her tears. She'd have plenty of time to cry later.

She watched him out of sight; then, picking up her skirts, she ran down the road to the Howards'.

Chapter Twenty-Eight

"Took him?" William Howard said, frowning. "Who took him?"

"Bounty hunters," Jenny exclaimed, and dissolved into tears.

"Here, now," Howard admonished, awkwardly patting her shoulder. "This is no time for tears. Tell me what happened."

Sniffing back tears, Jenny quickly told William and Nell everything that had happened.

"I need some money," Jenny said. "A lot of money. At least two hundred dollars."

"Two hundred dollars! Crikey, girl, I haven't seen that much money all at once in years."

"What do you need the money for?" Nell asked.

"I'm going to try and buy Ryder from the bounty hunters," Jenny replied, as if such a thing was done every day.

Will Howard stared at her as if she'd suddenly grown two heads. He was a big bear of a man, with a mane of brown hair and a shaggy brown beard. His eyes were a mild shade of gray beneath heavy brows.

"Buy him!" Howard exclaimed. "From bounty hunters! Have you gone plumb loco, girl?"

"It's worth a try," Jenny insisted. "Will you help me?"

"I ain't never heard of such a thing," Will muttered, shaking his head. "Where'd you ever get such a crazy notion?"

"I don't know, but I've got to do something!" Jenny cried. "I can't just let them take him. He'd hate being locked up. And what if they hang him!" She groaned softly and clutched her stomach, the image of Ryder swinging from a rope making her physically ill. "Won't you please help me, Will? Nell?"

Will Howard looked over at his wife, and she nodded.

"We've got to try, Will," Nell said, her expression solemn.

"You two stay here," Howard said. "I'll go see what I can do."

"Please hurry," Jenny urged.

At Nell's insistence, Jenny sank down on a kitchen chair while Nell filled a pot with water for tea.

Nell Howard was a tall, angular woman with long black hair and large dark eyes. Her heavy calico skirts swished softly as she moved around the kitchen, taking cups and saucers from the cupboard and placing them on the small pine table.

"I should have gone with Ryder," Jenny murmured. "What if something happens? I might never see him again."

Nell Howard shook her head. "No. He was right to make you stay. El Paso is no place for a woman alone. He will have enough to worry about without worrying about you, too."

"I know, but, oh, Nell, what if they hang him?"

"He will get a trial. Perhaps . . ."

"He's guilty, Nell. He did kill that man. He told me it was self-defense, but you know as well as I do that no jury is going to believe him."

Nell Howard nodded. Ryder Fallon was a half-breed. No jury this side of the Missouri was likely to find him innocent when they learned he had killed a white man.

It was almost an hour later when William Howard burst into the kitchen. "Let's go, Jenny," he cried, waving a handful of greenbacks.

"You got it!" she exclaimed.

Howard grinned. "The folks in this town think a lot of you and that man of yours. They came up with over two hundred dollars."

Ryder sat with his back against a tree, his hands and feet tightly bound, his thoughts dismal. Though he knew he'd been right to insist that Jenny stay behind, he couldn't help wishing she was here with him now. At the moment, she was the only constant in a world suddenly turned upside down.

Jenny . . . The last few months in the valley had been the happiest, most rewarding, of his life. She had taken a crude cabin and made it a home. She had taught him to laugh again, to have hope. She'd even taught him to dance. And late at night, alone in the privacy of their bed, she cocooned him in a world of love.

And now he might never see her again.

He wasn't fool enough to think he'd get a fair trial, if he got a trial at all. If he was lucky, they'd hang him. While he wasn't crazy about the idea of swinging from a rope, it beat spending the rest of his life behind bars.

He swore softly as he stared into the flames of the campfire. Why now? he thought bitterly. For the first time in years, he had roots, a home, a woman who loved him. A woman he loved. Doing time in prison would never have been a picnic, but now, knowing what he'd left behind, what his life could have been like, prison would be sheer hell.

And Jenny . . . what kind of life would she have if he was sent to prison? She was too young to spend the rest of her life waiting for a man she might never see again. Too young to be a widow . . . but she wouldn't remain a widow for long.

The thought of Jenny in the arms of another man cut through him like cold steel.

He slid a glance at the two men seated beside the fire. They didn't act like any bounty hunters he'd ever known. They'd treated him decently enough so far, and he no longer feared that they'd gun him down in cold blood somewhere on the trail; they were determined to take him in and claim the reward. And he had nothing to offer them to make them change their minds.

Damn. His captors would sleep in shifts, leaving him no chance to escape.

Resting his head against the tree, Fallon closed his eyes. He could almost hear the prison doors slamming shut behind him.

It was near dawn when Jenny and William Howard caught up with the bounty hunters.

Howard drew rein a good distance from where Jed and Vince had bedded down for the night.

"Hello, the camp," he hollered.

Jed jumped to his feet and drew his gun. "Who's there?"

"William Howard, from Twin Rivers."

"Come on in."

The two bounty hunters were standing well apart when Jenny and Will Howard rode up. Ryder sat cross-legged against a cottonwood tree, his hands and feet bound.

He straightened when he saw Jenny, a frown creasing his brow, a question in his eyes.

The bounty hunters weren't taking any chances, Jenny mused as she offered her husband a smile of encouragement. No chances at all. Jed's Winchester was leveled at William Howard's broad chest. Vince's rifle was aimed at Ryder's head. She let her gaze run over Ryder lovingly, assuring herself that he was all right.

"I hope you ain't thinkin' of doin' somethin' stupid, like tryin' to take our prisoner," Jed remarked.

"No," Will Howard said quickly. "We came to make a deal."

Vince took a step forward, his finger curling around the trigger. "What kind of deal?"

"We've got close to three hundred dollars here," Will said, holding out a brown paper sack. "More than the reward offered for Fallon."

Jed frowned. "So?"

"We want to buy him back. You'll be money ahead, and you won't have to haul him all the way to El Paso."

Jed and Vince exchanged wary glances.

"Don't sound quite right," Jed remarked, scratching his ear.

Vince shrugged. "Sounds good to me. Let's take the money and ride."

Jed shook his head. "I don't know. Might give bounty hunters a bad name if we start makin' deals."

"Who the hell cares?" Vince exclaimed. "Two hundred bucks is two hundred bucks. What difference does it make who we get it from so long as we get it?"

Jed grunted softly. "None, I guess. Okay, mister, you got a deal. I'll take the money. Vince, you untie the breed."

"Wait a minute," Howard said. "We want your word that you won't be coming back here to try and collect again."

"You'd take our word?" Vince asked in amazement.

Will Howard nodded.

"Well, I'll be damned," Vince muttered. Drawing his knife, he cut Ryder's hands and feet free. "You're a lucky man, Fallon."

Ryder nodded. "I never knew how lucky until now." Rising, he rubbed his chafed wrists. "Okay if I go?"

"Reckon so," Jed replied as he stuffed the counted greenbacks into his saddlebag. He grinned at Will Howard. "Nice doing business with y'all."

Fallon stared after Jed and Vince as they rode north, unable to believe they were letting him go.

"Ryder!" Jenny slid from the back of her horse and threw herself into her husband's arms. "Oh, Ryder!"

He hugged her close, his face pressed to the top of her head. The scent of her hair filled his nostrils. He drew her closer, pressing her against him, soaking up her nearness, her warmth.

"How?" he asked at last. "Where'd you get that money?"

"From our neighbors," Jenny answered. She rained kisses over his face. "Isn't it wonderful?"

"Wonderful," Fallon agreed, though *wonderful* hardly seemed a word strong enough to convey what he was feeling.

"Come on," Jenny said, beaming up at him. "Let's go home."

Chapter Twenty-Nine

As the days grew shorter and the nights longer, there were fewer chores to be done, at least outside. During inclement weather, Ryder taught Jenny how to play poker and blackjack. She was a quick study, and Ryder marveled at her keen mind and nimble fingers.

"You'd have made a terrific dealer," he mused one blustery afternoon. "With that innocent face and those hands, you'd have made a fortune."

"Maybe I'll open a saloon here in the valley," Jenny replied with a cocky grin. "We'll wager eggs instead of gold."

It had been raining for a week. Bored with just playing cards, Fallon had spent the time teaching Jenny the ancient art of cheating at poker.

He showed her how to palm an ace, how to stack a deck, how to mark cards.

As usual, she learned quickly.

"Are you sure you haven't done this before?" he asked as she adroitly shuffled the deck.

If he hadn't been watching her so closely, he never would have noticed that she was cheating. An amateur would be hard-pressed to catch her at it.

"I'm sure," Jenny answered, her face a perfect blank as she studied her cards.

Fallon picked up his hand. A pair of fours, a pair of tens, and a deuce.

"I'll take one," he said, tossing the deuce on the table.

She dealt him a card. "And I'll take two."

Ryder picked up his fifth card. It was another four, giving him a full house.

"Okay," he said. "Let's see what you've got."

One by one, Jenny laid her cards on the table. She had four aces, and the queen of hearts.

"Pretty slick," Fallon allowed. "Well, it's nice to know that if next year's crops fail, we can always head for Denver and make a killing at one of the poker tables."

"I'm not that good, and you know it," Jenny retorted. "You saw every move I made."

"But I was expecting it."

"My mother would be turning over in her grave if she knew I was learning how to be a card cheat," Jenny muttered. "She detested gambling."

"You've never mentioned her before."

"My parents died a few months before I met Hank. My mother was a gentle woman, delicate, soft-spoken. Serene is the word that comes to mind when I think of her."

"And your father?"

"He was a hard man, cold sometimes, but never cruel. I think you would have liked him." Jenny cocked her head to one side. "And he would have liked you."

"Are you saying I'm hard and cold?"

"No, no," Jenny protested quickly. "But my father had the same inner core of strength that you do. He always knew who he was, and what he was about. I always knew I could rely on him, that he'd be there when I needed him. And he was, until the day he died."

"Why did you marry Hank?"

"He needed me. But that's not the only reason. We were friends. Good friends. I could tell Hank anything, and he'd understand. And he loved me, as much as he could."

Fallon felt a twinge of jealousy. "Did you love him?"

"I thought I did. I know now it wasn't love. I was just lonely, and so was he. We sort of drifted together." Jenny gazed out the window. "If it wasn't for me, he'd still be alive. And Charlie, too."

"Jenny, don't."

"It's true."

"If anyone's at fault, it's me," Ryder retorted. "I've brought you nothing but trouble."

He picked up the cards, shuffled them and turned up the top card. It was the ace of spades.

He shuffled the cards again, and again turned up the ace.

"If it wasn't for me, you'd still be in Kayitah's camp," he said gruffly. "You'd have your son. And Hank would still be alive."

"No!" She whirled around to face him. "Don't say that. You're the best thing that's ever happened to me."

"Am I?"

"Yes." She winced at the pain reflected in his eyes. "Ryder, please don't think I'm blaming you."

"Maybe you should."

"I love you. I love our life together. I can't help missing my baby. I can't help feeling guilty for Hank's death. But I wasn't blaming you."

"Maybe I'm blaming myself," he muttered.

Rising, he tossed the cards onto the table, grabbed his coat and left the house.

"Ryder!" She called his name again, but he was gone.

Jenny stared at the door, wondering if she should go after him.

After a moment of indecision, she reached for her coat, then doubled over, her arms wrapped around her abdomen, as a sharp pain knifed through her.

"Ryder . . ."

She gasped his name as she sank to the floor. She shook her head in dismay as a warm stickiness trickled down her thighs. Blood . . .

Fear and a sudden blackness engulfed her. She murmured Ryder's name once more and then there was only darkness . . .

She woke to the sound of someone calling her name. Gradually, she realized it was Ryder's voice and she wondered why he sounded so frantic, so sad. It was an effort to open her eyes, and when she did so, she saw that she was in bed, and that Ryder was kneeling beside her, clutching her hand in his.

"Ryder, what's wrong?"

"Jenny, thank God."

"Why am I in bed?" She blinked at him several times, puzzled by the sorrowful expression in his eyes, and then, in a rush, it all came back to her. "I . . . what happened?"

"Jenny, why didn't you tell me you were pregnant?"

"Pregnant? Me?"

She shook her head. Could she have been pregnant without knowing it? She thought back to her first pregnancy. She'd had no symptoms then either, and her menses had always been irregular.

"Are you sure?"

"Laura Barnes has had some experience as a midwife."

Jenny let out a deep sigh. She couldn't have been more than a couple of weeks along; she hadn't even suspected she might be with child, yet she felt her loss deeply. Ryder's baby, and she'd lost it. Had it been a boy or a girl? Was she never to have a child to love?

Tears welled in her eyes and coursed down her cheeks, falling faster and faster until she was sobbing in Fallon's arms, her head buried against his shoulder.

"It's all right, Jenny girl," he murmured, lightly stroking her hair. "It's all right." He hugged her close, his lips brushing her cheek. "It's all right."

He held Jenny until she fell asleep; then, covering her with a blanket, he left the room and quietly closed the door.

Outside, he stared up at the snow-laden clouds, his heart heavy as he thought of Jenny's grief and pain. And then, slowly, he raised his arms toward heaven. He was not normally a praying man, but standing there in the stillness of a dark winter night, he lifted his voice in supplication, fervently beseeching Usen to heal the hurt in Jenny's heart and bless them with a healthy child.

Jenny recovered quickly, physically if not emotionally. Fallon was patient with her moods. He knew he could never fully understand how she felt, but he remembered all too clearly the loss of Nahdaste's child, and he wondered if he would ever sire a child that lived.

It was difficult trying to imagine himself as a father. He'd never had much to do with kids, never knew how deeply he had wanted a child until he buried his tiny stillborn daughter beside her mother.

As the weeks passed by, Ryder began to wonder if perhaps Jenny was grieving more than necessary for a child that she hadn't been aware she was carrying, and then he realized she wasn't grieving only for the child she'd miscarried, but for her firstborn son, who was also forever out of her reach.

With the coming of spring, Jenny's spirits brightened a little. There were flowers on the hillsides. Baby chicks paraded after their mothers, calves frolicked in the pasture.

A fit of spring cleaning had her turning the house inside out, shaking out the rugs, washing the windows, scrubbing the floors. It seemed to Ryder that she dusted, washed, waxed, polished or refurbished everything in sight.

She went readily into his arms at night, smiled at him with the coming of dawn, and yet he sensed the change in her, as if she were holding back a part of herself, a part she was afraid to give.

Now, as he held her close in the dark of a quiet night, he knew she was dying inside, a little each day. Some women could have a child, lose it, grieve, and put it behind them. But not his Jenny girl. She was soul sick, heartsick, and he couldn't bear to see the sorrow in her eyes any longer.

In the morning, he'd tell her he was going to El Paso to see about some cattle. Instead, he would go scout Kayitah's camp. Alone, he might be able to get in undetected, grab the boy, and get out with a whole skin. If not . . . he shrugged. What would happen if he failed didn't bear thinking about.

Jenny stared at him across the table, a frown puckering her forehead. "El Paso? Can't I go with you?"

"Not this time. The Pattersons will look after you while I'm gone."

"But . . ."

"I didn't break my back planting all those crops to have them die of neglect," Ryder said, tugging gently on a lock of her hair. "You need to stay here and look after things."

Jenny nodded, unconvinced. While she had thrown herself into a fit of housecleaning, Ryder had been working from dawn until dark, preparing the land, planting corn and beans and peas in neat rows, furrow after furrow.

"How long will you be gone?" she asked.

"I don't know. As long as it takes. Can I bring you anything?"

"Just bring yourself back to me as soon as possible."

"I will. Think you could pour me another cup of coffee before I go, and maybe throw some grub in a sack?"

She nodded, her mind whirling. It was all so sudden. What would she do here all alone? He'd be gone several weeks at the least, a couple of months at the most.

She glanced around the kitchen, thinking how empty the house would be without him.

"Ryder, I . . ." She bit back the words. She didn't want to be a nagging wife, or one who complained, but oh, how she was going to miss him.

"I know," he said, and taking her in his arms, he hugged her close, knowing that if things went wrong, he'd never see her again. "I'll bring you back a surprise," he promised. "Come on, walk me out."

The sight of his horse waiting at the hitching post brought a quick sheen of tears to her eyes. He was going, really going.

"Ryder . . ." She pressed her lips together, refusing to cry. "Have a safe trip."

He cupped her chin in his hand and kissed her. "Take care," he admonished.

For a moment, he gazed into her eyes, and then he smiled at her.

"Be well, Jenny girl," he said, and swung into the saddle, afraid to linger for fear he'd change his mind about going.

With a final wave, he turned the buckskin away from the house and rode out of the yard.

Chapter Thirty

Jenny was sitting outside enjoying the fading rays of the sun when Nell Howard paused to wish her a good evening.

The Indian woman had always been friendly, stopping to pass the time of day whenever she saw Jenny. She was a pretty woman, almost regal in bearing with serene black eyes and a ready smile. Her skin was the color of burnished copper, smooth and unlined save for the tiny laugh lines around her eyes.

"How are you, Nell?" Jenny asked. Rising, she walked down the road.

"I am well, Jenny. How are you?"

"Fine, thanks. A little lonely."

Nell Howard frowned. "Lonely? Where is Fallon?"

"He left for El Paso yesterday afternoon.

He . . ." Jenny's voice trailed off. "What is it, Nell?" she asked, seeing the look of dismay in the older woman's eyes. "What's wrong?"

Nell Howard shook her head. "I . . ."

"What?" A sudden nameless fear took hold of Jenny. "What is it? Tell me!"

"I had a dream last night."

A cold hand coiled around Jenny's heart. Nell Howard had been a medicine woman among her own people, one given to dreams and visions. It was a power that had not left her.

"What did you dream?"

"I saw a man riding a buckskin horse. He rode into a hostile village and took a small child."

The hand around Jenny's heart grew colder, tighter. Fallon rode a buckskin horse. "What else did you see?"

"Blood. And death."

Jenny swallowed hard, forcing the words from her throat. "Ryder's death?"

"I could not be certain, for the dream turned dark." Nell placed her hand on Jenny's arm. "You were there, and two children were with you. One born. One waiting."

Jenny folded her arms over her stomach, her heart pounding. How did Nell know about Cosito? How did she know that Jenny suspected she might be pregnant again?

"I've got to go after him," Jenny said. "I've got to stop Ryder before it's too late."

"William will take you."

"Ask him to hurry, please."

"He is ready now."

Jenny took Nell's hands in hers and held them tight. "Thank you."

"Be careful, Jenny. Do not worry about your house, or your fields. I will look after them until you return."

Nell gazed deep into Jenny's eyes. "May *Ta ahpu* guide your path."

Jenny nodded, unable to speak past the lump in her throat. Blood and death . . . please, God, don't let me be too late.

Fallon's thoughts were tumultuous as he made his way toward Kayitah's camp. He was taking a big risk, one that could cost him his life. He knew it, and yet he couldn't turn back. He couldn't live with the heartache he read in Jenny's eyes any longer, couldn't live with his guilt. Once, Jenny had accused him of giving Kayitah her son to save his own life. And in a way, she had been right.

He shook his head, remembering the implacable expression on Kayitah's face as he had sighted down the shaft of his arrow—an arrow pointed at Jenny.

Give me my son, Kayitah had demanded softly, *or the woman dies now, and then you will die, slowly, cursing the mother who gave you life.*

And if I give you the child?

You and the woman are free to go. But I will peel the skin from your body an inch at a time if you ever return to the rancheria.

Ryder shivered. It had not been an idle threat, but a promise. Perhaps he could have done things differently. He could have offered to return Jenny and the child in exchange for his freedom, but letting Jenny go had never crossed his mind.

He swore softly as he urged his horse across a shallow stream and up a sandy bank. He'd given Jenny's son to Kayitah, and now, by damn, he meant to get the boy back.

He put aside the thought of the fate that might be his if he failed to get the boy away from the Apache camp and thought instead of Jenny.

His Jenny, with hair like silk and a smile like sunshine. Jenny, who had melted the ice from his heart and filled it with love and understanding. Jenny, who loved him unconditionally, not caring that he was a half-breed, that he'd been a gunfighter. Jenny . . .

He closed his eyes and her image danced before him, bright as a summer day.

Doubts crowded his mind. What would she do if he didn't make it back? She'd never know what had happened to him but would spend the rest of her life thinking that he'd tired of her, after all, that he'd ridden out of her life because he'd been too big a coward to say goodbye.

Perhaps he should have told her where he was going, he mused, but even as the thought crossed his mind, he knew it would have been a mistake. She would have insisted on coming along, and he had enough to worry about without having to look after her, too. And if she'd been with him, and he failed, she would have been Kayitah's prisoner again . . . perhaps she wouldn't have minded that so much, though, he thought. At least she'd be with her son again.

Damn!

Opening his eyes, he shook her image from his mind. He'd made his choice, and it was too late to turn back now, too late to worry about what he might have done, what he should have done. If he succeeded, the light would shine in Jenny's eyes once again.

If he failed . . .

His mouth went dry.

If he failed, he wouldn't have to worry about making any more decisions.

Chapter Thirty-One

Jenny felt an increasing sense of urgency as they rode across the trackless desert toward the Apache camp. Ryder was out there, alone. She remembered all too clearly the day Ryder had given her son to Kayitah, and Kayitah's warning.

She berated herself again and again as the miles passed. Why had she let Ryder see her unhappiness? Why hadn't she tried harder to accept the fact that Cosito was gone? Why hadn't she tried harder to make Ryder happy, to concentrate on the good life she had instead of lamenting the loss of her son? She knew Kayitah would take good care of the boy, that he would be loved. The Apache doted on their children, never striking them, rarely speaking any but the kindest words. Children were a gift from Usen, meant to be cherished, protected.

Now, because of her, Ryder might be killed.

Blood. And death.

Like mist rising from the prairie, Nell Howard's words floated through Jenny's mind.

"How much longer, William?" she asked anxiously.

"Another day. The Apache make their camp in the next valley at this time of the year."

So close, Jenny thought. All this time, Cosito had been nearby.

As they bedded down for the night, she wondered if her son would remember her. She hadn't seen him for almost six months, she thought sadly. Not a long time, by any means, unless you were a baby less than a year old.

But as much as she yearned for her son, her last thoughts before sleep were for Ryder. *Please, God, keep him safe for me . . .*

Under cover of darkness, Fallon padded silently toward the entrance of the village, his moccasined feet making no sound as he crept slowly across the soft, damp ground.

Heart pounding in his ears, he made his way toward the sentry he knew was guarding the entrance of the rancheria. Sweat beaded across his brow as he neared the warrior. One outcry, and it would all be over. But not quickly. He would find no reprieve this time, no mercy. Kayitah would skin him alive.

Damn. Crouched in the shadow of the ravine,

he held his breath, waiting for just the right moment.

Time seemed to stand still. He heard the soughing of the wind as it sighed down the valley, the cautious chirp of a cricket. The muffled sound of footsteps coming his way.

Eyes narrowed, Fallon waited for the sentry to come within reach, waited until instinct took over. He sprang forward, one arm wrapping around the warrior's throat, shutting off the man's startled cry. Using his gun butt, he rendered the warrior unconscious, quickly bound his hands and feet.

Releasing his pent-up breath, he walked toward the village, his head high and his shoulders back, as if he belonged there.

A soft word, spoken in guttural Apache, quieted the dogs. The horses picketed in front of the lodges stirred at his passing, their nostrils quivering as they sniffed his scent.

His heart was pounding loudly in his ears as he made his way toward Kayitah's lodge. Stealthily, he lifted the lodge flap and slipped inside. Holding his breath, he listened to Kayitah's soft snoring.

As his eyes adjusted to the darkness, he saw Cosito sleeping on a small pallet beside Alope.

Two long strides carried him to the child's side. Gently, he placed his hand over the boy's mouth and picked him up, but the boy didn't awaken.

Fallon's mouth was desert dry as he turned and made his way out of the lodge. Slipping behind Kayitah's tipi, he blended into the shadows.

He was almost to the entrance when the moon broke through the clouds. Fallon swore softly as he slid a wary glance at the softly rolling hills that surrounded the valley. There were a couple of sentries up there somewhere, and he prayed that anyone who saw him would think he was on his way to relieve the warrior at the entrance to the rancheria.

Only a few yards to go, he thought, fighting the urge to run. Only a few more yards.

He blew out a deep breath of relief as he reached the cover of the narrow ravine, praying that his luck would hold just a few minutes longer.

The sentry was where he had left him. Shifting the boy to his shoulder, Fallon swung into the saddle and clucked softly to the horse.

So far so good, he thought, but he knew he wouldn't breathe easy until he'd left the rancheria far behind, until he'd placed Jenny's son in her arms.

Jenny rubbed her eyes, unable to believe what she was seeing. Could it be? Could it really be Fallon riding toward her? And Cosito . . .

She heard William Howard mutter, "I'll be damned" as she drummed her heels into her horse's flanks.

"Ryder!" She cried his name as she drew rein beside him. "Cosito! Oh, thank God!"

Ryder felt as if his heart might burst as he

handed the boy to Jenny, saw the tears of joy sparkle in her eyes as she cradled her son to her breast.

"Cosito," she exclaimed. "How you've grown! Do you remember me?"

The boy gazed up at her, his eyes wide and black, his expression pensive. When he smiled, tears cascaded down Jenny's cheeks.

"He does remember me. Oh, Ryder, how can I ever thank you?"

"You just did, Jenny girl," he murmured, and knew it had been worth the risk to put that glow back in Jenny's eyes.

"I hate to break this up," William Howard said, "but I think we'd best be headin' for home."

"You'll get no argument from me," Fallon said. "Let's go."

They all heard it at the same time, the low thunder of approaching hoofbeats.

"Kayitah," Ryder muttered. "Damn."

"Ryder . . ."

Jenny stared at him, her eyes afraid, her arms tightening instinctively around her son.

"William, take Jenny and ride like hell. I'll try and hold 'em off."

"You sure?" Howard asked.

"I'm sure. Go. There's no time to argue."

"Ryder, no!"

"Get her out of here, now!"

With a nod, William Howard grabbed the reins of Jenny's horse and lit out for the cover of a stand of timber a few yards away.

Ryder watched them out of sight; then, drawing his rifle, he turned to face the oncoming horsemen.

There were a dozen of them, armed and painted for war, and Kayitah rode in the lead.

With the Cheyenne war cry on his lips, Fallon sank his heels into the buckskin's flanks and the horse bolted, lining out in a dead run, leading the Indians away from Jenny.

He bent low over the buckskin's neck, urging the horse to greater speed, knowing that every mile he drew the Apache away gave Jenny and Howard that much more of a chance to get away.

The war cries of the Apache reached out to him, winding around him like an invisible web, making the short hairs rise along the back of his neck, sending chills down his spine.

You will die, slowly, cursing the mother who gave you life . . . I will peel the skin from your body an inch at a time . . .

Kayitah's words echoed like a death knell in the back of Fallon's mind.

He risked a glance over his shoulder. Kayitah, mounted on a big piebald stallion, was rapidly closing in on him.

Fallon swore under his breath as an arrow hissed past his ear. Damn! He heard the rolling report of a gunshot, felt the buckskin jerk beneath him, and then the horse was going down.

Ryder rolled clear of the buckskin and scrambled to his feet, but before he could turn and fire, he felt the hot sting of lead slam into his side, knocking him off his feet. And then Kayitah was there, glaring down at him over the barrel of a Winchester.

Fallon inhaled deeply, let it out in a long slow sigh of resignation, and dropped his rifle.

Moments later, he was surrounded by a dozen Apaches.

"My son," Kayitah said. "Where is he?"

"I don't know."

"This is not a time for lies, white man, but a time for truth."

Ryder pressed his hand over the bleeding wound in his side and slowly shook his head. "I don't know where he is."

With effortless grace, Kayitah slid from the back of his horse.

"I ask you one last time, Kladetahe. Where is my son?"

"And I tell you one last time. I don't know."

Hatred burned bright in the Apache chief's eyes as he smashed the butt of his rifle into Fallon's wounded side.

A hoarse cry of agony erupted from Ryder's throat as he sank to his knees, choking back the bitter bile that rose in his throat. Immersed in a red haze of pain, he was hardly aware of being spread-eagled on the ground, his hands and feet secured to war lances sunk deep in the earth.

Voices hummed around him. He felt the prick of a knife as someone cut away his clothing. And then a sharp stinging pain as Kayitah's blade lifted a small square of skin from his chest.

I will peel the skin from your body an inch at a time . . .

He began to shiver spasmodically as pain and loss of blood and a horrible creeping fear settled over him.

"Where is my son, white man?"

Fallon shook his head. He stared at Kayitah for a long moment, and then he looked past the chief, staring into the distance, trying to lose himself within himself, to close his mind to the pain, to the fear that threatened to strip him of his pride, his manhood.

Every muscle in his body grew taut as Kayitah's blade moved over his chest a second time. He had once seen what was left of a man who had been skinned alive. It had not been a pretty sight.

Fallon choked back the bile that rose in his throat as he imagined Kayitah stripping away every inch of flesh, then leaving him there, prey to the wolves and the vultures, the ants . . .

Trembling convulsively, he focused his thoughts on Jenny, on the look of exquisite joy in her eyes as she held her son to her breast.

He closed his eyes, remembering the lazy summer nights when he'd held her in his arms, feeling the warm silk of her hair against his chest, the eager touch of her hands moving over him, the sound of her voice . . .

Her voice . . .

He fought his way through the dark mist that hovered around him, drawn from the brink of unconsciousness by the sound of her voice.

It took him a moment to understand her words.

"Take the child," Jenny said, her voice thick with tears. "Take me. But please, please, spare his life."

With an effort, Ryder focused his gaze on her face. "Jenny, no . . ."

"I will have it all," Kayitah said, his voice harsh. "And the traitor's life, as well."

"No, please." Tears streaming down her face, Jenny took Kayitah's hand in hers. "Please don't hurt him any more. I'll do whatever you ask. Please, just let him go. He only took Cosito because of me, because he knew how I yearned for my son. Please, Kayitah, you must know how I feel. Have pity. For once in your life, have pity and let Kladetahe go!"

"He must love you very much," the chief mused.

"Yes."

"And you love him?"

"Yes."

"Enough to give up your son forever?"

Jenny gazed into her son's face. Could she give him up forever? Never see him again? She stroked Cosito's cheek as she glanced down at Ryder. He was watching her, his deep blue eyes filled with understanding, and she knew that, even if she chose to let him die, he would understand and forgive.

"Yes, even if I have to give him up forever," she said in answer to Kayitah's question. And giving her son a kiss on the forehead, she handed Cosito to his father.

Cosito snuggled comfortably, familiarly, in his father's arms, his inquisitive fingers reaching up to play in his father's long hair, a look of contentment on his face. It was easy to see that Kayitah and the boy were close.

As soon as Cosito had seen Kayitah ride up, he had cried for his father, his arms reaching out to him, and she had known at that moment that her son belonged with his father, that as much as she loved the boy, he would be happier living with his father's people.

Is it hard, being a half-breed? That was the question she had asked Ryder on the day of Cosito's birth. He hadn't wanted to answer her. *It's bad, isn't it?* she'd said, wanting to know, and when he'd finally said, *It's hard,* his curt response had spoken volumes.

"And would you stay with me, of your own free will, if I asked it of you?" Kayitah asked, his dark eyes probing hers.

Kayitah's voice drew her back to the present. "Yes, if you'll just let Kladetahe go."

Kayitah grunted softly. "What is to keep me from killing him and taking both you and my son back to rancheria?"

"Nothing," Jenny admitted, fighting down the panic rising in her breast. "Nothing but your honor."

A slow smile tugged at the corners of Kayitah's mouth. "Honor," he mused. "Whose honor? Apache honor, or the white man's honor?"

"There should be no difference."

"But there is. The word of the white man cannot be trusted. He makes his mark upon treaty papers and breaks his word before the ink is dry. He steals our land. He kills our women and children."

Kayitah stared down at Kladetahe. The half-breed was breathing shallowly, obviously in pain, yet he seemed oblivious to everything but the woman.

Jealousy edged its way into Kayitah's heart. "The word of the white man cannot be trusted," he said again, "but my word is my life, and I swore to peel the skin from Kladetahe's body if he ever returned to the rancheria."

"But this is not the rancheria," Jenny said.

Kayitah laughed softly. Even if he killed Kladetahe, even if he took Jenny back to the rancheria, she would never belong to him the way she belonged to his rival.

"Well met, Golden Dove. Kladetahe is yours. If he is wise, he will not let his shadow fall near mine again."

"Thank you," Jenny whispered fervently.

She blinked back her tears as four of the warriors cut Fallon's hands and feet free. Jerking their lances out of the dirt, they vaulted onto the backs of their horses and rode away.

Silent tears tracked Jenny's cheeks as she watched Kayitah place Cosito on the back of his horse, then swing up behind the boy, one arm circling Cosito's waist.

"Goodbye, Cosito," she whispered.

As if he'd heard and understood, Cosito scrambled to his feet and waved at her from over his father's shoulder.

"Jenny."

Wiping the tears from her eyes, she knelt beside Ryder, her hands moving over him. There were four bloody patches on his chest, but they seemed minor compared to the bullet wound in his side. She breathed a silent prayer as she examined the wound, grateful the bullet had passed cleanly through his side.

Tearing the bottom ruffle from her petticoat, she ripped it into three pieces. Moving quickly, she folded two strips into thick pads which she placed over the wounds, front and back. Then, using the remaining length of cloth, she wrapped it tightly around Ryder's midsection to hold the bandages in place.

A tight smile tugged at the corners of Fallon's mouth. "Seems like . . . you did this . . . once before."

"Don't talk, Ryder. Just rest. You'll be all right."

With a low groan, he reached for her hand. "Will you?"

"Yes."

Her voice was strong, determined, but he saw the lingering hurt in her eyes.

Jenny studied the raw wounds on Ryder's chest. There wasn't much blood, and she was wondering whether to try to bandage them or leave them exposed to the air when Ryder caught her hand in his.

"Leave them be, Jenny."

"Are you sure?"

"I'm sure. Stop fussing over me. I'll be all right."

She relented, but reluctantly.

"Where's Howard?"

"Right here," Will said, stepping from the saddle. "How're you feeling?"

"How do you think?"

Howard chuckled. "I suppose you've been better."

Fallon nodded. "And worse."

"Think you can travel?"

"Yeah." Gritting his teeth against the pain, Ryder sat up. "Give me a hand, Will."

"Sure." Howard took hold of Fallon's right forearm. "This is gonna hurt some."

"It already hurts," Ryder muttered. He grunted softly as Will pulled him to his feet.

"Ryder . . . ?"

"I'll be all right, Jenny girl," he said. "Just give me a minute to catch my breath."

"Maybe you should rest awhile."

"No."

"You're afraid Kayitah will change his mind and come back, aren't you?"

"I don't think he'd break his word," Fallon replied slowly. "But I'd rather not be around if he does." He glanced over his shoulder at Will Howard. "I think I'll need a little help mounting up."

Jenny watched anxiously as Ryder put his foot into the stirrup. He muttered a vile oath, his face turning fishbelly white, as Will Howard boosted him into the saddle.

Fearing he might faint, she scrambled up behind him, her arms sliding around his waist. "Are you all right?"

He grunted softly as he covered her arms with one of his own. "Let's go home."

Chapter Thirty-Two

Jenny hovered over him for the next week, insisting he stay in bed. No matter how often he assured her that he was fine, she remained adamant, feeding him even when he insisted he wasn't so damn weak he couldn't hold a spoon. Worst of all, she wouldn't even let him out of bed to relieve himself.

And Wyatt agreed with her.

"You've lost a lot of blood," the old sawbones had said when Ryder complained. "Won't hurt you to take it easy for a week or so."

It seemed as if the whole valley came by to see how he was doing and to wish him well. It was damned disconcerting, lying there in bed while women hovered over him, bringing him cakes and pies, exclaiming over what a brave thing he'd done.

"Dammit, Jenny, does the whole valley have to know our business?"

She shrugged. "I didn't mean to tell anyone. But Mrs. Johnson overheard Will asking me how you were, and one thing led to another, and the next thing you knew, it just seemed easier to tell her the whole story."

Jenny bent to examine the wound in his side, pleased to see that it was healing nicely. "Everyone's been so kind."

Ryder took her hand in his. "No regrets, Jenny girl?"

"No."

"You're sure?"

"I'm sure. Cosito belongs with his father. I know that now."

"Jenny . . ."

She heard it all in his voice, his uncertainty, his doubts. She knew he was afraid she would come to hate him, that one day she'd be sorry she'd given Cosito back to Kayitah.

She reassured him in the only way she knew how. "I'm pregnant, Ryder."

"Are you sure?"

"Yes."

His gaze swept over her slender figure, then settled on her face once again.

"How do you feel? Is everything all right?"

"I'm fine."

She was carrying his child. Tenderly, he cupped her face in his hands and kissed her.

Chapter Thirty-Three

Fallon laid his hammer aside and stood up, flexing his tired muscles. Another two dozen shingles and the roof on the baby's room would be just about finished.

From his lofty perch, he commanded a view of the entire valley, but he had eyes only for his own domain: the crops growing in neat rows, the horses standing head to tail in the corral alongside the house, the calf bawling in the pen behind the cabin, the chickens scratching for grubs near the front door.

Twenty-five head of prime white-faced cattle grazed on the verdant hills behind the house.

Fallon removed his hat and wiped the sweat from his brow. Things had been tight at first, but he'd scraped up a little cash and ridden to Canyon Springs. There, in an all-night poker game, he had parlayed a few dollars into a sizable bankroll.

They had put the money to good use, buying cattle and seed, clothing, a plow, a new hat for Jenny because he wanted to buy her something pretty and impractical.

They had accomplished a great deal in the few short months since he'd gone after Cosito, yet nothing had given him as much pleasure or satisfaction as carving the cradle that would hold their child.

The corners of Fallon's mouth turned up in a wry grin. Somehow, he could not imagine himself as a father. Occasionally, as now, he wondered if it was wise for them to have a child. Looking back over his life, he was suddenly afraid that they had made a terrible mistake, and that their son or daughter would suffer for it. Life as a mixed blood was never easy.

Unwilling to spoil Jenny's happiness, he kept his misgivings to himself, and as the golden summer days passed into fall, and his love for Jenny grew and deepened, he laid his doubts aside, determined not to let what might happen in the future mar the beauty of the present.

Standing there, he lifted his face toward heaven and uttered a silent prayer, beseeching Usen to bless Jenny with a healthy baby and an easy delivery.

He was still amazed that she'd been willing to give up her son to save his miserable hide, but she'd done it, and he knew he'd never be able to repay her for that, not if he lived to be a hundred.

Most amazing of all was the fact that she seemed to be truly at peace. Sometimes she asked him about his childhood with the Indians, and he knew she was thinking of Cosito, picturing him doing the things that he had done. But there were no tears.

She spent a good deal of time with Nell Howard, making tiny baby clothes and quilts, diapers and gowns.

"Please, God, please let this baby be all right. She wants it so bad. And deserves it so much."

He heard the front door open and, glancing over the edge of the roof, saw Jenny standing in the yard, her shopping basket over her arm.

Shading her eyes with her hand, she looked up at him and smiled.

"I'm going to the trading post for some salt and sugar," she called. "Can I bring you anything?"

"Yeah," he said with a grin. "How about a cold beer and a skinny woman?"

Jenny made a face at him, then turned and flounced down the path that led to the gate. Skinny woman, indeed, she mused, and then smiled because she knew he was only teasing, and that he would love her if she weighed three hundred pounds!

Fallon spent a pleasant moment watching Jenny's backside. She seemed to grow more beautiful with each passing day. Sometimes in the evening as he sat watching her mend one of his shirts, his heart ached with loving her.

A movement on the outskirts of the valley drew his attention and he frowned as he shook off a vague sense of foreboding.

Four riders, he judged by the cloud of dust they raised on the narrow trail. Settling his hat on his head, he watched their progress into the valley.

As they drew nearer, he saw they were Comanches. And they had a prisoner. Blond hair, long and unkempt, identified the captive as a white man. His hands were bound behind his back; a rope circled his neck like a leash. Head hanging, shoulders sagging in defeat, the prisoner shuffled listlessly behind the lead warrior's horse.

Fallon swung down from the roof as the Indians drew rein outside the fence that separated their homestead from the road that led into Twin Rivers.

He raised his hand in the traditional sign of peace. "Welcome, brothers," he said in the Comanche tongue. "You are far from home."

The lead warrior nodded as he raised his right hand, returning Fallon's gesture of peace.

"Come, step down," Fallon invited.

"I am Isawura," the warrior said as he dismounted. "And these are Kebakowe, Isananaka and Tabe Kwine."

Fallon nodded to each man in turn. "Welcome. Will you stay and eat with us? My woman will be back soon to prepare supper."

The warriors conferred briefly. "We will stay," Isawura announced, and tethered his spotted pony to the fence post.

Isawura gave a tug on the rope around the captive's neck and the man stumbled forward.

Ryder frowned thoughtfully. There was something disturbingly familiar about the prisoner.

Feeling Fallon's gaze, the captive lifted his head. Recognition flickered in the depths of his blue eyes. "You!" he gasped.

Ryder felt the muscles tighten in the back of his neck, felt his whole body grow tense as he stared into the ashen face of Jenny's husband.

Rage boiled up inside Fallon as he thought of all the pain, both mental and physical, that Hank Braedon had caused Jenny. He remembered how he'd found Jenny wandering aimlessly in the darkness the night after Hank had beaten her. There had been bruises on her arms, her left eye red and swollen, a souvenir of Braedon's fist. Fallon swore softly as he remembered Jenny's tears, how she had curled into his arms, needing him, trusting him.

Damn. Why wasn't the bastard dead?

Hank stared at Fallon, unable to believe his bad luck. When the Indians had turned down the valley, he had hoped to beg for help from one of the residents. But he'd find no mercy here, he thought bleakly. Fallon would be more likely to cut out his heart than help him.

Hank shook his head, trying to clear it. If Fallon was here, then Jenny must be here. Jenny . . . She'd always had a soft heart, taking in strays and caring for the weak and helpless. She had once cared for him. Maybe she still cared, a little, but even if she didn't, even if she hated him, she wouldn't let Fallon kill him. She might even be able to persuade the Indians to let him go.

For the first time in weeks, he felt a tiny surge of hope. If only he could see Jenny, talk to her, he might yet find a way out of this mess, he thought.

And then he looked into Ryder Fallon's cold blue eyes and knew he was a dead man.

Ryder jerked a thumb in Hank's direction. "Your prisoner," he said to Isawura. "Did you take him in battle?"

The warrior shook his head. "No. We took him in trade from the Kiowa. I am taking him home to my woman."

"He looks sick," Fallon remarked.

Isawura shrugged. "If he dies, it will be no loss."

"I couldn't agree more," Ryder muttered in English.

He led the warriors to a shady spot beside the cabin, bade them sit down and rest. Isawura tied his prisoner to a tree near the cabin before going to sit cross-legged with his traveling companions.

Fallon stared at Braedon, who sat with his back resting against the tree. For a moment, he imagined Hank hanging from one of the branches, his body swaying in the breeze, his face swollen and black.

Abruptly, he turned away and went into the house.

He was serving the warriors coffee when he heard Jenny call his name.

"Back here," he said, and walked toward the front of the house to meet her, wondering how to explain that Hank Braedon wasn't dead, and that their marriage was no longer valid.

Chapter Thirty-Four

Jenny was smiling as she rounded the corner of the house. "I couldn't find any skinny women," she said, "and the beer wasn't cold. Who do those horses belong to . . ."

Her voice trailed off when she saw the quartet of warriors sitting on the ground. "What's going on?"

"It's all right, Jenny," Ryder assured her, chiding himself because he couldn't bring himself to tell her about Hank. "How about rustling us up some chow? I promised them supper."

"Oh, you did, did you? Maybe I should make you fix it, then."

Ryder ruffled her hair affectionately. "Be a good wife, Jenny girl," he teased, "or I shall have to beat you to save face."

"Yes, my lord," Jenny replied saucily, and

dropped a proper curtsey before heading for the front door.

Fallon and the warriors passed the time in quiet conversation as they waited for supper. The Indians spoke of their growing concern over the increasing number of whites encroaching on their land, of great chiefs, of battles won and lost.

They were discussing the war talk spreading over the plains when Jenny appeared bearing a steaming platter of beef, potatoes, biscuits and gravy, and a pot of coffee.

The warriors grunted with pleasure as they helped themselves to the food, ignoring the silverware Jenny had provided in favor of their own knives.

Jenny was about to return to the house when she noticed the man tied to the tree. He looked quite pathetic sitting there, she thought sadly. His clothes were ragged and covered with filth, there were holes in his boots. A thin red line circled his neck, caused by the constant chafing of the coarse rope. He was so covered with mud and grime she couldn't see the color of his skin, but the color of his hair quickly identified him as a white man.

When it grew evident that no one was going to feed him, Jenny plucked a fat slice of meat from the platter, buttered two fluffy biscuits, and resolutely placed them on a plate.

Smiling timidly, she started toward the prisoner, wondering what she could say to put the man at ease, when Fallon placed a restraining hand on her arm.

"No, Jenny."

"But he's had nothing to eat," she protested.

"He's their prisoner. You mustn't interfere."

"Some water, then? Surely they wouldn't object to that?"

"Dammit, Jenny, stay out of it!"

"Don't listen to him, Jen," Hank croaked. "He'd like to see me dead."

Jenny gaped at the prisoner. "Hank?" It couldn't be. He was dead. Images of that awful night at the rancheria crowded her mind—the gunshots, the fear as they raced through the darkness, the hiss of unseen arrows. She remembered the hatred blazing in Kayitah's eyes, Hank's scream as one of those arrows found its mark, her last sight of him as he tumbled off the horse to be swallowed up by the night.

Hank. Time shifted backward and she recalled the day she had met Hank Braedon, the loneliness that had drawn them together, the sweet affection they had once shared, the slow deterioration of that affection, the recriminations . . .

Hank was alive.

He was her husband.

Ryder swore softly as recognition spread across Jenny's face, quickly followed by a variety of emotions ranging from mild affection to pity. He knew the exact moment when she realized that they'd been living a lie, that she was still Braedon's wife.

Before she could say or do anything else, he grabbed her by the arm, hustled her into the cabin and closed the door.

"Jenny, listen to me . . ."

"Ryder, you've got to do something. They'll kill him."

"Good riddance."

"How can you be so callous?" Jenny demanded, arms akimbo.

"Callous! After the way he treated you?" Ryder sucked in a deep breath and let it out in a long, slow sigh. "You don't have to worry. Isawura isn't gonna kill him."

"What then?"

"Isawura is taking Hank home, as a present for his wife."

"To be a slave, you mean?"

"Yes."

Jenny's green eyes were as turbulent as an angry sea. "How can you let that happen?" she demanded incredulously. "You, of all people! Have you forgotten Alope? Have you forgotten how you hated being her slave? How humiliating it was?"

"No," Fallon acknowledged quietly. "And I haven't forgotten how you looked after that bastard hit you, either."

"He didn't mean it, Ryder. He was hurt, and angry."

Fallon muttered a vile oath. How could she be so concerned about a man who had hit her hard enough to leave bruises on her arms, a man who had slapped her so hard she had carried the imprint of his hand for days?

"Please, Ryder," Jenny asked softly, "can't you do something?"

He couldn't ignore the pleading note in her voice, or the trust in her eyes, could not deny her anything that was in his power to give. And if she wanted Hank Braedon, he would get the bastard for her.

"I'll try, Jenny," he said heavily, "but I can't promise anything."

Outside, the warriors were getting ready to ride on. Hank stood forlornly behind Isawura's horse, expressing no interest in what was going on around him. He'd spent weeks as Kayitah's prisoner, living in abject misery, waiting for the Indians to kill him the way they'd killed Charlie.

To his regret, the Apaches hadn't killed him. He'd been ready for death. What he hadn't been ready for was the abuse, the constant mockery. Once it was discovered that he was less than a man, the women had belittled him constantly, the men had looked at him with pity. For a time, the Apaches had forced him to wear a dress, to sit with the women, to gather wood and water. It had been humiliating beyond belief or description. And when they finally tired of him, they had traded him to the Kiowa, where he'd fared little better. And then the Kiowa had traded him to the Comanche warrior known as Isawura.

He had felt a glimmer of hope when he saw Jenny, but Fallon had taken her inside and he hadn't seen her since. And what did it matter?

He had nothing to offer her. Nothing at all.

The sight of her, happy and swollen with new life, had pierced his heart like a knife. The jealousy he'd felt when he looked at Fallon, the envy, had been so strong it had been almost physical.

But it didn't matter, he thought, too tired and ill to care what happened to him. Nothing mattered. Charlie was dead. Jenny had found someone else. And in a few months, he'd be dead.

Fallon watched the warriors for a few moments; then, with a sigh of resignation, he approached Isawura.

Stopping beside the warrior, he patted the Indian's horse on the shoulder. Of the four men, Isawura had the poorest mount.

"It is a long ride to the land of the Comanche," Fallon commented. "I doubt this horse will make it."

Isawura nodded. He had started the journey on a sturdy mustang stallion, but the foolish beast had stepped into a prairie dog hole and broken its leg. The pinto had been stolen from a Mexican peasant. It was a sorry animal, but better than being afoot. No warrior worthy of the name walked when he could ride.

"I have a fine roan mare that runs like the wind," Fallon remarked.

Isawura's eyes gleamed like polished obsidian as he glanced with interest at the roan mare standing in the corral.

"Would you be willing to make a trade for the mare?" the warrior asked.

Fallon nodded. "I will give you the mare in exchange for the white man."

Isawura glanced at the prisoner, then at the roan.

"I will trade," the warrior said quickly, and thrust the prisoner's tether into Fallon's hand.

Minutes later, Isawura was mounted on the roan and the Comanches were riding out of the valley.

Fallon made no effort to conceal his disgust as he dropped the rope at Hank Braedon's feet. As far as he was concerned, Isawura had definitely gotten the better end of the deal.

Muttering an oath, Fallon turned on his heel and stalked into the cabin.

Jenny was waiting for him, a question lurking in the depths of her lovely green eyes.

"He's outside," Ryder said curtly, annoyed by Jenny's visible relief, and by the way she picked up her skirts and hurried outside to invite Hank in.

Fallon swore softly as Hank followed Jenny into the house. What a cozy threesome they made!

Jenny seemed oblivious to Fallon's mood as she ushered Hank into the bedroom, pulled off his boots, then bade him lie down and rest.

Fallon scowled irritably as she scurried about the kitchen, putting a pot of soup on the stove for supper, heating water for Hank to bathe in, filling the laundry tub so she could wash his clothes.

"I don't want him here," Ryder said, trying to

hold back his anger. "Feed him if you must, then tell him to get the hell out of my house."

"I can't ask him to leave," Jenny protested. "He's sick."

"I don't care if he's dying," Ryder retorted flatly. "Dammit, Jenny, it's all I can do to keep from tearing him apart with my bare hands."

"It will just be for a few days, just until he gets his strength back."

"No. Either he goes or I do."

"You can't mean that!" Jenny gasped. She shook her head incredulously, unable to believe he meant it.

"Jenny . . ."

Hank's voice, weak and uneven, sounded from the bedroom, calling for help.

Jenny stared at Ryder, her eyes pleading with him to understand.

A sense of bitter frustration swept over Ryder Fallon. "Go on, go to him," he said angrily, and turning on his heel, he walked out of the cabin.

Whistling for Jenny's horse, Fallon vaulted onto its bare back. Clear of the road, he urged the gelding into a hard gallop, closing his mind to everything but the surging power of the horse.

The sting of the wind in his face and the serenity of the rolling hills cooled his anger, and he reined the horse to an abrupt halt.

What the hell was he doing, anyway? He couldn't just ride off and leave Jenny alone with a sick man, not when her baby was due any day.

Damn, he had never hated a man as much as he hated Braedon. The man had married Jenny when he had no business marrying at all, had dared to strike her, not once but many times, for something that wasn't her fault. Just thinking of it, remembering the bruises on her arms, the imprint of Braedon's hands on Jenny's cheeks, filled him with a cold and fierce anger.

The man had hit her, and she felt sorry for him. It was beyond his understanding.

The moon was high in the sky when he rode into the yard. Jenny was a dark shadow beside the front door. He felt her gaze on his back as he dismounted and led the gelding into the corral.

"Ryder . . ."

"Do you still care for him, Jenny?"

"Of course not. But I do feel sorry for him."

"Sorry for him? Dammit, Jenny, you'd feel sorry for a snake!"

"Maybe," she admitted, "if he was sick and hungry and all alone in the world. He's had a bad time, Ryder."

Jenny laid her hand on Fallon's arm. Tears sparkled in her eyes as she sobbed, "Oh, Ryder, I was afraid you'd left me!"

With a sigh, Fallon gathered her into his arms and stroked her hair.

"I'll never leave you, Jenny girl," he promised softly. "Not as long as you want me around."

He sat up long after Jenny was asleep. In the dim light cast by the coals in the fireplace, he could see her lying on the sofa, her rounded belly rising and falling beneath the blankets. She was so beautiful, so damnably sweet, and he loved her so much.

In the bedroom, Hank moaned, tossing fitfully on their bed.

Fallon stared into the fireplace, annoyed by the deep resentment that Hank Braedon's presence aroused in him.

He scowled darkly as Hank cried out in his sleep. Though he hated like hell to admit it, Ryder supposed he was jealous of the time and attention Jenny expended in Hank's behalf. Yet the man was still her husband. Damn, the whole situation was ridiculous.

"Ryder?"

"I thought you were asleep, Jenny. Is anything wrong?"

"No, I just don't like sleeping alone. Do you think you could find room for me down there with you?

He rose swiftly to his feet and went to her. Gathering her in his arms, he carried her to the buffalo robes spread before the hearth.

"We slept here before," Jenny said. "Remember? When we first came to the valley."

"I remember."

"Are you still happy here?"

Ryder cradled Jenny's face in his hands. "What's troubling you, Jenny?" he asked tenderly.

"I don't know."

"Go to sleep, darlin'," he murmured, gently stroking her hair, the curve of her cheek. "Everything will be all right."

Smiling faintly, she rested her head against his shoulder, her hand clinging to his.

Moments later, she was asleep.

Jenny summoned the doctor first thing the following morning.

Dr. Wyatt's face was grave when he finished examining Hank.

Jenny closed the bedroom door before asking, anxiously, "He'll be all right, won't he, Dr. Wyatt?"

"I'm afraid not," the doctor replied matter-of-factly. "It's just a matter of time. A week, perhaps two or three. Just make him as comfortable as you can."

Wyatt snapped his bag shut with an air of finality, as though there was nothing more to be said or done. After giving Jenny a brisk pat on the arm, he settled his hat on his head, nodded briefly in Fallon's direction, and left the house.

Hank Braedon declined rapidly during the next few days until even Ryder, who thoroughly disliked the man, could no longer begrudge him the time Jenny spent at his bedside.

Braedon seemed to have lost the will to live, and only seemed aware of his surroundings when Jenny was with him. He often talked about his old life before the war, when each day carried the same promise of happiness and serenity as the day before.

He talked about his parents, and reminisced about the good times he and Charlie had shared when they were growing up.

And then, as he grew weaker, he hardly spoke

at all. His only comfort was having Jenny nearby. Sometimes he was troubled by wild nightmares, reliving the battles he had fought during the war, sobbing as he saw men he'd known blown to bits, reliving his own agony as a shell fragment destroyed his manhood. At those times, only Jenny's voice and the touch of her hand could soothe him.

Now, holding Jenny close under the buffalo robes a week later, Ryder marveled at what a remarkable woman Jenny was.

In a moment of crystal clarity, he realized Jenny would have extended the same hospitality and kindness to any passing stranger, male or female, red or white, who needed her care.

Yes, he thought, she was a truly remarkable woman. With a sigh, Ryder buried his face in Jenny's hair, delighting in its fragrant softness.

"I love you, Jenny girl," he whispered fervently. "Forgive me for being such a fool."

Jenny stirred in his arms. "I love you, too," she murmured sleepily, and curled deeper into his arms, asleep before the words were barely spoken.

"Ryder!"

He woke instantly, aware that he had been asleep for only a short time.

"What is it, Jenny?" he asked, alarmed by the note of panic in her voice.

"The baby . . . it's coming."

"Are you sure?"

Jenny managed a weak smile between contractions. "Yes, I'm sure."

"Okay, darlin'. Just rest easy. I'll go after Mrs. Barnes."

"Hurry!"

Fallon slipped on his trousers, bent to give Jenny a hasty kiss of reassurance before he padded barefoot out of the cabin.

Jenny's horse came at his call, and after slipping a hackamore over its head, he swung onto the horse's bare back and turned the animal south, riding down the dark trail toward the midwife's house, remembering another night, and another man's child.

Jenny sat up, her hands pressed against her belly as another contraction swept through her. She had forgotten how painful childbirth was. And then she smiled, remembering her joy when Ryder had placed Cosito in her arms. Surely any pain was worth the joy of holding a new life.

She gasped Ryder's name as another contraction knifed through her. She had once asked him how he had stood the pain while she dug the bullet out of his thigh, and he had told her the trick was to focus on something else.

She groaned as the pains grew worse. Ryder. She concentrated on Ryder, summoning his image to mind, remembering the first time she had seen him in the Apache camp. Even then, wounded, with his hands bound, he had exuded an aura of strength and self-confidence few men possessed.

She recalled how stoically he had endured the days and nights he had spent tied to the log, the way he had silently endured the pain when she probed for the bullet lodged in his thigh. Surely if he had been strong enough to endure such agony, she could bear the pain of childbirth, which was, after all, a perfectly natural part of being a woman.

Oh, it sounded so easy, but it wasn't! The future joy of holding her child was swallowed up in the pain of now.

She wished suddenly that Ryder would hurry back. She could bear anything so long as he was beside her.

Laura Barnes answered the door clad in a long pink flannel robe, her hair twisted into rag curlers. She was a woman in her late forties, plain of face, with placid brown eyes and a motherly smile.

"Mr. Fallon," she said pleasantly. "Is it time?"

"Yes. Hurry, please."

"Don't worry," Mrs. Barnes said, stifling a yawn. "We've plenty of time. Just let me put on my slippers and we'll be on our way."

She disappeared into the darkened house, reappearing a few minutes later carrying a flowered carpetbag, her feet encased in furry mules.

Outside, Fallon lifted the woman onto the back of his horse, swung up behind her, and urged the bay into a gallop.

"Gracious, Mr. Fallon," Laura Barnes admonished nervously as she bounced up and down. "There's no need to rush so."

Jenny felt a quick surge of relief when she heard Ryder's footsteps. At last, he was here!

Ryder knelt beside Jenny, his expression worried. Her face was sheened with sweat, her breathing was hard and fast. The blanket beneath her showed a dark, wet stain.

"Oh, my," Laura Barnes murmured. "I think perhaps you were right to hurry so, Mr. Fallon. Quick, put the kettle on, and bring me a clean sheet."

While Fallon went to do her bidding, Laura Barnes smiled reassuringly at Jenny.

"Everything will be fine, Mrs. Fallon dear," she said cheerfully. "You'll be cuddling your wee one in no time at all."

The midwife offered Ryder a motherly smile as she took the sheet from his hand.

"Why don't you go along into the other room, Mr. Fallon?" she suggested. "This is no place for a man."

With a curt nod, Ryder left the parlor.

Hank stirred, rubbing his eyes, as Fallon entered the bedroom and closed the door. "Jenny?"

"No, it's me."

Pale yellow light flooded the room as Ryder lit the hurricane lamp beside the bed, then dropped into the rocking chair beside the window. He stared out into the darkness, praying that God or Usen or whoever was out there would keep Jenny safe and strong and give them a healthy child. A boy or a girl, it didn't matter, so long as the baby was born alive and well.

"Why'd you do it, Fallon?" Hank asked after a long while. "Why'd you buy me from the Comanche?"

"Because Jenny asked me to," Ryder replied curtly.

"You love her, don't you?"

"Yeah."

"I never meant to hurt her," Hank said. "I loved her. I still do."

"That's why you hit her? Because you love her?" Ryder snorted softly. "You've got a funny way of showing it."

"I couldn't help it. Every time I looked at her, I saw her bedded down with that damned savage. And always, I knew people were whispering behind my back, calling me a squaw lover, snickering. If they only knew!" His voice turned bitter. "And then there was you. I knew she cared for you, though she denied it. I thought that she . . . that the two of you . . ."

"I know what you thought." Ryder glared at Braedon, but try as he might, he couldn't hate the man. Not anymore.

"She was never unfaithful to you," Ryder said quietly. "Nothing ever happened between us until that night you beat her. I found her wandering around out in the dark and . . ." Fallon shrugged. "It just happened."

"She saved my life," Hank said. He stared up at the ceiling, his thoughts turned inward. "I was wounded during the war. Maybe Jenny told you? They sent me home to recover from my wounds."

He laughed softly, bitterly. "Recover! As if a man could recover from . . . from losing his manhood. Jenny nursed me. She came to the hospital every day, always smiling. She read to me, books, newspapers. Sometimes she just sat there, holding my hand, keeping me company. I didn't want her help! I didn't want her pity!"

A single tear trickled down Braedon's cheek. "She refused to give up on me, and we became friends. She'd lost her parents, and I'd lost my will to live, but somehow we became friends. She was so beautiful. She was lonely. I was lonely."

Hank shrugged. "When I got out of the hospital, we started keeping company, and after a while I asked her to marry me, never dreaming she'd accept. What woman would want a man who couldn't . . . couldn't . . . but she said yes." He sighed softly, as if still unable to believe his good fortune. "She said yes."

Hank began to cough, a deep rasping cough that drained what little color he had in his face, leaving him pale and breathing heavily. When he wiped his hand across his mouth, it came away stained with blood.

"How long you been sick, Braedon?"

"Six months, maybe more."

"I guess you've had a hard time of it with the Indians."

"Yeah. I thought the Apache would kill me, like they did Charlie." He shuddered at the memory. "It was horrible, what they did to him. It took him two days to die, and it was still a better way to go than this."

Ryder stared out the window again. He had no words of comfort, spiritual or otherwise, to offer the man. Oddly enough, he wished he did.

"Promise me," Hank rasped. "Promise me you'll take good care of her."

"I promise."

"I envy you," Hank said. "You've got everything I ever wanted," he said, his voice filled with resentment. "Everything that should have been mine. Jenny. A baby . . ."

A ragged sob tore at Hank's throat and he turned his face away so Fallon couldn't see his tears.

"You'd best get some rest, Braedon," Ryder said gruffly.

Sitting back in his chair, Fallon stared out the window into the darkness again, wondering at the strange twists and turns of life. If Hank had stayed in the East, Jenny would never have been captured by the Apache, and Ryder would never have met her.

He didn't know whether it had been fate or destiny that had brought them together in Kayitah's camp. He only knew it had been meant to be, that his life had been incomplete without Jenny.

The first faint light of dawn was stealing away the night when a baby's lusty cry sounded from the parlor.

Ryder jumped to his feet and rushed into the other room as Laura Barnes wrapped the infant in a blanket.

"Ah, you're just in time," she beamed, and thrust the mewling bundle into Ryder's arms.

Fallon stared down at the baby, seeing a thatch of thick black hair and a pair of unfocused blue eyes. He felt a sudden tightening in his chest. His child. It was a miracle wrapped in a blue blanket, the sum of a man's dreams, the proof of a woman's love.

He knelt at Jenny's side, awkwardly cradling the squirming baby in the crook of his arm.

"Jenny girl, are you all right?" he asked anxiously.

"Fine," Jenny murmured. "A little tired is all." She yawned hugely, her long lashes fluttering down. "It's a boy, a beautiful boy."

"Jenny, I . . ."

But she was already asleep.

Ryder shot Laura Barnes a worried look. "Is she all right?"

"Yes, she's a fine healthy girl. Only tired now, and a bit sore. It's hard work, you know, bringing a new life into the world. Not so easy, or so much fun, as the fathering," she added, a twinkle in her eye. "Here, now, let me take the wee one and clean him up a mite."

Reluctantly, Ryder handed the baby to the midwife.

"A son," he said aloud, and the words sent a shiver down his spine.

Suddenly, the cabin was too small to hold him and he strode briskly outside into the light of a new day.

It was a bright and beautiful morning, all

golden sunshine and brilliant blue sky. He heard the lilting dawn song of a sparrow, the crowing of a rooster, the lowing of cattle in the hills.

"My heart soars and my spirit sings," he murmured, and smiled as he recalled that his father had used the same words years ago, on the day Ryder had become a warrior of the Cheyenne nation.

Filled with joy and a deep sense of well-being, awed by the miracle of birth and the wonder of life renewing itself, Ryder lifted his face to the sun and loosed the ululating victory cry of the Cheyenne. He laughed aloud as he imagined the momentary panic the shrill cry would arouse in the hearts of his neighbors.

"You're a lucky man, Ryder Fallon," he mused.

Whistling softly, he hurried through the morning chores, then returned to the cabin.

Inside, Laura Barnes was singing an Irish lullaby as she whipped up a hearty breakfast of bacon and eggs, fried potatoes, baking powder biscuits and gravy.

Jenny was sitting up on the sofa, nursing the baby. She smiled at Ryder as he came to sit beside her.

"So, how are you feeling, darlin'?" he asked.

"Wonderful." She gazed lovingly at the child cradled against her breast. Ryder's child. "Isn't he beautiful?"

"You're beautiful," Ryder said. "The best, sweetest, most extraordinary woman I've ever known."

Jenny blushed prettily, pleased by his words, and by the love shining so pure and clear in the depths of his midnight blue eyes.

She leaned forward for his kiss, felt her heart beat a little faster as his mouth covered hers. Silently, she thanked God for sending her a man like Ryder Fallon. Ryder, who had strong arms to hold her when she was sad, whose very touch filled her with peaceful fire.

"Ryder, would you do something for me?" Jenny asked. "Would you look in on Hank and make sure he's all right?"

"Sure, honey."

Ryder kissed her one more time. He could afford to be tolerant of Hank Braedon, he mused. The man had nothing, while he, Fallon, onetime gambler and gunman, had everything he had ever hoped for, and more.

The bedroom was cool and dim. Outside the window, a bird warbled cheerfully, and from the parlor came the faint cries of his son, but in this room there was only silence, and the faint, musty smell of death.

The Indians believed that life was a circle, that nothing was ever lost. A man had died, but in the next room a baby's cry could be heard. It was a good sound, filled with hope and the promise of a new life.

With a sigh, Ryder Fallon covered the face of Jenny's husband.

She was free now. As soon as she felt up to it, they would ride into the next town and be married again. No one in Twin Rivers need ever know that their child had been born out of wedlock.

Closing the bedroom door behind him, Ryder went to tell Jenny that their last link with the past was gone.

Epilogue

Jenny sat on the top rail of the corral, watching as Ryder sacked out a young spotted stallion. The mustang, fresh off the range, tossed its head, shying as Ryder rubbed the heavy burlap bag across its withers and down one shoulder. She could hear Ryder talking softly to the horse, telling it not to worry, that everything would be all right.

The horse, tied to a snubbing post in the middle of the corral, watched the man's every move, its eyes showing white, its whole body tense, quivering.

Ryder was infinitely patient, rubbing the burlap over the horse's back, down its flanks, over each leg, up its neck and over its head.

Four-year-old Dorinda gasped, her tiny hands covering her mouth, as the horse reared up, its forelegs slicing dangerously close to Ryder's head.

Six-year-old Dusty shouted, "Pa, watch out!"

"Ryder, be careful," Jenny cried, adding her warning to her son's.

Fallon waved at Jenny and smiled reassuringly at Dusty and Dorinda. Despite the difference in their ages, his son and daughter looked much alike with their wavy black hair and deep green eyes.

Another thirty minutes and the horse accepted the touch of the burlap bag without flinching, though it continued to watch Ryder's every move.

After another thirty minutes, the horse endured having the sack waved in front of its face.

Giving the stallion a pat on the shoulder, Ryder called it a day.

Jenny let out a sigh as Ryder walked the horse around the corral to cool him out. How good life was! They had two happy, healthy children, a crop in the field, dear friends in the valley. The little town was growing each year. More people meant more homes, churches, schools, stores. And yet Twin Rivers remained a close-knit, friendly place.

Jenny glanced over her shoulder, admiring the home that she and her husband had built together. In the past five years, they'd added several rooms and a spacious veranda to the cabin. Ryder had painted the house the summer before, a soft yellow with white trim.

Jumping down, she lifted Dusty and Dorinda from the fence rail and sent them into the house to wash up for supper. She watched them for a moment, smiling with a mother's pride as they skipped up the path to the back door; then, with a sigh of contentment, she walked over to the gate to wait for Ryder.

He was smiling when he joined her. "He's a beauty," Ryder said, jerking a thumb in the stallion's direction. "I can't wait to ride him."

"He still looks wild to me."

Fallon shook his head as he draped his arm around Jenny's shoulders. "He's just young and skittish."

"Well, I guess you know what you're doing."

"You guess!" Ryder grinned down at her, knowing she was teasing and loving her for it. Loving her for the warmth she'd brought into his life, the sense of home, of belonging.

They had a good life, he mused as they strolled toward the house. He farmed the land because it gave him a certain sense of satisfaction to grow food for his family with his own hands, but his real love was breaking mustangs for the townspeople. His reputation as a horse trainer had spread beyond the valley, and people from as far away as Texas and Nebraska came to Twin Rivers to buy a horse that had been gentled by Ryder Fallon.

It had amused him, having a reputation again, and he sometimes kidded Jenny that he didn't know which was more frightening, the thought of being stomped by a wild bronc now that he had a reputation as a horse trainer, or the possibility of being gunned down by a wild kid out to make a name for himself back when he'd had a reputation as a fast gun.

"Come here," he murmured. Stepping behind a tree out of sight of the house, he drew her into his arms, lowered his head and kissed her.

A slow heat crept over Jenny as she melted against him, her eyelids closing, her heartbeat increasing as Ryder kissed her with infinite sweetness. As always, she warmed to his touch, forgetting everything but the man who held her, who loved her. The man she loved.

He kissed her deeply, thoroughly, possessively. "Tonight," he whispered, his voice tickling her ear, "I'll meet you down by the creek when the kids are in bed."

Jenny nodded and then she pressed her lips to his once more, wanting him, needing him, still surprised that the desire between them had not dimmed with time.

"Mom! Hey, Mom, Dorinda's pinching me again."

Chuckling, Ryder dropped a kiss on Jenny's cheek, then took her by the hand and headed for the house.

"Tonight," he reminded her as they reached the back door.

Jenny smiled up at him, her heart aglow with happiness. "And every night," she murmured.

And hand in hand, they went into the house and closed the door.

SEVEN BRIDES
LEIGH GREENWOOD

LAUREL

Chapter One

Arizona Territory, 1877

The shrill cry was out of place in this peaceful desert canyon filled with towering sycamores and a myriad of singing birds. Hen Randolph thought at first it must have been an eagle or some small animal. When it came a second time, he knew it was a woman. Unsure where he was going or what lay ahead, he ran forward along the narrow path that hugged the canyon wall.

Hen didn't hear the deeper male voice until he rounded the bend. The canyon opened up into a small, boulder-free clearing on the steep incline of the creek. Back up against the sheer canyon wall, well away from the stream, Hen saw a small adobe. In front, a man and a woman argued, lashing each other with their voices, striking out with open hands. Hen's steps slowed, then stopped. He had been told Laurel Blackthorne was unmarried, but this looked like a domestic quarrel. Just as he started to turn around, she cried out again in a voice that spoke to him of danger and desperation.

"Touch my child, and I swear I'll see you dead!"

The man shoved her aside, but she ran ahead of him.

"Adam, hide!" she screamed.

The man was faster, and he caught up. Laurel threw herself at him, grabbing his arm to hold him back.

Hen started forward again.

The man seemed to be trying to get away from Laurel. Though she was much smaller, she held on tenaciously. Then he hit her. He simply drew back his fist and hit her in the face.

She fell to the ground.

In a flash Hen felt himself fill with hot rage. He had few principles, but he held to those with fierce tenacity. Among the most important was that a man should never strike a woman.

Hen drew his gun and would have shot the man right then. But even as the woman summoned the energy to shout one last warning, the man disappeared inside the adobe. A moment later he came out dragging a small boy.

"Let me go!" the child cried as he kicked and hit at the man.

Laurel struggled to her feet and tried to take the child from him. He hit her again. She staggered, but refused to give up. She followed him as he tried to reach his horse.

Holstering his gun, Hen started forward as fast as he could run. He couldn't fire at the man and risk hurting the woman or child. Caught up in their struggle, they didn't hear Hen's approach.

"Let them go," he called out, still several yards away.

The man froze; the child continued to struggle; Laurel hit the man with her balled-up fist. The man put his hand in her face and pushed her to her knees. Reaching him, Hen grabbed him by the arm, turned him around, and hit him so hard he slumped to the ground, dazed. The child broke away and ran to his mother.

"Here, ma'am, let me help you up," Hen said and extended his hand.

The woman made no attempt to rise. As she leaned forward, holding herself off the ground with one hand, her other arm around her son, her body heaved in its struggle to fill her lungs. She lifted her head to look at him. Hen's stomach turned over and rage welled up inside him more ferociously than before. Her face was covered with bruises and contusions. She had put up a good fight, but the man had beaten her unmercifully.

Turning, Hen found the bastard staggering to his feet.

"Only a coward hits a woman," Hen growled

and backhanded the man so hard he sprawled on the ground once more. Hen reached down and jerked him to his feet. "Only a rotten yellowbelly hurts a kid." A series of methodically rendered blows left the man unable to stand, but Hen held him up so he wouldn't fall.

"If I ever find you here again, I'll put a bullet in you. Touch this woman or her child, and I'll kill you." A last backhand sent the other man to the ground. Hen kicked the gun well out of the fallen man's reach. Then he took a rope from his saddle, rolled the man over, shoved his face in the dust, and tied his hands behind him.

"I'll kill you," the man bellowed from between bloody lips.

"You might try," Hen said as he jerked the knot tight.

"Nobody touches a Blackthorne and lives."

Bending down, Hen spoke in his ear, low and menacing. "This nobody has a name. Randolph. Hen Randolph. Remember it. If you bother this woman again, I'll brand it on your forehead." Hen turned the man over. When he kicked at Hen and tried to scramble to his feet, Hen yanked on the rope and pulled the man's shoulders back until he screamed. Pushing him to his knees, Hen trussed him like a calf about to be branded.

Hen turned back to Laurel. She still sat on the ground, her arm protectively around her son.

"Let me help you up. We need to do something about those bruises."

"Who are you?" she asked.

"I'm the new sheriff of Sycamore Flats. I take it you're Laurel Blackthorne."

Laurel's gaze gripped him in a narrow focus. "You realize you've signed your death warrant, don't you?"

Her tone was sharp and without a trace of appreciation for what he had done. It wasn't exactly the response he had expected.

"No, ma'am, I didn't. I thought I was helping you and your son. Didn't look to me like you were having a whole lot of fun."

"That's Damian Blackthorne." She still sounded stiff and ungrateful.

"So?"

"He's got at least two dozen brothers, cousins, and uncles."

Maybe she was too scared to show her real emotion.

"It figures. Trouble never shows its face but when it's got a whole lot of company."

Laurel continued to eye him. "Either you're crazy or you're a fool."

Hen smiled. "I've been accused of both. Now I'd better get started on your face. I was told you were a right pretty woman, but you don't look too pretty right now." He extended his hand once more, but she still didn't take it.

"At least you're nicer than the other gunman who tried to be sheriff," Laurel said, continuing to stare at him. "I hope they give you a big funeral."

"Ma'am, being sheriff hasn't taken up a whole lot of my time so far, but if you don't get up off that ground soon, I expect I'll have Hope up here wondering why I'm late for dinner. Besides, all that blood's a lot easier to clean off before it dries."

Laurel finally accepted his help. Her hand felt rough and dry, not soft like those of the ladies he had known.

"This is my son, Adam," Laurel said as she got to her feet.

Adam continued to cling to his mother, apparently unsure of whether he could trust Hen.

"What was he doing here?" Hen asked, indicating Damian.

"None of your damned business," Damian shouted. "When I get free, I'm going to fill your ass so full of holes the—"

Hen stuffed Damian's bandanna in his mouth. "That fella sure doesn't know how to talk in front of a lady," he said, turning his attention back to Laurel.

"Don't you ever get upset over anything?" Laurel asked.

"It's a waste of energy and doesn't change anything. Now let's see if I can do something about your face."

"I can take care of myself."

It upset Hen that she seemed afraid to let him touch her. "I'm sure you can, but you don't have to."

"I would prefer it."

"People don't always get what they prefer."

"Didn't anybody tell you that you were supposed to protect people, not bully them?"

"I guess they didn't get around to that. They seemed too anxious to pin the badge on me to say anything that might cause me to change my mind."

"That sounds like Sycamore Flats," Laurel said, disgust in her voice. "If they don't see anything wrong, there can't be anything wrong."

"A lot of people are like that. It's easier than doing something about it." He looked around until he saw a shallow pan. "I'm going to get some water. While I'm gone, see what kind of medicines you can rustle up."

As Laurel watched him go, she marveled at his confidence. Either he was a great fool, or he was more of a man than half-a-dozen Blackthornes rolled together. She felt a tiny shiver run down her spine, the same shiver she'd felt when he'd touched her.

From the way he'd handled Damian, she had no question he was a man. But only a fool would try being sheriff of Sycamore Flats.

Laurel was inside the adobe when Hen returned. Adam stood by the door as if guarding his mother. He watched Hen uneasily, but he didn't shrink from him.

"Are you hurt?" Hen asked the boy.

"No."

"Damian wouldn't hurt another Blackthorne," Laurel said, coming outside. "Adam is his nephew," she explained, seeing Hen's confusion.

"Too bad he doesn't feel that way about you."

"He might if I'd given him what he wanted."

Hen moved a chair from beside the house to a spot where an opening in the canopy overhead offered the most light. "Sit."

Laurel didn't think she'd ever met anyone as coldly impassive. Or as incurious. "Aren't you going to ask what he wants?"

"I figure it's none of my business."

"It isn't, but Damian is going to make you his business." Laurel winced when Hen took her face and turned it toward the light.

"Don't talk."

Laurel sat absolutely still, trying to give no sign of how much her face hurt. The shock was wearing off and the dull throbbing had become intensely painful. The cool, moist cloth Hen pressed to her face did little to ease the pain or remove the marks that would make her unfit to be seen in public for weeks.

"What did you find?" Hen asked.

"Yerba mansa," she replied.

Laurel handed Hen a small bottle. He passed it under his nose. Seemingly satisfied, he carefully cleaned the blood and dirt from one side of her face, then generously anointed it with the herbal tincture to disinfect the wound.

He worked in silence.

Laurel marveled at his gentleness. She had never met a man who would even consider caring for a woman. Womenfolk had to take care of themselves. Nor had she imagined a man tough enough to handle Damian would take such care not to hurt her. Yet beneath his easy touch, she sensed a hardness that seemed to go to the core of this man.

"What was all that about?" he asked at last.

"I thought you weren't interested." She didn't know why, but his failure to ask earlier irritated her.

"I'm not. The sheriff is."

"Is there a difference?"

"Sure."

She believed him. If anybody could divide himself in two, this man could. How else could his touch be so gentle and his heart so cold?

"My husband died before Adam was born. None of his relatives paid any attention to him when he was a baby. But now that he's six, they think he ought to go live with them."

"I gather you disagree."

"Wouldn't you?" In her agitation, Laurel twisted in Hen's grasp. She winced.

"Keep still."

Gentle he might have been, but there was no compassion in him. She was sure he would show more feeling for his horse.

"I know nothing about your situation," Hen said without taking his eyes off his work, "but in my experience, a boy who's around nobody but women is liable to grow up soft. That could get him killed."

Laurel jerked away from Hen. "Has your experience shown you what happens to boys who grow up like Damian?"

"They generally get themselves killed."

He acted as though he were talking of the

weather instead of life and death.

"And you think Adam ought to grow up like that?" she snapped.

"I never like to see anybody get killed, not even those who deserve it." Hen took Laurel's face in his hands once more and resumed his work.

At least, Laurel thought, he didn't approve of killing. That was something. "I have no intention of letting Damian or any other Blackthorne get his hands on Adam. I don't want him growing up soft, but I mean to see he grows up with some principles."

"Nice if you can do it."

"You don't think I can?" Why did she care what he thought? She was mad at herself for asking.

"I don't know. You seem like a remarkably stubborn woman, but I don't know if you're any good at getting things done."

Laurel pulled away again. "I've gotten a lot done, including taking care of myself for nearly seven years."

"Weren't doing such a grand job a while back."

Hen turned her toward the light. She flinched when he touched her shoulder.

"You've got a bruise under your dress."

"I hit a rock when I fell."

"Let me see it."

"No."

"You afraid I'd try to take advantage of you?" His gaze was riveting, uncompromising.

"N-no."

"You think it would be indecent?"

"Of course not."

"Then let me see it."

No sensitivity either, Laurel thought to herself as she slipped the dress over her shoulder. He clearly didn't understand how humiliating it was to have to submit to his care.

When he touched her, she practically rose off the chair. His touch was too light to hurt. Rather it seared her with a jolt of energy that left her feeling a little dazed. She forgot the pain in her face. She was aware only of his fingers on the warm flesh of her shoulder. She couldn't bring herself to look at him. She was suddenly, acutely, achingly aware that he was a man and she a woman.

Stop being a fool. You're only acting this way because you've been seven years without a man's touch.

Regardless of the reason, it was impossible to feel indifferent.

"The skin's not broken," Hen said. He pressed ever so slightly. Pain as sharp as a pin shot through her shoulder. He must have seen her wince, but he offered no apologies. "You're going to have to be very careful for a few days."

"Can I put my clothes back on now, Doctor?"

He smiled. "Do you have any prickly pear around here?"

"Farther up the canyon," Laurel said as she righted her dress.

"I'll be right back." He headed off at a leisurely pace.

She was glad he was going. She needed time to calm down. She couldn't be calm, or she wouldn't be having this ridiculous reaction to him. This sense of not wanting him to touch her, yet somehow wanting him to. Of looking for comfort in a place she didn't expect to find it.

"Where's he going, Ma?" Adam asked. He hadn't left his mother's side the whole time.

"To find some prickly pears, though what he wants with them is a mystery."

But that mystery didn't interest her so much as why his touch had such a powerful effect on her. She had never enjoyed Carlin's caresses. Even in the beginning, when she was still wild and foolish and believed she was in love with him, she had found his nearness strangely unsatisfying. But with a single touch this stranger had caused her body to ache and yearn, her skin to feel scorched, her nerves to become uncomfortably sensitive.

It must have been the shock. Damian had been brutal. It would be days before she felt like herself again.

"Is anybody else going to come after me?" Adam asked. He looked scared.

Laurel had always been afraid the Blackthornes would come for Adam someday. She had expected it to be later. It had been a cruel shock when Damian had showed up today.

"Maybe," Laurel said, "but we'll be ready next time."

She hadn't been ready today. Adam would be beyond her reach right this minute if it hadn't been for this unusual man. Okay, he was the sheriff and maybe protecting her was his job, but she didn't think she had ever met anybody remotely like him.

"He's coming back," Adam warned her.

Hen came down the canyon, his arms loaded with prickly pear fruit.

"Here, hold these," he said and dropped the fruits in her lap. He took a knife from his pocket and sliced a piece of fruit in half, then filleted it. "Do you have any cheesecloth?"

"Yes."

"Cut the rest of these just like this one. Then put them on your bruises and wrap your face in the cloth. You'll heal up twice as fast."

"I'll look like I'm being readied for burial," Laurel objected. She broke off, staring at him. "Why did you come up here?" she asked.

"I wanted to ask you to do my laundry." He looked around. "I dropped it back there."

"I'll get it," Adam said and ran off. He had regained some of his confidence.

"I'm not sure when I can get to it," Laurel told him. "I've got a lot to do." She knew she ought to do his first, out of gratitude if nothing else, but a feeling of disappointment, of irrational irritation, had taken hold of her.

"You shouldn't do anything else today."

"Except pickle myself in cactus fruit."

"Except that."

She thought she saw a smile, a glint in those blue eyes, but maybe it was only a trick of the sun. She smiled back anyway. "I'll tell people to see you when they want to know why their laundry isn't done on time."

"Seems telling them to see Damian would be more appropriate."

The humor faded from her expression. "It wouldn't make any difference. The Blackthornes don't care what anybody else wants."

"You ought to see if you can work out a compromise. It won't do that boy any good to be caught between the two of you."

"You don't know anything about the situation," she said, her voice cold and sharp.

"True, but you can't change who his father was."

"But I can see he grows up with some principles," she said stubbornly, "that he doesn't think it's okay to take what he wants just because he's bigger and willing to use a gun."

Adam came up, carrying the bag of clothes. He was a big boy for his age, and he handled the heavy bag well.

"You carry a lot of clothes with you," Laurel said when she saw the heavy bag.

"I'm a long way from home."

"Maybe you ought to consider going back." Even though he had made her angry, she meant it as a kindness. She didn't want to see him killed. No one had ever been this nice to her.

"You going to consider letting that boy see his uncles once in a while?"

Laurel glared at him, all desire to be kind gone. "That's none of your concern."

"Nor is where I go yours."

"It is when you're on my property," she shot back. "I'll do your clothes, but I mean to see the back of you disappearing down that canyon before I stir from this spot."

"It'd be more to the point if you'd clap a couple of those cactus fruit to your face and lie down. You'll be a whole lot happier about what your mirror shows you tomorrow."

"Leave!" Laurel practically shouted. "And take your clothes with you."

"I'll be back tomorrow to see how you're doing," Hen said.

"I've got a shotgun."

"Good. A woman living alone needs to be able to protect herself." Hen turned to Adam. "Watch out for your ma, son. In her present frame of mind, she's liable to attack anything, including a panther. Poor old cat would be chewed to little bitty pieces before it could let out a screech. You'd have cat fur all over the yard. Take you the better part of a day to sweep it up."

Laurel had to struggle to preserve her frown. "I'd appreciate it if you'd go before you ruin my character with my own son."

"See, you can talk nice when you try," Hen said. There wasn't a trace of humor in his eyes. "I enjoyed the visit, too."

Hen walked over to Damian and untied his feet. He practically threw the other man into the saddle. Tipping his hat, Hen sauntered out of the yard leading Damian's horse.

"You forgot your clothes," Adam called.

Hen merely waved without looking around.

"Ma, he forgot his—"

"He didn't forget," Laurel said. "He had no intention of taking them."

"What are you going to do with them?"

She sighed. "Wash them, I guess."

"But you said you wouldn't."

"I know, but Mr. Sheriff doesn't seem to hear very well."

"He said his name was Mr. Randolph. I heard him."

"I know. Hen Randolph. What kind of name is that for a grown man? Hen. That's a chicken. It makes you think of some animal covered with feathers scratching in the dirt for worms and squawking for all she's worth when she's laid an egg in the bushes."

Adam was suddenly overcome with giggles. "He don't have no feathers, Ma. And he don't squawk."

"Doesn't squawk," Laurel corrected. "No, but he sure does talk a lot of nonsense."

"I like him. He beat up that man."

"Yes, he did, didn't he?" But violence frightened her, and Hen had been brutal.

"Do you think he'll come back?"

Laurel let her gaze linger on the spot where Hen had disappeared down the canyon. "I doubt we'll ever see him again."

"I didn't like him. If I had I gun, I'd shoot him."

"Oh, you mean Damian," Laurel said, jerked back to reality. "I'm afraid he will come back. And you will not shoot anybody. Now you'd better get some water and gather wood if I'm going to do Mr. Randolph's clothes."

"He told you to lie down."

"I know what he said, but you can be sure he expects to see his clothes done by tomorrow."

But as Laurel watched Adam heft the wood bucket and head toward the stream, she wondered if Hen really did expect to have his clothes laundered by morning. She had never met a man like him. She really didn't know what he'd expect. Except for her father, whom she could barely remember, every man she'd ever met believed a woman existed solely to provide for his comfort and pleasure.

Hen acted like that when he talked about Adam needing a man's influence. But when he'd cared for her bruises, his touch had been gentle.

Still, she hadn't missed the fury in his eyes when he had systematically beaten Damian into helplessness. It reminded her of her stepfather. She could still remember the blows raining down, the feeling of helplessness. She shivered. She had vowed she would never tolerate that again. Yet despite what he had done to Damian, she felt sure Hen would never strike a woman.

"I'll need at least two more buckets," she said when Adam poured the first into the kettle. "He has an awful lot of clothes."

She watched her son return to the stream. He was a good child. She didn't care what Hen Randolph thought, she intended to keep him out of Blackthorne hands no matter what she had to do. And that included using the shotgun she kept by her bed. She didn't think Hen would approve of the Blackthornes even though he felt Adam needed a man, but how could she know that? There was no law that said a man had to be good just because he was so good-looking it made a woman feel weak just being near him.

She remembered white-blond hair showing under his hat, skin tanned to the color of new leather, lean features chiseled into an expression that gave no hint of his thoughts, a tall, powerful body capable of knocking Damian Blackthorne to the ground with one blow.

But it was his eyes that had exercised the most powerful effect on her. As intensely blue as the sky, they showed no sign of warmth, amusement, sadness. Nothing. Even though he had defended her, taken care of her, he appeared completely cold and unfeeling. But he couldn't be, could he? Not and risk his neck for her.

Stop acting like a fool. All this wondering is a waste of time. If you had spent half this much time thinking about Carlin before you married him, you wouldn't be in this mess now.

Putting her former husband out of her mind, Laurel picked up the bag of clothes and put them on the chair. Even that effort caused the blood to rush to her face and her bruises to ache. She leaned against the back of the chair. Maybe she wasn't well enough to do any more work today.

She thought of the nearly bare cupboard inside and knew she didn't have any choice. Not everyone in town was as careful to pay their bills as they were insistent their laundry be done on time.

"I wish we were closer to the creek," Adam said as he poured the last bucket into the pot. His face was pink from the exertion of lugging three buckets of water up from the creek.

"I know, but then the creek would flood the house every time it rained." Adam knew that, but she didn't mind his complaining a little. He did it so seldom.

Laurel opened the bag and began to pull out one shirt after another. She was amazed that any man would use so many. More than the number, she marveled at their quality. She examined the fabric more closely. Fine linen, the best she had ever seen. She inspected the needlework and tested the seams. Better and more expensive than anything she got from town. She kept pulling shirts out of the bag until she had twenty-two. His underwear, pants, and socks were of the same quality. He even had a stiff collar. He must have a dress coat in his wardrobe.

This man hadn't been a sheriff before. At least not for very long. A sheriff had to be calculating and careful. He had to know who wielded the power. Hen seemed to be the kind of man who did whatever he wanted and damned the consequences.

Laurel wondered if her life would have been any better if she had married a man like Hen rather than Carlin?

She was certain Hen wouldn't have abandoned her for a cheap whore or gotten himself killed trying to steal a bull. He would have married her in a church in a decent wedding instead of rustling some preacher out of bed in the middle of the night, a preacher she hadn't been able to locate in seven years. And he wouldn't have left her with a son to raise by herself and no means of support.

But she hadn't married a man like Hen. She had married Carlin Blackthorne and had spent the last six years raising her son alone. She didn't mean to give him up now. Nor did she mean to let him starve. She would wash this man's clothes. Then she would lie down. He would pay her. Then she could buy some food.

Chapter Two

Hen didn't feel the indifference he'd shown Laurel. Inside him simmered a dangerously hot anger toward Damian. Only remembering he was now the sheriff had kept him from administering the brutal beating the son of a bitch deserved, the beating he would get if he ever touched Laurel again. While Hen was sheriff, no man would get away with beating a woman.

He probably shouldn't have hit Damian more than once, maybe not at all. Well, that was too damned bad. He had hit him, and if Damian aggravated him any more, he'd do it again.

Hen knew that wasn't the right attitude. The very fact that it wasn't irritated him. He wasn't used to restrictions. He and Monty were used to delivering their own brand of justice and making it stick with guns and fists. It wasn't going to be easy to change his habits now.

Why the hell had he agreed to be sheriff anyway? Nobody paid 250 dollars a month unless it was a job only a fool would take, or unless the last three sheriffs rested under six feet of desert sod. He ought to get the hell out and let them worry about their own hides.

But he couldn't do that, and he knew it. He might not like this damned job, he might wish he had never set foot in Sycamore Flats, but he couldn't back out until he'd done what he'd promised—cleaned out the rustlers. In the meantime, it was also his job to keep the peace, enforce the law, and protect the citizens.

And Damian Blackthorne was a citizen. But so was Laurel.

Hen didn't know what he should do about her any more than he knew what he wanted to do. She seemed ordinary enough, a bit sharp-tongued and short of temper, but no more than you'd expect of a young woman saddled with a kid and forced to make her living washing clothes. But it was the Laurel who had fought Damian Blackthorne with the determination of a lynx, the Laurel who never uttered a whimper of pain when he cleaned her wounds, who was so far from ordinary she lingered in his thoughts.

She was a pretty woman. Not even the bruises and blood could hide that. She reminded him of a woman he once knew who claimed to be a gypsy. She had that same thick black hair and huge, dark brown eyes combined with skin the color of moonlight. She was unnaturally thin—probably from giving her son most of her food—but a lushness still clung to her. Maybe it was her sinuous movement. It certainly wasn't her seductive behavior. She had looked him square in the eye, challenging him, defying him.

Yet still a little frightened. No, unsure. Uneasy. He couldn't imagine Laurel Blackthorne being frightened of anyone. She might have been when she was younger, but then lots of people had been different when they were younger.

He had been, but he didn't let himself think about that anymore.

He didn't think Laurel had been prettier. She was the kind of woman who would grow more attractive as she matured, the kind whose beauty would benefit from well-chosen clothes and a proper setting, the kind who in her mid-thirties would make younger women look shallow and insignificant. Not that it mattered to him. He wasn't interested in women, young or old. They represented ties, responsibilities, restrictions—all the things he meant to avoid.

It wasn't that he disliked women, just that they were always demanding, expecting, wanting, needing. There was no end to it. They were always after something he didn't have to give. It wasn't that he didn't want to. He didn't have it. There was nothing to Hen Randolph but a shell.

He wondered if Laurel might not be the same.

"This is a good place to let me go. You can't see into this wash from town," Damian explained when Hen just stared at him.

"You're going to jail," Hen said.

"You're new here. I guess you don't know."

"Know what?"

"Blackthornes don't go to jail."

"Why?"

"It'll get you killed."

"Sounds like an empty threat."

"There's people who could advise you otherwise."

"I never take advice. It always seems to be for somebody else's comfort."

"You're a fool!"

"Maybe, but you're the one who's going to be sitting in jail."

Damian threw his leg over the saddle. He stumbled when he hit the ground, but tried to make a run for it. Hen pulled on the rope so hard it nearly twisted Damian's arms out of their sockets.

"I'll kill you!" Damian managed to gasp from between clenched teeth. "I'll gut-shoot you and leave you to die."

"You'll have plenty of time to work out your plan," Hen said. He led Damian out of the wash and up to the back of the jail. Damian didn't say anything until Hen dragged him inside, shoved him into one of the cells, and locked the door.

"My family will get me out." The bruises from Hen's knuckles were beginning to show plainly on his face. "Then they'll kill you."

"Knock real loud," Hen said. "I'm a sound sleeper."

Passing into his office in the front part of the jail, Hen closed the door on Damian's profane response. The frame building had a door and two windows that faced the street. A desk sat to one side, a potbellied stove to the other. The floor was of local rough-hewn oak. It was a tiny building, but then the sheriff didn't need much space. There wasn't much to do indoors.

Hen wondered what his brothers would say if they could see him now. He had sent George a telegram. He ought to know where to come in case he had to collect Hen's body. Not that Hen expected to be killed. Or to stay here long. But it would give him something to do while he decided what the hell to do with the rest of his life.

He could have decided in Texas with George, in Wyoming with Monty, or in Colorado with Madison, but he was trying to avoid his family. No, he was running away from himself. He had accepted the job of sheriff because he thought, if he kept busy, he might not be plagued by questions he couldn't answer.

The Widow Blackthorne offered him a problem to occupy his mind. Hen welcomed her intrusion into his life.

Author Of More Than 4 Million Books In Print!

"Powerful, passionate, and action packed, Madeline Baker's historical romances will keep readers on the edge of their seats!"
—*Romantic Times*

Callie has the face of an angel and the body of a temptress. Her innocent kisses say she is still untouched, but her reputation says she is available to any man who has the price of a night's entertainment.

Callie's sweetness touches Caleb's heart, but he and the whole town of Cheyenne know she is no better than the woman who raised her—his own father's mistress. Torn by conflicting desires, the handsome half-breed doesn't know whether he wants her walking down the aisle in white satin, or warm and willing in his bed, clothed in nothing by ivory flesh.

_3581-2 $4.99 US/$5.99 CAN

LEISURE BOOKS
ATTN: Order Department
276 5th Avenue, New York, NY 10001

Please add $1.50 for shipping and handling for the first book and $.35 for each book thereafter. PA., N.Y.S. and N.Y.C. residents, please add appropriate sales tax. No cash, stamps, or C.O.D.s. All orders shipped within 6 weeks via postal service book rate. Canadian orders require $2.00 extra postage and must be paid in U.S. dollars through a U.S. banking facility.

Name____
Address____
City ______________________________ State______ Zip______
I have enclosed $______in payment for the checked book(s).
Payment must accompany all orders.☐ Please send a free catalog.